To the death. . . .

Panting with fatigue, Fargo twisted away from the Kiowa brave, feeling the tomahawk whistle by his face. The man pressed forward with short, chopping blows, and Fargo had to give ground—ducking and twisting as the blade came increasingly closer to hitting home.

Suddenly, he saw an opening, dropped low, and risked lashing out with a tremendous blow to the brave's ribcage. He heard the grunt of pain, saw the warrior drop to one knee, and then Fargo stepped in with a long roundhouse that smashed into the man's jaw. The Kiowa went down, but managed to hold on to the tomahawk. Fargo dove recklessly forward, hoping to get to the man before he recovered. As he did, the Kiowa found the strength to whip his tomahawk in a brutal uppercut.

Fargo saw the gory blade flash upward, ready to split his jaw in two. . . .

THE
TRAILSMAN
#225

PRAIRIE
FIRESTORM

by

Jon Sharpe

A SIGNET BOOK

SIGNET
Published by New American Library, a division of
Penguin Putnam Inc., 375 Hudson Street,
New York, New York 10014, U.S.A.
Penguin Books Ltd, 27 Wrights Lane,
London W8 5TZ, England
Penguin Books Australia Ltd,
Ringwood, Victoria, Australia
Penguin Books Canada Ltd, 10 Alcorn Avenue,
Toronto, Ontario, Canada M4V 3B2
Penguin Books (N.Z.) Ltd, 182–190 Wairau Road,
Auckland 10, New Zealand

Penguin Books Ltd, Registered Offices:
Harmondsworth, Middlesex, England

First published by Signet, an imprint of New American Library,
a division of Penguin Putnam Inc.

First Printing, July 2000
10 9 8 7 6 5 4 3 2 1

The first chapter of this book originally appeared in *Texas Tinhorns*,
the two hundred twenty-fourth volume in this series.

 REGISTERED TRADEMARK MARCA REGISTRADA

Printed in the United States of America

PUBLISHER'S NOTE
This is a work of fiction. Names, characters, places, and incidents either are
the product of the author's imagination or are used fictitiously, and any
resemblance to actual persons, living or dead, business establishments,
events, or locales is entirely coincidental.

The Trailsman

Beginnings ... they bend the tree and they mark the man. Skye Fargo was born when he was eighteen. Terror was his midwife, vengeance his first cry. Killing spawned Skye Fargo, ruthless, cold-blooded murder. Out of the acrid smoke of gunpowder still hanging in the air, he rose, cried out a promise never forgotten.

The Trailsman they began to call him all across the West: searcher, scout, hunter, the man who could see where others only looked, his skills for hire but not his soul, the man who lived each day to the fullest, yet trailed each tomorrow. Skye Fargo, the Trailsman, and the seeker who could take the wildness of a land and the wanting of a woman and make them his own.

The Great Plains, 1860—where the great untamed stretches of the New Land brought out both the best and the worst in men, and proved that savagery can wear many faces. . . .

1

The town outside the window had a name: Sandstone. The girl in the bed beside him had a name: Betsy. Strangely enough, they had certain similarities. The town was one of those he called "not quite" towns. Not quite close enough to a wagon trail to grow and prosper, not quite large enough to have a sheriff, not quite in a location good enough to attract people to settle in and around it, and not quite able to do more than simply exist. There were many like it scattered along the edge of the Great Plains.

Betsy was a "not quite" girl as well; not quite pretty, not quite voluptuous, not quite ambitious enough to pick up sticks and move on. Yet she had been pleasant enough, warm and willing, and it had been a hot, hard trip breaking trail for Ted Olson's herd all the way from the Texas panhandle. When he'd finished, he'd ridden on to Sandstone only because Miles Davis had asked him to meet there. When he reached Sandstone, Betsy had been waiting tables at the saloon and she had been sweet and one thing led to another, as it often does. That had been three days ago, much of it spent in Betsy's bed in the small house not far from the saloon. He rose quietly, his lake-blue eyes peering through the window as another day rose. A tiny furrow touched his brow. Miles was late and it wasn't like General Miles Davis, U.S. Cavalry, to be late.

Skye Fargo turned from the window as Betsy stirred, opening her soft brown eyes, sitting up and wrapping herself around him at once. "Mmmmmm-mmm, I like it in the morning," she whispered, her breasts pressing into him, her muscled thighs lifting to wrap around him. She lay back, pulling him down with her. Betsy had warm, tingling skin that could start an instant, tactile fire to which he instantly responded. His fingers painted an invisible line across her shallow breasts, pausing to circle her small, dark red nipples set against larger matching circles. Betsy groaned happily. He continued to wander downward, over her small but puffy little belly, down to the curly down that she pushed upward at once to meet his touch.

"Oh, God, oh yes," Betsy murmured, her soft moans illicited by the touch of his hand, moans that grew louder as he moved lower, taking on a new note of pleasure when he reached the dark apex. Betsy was a creature of instant wanting. There was no coyness to her, no games, and it was perhaps that plain, unvarnished sincerity that gave her a special quality; a simple, uncluttered sexuality that had its own power. When her soft murmurings grew into rising groans, he felt her eager warmth around him, lifting her entire body to move in sublime harmony with his, finally finding that too-short moment of ecstatic intensity that was forever the same and forever new.

She screamed her pleasure and satisfaction and her body jiggled against him until finally she sank back onto the bed, spent and satiated, her arms and legs still clinging to him. Only when her breath returned in full did she relax her limbs. Her soft brown eyes peered at him, the hint of a private thought edging her lips. "Maybe your friend isn't coming. I'd like that," she murmured smugly.

"If he doesn't, he'll send somebody," Fargo said confidently. As an officer in the United States Cavalry, Miles Davis's position demanded no less. His personal code of behavior wouldn't let him do otherwise. Fargo lay back and Betsy put her body over him.

"There's always a first time," she said, unwilling to relinquish hope. "You could stay on then," she added, not that she needed to. He smiled but knew he'd not be staying. A list of jobs awaited him, each needing someone who could find what others missed, who could read what others only saw, each needing the Trailsman's knowledge and special gifts. Even if Betsy were the most beautiful woman in the world, he'd not stay. His world, his life, his love of searching the land, still beckoned him with an undiminished song. And despite what she wanted, Betsy knew that. Perhaps that was why she wanted so much so often. Storing memories was the next best thing to reality.

Her soft-fleshed body slid against him again and in moments the room once more echoed her soft moans. The sun was in the midmorning sky when Betsy made breakfast, wearing only a thin, loose shift. Fargo dressed, and had just finished his coffee when the sound of hooves rumbled through the room from outside. Betsy went with him to the window and gazed out at the double column of blue-and-gold uniforms astride sturdy, dark sable mounts. A second lieutenant led the column, Fargo noted. "Told you Miles would send somebody," he commented.

"Jeez, he always send a hundred troopers?" Betsy murmured.

"No," Fargo admitted as Betsy clung to him.

"Will you come back?" she asked.

"I'll try," he said, tasting her kiss before hurrying from the house. The troopers had halted at the stage depot as Miles had arranged. Fargo strode up to the second lieutenant. "Skye Fargo," he introduced himself.

"Lieutenant Boomer," the young officer said.

Fargo's eyes swept the long column. "I don't see General Davis," he said.

"He's at the field camp. We're on our way there. You're to come with us," the officer said.

"I'll get my horse," Fargo nodded, and hurried to the town stable and retrieved the Ovaro, its jet black fore-and-rear quarters and its pure white midsection glistening in the sun. He swung in beside the lieutenant as the officer waved the column forward. "Why the whole platoon?" he questioned.

"We're joining the others at the field command. We'll all be going on together," the lieutenant said.

"Going on where?" Fargo questioned.

"The general will tell you that if he wants to," Boomer said and Fargo smiled. Never give information you're not authorized to give, part of every officer's manual. He rode on in silence as he wondered what had made the general send for him this time. He knew one thing: Miles never called him in for something trivial. He'd worked enough with Miles Davis to know that. Lieutenant Boomer kept the double column at a trot, but it was already mid afternoon when they reached a dip in the land, and Fargo saw the neat rows of pup tents that marked a field camp, horses

4

tethered along both sides of the tents. Miles Davis emerged from the larger command tent as Fargo drew to a halt, his thick, silver white hair topping a handsome, still-youthful face.

"Been waiting, old friend," the general boomed. "How are you?"

"Can't complain," Fargo said, grasping the general's outstretched hand, then followed his tall, straight figure into the tent. Sinking into a canvas-backed chair, Fargo watched the general allow a wry smile to edge his lips. "What're you cooking for me to taste?" Fargo said.

"Maybe I just wanted to see you. You're growing cynical," the general said.

"I'm growing smart," Fargo replied. "You've your whole damn command in a field camp. Why?"

"They're moving me," Miles Davis said unhappily. "Want me to take charge of the Department of Texas. They want me on-hands there, for a while, at least."

Fargo's brows rose. "That's a lot of territory, all of Texas, New Mexico, the Oklahoma Indian Territory— along with the Comanche, the Chiricahua Apache, the Jicarillo, and all those wild Comanchero bands. Why the move?"

"There's increasing talk of war between the states. The army's pulling out all the men it can spare. They need someone who knows how to run a lot of land with a handful of men," Miles said.

"Which is pretty much what you've been doing for years up here," Fargo put in.

"I'll still technically be in command of the plains territories, but it'll be mostly in name only. I won't be really able to know what's going on and that's what's bothering me," Miles Davis said.

"How do I figure in this?" Fargo questioned.

"I'm worried about what I'm leaving behind, mainly General Robert Carlton," the general said and again Fargo's brows lifted.

"You're worried about one of your own people?"

"General Carlton's been running things but I've always held a tight rein on him. I won't be able to do that now. Carlton's a desk general, never been a field commander, but with his own personal connections and the army's need for filling posts, he was appointed. He doesn't know the plains, doesn't understand the dynamics that go on there. He's voiced ideas on how to keep control of the tribes that scare me."

"You outrank him. Why didn't you just slap him down?" Fargo asked.

"He hasn't done anything to allow me to do that. It's all been in the area of talk and memorandums, suggestions, and opinions. He's clever with words. He kept putting me in the position that if I disagreed with him, I'd sound as though I didn't want to take action against the Indians. But now with my moving south, he'll have a free hand. I need someone I can trust to keep an eye on General Carlton and keep me informed, at least until I can get back there."

"That's me?" Fargo frowned.

"Bull's-eye," Miles Davis said.

"No general, especially one such as him, is going to take orders from a civilian," Fargo said.

"I don't expect that. I want you on the scene to evaluate with your own eyes, in the way only you can, and report back to me. I'll have two couriers stationed in Elbow Flats. You can use them to get reports back to me."

"Why don't you just remove him?" Fargo queried.

"I can't, not without real proof. Right now I've a lot of uneasiness but no real evidence of anything to go with it. I've been looking over his shoulder up until now and he's had to be careful. But Carlton's the kind of man to let personal ambition destroy judgment. You know the army's full of small dictators. It's only when they get into a position where they can do some real harm that they became dangerous. Because of my orders to move south, Carlton's been put into that position. That's why I need your eyes and ears," Miles Davis said as he opened a file folder and drew out a letter on official army stationery. "You'll take this with you," he said and read the letter aloud.

Brigadier General Robert Carlton, USA:
This will introduce Mr. Skye Fargo, who is widely known as the Trailsman. He has served the army on numerous delicate assignments. I have always found his special knowledge, instincts, and experience to be of tremendous value. I hope you will find him equally helpful. Please extend him every courtesy.
Major General Miles Davis, U.S.A.

Fargo smiled. "That's sending a message. Subtly. You think he'll take it?" he asked.

"Anybody's guess." The general shrugged. "But he'll have to be careful." He rose as he handed the letter to Fargo, and Fargo pushed to his feet with him, walking beside him from the tent. "Same rates as always, old friend," the general said. "More than the army pays any other civilian."

"And they should." Fargo laughed as they reached the Ovaro.

"Won't argue that. Good luck," Miles Davis said as Fargo swung onto the horse. "Remember, those two couriers will be at Elbow Flat just for you."

"How long are you going to be holding things down south?" Fargo questioned.

"Until Washington decides different. I'll be head-quartered at Fort Ransom, Oklahoma Territory, but I'll be moving around. The two couriers will be kept informed where I'll be," Miles said, and raised his hand in a salute as Fargo sent the Ovaro off into a canter. Fargo kept the horse at a good pace in the late afternoon haze, headed north and west, holding steady until night descended. He found a place to stretch out in a cluster of black walnut and lay awake on his bedroll. The distant cry of timberwolves circled through the night and he smiled as he saw a mental picture of the land that lay in the darkness ahead of him.

The Great Plains were a vast and untamed area, a place of contrasts; beauty and cruelty, richness and sparseness, a place that could offer great rewards and provide a sudden death. The Great Plains were an area that teemed with life of every kind, from the tiny vole to the mighty buffalo, from the soft chatter of the goldfinch to the scream of the golden eagle. It harbored every kind of gift a man could want, and every kind of danger a man could face. But this vast land was made of balances, every creature playing its role, from predator to prey, every tree, bush, flower, and creature in its place, all part of the vast balance that was the Great Plains.

Only man had come to intrude on that balance, disturbing that ecological equilibrium. And not all men, Fargo grunted. The red man lived inside the vast balance, had become part of it, until now he, too, had torn himself out of his place. Fargo closed his eyes, letting sleep wash over him as he thought about the unknown dangers that lay waiting when the natural order of things was upset.

When the new day woke him, Fargo found a stream and washed and was in the saddle when the sun blanketed the land, the day dry and hot. It was under a noonday sky when he halted the gleaming Ovaro. He stayed in the saddle as his eyes peered out across the Great Plains that stretched before him. It was not unlike standing at the edge of an immense sea of green, he reflected, beckoning yet silently warning. I can be yours, it murmured, if you are wise enough and strong enough. I can be yours, or I can make you mine.

Elbow Flats lay some fifty miles west of the edge of the plains. Nestled at the lower edge of the great prairie, the town played host to plenty of dreamers who needed to take on fresh supplies before setting off across the heat of the plains. From Elbow Flats, wagon trains could roll northward to the Santa Fe Trail, the Oregon Trail, and the Mormon Trail. On these trails, most would push westward, some to connect with the Old Spanish Trail, the Gila River Trail, and the California Trail. But there were many who'd push west, forging their own trails, convinced there were better places to find than following the old trails. Sometimes they were right. Sometimes they were wrong. And too often, being wrong meant being dead.

But he'd get to Elbow Flats later, Fargo told himself. His goals were not limited to towns, nor to wagon trains. His goals included both and a lot more and he sent the Ovaro forward onto the vast plains, a land he knew perhaps better than any other man, and he allowed a wry smile at how little that really meant. His gaze swept the prairie as he rode, not hurrying. Legislators and local governments created states and territories and gave names to their creations. But the army paid little heed to that and divided the plains—indeed, all of the new western lands—into its own divisions. They drew their own boundaries based on their own strengths and estimates.

The lower plains they titled the Department of the Missouri. That division took in not only Missouri but Illinois, Kansas, Colorado, and Utah; an area the Pawnee, the Shoshoni, the Kiowa, the Utes, the Missouris, and the Osage also called their own. Above that, the army created the Department of the Platte, anchored by the Platte River. Here they took in Iowa, Nebraska, and Wyoming. In these states and territories, the Cheyenne and the Arapaho ruled the plains. Above that, reaching northward, the army established the Department of Dakota, which covered the entire northern plains territories of North and South Dakota, Minnesota, Montana, and on up to the Canadian border. In these northern plains states the Sioux and the Crow were the most powerful of the tribes, with the Poncas, Assiniboins, and the Nez Percé close behind, then the Sauk and Fox.

This was the geography the army had set for itself, defining the expansive tinderbox of delicate balances. It was no place for the inexperienced or the amateur, and no place for fools or ambitious egotists. Fargo let grim thoughts slide into a corner of his mind as he rode on, pausing to pick up a torn piece of armband. Kiowa, he noted by the design, and he'd gone on for another half hour or so when, moving just inside a long line of cottonwoods, he suddenly felt the ground vibrate with the pounding of hooves. The Ovaro felt it at the same moment and immediately tensed. Fargo stroked its jet black neck as he swung from the saddle and knelt one knee on the ground, letting every inch of his body become a sounding board.

Not Indian ponies, he muttered as he absorbed the thundering sound. This was the pounding of shod hooves. His ears picked up the next sound, that of rein chains, then the slap of leather chaps against horseflesh. He continued to pick up vibrations and this time they told him who the riders were that rode hard toward where he waited. It was not a mixture of individual riders, each setting their own pace and gait for their horses. These horses moved at a steady, uniform pace, almost in rhythm. "Cavalry," he said to himself and climbed back onto the Ovaro. As he peered out through the trees, only minutes later the blue-and-gold uniforms appeared in the sunlight, a platoon led by a lieutenant. Fargo watched the troopers pass by, noting the letter *B* on their small, triangular platoon banner.

They continued to ride hard, almost at a gallop, plainly with a goal in mind. Staying in the trees, Fargo moved the Ovaro forward and followed. The platoon had outdistanced him but the column of dust they sent up was easy enough to follow. Only a few minutes more passed when a fusillade of shots split the air, all the heavy explosions of army carbines. Fargo put the pinto into a canter and hurried forward inside the cottonwoods, slowing when he saw the scene unfolding on the open land to his left. The platoon was pouring fire into a small Kiowa camp. Fargo's quick glance saw only squaws, naked children and a half-dozen old men in the camp. The women, some clutching children in their arms, tried to flee and Fargo scowled in disbelief as the troopers poured lead into them.

An old man with long, gray, straggly hair tried to fire his bow and was cut down by a hail of bullets. A young woman fell with her arms still wrapped around her child. Fargo, the frown digging deep into his forehead, reached back and drew the big Henry from its saddlecase, and brought the rifle to his shoulder. He'd no desire to shoot U.S. cavalrymen but a massacre was a massacre, no matter who was doing it. He swung the rifle at two troopers riding down a young squaw with an infant in her arms. Using his superb marksmanship and the accuracy of the big Henry, he fired and one trooper's hat flew from his head. Another shot sent the second trooper's carbine spinning from his hands. Both soldiers reined up at once, surprise flooding their faces as they wheeled their mounts and stared toward the trees.

Fargo shifted position in the cottonwoods, firing at a trooper about to bring his carbine down on an old woman. His gun fell from his grip as Fargo's shot creased the top of his forearm. Fargo shifted position in the trees again, and fired. Another trooper's saber flew from his belt. Fargo saw the soldiers turning, surprised and confused, the young lieutenant moving forward to peer into the trees. It was enough time for the remaining squaws, children, and old men to reach a stand of shadbush behind the camp, and Fargo waited as the lieutenant drew his troop back to form a line that faced the cottonwoods. They waited, rifles ready to lay down a barrage, plainly expecting to face a Kiowa charge.

Fargo slid the Henry back into its saddlecase and slowly walked the Ovaro out of the cottonwoods. He let the horse amble toward the line of troopers and the lieutenant moved forward to meet him. Fargo saw a young face, dark hair poking from under his cap, dark brown eyes, and a face that was probably always serious, he guessed. It was a clean-shaven face, with a young man's skin that held no marks of age. The army was commissioning them younger and younger, Fargo noted. "You see any Kiowa in those cottonwoods?" the lieutenant frowned.

"Can't say that I did," Fargo answered.

"Maybe only three or four of them. You see any signs of anyone near where you were?" the lieutenant said.

"There wasn't anybody in those cottonwoods except me," Fargo said. "I did the shooting."

The lieutenant's mouth fell open as he stared back at Fargo. "You?" he said, finally, swallowing hard.

"That's right. Just little old me," Fargo said blandly.

The lieutenant drew his indignation around himself. "Why in hell were you shooting soldiers of the United States Cavalry, Mister?" he flung out.

"I didn't really shoot at your boys. You'd have six dead troopers it I'd done that," Fargo chided.

"Dammit, you interfered in an army attack," the lieutenant snapped.

"That was no attack. That was a massacre. There's a difference. I don't sit by for massacres, whether it's the Kiowa or the cavalry doing them," Fargo returned.

"Massacre is your word, mister. That doesn't make it so."

"I know a massacre when I see one. You were shooting down helpless squaws, children, and old men. What would you call it?" Fargo said.

The lieutenant was either too honest or too young to hide the moment of discomfort from his face. "I'd call it following orders," he said. "Who are you, mister? Lieutenant Thomas Nickles asking, Third Regiment, Platoon B."

"Skye Fargo answering. Whose orders were you following?"

"My commander's. General Robert Carlton," Lieutenant Nickles answered.

"I'd like to hear him explain ordering a massacre," Fargo remarked.

"I'm sure he'd enlighten you as to his orders."

"I'd like hearing that. Why don't I just follow you back?" Fargo suggested.

"The general's in the field. Pay him a visit in a few days. Fort Burns," Lieutenant Nickles said, letting his eyes bore into Fargo. "I don't know if I should just forget this," he muttered.

"Forget what?"

"You shooting at the U.S. Cavalry."

"I told you, I didn't shoot at your boys or they'd be dead," Fargo returned mildly.

"You came awfully close."

"That's called fancy shooting."

"Maybe too fancy. Maybe it was just dumb luck you didn't hit anybody. That kind of shooting's pretty hard to believe."

Fargo smiled as he drew the Henry from its case, and turned toward one of the teepees a few dozen yards away, aiming the rifle at the poles that rose up from the top of the teepee. "Pick a pole," he said.

"The center one," the lieutenant said, smiling doubtfully.

Fargo fired one shot, and the top of the center pole snapped off. "That help you believe?" he said laconically.

"Guess so," Nickles said, a touch of awe coming into his voice. "I've a feeling I'll be seeing you again, Fargo," he said as he turned his mount.

"Now, there's something else you can believe," Fargo said, and stayed in place to watch the lieutenant lead Platoon B northwest. When they were out of sight, he sent the pinto forward, passing the small Indian encampment and continuing on his way. Those hiding in the shadbush would return. What had taken place here would not be kept silent, he knew, and he felt a stab of grim apprehension through him. He rode slowly, reaching a narrow river, and let the pinto drink as he refilled his canteen while a pair of golden eagles wheeled overhead. A mild breeze bent the long field of sweet clover that stretched out before him as he crossed the river and rode on into a thick stand of bur oak.

He climbed a low ridge heavily overgrown with oak and hackberry that just let him see into a long, shallow dip in the land, both sides heavy with dense foliage. Three deer, one a big buck, suddenly flashed across from him as they burst into the open. Fright was plain in their sudden, darting movements and seconds later, a half-dozen Indian ponies raced from the side of the rise. Fargo watched the six bucks send a hail of arrows at the three deer, every shaft hitting its mark. Moments later, the three deer lay lifeless on the ground. The six braves, one wearing a Kiowa arm-band, immediately leaped from their ponies and began loading their prizes onto their mounts. They laughed, exulted, their voices easily carrying to where Fargo watched from the trees across from them.

They were busy chattering as they secured the deer. "Plenty meat. Plenty good hides," one said. They were too busy to be aware of the brush that moved on the rise just behind them, but Fargo's eyes caught the faint movement. He was the first to see the blue-uniformed riders that burst from the trees, laying down a withering barrage of gunfire as they did. The six braves leaped onto their ponies to flee but the attack was too fast, the hot lead too heavy. Only two managed to send their ponies racing away and only one of those disappeared into the thick foliage.

Fargo watched the cavalry platoon as it emerged fully on the scene and noted the letter *A* on the platoon banner. He put the Ovaro into a trot, came out of the trees, and went down the shallow hillside. A young lieutenant on his dark mount came forward. He was just as young as Nickles, Fargo saw, but with blond hair, a wispy mustache, and light blue eyes. He, too, tried to let serious formality mask his age. "Where'd you come from, mister?" he questioned.

"Back up there in the trees," Fargo said.

"The shooting bring you out?" the officer asked.

"No. I saw them bring down the deer," Fargo said, his glance sweeping across the slain braves. "They were a hunting party."

"I'm aware of that," the lieutenant said.

"Since when is the cavalry ambushing hunting parties?" Fargo asked.

"Since we got orders," the young officer said stiffly.

Fargo's glance went to the platoon banner. "Let me guess. Platoon A, Third Regiment," he slid out and the lieutenant's eyes widened.

"That's right," he said.

"Met up with Platoon B. They were following orders, too. Mighty strange orders," Fargo commented.

"That's not for me, nor Lieutenant Nickles to say," the officer answered. "Not for you, either, I'd say, mister."

"Sure it is. I can have an opinion. I'm not in the army. I'm not under orders," Fargo returned. "Name's Fargo. . . . Skye Fargo."

"Lieutenant Buzz Alderson," the young officer answered.

Fargo glanced at the silent figures on the ground again. "One of them got away, you know," he said and the lieutenant nodded. "He'll be saying plenty about this to his friends," Fargo mentioned.

"Oh, General Carlton expects there'll be a reaction," Alderson said a trifle smugly.

"He does, does he? And what kind of reaction does he expect?" Fargo pressed.

"Increased attacks on our patrols. The regiment's been fully prepared," the lieutenant said.

Fargo spit in disgust. "I'll tell you what the general ought to expect. He ought to expect the Indian not to do what's expected."

Alderson frowned. "I'll pass that on to him when I get the chance," he said.

"You do that, sonny, before it's too late," Fargo shot back. "Meanwhile, you might just go easy on following orders."

"I couldn't do that," the lieutenant said, visibly recoiling at the thought. "That'd be against regulations."

"Guess so, but they're regulations, not commandments. You could be saving a lot of lives."

The lieutenant frowned for a long moment. "I'll keep that in mind," he said dismissively and motioned to his troopers. Fargo watched as he led Platoon A, Third Regiment U.S. Cavalry, from the little hollow of land. Turning the Ovaro, Fargo rode north and swore under his breath at the excellent job the army did of instilling its rules and principles. Miles Davis had more reason than he realized to be uneasy.

Riding slowly, Fargo set out to explore the lower plains, to read the signs and markings that would let him see what others failed to see. He rode north, then west, then back south, carefully searching the terrain. He probed the flat prairie, followed the rolling sagebrush, explored low hills with thick tree cover and dense ridges, went down deer trails that were used by a lot more creatures than just deer. He found pieces of wristbands, gauntlets, moccasins, broken arrows, all Kiowa except for a few Osage, and he was grateful for that. He glimpsed a few distant bands of near-naked riders and quickly took refuge, wanting no unnecessary encounters.

When the day began to slip away, Fargo doubled back across the Great Plains that remained unchanging yet never the same. The day had been not unlike an unfinished sentence, its real meaning not what had been said but what hadn't been. He found a thick stand of shagbark hickory growing in moist soil beside a riverbank and set out his bedroll. A row of low hills rose up on the other side of the river and Fargo lay down and closed his eyes while a blanket of uncertainty stayed over him. Finally, he found sleep until the morning sun awoke him. He rolled up his gear, stepped to the river's edge with the Ovaro, and an oath fell from his lips. Staring across the river, he saw four plumes of gray smoke rising up just beyond the row of low hills.

"Shit," he swore as he vaulted onto the horse, sending the pinto racing across the river, grateful for its shallowness. The terrible feeling had already curled into the pit of Fargo's stomach as he reached the other bank and charged up the incline.

2

The smoke had grown thicker by the time he reached the top of the hills. He heard the fitful sounds of rifle fire, first, then the high-pitched war whoops. He kept in a line of hackberry as he saw six houses stretched out in a loose settlement along the flat plain that stretched beyond the hills. All six were afire, some forty Kiowa braves pouring arrows into the houses and the hapless occupants. Fargo saw the bloodied bodies of at least six children on the ground, along with a dozen men and women. As he watched, five Kiowa dragged three women from one of the houses, pulling clothes from them as they did. The women's screams mingled together to become one long, torturous cry as the Kiowa set on each, some two at once on a naked form. When they finished with the first woman, two pinned her naked body to the ground while a third took a hunting knife and began to cut off her nipples.

Fargo found the Henry in his hands and he fired a volley. The three Kiowa holding the woman went down but two others wrapped around another of the women. Racing the Ovaro through the trees, Fargo fired off another volley. Four more Kiowa spun and whirled as they went down. Reversing direction, he fired again as he raced back and three more of the attackers went down. As he paused to reload, he saw the Kiowa draw back, some climbing onto their ponies. He fired again and two more flew from their ponies. Racing in the other direction again, he let loose yet another volley. Two more attackers went down but others drew back still further. But it was enough. The attackers turned and began to race away from the burning houses, leaving the scene of carnage behind them.

The Kiowa, like most Indians, abhorred being trapped, caught by unexpected forces that might be superior. They always wanted to know the strength of their enemy. They were willing to be outnumbered so long as they knew it. Besides, these had done their work here. They had no reason to take chances and stay. For all they knew, the attacking bullets might be the advance of a full cavalry troop. The Kiowa raced away, disappearing across the flat plain with their wild shouts of triumph lingering in the wind. Fargo sent the pinto out of the trees toward the devastated settlement, dismounting when he reached it. The three women wandered nakedly through the terrible scene, dazed, trying to find loved ones.

Fargo stepped into some of the houses that were now mostly charred remains. He saw three men in one, two in another. All had been stripped, spread-eagled, their private parts cut off and stuffed into their mouths. No ordinary scalpings, Fargo saw as his stomach churned. He found a woman so riddled with arrows she resembled a pin cushion. But her long, blond hair was still with her. Frowning, he wandered outside as thoughts whirled inside him. An Indian attack was always stark and brutal, and carried certain marks in it. Hate, fury, defense of their lands, wrath and savage passions—those elements were always part on an Indian attack.

But this was different, some of the usual characteristics missing, the special savagery like a statement of revenge. He pondered the thought. It would be the Kiowa way. They'd not strike directly at a full regiment. They had many other ways to wreak revenge. He hadn't the time to sort it through but he was certain of one thing. This attack had carried a special message, a brutality that went beyond the ordinary. He put aside further thoughts and turned his attention to those few survivors, six women, two men, and two children. He found enough pieces of clothing and blankets for them and behind the charred remains of one house he found an Owensboro Kansas-Nebraska wagon with its peculiar high seat, its two horses tied to a stake. He hitched up the horses, brought the wagon around, and led the still-dazed survivors inside it.

"I'll take you to Elbow Flats. They'll send people back to take care of things," he said to one of the men who was not completely dazed.

"No, too far. Go to Greenville . . . it's closer. Due east," the man said and Fargo sent the brace forward, the Ovaro trotting alongside. Fargo left the open plains and steered the wagon through a line of hackberry and was glad of his decision when he spotted a sizeable band of braves riding in the open. He halted in the trees, unwilling to risk the creak of a wagon wheel. As he peered out at the band of braves, a frown spread across his forehead. They were not Kiowa, he saw. These were Pawnee. And they were no idle band out exploring far from their lands. They rode with a purpose, each man equipped with extra quivers. They were far from their homelands.

When the Pawnee moved from sight Fargo sent the wagon forward again with its huddled, sobbing band of survivors. When he reached Greenville he found the small town neat and orderly, and people came racing up to them. Fargo spoke to a man wearing a sheriff's badge. "We'll send a burying party out," the sheriff said when Fargo finished recounting what had happened. "Damn, another one," he added.

"Another one?" Fargo echoed.

"They wiped out the settlement by Thompkin's Lake last week, damn Shoshoni," the sheriff said.

"Shoshoni?" Fargo frowned. "You sure? They'd have to have come a long way."

"One of them was Shoshoni. Found him dead. Can't say for the rest," the sheriff said. Fargo grimaced. One Shoshoni? Or more? Even one made his stomach churn.

"Thanks for taking over, Sheriff. I'll be moving on, now," Fargo said, and swung onto the Ovaro and rode from the town. He turned west and headed for Elbow Flats, reaching it with the midafternoon sun. The town had grown since he'd last visited it, he saw, the main street crowded with Conestogas, heavy mountain drays, and a sprinkling of one-horse farm wagons. A corral with horses for sale was another new addition, he noted. Fargo's first impulse was to find the two couriers and send Miles a message but he quickly discarded the thought. He'd need more to give Miles. He'd have to meet with General Carlton first, he decided, and moved slowly on through the town.

He was walking the Ovaro through the center of

town when the shout reached his ears. "Fargo . . . by God, Fargo! I'd know that Ovaro anywhere." Fargo halted, turned, and saw the small, wiry figure rushing toward him with that special half-running, half-hopping gait he hadn't seen in too long.

"Jiminy Cricket," he gasped and felt the special rush of warmth that comes with seeing old friends. He swung to the ground as the little figure reached him, hardly over five feet tall, with a weathered, wizened face that had looked old even when it was young. Fargo swung the small figure into the air as though he were a child. "God, it's good to see you! It's been a long time," Fargo said as he set the little man down.

"Too long," the little figure agreed. "This calls for a drink, and we just happen to be in front of the Elbow Flats Saloon."

"Lead the way," Fargo said and followed the little man into the saloon. Jiminy Cricket had a proper name, Jimmy Johnstone, but when he was still a young cowhand, with his diminutive frame and unusual way of walking, the others quickly hung a nickname on him. Hanging nicknames on people was a long-standing cowhand practice and Jiminy Cricket stuck with him all through the years. Fargo often wondered if he ever used his real name anymore. But Jiminy had become one of the finest wagon drivers in the business, able to be one with any team he was driving, somehow able to sense every little thing about any of the horses.

"You out here to break a trail for somebody, Fargo?" Jiminy asked after they got their drinks at the long bar.

"Not at the moment. Doing a job for Miles Davis.

You remember General Davis, don't you, Jiminy? You did some special driving for him, once," Fargo said.

"Sure do, back a few years, though. Good man, for a general," Jiminy said.

"He is." Fargo laughed. "How about you? You driving for somebody out here?"

Jiminy Cricket crinkled his already crinkled face even further. "You could say that," he said.

"What's that mean?" Fargo questioned.

"It means I couldn't turn down the kind of money she offered me. But I'm wondering what I've got myself into."

"She?"

"Young woman named Melinda Tanner."

"Fill me in," Fargo said.

"She came to me in Missouri, and threw a year's worth of ordinary wages at me to be her driver. Two wagons. I'm to drive the supply wagon, a big, converted hay wagon with steel bow tops and canvas. She also pays me to take charge, handle all the supplies, equipment, extra horses, everything. She's going to drive the other wagon, a Conestoga," Jiminy said.

"Sounds all right to me," Fargo commented.

"It did to me, too. But I was all signed up when I found out she was taking six little girls in the Conestoga," Jiminy said.

"How little?" Fargo asked.

"From ten to twelve years old, she tells me. She keeps them away from everyone, keeps them in bonnets and long dresses. I've only had glimpses of them. Then she tells me she's taking them to Montana."

"Montana?" Fargo frowned. "Why in hell would

anyone take six little girls to Montana? It's crazy, and dangerous, even in a twenty-wagon train."

"She told me their folks were paying her a top price to take them to a fancy girls' school in Montana," Jiminy said.

"Shit, there are no fancy girls' schools in Montana. There's some real good ranch land if you can avoid a Sioux or Crow arrow," Fargo said. "I don't buy what she's handed you."

Jiminy threw his hands up helplessly. "All I know is what she's told me. She's real strong about it," he said.

"Doesn't make any damn sense. It's plumb crazy to try, anytime and especially now," Fargo said.

"Meaning what?" Jiminy asked quickly.

"Something bad's stirring. I'm not sure how bad yet but the Kiowa are on the warpath, I can tell you that," Fargo said.

"That's not making my ulcers calm down," Jiminy said. "But I can't back out. Wouldn't, anyway, not after I agreed. Besides, I already sent the money she paid me to my sister back in Missouri. She's hired a trailsman to take us through, feller named Matt Barlow."

"Never heard of him," Fargo said. "Maybe I ought to talk to her, convince her to call this thing off, at least for now."

"That'd be good but I don't expect she'll listen. But it's worth a try. She's paying for some supplies I bought at Willoughby's General Store. I'm to meet her there. Come along with me," Jiminy said as he downed his drink. Fargo emptied his glass and left the saloon beside the little man. They had just reached the general store when he saw the young woman emerge, a tall figure, held a little stiffly, with narrow hips and long legs encased in black riding britches. Her longish breasts were mostly obscured by a loose, white shirt. Blond hair, almost straw-colored, topped a narrow face with a straight, finely etched nose, a beautifully shaped mouth, and prominent cheekbones. Sharp, blue eyes sized Fargo up instantly. "This here's an old, old friend of mine, Skye Fargo, the best damn trailsman in the whole country," Jiminy introduced. "Melinda Tanner, Fargo."

The beautiful mouth managed a smile that was both warm and cool at the same time. "Unfortunately, Fargo, I've already hired a trailsman. Jiminy should've told you."

"Didn't come by for that. I'm all spoken for." Fargo smiled. "But Jiminy told me about your trip. This is no time for it." Melinda's brows arched, faint disapproval in her sharp, blue eyes. "There's Indian trouble brewing," Fargo explained.

"There's always Indian trouble, I'm told," Melinda Tanner said, her tone chiding.

"That's so," he agreed, "but there's trouble and real bad trouble. I sure as hell wouldn't try to reach Montana now, not with six little girls and two wagons, not even with a cavalry escort."

"I'm afraid I've no choice. I have to get there by a certain time," Melinda Tanner said firmly.

"You won't get there at all it you're dead," Fargo returned.

She allowed a faintly deprecating smile. "We'll get there alive," she said, flicking a glance past him. "Here comes Matt Barlow, now. He's a great deal more positive in his thinking than you." Fargo glanced at the tall man walking toward him, with black hair, and a face that edged surliness. Four men strode at his heels and all halted before Melinda. "This is Skye Fargo, Matt," she introduced. "Fargo has been telling me it's too dangerous to make the trip."

"I'll get you through, me and the rest of the boys here," Matt Barlow said. Fargo swept up the other four men in a quick glance. Two had the bloodshot eyes of men who spent too much time with a bottle. The other two had trouble looking him straight in the eye.

"You all going to break trail together?" Fargo asked Matt Barlow.

"That's right. More eyes see more," Barlow said.

Fargo fought down the impulse to snap an answer at Barlow. "You do much trailbreaking?" he asked, instead.

"Sure. Why?" Barlow frowned.

"Always looking for tips," Fargo said pleasantly. "Like I keep losing leads when they take to streams or rivers. Thought you might know something to help me out."

"Everbody loses leads in water. Can't do anything about that," Barlow said.

"Ever trail anybody on rock?" Fargo asked blandly.

"Nobody can trail on rock," Barlow said almost contemptuously. "Guess you haven't done much trailing."

"Now, hold on, Barlow," Jiminy cut in.

"That's all right," Fargo said quickly, cutting him off. "Man's entitled to his opinion."

Jiminy frowned back as Melinda Tanner spoke to Barlow. "We're about ready to leave, Matt," she said.

"I'd say by tomorrow morning. Right, Jiminy?" she asked the little man.

"Guess so," Jiminy muttered and Barlow strolled away with his four cronies. Fargo turned to Melinda Tanner.

"I told you Matt would be more positive in his thinking, Mr. Fargo," she said, a satisfied smugness in her voice. She needed her attitude shaken, Fargo murmured silently.

"I'm positive he doesn't know shit about being a trailsman," Fargo flung at her, seeing her face change expression. "He gave me all the wrong answers. You can trail in streams and rivers if you know how. You can trail on rock if you're good. And a good trailsman doesn't have four helpers. Doesn't, shouldn't, wouldn't."

"Why not?" Melinda Tanner frowned.

"Trailing is working alone. No real trailsman, no Indian scout, no woodsman, trails by committee. They'd get in each other's way. A trailsman has to have a special kind of focus. He has to believe in what he sees, what he hears, what he senses, one man in tune with himself and everything around him. That's the only way it can work," Fargo said, falling silent when he saw he had reached her by the way the sharp, blue eyes were narrowed at him.

"Very impressive," she murmured.

"I don't know about impressive but I know about true," Fargo said.

She thought for a moment more. "Would you take me through?" she asked.

"No, I've a job. If I didn't, I still wouldn't take you, not now," Fargo told her.

"Then I'll be trusting in Matt Barlow and his people," she said. "I'm going on. I must." She turned to Jiminy. "Everything you ordered at Willoughby's will be delivered in the morning." Jiminy nodded and she flashed a glance at Fargo. "I have to get back now. I've left the girls longer than I intended to." She turned on her heel and strode away. Jiminy followed and Fargo went with him, the Ovaro at his heels. When she reached the end of town she turned to two wagons pulled off to the side of the road. Two large blankets strung on poles largely closed the Conestoga from sight but Fargo glimpsed three of the little girls. All wore the long dresses and bonnets Jiminy had mentioned, only a small part of their faces visible. Melinda Tanner turned to him. "Thank you for your advice, Fargo. I'm sure we'll be fine," she said, dismissal in her tone.

"I'm glad you're sure," Fargo growled.

Melinda's eyes flashed. "Are you always so unpleasant?"

"Only around damned fools," he said. She spun around and pulled the curtain of blankets closed. Jiminy shrugged at Fargo's glance.

"Told you she was a hardnose," he said.

"It's more than that. Something's driving her," Fargo said. "Why's she keeping the little girls under wraps?"

"Says she doesn't want them exposed to things they don't need to see. Says it's best for them and everyone else," Jiminy answered.

"But she's willing to risk their necks on this foolish trip. Doesn't make any sense," Fargo said. Jiminy shrugged again. "Can you delay things, give me some more time?" Fargo asked.

"Can't see any way to do that. Barlow's anxious to move, too," Jiminy said.

"Maybe you'll get lucky and break a wheel," Fargo muttered.

"Any way you can maybe keep an eye on us?" Jiminy asked.

"Not likely. I'm going to have my hands full. But I will if I can," Fargo replied.

"I'll keep hoping you find a way. Barlow's going to start by heading straight north, he told me," Jiminy said.

"I'll remember. Good luck, Jiminy," Fargo said and climbed onto the pinto, riding off with a wave of his hand as dusk began to settle. Glancing back at the curtained wagons, he saw the straw-colored hair of one of the bonneted little girls sitting beside the Conestoga. He rode on through town and turned north, found a small cut of ironwood, and bedded down as night fell. Once again, a grimness settled over him. Melinda Tanner's lovely face swam into his mind.

He'd called her a fool. But she wasn't the ordinary kind, he realized. She was neither naïve nor stupid. She was driven by the kind of determination that made reason, caution, and logic, crumble away. She was a very attractive enigma he'd enjoy unraveling at another time but he had a lot more to unravel, priorities that concerned many more lives. He had to push aside further thoughts of Melinda Tanner and her strange little expedition and he drew sleep around himself with an effort. When the new day came, Fargo once again rode across the plains, searching underfoot and far away. When he came upon a torn parfleche he dismounted and studied the beadwork. "Pawnee," he spat and returned to the saddle. Besides the one item

31

from the Pawnee, everything else he'd seen had been Kiowa. Still it was more than enough to disturb him. Like swallows, the Pawnee never traveled alone.

It was time to visit General Robert Carlton and he turned northwest. He'd ridden another hour when he came onto a line of wagon tracks and dismounted to press his hands to the edges of the wheel marks. They were still firm, still holding moisture. Not more than twelve hours old, he guessed. It was difficult to read the size of the train by the wheel marks that followed each other in almost the exact same line. Instead, he counted the hoofprints that were part of each line of wheel marks and came up with a twelve-wagon train. But four sets of hoofprints were deeper than the others, he noted. These teams pulled wagons heavy with supplies. That left eight wagons of settler families. Fargo followed the tracks as they turned northwest.

He decided to catch up to the wagons, warn them of the extra dangers they faced, and urge them to turn back. Maybe they'd listen, he muttered, though he didn't hold out much hope for that. The men and women who rolled across the untamed, new lands in their Conestogas were a breed who had already accepted danger as a part of their journey. They embarked on their trek confident they could prevail. Courage was as much a part of their trip as the supplies they loaded. They simply didn't comprehend the variety and the magnitude of the dangers that waited for them. And now there were new ones brewing. He'd try to make them see that much, Fargo promised himself as he continued to follow the wheel tracks. They'd no doubt camped for the night, as he had. They weren't too far ahead, he felt certain.

A piece of headband on the ground caught his attention when the quiet of the morning was shattered by high-pitched war whoops, first, then the sound of rifle fire. The noise came from beyond a distant ridge thickly grown with shadbush. He put the pinto into a gallop, cursing as he heard the shouts grow louder, the rifle fire weaker, and soon stopping altogether. He reached the ridge and drove upward through the scrubby brush until he reached the top and could see through the leaves. His stomach turned. The prancing, whooping figures circled the wagons that were there, but not as they usually would be. In an Indian attack, wagons were usually stripped of blankets, sheets, guns. Then they were set afire, sometimes the horses taken. But none of that had happened here. The wagons were intact, nothing strewn upon the ground, nothing set afire.

But on each wheel, a naked man or woman was strapped, each body riddled with arrows. Fargo saw a half-dozen children huddled together, guarded by a Kiowa holding a rifle. Pulling the big Henry from its case, Fargo fired from inside the shadbush. The Kiowa guarding the children flew backward as his chest exploded. The six children stayed huddled together. Fargo swung the rifle, firing furiously and six of the Kiowa went down. He brought down three more as the others leaped onto their ponies. Three more started up the ridge toward the shadbush. None made it more than halfway up the incline. Fargo reloaded as the others wheeled their ponies and began to flee. He brought down two more before the others vanished over the western ridge, the sound of their cries quickly dying away.

Fargo sent the pinto down the slope toward the wagons. He didn't hurry. There was no need. Only the six youngsters were alive. Reaching the wagons, he dismounted, unhitched three of the horses, brought them over to the children, and sat two on each horse. He took another few minutes to walk around the wagons, pausing at each figure on each wheel. He studied the arrow shafts that protruded from each body. Most had Kiowa markings. A dozen bore Pawnee and Osage. Returning to the Ovaro, he led the three horses and their small, silent riders away, slowly climbing up the slope and through the trees until they were on the plains again.

The terrible scene rode with him, an attack unlike any he had ever seen, an attack that was unmistakable in what it said, unmistakable for what was missing. This had been a deliberate exercise in savagery, a statement that was now beyond questioning. Its meaning made Fargo's blood curdle as he rode and he cast a glance behind at the three horses and their riders. He had no words for the children, none that would comfort, and shock had robbed them of words. Silence was its own terrible blessing, he decided, as he rode on. He had gone on another mile when he suddenly spotted a distant spiral of dust rising into the air. It rose in a straight line, moving at a steady, even, pace and that meant only one thing in this country—a cavalry patrol.

He drew the Colt and fired three shots into the air, then another three. The thin spiral of dust changed direction, and started toward him and a few minutes later, the column of troops came into sight. As they drew closer he made out the letter *A* on the triangular platoon pennant. He stayed in place as Lieutenant Alderson drew his column to a halt, his glance going to the children. Fargo spoke in a terse, low voice and was glad to see horror pass through the young officer's face. "My God," Alderson breathed.

"Take the children to Greenville. There are womenfolk there who'll see to them," Fargo said.

"Where are you going?" Alderson asked.

"To visit General Carlton," Fargo said.

"I know shortcuts. I can get you there faster," the lieutenant said, and turned to an older trooper wearing sergeant's stripes. "Take the children. See to them when you reach Greenville. Resume patrol when you've finished and return to the fort as usual." Fargo waited until the Sergeant rode off with the six children, the column flanking the three horses. He then turned to the lieutenant.

"What have you and Troop B been doing the past few days?" Fargo asked sharply.

"Patrolling, as per orders," the lieutenant said.

"I want details, descriptions," Fargo said.

"We pursued and engaged hostiles when we found them," Alderson said stiffly.

"No official army talk, dammit," Fargo barked. "Plain language. What did you and Troop B do exactly?"

The lieutenant looked uncomfortable for a moment, then pulled himself together formally. "Troop B came upon a dozen squaws at a place set up for scraping and fleshing hides," he said.

"Lieutenant Nickles in command," Fargo said.

"That's right," Alderson said. "There were almost twenty hides stretched and staked out on the ground. Another two dozen were hanging on drying racks. I'd guess there were enough hides to make clothes for everybody for the entire winter."

"What did you do?" Fargo pressed.

35

"We destroyed every one of those hides, ripped each one to shreds," Alderson said.

"And the squaws?"

"They tried to run. We couldn't let them."

"Meaning you killed them."

"General's orders," Alderson said crisply.

"So much for Troop B. What about you? You had your own sector to patrol," Fargo said.

"We came upon a big field, sort of a natural farm field, you could say. There were at least two-dozen squaws and children filling baskets and sacks with berries, camass root, corn, squash, beans, prairie turnips, wild onions, and leeks and potatoes. They were gathering a whole winter's supply of food. The general had told us to watch for just this kind of place."

"You attacked, of course," Fargo snapped.

"Yes, sir. Some of the squaws tried to fight. We had to take care of them," Alderson said.

"You killed them. Don't sugarcoat it, soldier," Fargo bit out.

The lieutenant nodded. "Then we took care of the whole field," he said.

"You mean you destroyed what they'd picked," Fargo said.

"We did more than that. We burned the whole thing, set it on fire, and torched it to the ground. They won't be getting any food from that field for a couple of years," the lieutenant said.

Fargo groaned as he cursed. "Fort Burns, dammit," he snapped and the lieutenant put his mount into a fast canter. He rode at least twenty minutes in silence before he spoke.

"It's not as though the general hasn't thought this out, Fargo. He has a plan, a concept," Alderson said.

"Concept. That's a fancy word for ambition," Fargo tossed back. "And his plan is a recipe for disaster."

Alderson didn't speak again but he made good time on trails he knew well and they reached Fort Burns in the early afternoon. Fargo took in a fort with only one corner blockhouse but plenty of space for men and horses. But it was set out in the middle of nowhere, no settlements anywhere near it, not even a single sapling near the stockade walls, with only a stream some fifty yards away from which water had to be trekked. He knew at once what it was—one of those forts that the army had put up because it had to, that Washington had commissioned to salve some politician's feelings. The lieutenant led Fargo directly to the structure with the commander's flag outside, and Fargo followed him inside.

A tall man rose, his black hair cropped short, a prominent nose and a face that wore condescension in its every line. Cold, gray eyes barely avoided impatience as Alderson made the introductions and Fargo handed him Miles Davis's letter. Carlton read it, a faint sneer coming into his face as he handed it back. "I've heard of you, Fargo. You've done a number of jobs for Miles Davis. Is this another one?" he asked.

"I don't follow you," Fargo said evenly.

Carlton's smile was thin. "No games, Fargo," he said.

"Didn't come for games. The general thought I might be of help," Fargo said, holding on to his posture.

"Help? What a nice word for spying." Carlton sneered. Fargo cursed silently. Subtlety had plainly failed, as he'd feared it might. Carlton was a man made of defensiveness and suspicion.

"I'm not spying. I came looking. Now, I've come asking," Fargo said.

"Asking what?" Carlton snapped.

"Do you have any idea of what you're doing? Do you know what you're playing with?" Fargo tossed back, deciding that time for politeness was past.

"I know exactly what I'm doing. I've made careful plans. I'm going to do what no one else has done. I'm going to destroy the Kiowa, grind them into the ground. The other tribes will see and lay down their arms. I'm going to hit the Kiowa as they've never been hit before," the general said with calm certainty.

Fargo peered at the man's disdainful, superior attitude. "You don't have a clue, do you? You don't understand," he said.

"Understand what?" Carlton returned.

"The forces you're playing with. The dynamics of the plains, the delicate balance that keeps this land from erupting into a firestorm of killing."

"What is that balance? Tell me." Carlton almost laughed.

"A kind of unwritten rule, a silent understanding," Fargo said.

"You mean an understanding to let the Indian indulge in his savagery, his attacks on wagon trains and settlers?" Carlton snapped.

"No, I mean a silent understanding that there are limits even on savagery and brutality. To the Indian, there is honor in killing your enemy. But that killing must be done with honor, in an attack motivated by hate and pride. To the Indian, there is honor in hate. I'd say the white man has adhered to the same code for centuries. There is honor in battle and there is dishonor. There are things done and things not done. You're out to destroy all that and innocent people are going to pay the price. Some have already," Fargo said.

"There's always a price for victory. You, Miles Davis, and all the others have been wrong with your tacit understandings. I'm changing all that. I'll destroy the Kiowa completely," Carlton said.

"You don't know the Indians. They'll come together to fight you. your tactics will bring them together, something Miles Davis has been careful to avoid. Other tribes are already here."

"A few stragglers, perhaps. But no major force. I'd know if there were."

"How?"

"I've posted lookouts at the edges of the Kiowa territory. No sizeable outside tribes can come in without my lookouts seeing them."

"Your lookouts have failed. They're already here and more will come," Fargo said.

"Impossible!" Carlton said. "My lookouts are strategically posted. They'll see any tribes coming in to join the Kiowa. And if they come, so much the better. I've an ace in the hole. I've put in a request for five hundred new troopers. They'll be here any day now."

"Five hundred won't be enough. You keep on and you'll set the plains on fire. You'll see hate and fury no one has ever seen," Fargo said.

"Nonsense. They'll be giving me medals for taming the lower plains," the general said with a snort.

Fargo grimaced inwardly. Carlton was a man consumed with his ambition, a man charging headlong after glory. But perhaps there was still a spark of reason and humanity left in him. Fargo knew he had to try. He had to buy time. "Look, Carlton. There are a lot of wagon trains on the move across the plains and there are a lot of new settlements. They're all extremely vulnerable. They'll pay a terrible price. Hold off for a spell. Let things settle down some," Fargo tried.

"That's exactly what I won't do. I've plans that will send the Kiowa into a frenzy, make them attack the regiment. That'll be the end of them. I'm going to shatter all their primitive rituals. I'm going to break their spirit as well as their bodies," Carlton said, his gray eyes taking on the light of a zealot. Fargo turned the man's words over and wondered if they were just more rhetoric or it they had a more terrible meaning. "That's all I'm going to say, Fargo. This conversation is at an end," Carlton said.

"Nothing's at an end," Fargo said, casting a glance at Lieutenant Alderson. The lieutenant had listened in silence. Fargo hadn't expected him to say anything but he was glad Alderson had been there. Turning, Fargo strode from the small office to see Lieutenant Nickles returning with his platoon. "Lieutenant Alderson will fill you in," Fargo said curtly as he climbed onto the Ovaro.

"You met with the general, I take it," Nickles said and Fargo nodded.

"You and Lieutenant Alderson have something unusual here," Fargo said. "It's not often you get a commanding officer who's both an idiot and a madman," Fargo finished and left Lieutenant Nickles with his mouth open. Riding from the post in the late afternoon sun, Fargo headed east and then north when the land stretched low, rolling hills heavy with red cedar and bitternut. He hoped it was the way Barlow had taken Melinda Tanner and her little girls. Mostly, he wanted to meet with Jiminy. Time had grown suddenly important and unsettling. He rode alongside the trees until night fell, and then he bedded down.

Carlton's cryptic words still stabbed at him as he waited for sleep. Were they just the rantings of an obsessed man? He wanted to think that but he was afraid they meant a great deal more. If his fears were right, he had to find out what lunacy Carlton was planning. And he had to get a message to Miles Davis. Not that Miles could help. He was too far away now and too tied down. But perhaps he knew a place to find help, a way to reach Carlton through army channels. Fargo finally found sleep with bitter misgivings by his side.

3

When he rode with the new day Fargo felt that he suddenly understood why animals sensed a terrible storm or an earthquake coming. They felt the electricity, vibrations, psychic messages, picking up the subtle warnings of catastrophe. Yet they only knew their fear, the nervous tension that seized them, the knowing that was not knowing. He could empathize with that burden, now. It was exactly how he felt. He could feel disaster looming but he knew not where, when, or how. Staying close to the edge of the red cedar and entering the trees, he spotted wheel marks.

They had to go slow to stay in the cedars, the trees grown so thick that they left little space between their red-tinted bark. Barlow was smart enough to stay in the tree cover and pay attention to the warnings that had been given him, Fargo noted. He rode on another half day when he spotted the two wagons. They had been forced out onto the open land, the cedars too thickly overgrown to negotiate through. Fargo reached Jiminy first, in the big converted hay wagon following the Conestoga. "Jeez, am I glad to see you," Jiminy said as Fargo reached the wagon.

"Trouble?" Fargo questioned.

"Of sorts. Melinda's been jawing at Barlow for making such slow time," the little man said.

"That's pretty damn dumb of her." Fargo snorted. "Where's Barlow now?"

"Rode on ahead to break trail with his friends," Jiminy said.

"At least he's being careful," Fargo said.

"He's more than careful. He's afraid. I know a man that's afraid and nervous when I see one. We met two riders who told us what happened to that wagon train. Ever since, Barlow's spent more time watching for Kiowa than breaking trail."

"That news didn't affect Melinda?"

"Made her want to move on faster." Jiminy snorted.

"She's never said why she's so desperate to get those little girls to that fancy school I don't think exists has she?" Fargo queried.

"Never. But Barlow and his buddies have done a lot of talking off by themselves. I don't like it, Fargo, got a bad feeling."

"Maybe I can get a handle on it," Fargo said and sent the pinto forward, coming up to the Conestoga. Three bonneted faces peered out the back of the wagon at him as he rode past and drew alongside Melinda. The heat had grown oppressive and she had her sleeves rolled up. He saw the outline of her breasts as the white shirt clung to her.

"What are you doing here?" she asked in surprise. "Thought you had a job."

"I do. It brought me this way," Fargo said. "I picked up your trail. I'm glad you're not further along."

"Why?"

43

"You can still go back to Elbow Flats or Greenville," Fargo said.

Melinda's face grew tight at once. "Absolutely not," she said. "I'm going on. Barlow's been setting too slow a pace. I'm going to insist he pick it up."

"What's pushing you?" Fargo inquired.

Melinda's eyes became twin blue masks. "You say you've commitments. You're not the only one," she said.

He was going to press further when Barlow appeared, his four cronies behind him. Riding to a halt, Barlow immediately glowered at Fargo. "What are you doing here?" he growled.

"Passing by," Fargo said. "How are you doing?"

"Fine, just fine," Barlow said.

"You find a trail to make up time?" Melinda asked the man.

"A good one. We'll talk about it in the morning," Barlow said. "Alone," he added pointedly. Fargo smiled, turned the pinto, and rode back to Jiminy.

"You're right about Barlow. He's real nervous. He shouldn't have been so upset seeing me," Fargo mentioned.

"Maybe he knows you've got him tagged," Jiminy offered.

"That could be part of it. But there's more. He acts like a man with something on his mind. His friends, too. They're all on edge, too," Fargo said.

"Wish you could stay around, Fargo," Jiminy said.

"We'll talk about that tomorrow. I'm going to need your help," Fargo said.

"If I can. You know that," Jiminy said.

"Meanwhile, I'm going to disappear," Fargo said and returned to Melinda, seeing that Barlow and the others had left again. "He go looking for another trail?" Fargo remarked blandly.

Melinda's eyes flashed blue fire. "Don't bother saying it," she snapped.

"Saying what?" Fargo asked innocently.

"I told you so," she flung at him.

"Wasn't going to," he said.

"You were thinking it," she muttered and his half shrug was an admission.

"Call it off for now. Turn back," Fargo said.

"I told you, no," she said.

"Good luck, then," Fargo said.

"Thank you," she returned, cold politeness coating her words, her attractive face strained. Fargo turned the pinto and rode away, waving to Jiminy and watching the sun lowering over the horizon. He made a wide circle, returned to the trees, and once more trailed the two wagons. He caught up to them as dusk began to settle, seeing that Barlow and the others had returned, the wagons pulled in just at the edge of the trees. Melinda had strung her curtain of blankets all around the Conestoga, securing them on low branches, and he saw her taking packages of beef jerky from Jiminy and the supply wagon. She disappeared inside the ring of curtains with the food and Fargo peered through the trees and found Barlow and his four cronies sitting off by themselves.

Retreating deeper into the cedars, Fargo set out his bedroll as dark fell. He'd have to approach Jiminy and Melinda in the morning, he decided. He couldn't let any more time go by. Melinda would resist, he was certain, but he put aside thinking about it and slept as the moon rose higher. He rose with the new

45

day, used water from his canteen to wash up, and gave the others time to wake. When he crept back to where he could see the wagons, the curtain was still up around the Conestoga. Jiminy was feeding the horses and he found Melinda facing Barlow and his four men.

"This is outrageous!" he heard Melinda say, fury in her voice, and he crept closer. "We have an agreement. I paid you," she said.

"That agreement's off," Barlow said. "This job's become a lot more dangerous."

"There was always danger. You knew that," Melinda said.

"Not like this. We deserve more money. You heard about what's been happening," Barlow said.

"This is blackmail," Melinda fired back.

"Call it whatever you like, honey. Fork over more cash or we're gone," Barlow said.

"You can't do that. I paid you to take us through. This is despicable," Melinda returned.

"No more lip, girlie," one of the others cut in. "Pay up or you're on your own." Fargo's eyes went to the other four men, making note of each one's position.

"You can't make it on your own," Barlow added with a confident sneer. Fargo saw Melinda glare at him, her fists clenched at her sides, deep breaths making her breasts press tightly against her shirt. He knew she desperately wanted to tell Barlow to go to hell but she also knew she needed help to make the trip. It was a devil's choice. But she really hadn't a choice, Fargo knew. Her decision didn't really matter. She had been a mark from the beginning. Barlow was about to make her one for a second time.

"Hurry up. Make up your mind," one of the others said gruffly.

Barlow tried to make his voice soothing. "Look at it as just another agreement," he said. "Pay up and we'll start rolling right away."

Fargo grimaced but he had heard more than enough. He knew what would follow. Barlow had no intention of taking Melinda further. No intention and no ability to do so. Fargo pushed through the trees. "How far?" he asked mildly as Barlow spun, his eyes widening in surprise.

"What are you doin' here again?" Barlow growled.

"How far are you going to roll?" Fargo said.

"This is none of your business. Butt out," Barlow ordered.

"I'm waiting for an answer," Fargo said.

"You're waiting for a bullet," Barlow snapped.

Fargo slid sideways, edged against one of the cedars, and his eyes flicked once more to the other four men. They hadn't changed their positions. "Tell her what you really figure to do as soon as you get the money," Fargo said to Barlow.

"Son of a bitch!" Barlow roared and reached for his gun. But he was slow, Fargo saw at once, his motion uneven. Fargo's eyes snapped to the other four men. One wearing a black kerchief was quicker, his draw smoother. Fargo's hand moved with the speed of a rattler's strike and the Colt fired in split seconds. The man with the black kerchief almost bent in half as he flew backward and went down. Barlow had managed to get his gun out, half raised it to fire, but Fargo's second shot already split the air. Barlow's chest shattered and he clutched at himself as he fell face forward.

The other two men had found the seconds they needed to fire but Fargo had ducked behind the tree as their shots tore chunks of bark from the trunk. Fargo dropped to the ground, fired around the tree from an almost prone position before the two men adjusted their sites to find him. Both seemed to be performing a strange dance together as they swayed and bucked and finally collapsed into a heap to lay side by side. Fargo pushed to his feet and stepped into the clear, seeing four bonneted heads poking through the curtain.

"Get back," Melinda ordered sharply and the heads vanished. She turned to Fargo as Jiminy came running up.

"That was too close for comfort," Jiminy said.

Melinda's eyes held Fargo with a steady gaze that offered relief, gratitude, and something else he couldn't define. "They would have killed you. Everybody else, too. They were never going to take you on and they couldn't leave anyone to tell," Fargo told her.

"We all owe you, more than any of us can repay. Thanks for following. How'd you know?" Melinda said.

"Rotten apples aren't hard to spot," Fargo said.

"Except for fools like me." She snorted.

"It takes a little practice," he said and felt a furrow touch his brow as he saw her eyes change expression, a kind of sly triumph come into the blue orbs.

"There's a good side to everything," she murmured.

"How do you mean that?" Fargo questioned.

"Now you have to take me," she said.

"I don't and I can't," he said.

"You wiped out my trailsman. It's your obligation to replace him," she said smugly.

"The hell it is. They drew on me. You saw that. I had to fire." Fargo frowned.

"That doesn't change anything. You have to take us. It's only right, only fair. It's your moral obligation," she insisted.

"Good try, Melinda, but it won't work," Fargo said.

"Don't you have a conscience?" she flung back.

"I've told you to turn back. That satisfies my conscience," Fargo said.

Her eyes narrowed at him. "If that's what you want," she said.

"What's that mean?"

"We'll go on alone."

"You won't have a chance in hell," Fargo snapped.

"Maybe not but I'm going to try," Melinda said, her chin lifted firmly. He peered hard at her; she met his probing stare. There was no acting in her eyes, no wavering, no smugness now, nothing but stubborn determination.

"It's not just your life you're throwing away. What about those six little girls?" Fargo pushed at her.

"My responsibility," she said adamantly and Fargo swore silently. She was going to go on. There was no question about it. He didn't understand her, couldn't accept her foolish willfulness. But he couldn't accept abandoning her and the little girls, either. A loose plan was forming inside him as he turned to her. "Only one way. My rules, my decisions. I say where we go and when, where we stop and when, what we do and when we do it. No arguments, no tricks. Those are the conditions," he said.

She took a long moment to answer but finally nodded. "Except for the girls and the Conestoga. I'm in charge there," she said.

"Fine with me. Get ready to roll," he said and strode into the trees to retrieve the Ovaro. Jiminy fell into step beside him.

"What are you figuring to do, Fargo?" he asked.

"Do what I have to do and maybe keep her and six little girls alive," Fargo said.

"Sounds like a pretty big order," Jiminy said.

"I know," Fargo said quickly and Jiminy went to the supply wagon as Fargo brought the Ovaro from the trees. When he walked the horse into the open, the curtain around the Conestoga was down and Melinda held the reins of the team. He saw two bonneted heads peek out at him as he rode past Melinda. "Stay north," he called to her and rode on, his eyes sweeping the plains to his left. Edging the trees, he found a well-worn deer trail, wide enough for the wagons to negotiate through the thick forest of cottonwood. When he returned to the wagons, the late morning sun was burning and once again Melinda's shirt was soaked with perspiration, clinging delightfully to her long, lovely contours and outlining little points.

She tossed him a glare. "You don't have to enjoy looking," she said.

"If it's worth looking, I look. Force of habit." He shrugged. "Beauty is made for looking, whether it's a tree, a flower, a sunset, a stallion, or a woman." She didn't soften her glare and he motioned for her to follow and led the way to the deer trail. "Stay on this till it ends," he said. "Wait there until I get back."

"Where are you going?" she asked, alarm in her voice.

"To take care of other things," he said and hurried

50

away with a nod to Jiminy. Fargo put the pinto into a fast canter, leaving the cottonwoods and riding hard onto the plains. He crisscrossed the land, ducking into a small clump of hawthorn as a large band of braves appeared and went on. He followed their tracks, slowing his pace as he saw the tracks spread out, becoming shallower. They were slowing and he halted and dismounted when he spied a long field of burdock, the weeds standing some five feet tall. He dropped down and began to make his way through the foliage, pushing aside the long, oval leaves and the reddish purple flower heads that sat atop bulbous growths.

Fargo crawled carefully, taking pains not to disturb any of the weeds. Suddenly he heard voices and inhaled the scent of water, fresh yet slightly musky. Staying low, he crawled forward until he could see a large, circular pond around which the Indians had halted. He counted some thirty horses, his eyes moving to the braves as they cooled themselves in the pond and began to step out of the water. He focused on their moccasins and armbands and cursed silently as he saw the Shoshoni markings. He lay still, waited as they climbed onto their ponies and rode away, riding directly north. When Fargo rose and returned to where he had left the Ovaro, he retraced his steps at a fast canter as he headed for the fort. He was almost there when he met Lieutenant Nickles and Troop B, and they rode with him to the fort.

General Carlton met Fargo as he halted outside the command office, the man's eyes gray ice floes. "Back again, Fargo? I told you our conversation was finished," Carlton said.

"The Shoshoni reopened it. I saw thirty of them, on their way to join the Kiowa," Fargo said.

"Impossible. They couldn't get through without my lookouts seeing them," the general said. "You see any other tribes before you met up with them?"

"Not that many," Fargo admitted.

"Then they were Kiowa wearing moccasins they found or stole. That's common enough," Carlton said.

Fargo didn't answer. The man's explanation held a thin edge of possibility, a very thin edge. "Maybe your lookouts can't cover all the ground you think they can," he said.

"They're strategically placed. They'd see any sizeable force coming into Kiowa territory," Carlton said and motioned to Lieutenant Nickles. "Show Mr. Fargo out, Lieutenant, " he said and turned back into his office. Nickles went to the gate with Fargo, his face careful not to betray any of his thoughts. But he and Alderson had talked, Fargo felt certain of that.

"Last time I talked with the general he said he was going to shatter the Kiowa, break their spirits as well as their bodies. You know what he meant by that?" Fargo questioned.

"That's for the general to tell you if he so wishes," Nickles said.

Fargo eyed him with a long, sideways glance. "It's hard to do isn't it?" he said and the lieutenant frowned back.

"What is?" he asked.

"Stop following the rule book. Think for yourself. Forget army protocol," Fargo said and saw the young lieutenant's mouth tighten. "See you soon," Fargo said and put the pinto into a fast trot as he rode from the fort. He rode back across the plains as his thoughts chased themselves inside him.

Fargo had no doubts that Carlton was setting wheels of horror in motion and he had seen enough to be convinced that other tribes were joining with the Kiowa. But he admitted to being mystified. They were arriving, yet they'd left no signs of their travels. Obviously, Carlton's lookouts hadn't seen any and Fargo admitted he hadn't picked up the kind of tracks he should have. Yet Shoshoni were here, Pawnee and Osage, too. How were they getting to Kiowa territory without being seen or leaving any tracks? The question stayed with him as he examined every inch of ground as he crisscrossed the land. He finally reached the cottonwoods with no answer and swung onto the deer trail. It went on for longer than he had estimated but he finally came to the end where the two wagons waited. A dense growth of hackberry ended the trail and climbed up a low hill.

Melinda frowned at him as he rode to a halt. "Expected you back long before now," she muttered. "We've wasted valuable time waiting around."

"There's a time for waiting and a time for not waiting," he said.

"Spare me the simple philosophic sentiments. I don't want to wait around," Melinda tossed back sharply.

"You forgetting the conditions so soon?" Fargo inquired mildly.

"I agreed to them. I didn't say I had to like them," she said.

"No, you didn't," he conceded, looking past her at the wall of hackberry. "Follow me," he said as he started to edge past the trees and saw a narrow, curving pathway just wide enough for the wagons. He led the way slowly, searching out fit passages, and it was nearing dusk when he found a circular arbor that bordered on a wide mountain stream. Peering beyond the stream, Fargo spied open high land along with a rocky formation that rose up still higher. But the little arbor was perfect for what he wanted—it was secluded, with fresh running water.

"Make camp here," he said, dismounting. Melinda pulled the Conestoga a dozen yards into the arbor and Jiminy halted back along the stream. Melinda swung from the wagon as he watched, a smooth, graceful movement that made her long, narrow body sway as though it were a willow wand in a breeze. "You'll be safe here while Jiminy's away," Fargo said.

Melinda's frown was instant. "What do you mean, while he's away?"

"He's going to deliver a message for me," Fargo said. "I'll scout a trail for you in the morning and come back and drive Jiminy's wagon. That way, he'll deliver my message and I'll keep you moving. Sort of killing two birds with one stone," he added soothingly. It had the effect he hoped for as her face softened.

"So long as we keep moving," Melinda said.

"You know, you're right pretty when you're not keeping yourself all tied up in knots," Fargo said offhandedly.

"That's almost a compliment," she said. "But I'll take it." He watched as she turned away and began to string the curtain of blankets around the Conestoga, again using low branches to secure the corners. Fargo went to Jiminy, who had been listening. The little man fixed him with a quizzical smile.

"You got her to swallow that one," he said.

"Meaning what?" Fargo asked innocently.

"I know you, Skye Fargo. This is a really safe, quiet, tucked-away spot. You didn't pick it just to have her move out come morning."

"You're getting suspicious in your old age, Jiminy." Fargo laughed.

"Damn right. Now, what's this message and where do I deliver it?"

"Elbow Flats. There are two army couriers waiting there. One of them will take it to Miles Davis. You wait there for an answer." Jiminy nodded and Fargo rummaged through his saddlebag, and came up with a small square of paper and a small bottle of ink with a horn stopper. He sat down, using the top of a log as a writing table, and penned the note to Miles Davis.

It's everything you were afraid of. He's an ambitious fool that doesn't want to listen. He's going to set the plains on fire. Other tribes are joining the Kiowa. He's doing all he can to make the tribes explode. He's requested five hundred men he figures will give him enough power to win. It won't. You've got to remove him from command before it's too late. He's planning something to blow the lid off things and I'm scared as hell about it. I'll wait for your answer.

Fargo

Folding the note, he gave it to Jiminy. "Leave at dawn. I don't have to tell you to stay in cover as much as you can," he said and Jiminy nodded soberly. When he strode away, dusk was giving way to night and Melinda had the circle of curtains up. He saw the glow of two kerosene lamps behind them. Melinda slid from between the curtains and started for Jiminy and the supply wagon.

"Time for supper," she said.

Fargo's eyes narrowed at her. "Jiminy told me you wanted to keep the girls from seeing things they didn't need to see. I'll buy that while you were in town. You're not, now. So why the curtains?" he questioned.

"There are still lots of things that could happen to upset a young girl, attacks by animals on other animals, cougars, grizzlies, even eagles. Nature can be very cruel and upsetting. I'm sure you know that. Then there's always the unexpected, such as what took place with Barlow. Other men might come by or we might come into another town. I prefer to keep them safe," she answered.

Fargo turned her words in his mind. They had been wrapped in tenuous reasoning that carried only a surface plausibility. She was manufacturing reasons and he returned a slow smile. "Nice try. Now, what's the real reason for keeping them under wraps? Something wrong with them?"

"I gave you the real reason," she said tensely. "You ought to learn to believe people."

"I know, but I keep being disappointed," he said and watched her stride away, wrapping indignation around herself as though it were a cloak.

"You going to stick with that story about a fancy school in Montana?" he called after her.

She paused to turn and glare back at him. "Of course," she snapped.

"What's the name of it?" he queried.

"That's not your concern. You just get us to Montana," Melinda snapped and strode on. He smiled as he went on up the stream and set out his bedroll. She'd never be able to keep up her little game all the way to Montana, if she made it that far. Too many things could happen to shred her efforts. He had no need to press her. He'd learn the truth of it all before the trip was over, he felt certain.

He fell asleep quickly and when morning came he rose with the new day to see that Jiminy had left. He was dressed, the Ovaro saddled when Melinda stepped from behind the curtains around the Conestoga. She wore a light blue cotton dress that let him enjoy the long curves that rose up from a very low and loose neckline. Surprised to see him, she hastily pulled the neckline up. "I'm not ready to travel," she said.

"That's all right," Fargo said and she frowned at once. "There's been a change in plans," he said evenly. "This is a good, safe place. You can hole up here till I get back."

The sharp blue eyes peered suspiciously at him. "Nothing happened last night to cause a change in plans," she said.

"I did some more thinking," he offered.

"Hell, you did," Melinda flung back. "You planned for me to stay here."

"You ought to learn to believe people. I heard that somewhere," he said.

"I keep being disappointed. I heard that somewhere too," she chided. He didn't answer as he grudgingly admired her quickness, and started to swing onto the pinto.

"This isn't fair. I can't get to Montana sitting here," Melinda said angrily.

"You want to get there alive, don't you? Sitting here might let you do that," Fargo said. "If I don't do what has to be done, you won't get to Montana at all. I can promise you that."

She glowered back. "I don't like being tricked," she muttered.

"That makes two of us," he said. "Now relax and enjoy the arbor." Putting the horse into a trot, he rode from the secluded spot, immediately climbing a low hill that let him see a broad expanse of the plains when he reached the top. The land directly ahead of him was the heart of Kiowa territory but he saw no signs of riders, neither near-naked ones nor those clothed in blue-and-gold uniforms. He let his gaze slowly sweep the plain and was just about to move from the top of the hill when he caught movement at the east edge of the terrain. He saw a swath of mullein growing amid the buffalo grass in seven-foot high stalks. The tall mullein stirred, a wide movement but without the sweeping motion of windblown grass. He sent the pinto down the hill, swinging in against a narrow line of hawthorns and when he drew closer to the moving mullein, he dismounted and went forward on foot in a crouch. He reached the mullein, letting the tall stalks hide his crouched form, and found himself peering at some fifty Indian ponies being led by their loinclothed masters.

As he watched, the mullein came to an end and the lithe, red-brown figures swung onto their ponies and began to ride on deeper into Kiowa country. But they were not Kiowa. Fargo's eyes focused on their moccasins and armbands, noting the beadwork on each and seeing the geometric designs of the Arapaho. He cursed softly. The Arapaho had to come all the way from beyond the Platte. They gathered speed as they rode and Fargo didn't try to follow across the low, open prairie grass. Instead, he moved back into the mullein, and dropped to one knee as he studied the tracks they had left. He followed the prints back the way they had come, carefully stealing through the weeds as they had. He halted when the tracks ended abruptly and frowned down at the ground. There had been tracks and now there were none. It was as if they had dropped down from the sky.

Staying on his knees, he examined the ground, the base of the grasses, the stronger, hardier mullein, and ran his hands over loose leaves, letting his fingers feel the touch of the soil until he finally came across the marks he searched to find. Tracks had been wiped away, soil carefully brushed, leaves, grass, and roots used to erase tracks. But that meant only one thing. There had been tracks there before. They had come the long way from above the Platte into Kiowa territory and none of Carlton's lookouts or patrols had seen them. Nor had they seen tracks. They were getting deep into Kiowa territory without being seen or leaving the kinds of tracks large groups of riders had to leave.

If they traveled by night they'd have left tracks. They'd never have been able to cover that many tracks by night, certainly not with the care with which these had been covered. Yet they were here to meet with the Kiowa without being seen or leaving tracks. How? The question shimmered in his mind. It was not simply a matter of curiosity, he realized. Finding the answer might tell him how to stop more from coming and how many had already arrived. The fact that they were here sent shivers through him. The Kiowa had recruited help from other tribes. That prospect held the seeds of carnage. It could mean a cooperation that had never happened before, a pact that signaled killing and terror for all the plains if it proved victorious.

Fargo rose and returned to where he had left the Ovaro and climbed into the saddle. He backed from the mullein and again let his eyes sweep the plains. It wasn't long before he spotted the dust plume of a cavalry patrol, then a second one far on the other side of the Kiowa heartland. His eyes followed both plumes and his brow furrowed. They didn't move in the usual long line. Instead, both went back and forth, cutting across the land, disappearing and then coming into sight again. He spurred the pinto forward when the plume at his right veered closer, and sent the horse at an angle and cut in front of the column. He found himself riding up to Lieutenant Buzz Alderson with Platoon A.

"What are you looking for?" Fargo asked casually. "You're searching for something special."

"What makes you think that?" the lieutenant asked.

"I know a search pattern from a regular patrol," Fargo said. "What are you looking for?"

"That's classified information," Alderson said.

"The general's orders, huh?" Fargo said and Alderson nodded. "Maybe I'll just ride along with you," Fargo said.

"We've orders not to allow that," the lieutenant said.

"Platoon B has the same orders?" Fargo queried.

"Yes, sir," the lieutenant said.

Fargo studied the lieutenant's young face. Alderson was still owned by the army, by training, indoctrination, ideals, and his patriotism. He was still filled with words such as honor, loyalty, duty. All good things, all necessary in the army's officer corps. Yet with all that, Fargo could see the man wasn't brainwashed. He was bright enough to think for himself, young enough to want to live. He, and perhaps Nickles, were the only hope he had, Fargo realized bitterly. "I'm going to tell you something, Lieutenant. Fifty Arapaho have come to join the Kiowa. I saw them with my own eyes. I don't know how many others are already here," Fargo said.

The frown slid across Alderson's young face. "The lookouts would have seen that large a force," he said.

"They're getting through without being seen. I don't know how but they are," Fargo said.

"You should inform General Carlton," Alderson said.

"He won't believe it. He doesn't want to. You know that. So I'm telling you."

"The general has reinforcements coming," Alderson said with defensive conviction. "He's prepared for attacks."

"You better hope so, soldier," Fargo said as he turned the Ovaro and rode away at a trot. He had tried to plant seeds. It was all he could do as he grimly rode back across the plains. But he had learned one thing. Carlton's plans weren't ready to be put into motion yet. He was still searching for a missing piece and Fargo's lips tightened as he wondered what it was. The day had moved into late afternoon when he reached the hills of hawthorns and he halted, gazing back across the open plains. But nothing moved and he finally turned and rode on. He was still on the top ridge of the hills when he neared the arbor below.

He could see down to the stream, and followed its path and came to the Conestoga. The curtains were still up around the wagon but as he looked down at the stream, he saw naked figures coming out of the water. A few were already onshore, drying themselves with towels. He stared, dimly aware that his mouth had fallen open. "I'll be damned," he breathed after a long moment. "I'll be damned."

4

Fargo continued to stare, hardly able to believe what he saw and realized that he was gazing down at the most unusual ten-year-olds he had ever seen. Each had beautiful, full breasts, curvaceous thighs, and dense, bushy thatches between her legs. Some were blond, some brunette, two auburn-haired, each emerging from the stream with a slow, sensuous movement. The youngest might be eighteen, Fargo guessed, the others not more than twenty-one. As they finished drying themselves, they started to pull on their long dresses and strap on their bonnets.

Fargo felt the anger push through him. He had seen enough and sent the Ovaro racing down the hill, reached the stream with a noisy splash, and saw two bonneted heads spin, others peering out at him from between the curtain of blankets. He spurred the pinto forward, reached up, and pulled the blankets down as he charged through the first line of curtains, then the second. As he reined to a halt he saw the straw-colored hair emerge from the Conestoga, surprise and alarm mixed in her face. "The masquerade's over," Fargo flung at her as he dismounted and strode to the costumed figures that had stepped forward. He yanked the bonnets from two of them, then a third. "You can all take them off," he said to the others.

The young woman nearest him shook a thick head of auburn hair. "At last," she said, her eyes reflecting her relief and welcome in their deep blue depths.

"Ditto," the next girl said, a dark blond. Fargo's eyes cut to Melinda as she came toward him, her own eyes narrowed.

"How'd you know?" she queried.

"Didn't. Came along up in the hills and saw down to the stream," Fargo said and his glance swept the six young women, who were now all bareheaded—and all very attractive, he took note. "Name's Fargo . . . Skye Fargo," he said.

"We know," the auburn haired one said. "We see a lot peeking out from inside the wagon." She turned and started for the Conestoga. "We're going to get out of these damn dresses," she said and the others followed her.

"Be my guest," Fargo said and brought his gaze back to Melinda.

"You'd no right," she said angrily. "You should have come to me first."

"I don't like being tricked," Fargo said. "Start leveling, honey. Why the masquerade?" He followed Melinda's eyes as she watched the young women emerge from the Conestoga. Some wore jeans, a few skirts. All wore blouses and shirts that fit tightly to their amply endowed figures. They were all lovely, Fargo saw, each in their own way, all smoldering with the vibrant sexuality of youth, as fresh and alluring as a newly blossomed trumpet honeysuckle. Melinda's voice cut into his thoughts.

"It's in your eyes," she said and he frowned back.

"The answer to your question. It's there in the way you're looking at them. Do you think I would have made it this far with them as they are now?" she said pointedly. His lips pursed, her answer not unreasonable.

"Maybe you've a point, but it shouldn't have included Jiminy or those you want to work closely with you," Fargo said.

"I decided on no exceptions. I'm glad I did after the way Matt Barlow and his friends turned out," Melinda said.

Fargo's eyes fastened on her. "That's only part of the masquerade. Who are they? Who are you? Why are you taking them to Montana and you can forget that fancy school routine," he said.

"Let's talk over here," Melinda said and strode to a tall cottonwood away from the young women. "I'm just who I said I am, Melinda Tanner, and they are my charges," she said, facing Fargo with her chin tilted upward.

"Not good enough," Fargo said.

"They are all young women from very good homes. Their parents, in some cases their fathers, are paying me to take them to Montana," Melinda said.

"Why in hell would they do that?" Fargo queried.

"These girls are very willful, headstrong, and disobedient, a problem to their parents or guardians. They've defied their parents' wishes. Excellent marriages to wealthy, socially acceptable young men were arranged for each of them. They refused to go along with everything."

"Can't say I blame them. I'm for letting people pick their own partners," Fargo said.

"Even when they want to pick nobodies, wastrels,

fortune hunters? Hormones over common sense? Parents want what's best for their daughters. Besides, in wealthy social circles, arranged marriages are the norm. They'll maintain the same economic, social, and cultural class. The parents of these rebellious and headstrong girls decided to send them away till they matured."

"They picked Montana?" Fargo frowned.

"One of the fathers has a very secure ranch out there. They'll all stay there."

"They're old enough to run away," Fargo commented.

"There's no place to run to in Montana," Melinda said.

"Sort of a prison without walls?"

"Your description. Many people would see it as a place to gain maturity, a time to grow, to find common sense," Melinda said.

"It's also a place to get a Sioux arrow," Fargo said. "Seems a damn fool thing. Why'd they pick you? What do you bring to this?"

"I was a headmistress at Chauncy School in Ohio," Melinda said. "I had a reputation for not tolerating nonsense. They wanted someone who'd be strict."

Fargo's glance flicked to the half-dozen young girls. "Why didn't they just run off before this? You couldn't have stopped all of them," he queried.

"Not physically. But I had other weapons. I told you they were each quite wealthy. They each have trust funds of their own of some ten thousand dollars. But they can't draw on them until they're twenty-five. Their accounts were signed over to me. If anyone runs away, I get her account."

Fargo's brows lifted. "A good reason for them not to run away," he agreed.

"Exactly. Much as they might want to run away, they don't dare," Melinda said with a touch of smugness.

"What happens if you don't get them there?" Fargo asked.

"I don't get paid. My contract reads that I get them there safe and sound and in the condition they are now," Melinda said.

"Meaning what exactly?" Fargo probed.

"Meaning young women who will be respectable, desirable, proper brides for proper husbands one day, not girls who've been frolicking with every cowhand in every saloon. But you've made that considerably harder, now," Melinda thrust at him.

"Why?"

"You've ruined the masquerade, as you call it. They never liked it and now they feel there's no point in going back to it," she said. "Now it's even more important I get them to Montana as quickly as possible."

"You try it now and they won't be safe or sound. They'll be dead," Fargo said harshly.

Her face tightened and she turned away. Night had descended on the arbor. He saw three kerosene lamps brought out by the six young women, who put them down in a bright circle. A tall girl came up to Fargo, her figure curvy with a softness that was almost tactile, breasts that seemed pillowy under a white blouse. Dark brown hair and matching eyes framed a soft face that nonetheless carried an inviting openness. "Hi. I'm Amy," she said, resting her hand on his arm and holding it there for just a moment too long before letting it drop.

"I'm Chrissee," the next one said, stepping forward with a quick smile. Fargo took in a small girl with pale blond hair and pale blue eyes but there was nothing pale in the smoldering message she turned on him. Her small body was perfectly balanced, every part fitting beautifully. A third girl came forward, her hair a dark auburn, her eyes the green of a pool table. She stood with her hips thrust forward, a sensuous challenge in every part of her.

"I'm Velma Dorrance," she said, her voice low, throaty.

The fourth girl had jet black hair and large breasts that seemed to want to push out of a loose, low-cut blouse. Large, liquid brown eyes gazed at him with dark fire. "Josie Howard," she said softly.

"Lena Baxter," a fifth girl said, pushing forward and Fargo saw a vivacious, peppery figure with flashing black eyes and a figure that seemed to exude motion even standing still. The last girl moved forward, her hair a lighter shade of auburn than Velma's, her face broad-cheeked. Sloe eyes slanted upward at their outer corners to give her a faintly oriental cast. A very tight shirt outlined her lovely contours, and her skirt showed off her smooth, well-curved legs

"Maxine," she said with a slow smile. Violet eyes held their own, very private smile. "Been wanting to meet you," she said, the words wrapped in a soft purr.

"How nice," Melinda cut in sharply "Now that you're all finished introducing yourselves you can help get supper ready. You, Lena, and Amy can go get supplies from the wagon."

"Will you be eating with us?" Maxine asked Fargo. "We'd like that. We'll fetch some extra tins of beef."

"Our supplies won't allow for guests," Melinda answered flatly. "Fargo will be using his own supplies."

"That's right," Fargo said.

"You could still eat with us," Amy put in as she came up to him, her soft figure shimmying under her blouse and skirt.

"Perhaps some other night. Please get to the wagon," Melinda answered curtly and the three girls strolled away, but not without casting quick smiles back at Fargo. Melinda beckoned to him, and drew him aside.

"They're shameless flirts. They enjoy teasing. They are a problem and like being so. I expect you to ignore them," she said, sounding very stern. "Just as I expect you to be a proper gentleman."

"Proper. One of my favorite words." Fargo smiled and drew a scowl from Melinda.

"Don't be condescending with me," she snapped. "I doubt that you have ever had anything to do with the word."

"Now, what makes you say a thing like that?" He frowned in mock protest.

"I have my own sensitivities," she said.

"That's good. I like a woman with sensitivities," he returned. She was about to snap an answer when the three girls returned carrying the supplies for supper. "Good night, ladies. I'll be bedding down upstream in the hills. Want to get an early start come morning."

"How much longer are we going to have to wait here?" Melinda asked, annoyance coating her tone.

"Tell you when Jiminy gets back," Fargo said and led the pinto away. He walked alongside the stream to the first rise of the hills, climbing a dozen yards up to a patch of soft Indian Brave moss and set out his bedroll. It seemed an appropriate spot, he reflected wryly. He munched a cold strip of beef jerky and undressed to his shorts. The night stayed warm as he lay awake, his thoughts consumed with the specter of an explosion of bloodshed that could turn the prairie from green to red. Had he any chance to stop it? he wondered and found little cause for hope. But he knew he'd try. He had no choice. Maybe somehow, some way, something would happen to change what seemed an inexorable path toward disaster.

He wanted to sleep but the dark misgivings kept him awake and restless as a half-moon rose to cast a pale light. The high-pitched cries of kit foxes squabbling and the deep bays of timber wolves drifted up from the distant plains below. Fargo was resting on one elbow, peering into the night, when he caught movement at the bottom of the hill. The leaves of low bushes shook and his hand silently slid to the Colt that lay in its holster at the side of his bedroll. He continued to peer down the slope, the Colt firmly in hand, when he saw a figure detach itself from the bushes and move upward in a vague path. Waiting, watching, he finally raised his voice. "Over here," he called softly.

The figure immediately changed direction and came toward him, taking on shape as it drew closer. "Maxine," he murmured as her tall figure reached him and dropped to her knees at the edge of the bedroll. He saw the young woman wore a thin nightgown of light blue silk with a low, lacy neckline.

"Susrprised?" Maxine asked in her low purr as she leaned forward. The neckline of the nightgown dipped low and Fargo saw her two lovely mounds hang forward like twin peaches waiting to be plucked.

"Yes," he admitted. "I'm sure Melinda doesn't know you're here."

"You can say that again." Maxine smiled, her eyes appreciatively taking in the muscled contours of his torso.

"Couldn't sleep?" Fargo asked innocently.

"Not knowing you were up here," Maxine said. "We've all been watching you since you took over."

"The others know you're here?" Fargo queried.

"Yes," Maxine said.

"They send you?" he asked.

"Not exactly," she said and moved closer to him.

The answer was evasive but he decided not to pursue it further at the moment. "You come for a reason?" he asked.

"The best one," she said and her arms slid around his neck, her lips finding his with a wet, warm touch.

"You don't waste time, do you?" he murmured as she drew back.

"That's all I've been doing. Melinda's seen to that for all of us," Maxine said. "It's time to stop."

"Seems I'm convenient," Fargo said.

"You're not convenient. You're a gift, one I can't pass up," she said. Questions edged each other inside him but her mouth found his again, pressing with a soft urgency, her tongue sliding forward, touching, tasting, teasing. He answered in kind. Questions could wait. Besides, it was against his principles to turn from a willing woman. His hands came up and slid the nightgown from her shoulders. It fell easily from her and he took in her beautiful, teardrop-shaped breasts, each crowned with the tiniest of pink

71

points centered on pale pink circles. A flat abdomen slid down to a slightly convex little belly, just fully round enough to be quietly provocative.

Beneath it, a bushy little triangle held an echo of the auburn of her hair, and her long legs were magnificently curved, smooth willow wands that invited touching. Her lips found his again and she murmured at his response. His hands strayed down, caressing first one teardrop breast, then the other. Both were very soft, almost cottony to his touch. His mouth edged across her pronounced clavicles, and nibbling further, he came to a breast and drew it in. "Oh, God, oh, God," Maxine purred and her torso pushed upward to offer her breast. He drew the teardrop mound deeper into his mouth, let his lips circle the tiny pink crown, and felt it rise under his tongue.

He sucked gently and Maxine's purr became a low growl and he felt her torso rock from side to side, lifting upward and falling back down onto the bedroll. His hand was slowly sliding downward across her little convex belly when her hand rose, clapping itself down upon his. She pulled his hand down to the soft pubic mound, and pressed it into her faintly auburn bush. "Here, here, oh God, here. Please . . . oh, please," Maxine growled, her hips twisting. He explored the soft-wire tendrils, letting his fingers slid through their thick bushiness, over the soft rise of her Venus mound. Maxine's growl became a low groan. "More, more, more," she breathed. He glided further down and felt the warm moisture of her inner thighs as they parted, then came together to grasp his hand in a soft, sweet vise. "Oh, oh, oooooh," Maxine moaned and again her hips rose, offered.

He felt her hands sliding across his groin, grasping

his own throbbing erectness and her purring sounds broke off, becoming a guttural cry of excitement. "Yes, oh, God, yes, yes . . . ah, ah . . ." she managed as she drew him to her, clasping and pulling on him. He moved with her, brought himself onto her, and felt her wetness now moistening her bushy triangle. She was lifting her hips again, moving almost frantically, the lock trying to find the key as he slid forward, touching the edge of her warm darkness, Maxine screamed. He saw her shaking her head up and down frantically as she cried out. "Yes, yes, yes, yes, oh, my God yes!" she half screamed.

He slid forward, into the sweet, warm, wet tunnel and felt the tightness of her grip around him. Her hands had become little fists that pounded into the bedroll as he moved inside her, and her cries were wordless little bursts of purest pleasure. She moved with him, slowly thrusting as her long legs rose and encircled his hips. As they rubbed and pressed, he saw her auburn hair flash in the moonlight as she tossed her head up and down. Unclasping her hands, she pulled his head down to her and buried his face into her belly as she heaved and twisted with him. Her cries and low guttural groans came in rhythm with her every thrusting motion, and he reveled in his own pleasures of the eternal horizontal dance.

He was ready when he felt her thighs and arms grow tight around him, her body begin to stiffen, her groans turning to sharp little cries. "Oh, my God, my God, yes, yes, now, oh, now, now, now!" Maxine screamed out in an explosion of sound as she suddenly bucked under him, her body quivering in place as he pumped harder and harder. He held her as he exploded himself, and felt her teeth digging into the base of his neck as she held onto him as a limpet clings to a stone. He was surprised at how long she stayed against him, her long body consumed with tiny little motions, miniature thrustings against his crotch.

But finally, her thighs fell away and her arms loosened and she slowly sank down onto the bedroll. But she pulled him with her, unwilling to let him leave her place of consummate pleasure. He was happy to stay with her, enjoying the sensual pleasure of her enveloping warmth, until she finally drew back with a little groan of despair. She brought her long body up against him at once, pressing herself against his groin as she lay over him. She moved to let her breasts rest against his face.

"That was very special," Fargo murmured into her ear and meant the words. Maxine had been a volcano of warmth in a smoothly sultry way he had seldom encountered, and certainly hadn't expected.

"You were very special," Maxine purred. "But then I expected that."

"Did you?" Fargo smiled. "You're that much a woman of the world?"

"You don't have to be to know some things. You feel them," she said. "I wish I could stay," she said almost as an afterthought.

"But you have to get back before someone sees you're gone," Fargo agreed.

"Only Melinda. The others know I've gone," Maxine said with a slightly smug little smile.

"They know you're here? Is that what you meant when I asked if they'd sent you?" Fargo probed.

"Not exactly," she said.

"You're being cute," he growled.

"We drew straws for who'd go find you," she said. "I won."

Fargo paused to choose from the questions that tumbled through his head. "Guess I should be flattered. Never been the prize in a contest. But I keep wondering why?"

"You don't need a why to want," Maxine said. "We've all been wanting. We've been prisoners in bonnets."

He smiled. It was a good answer but he had the feeling that there was more. He also had the feeling that more direct questions wouldn't get him the real answers. He decided to wait and get the answers in bits and pieces. "Melinda wouldn't be happy if she knew you were here. She'd be furious at both of us if she knew more," Fargo said.

"Oh, God, yes, she'd be crazy mad," Maxine said, enjoying the thought. "She's always been against having fun. They used to call her Miss Chastity Belt at the school where she was headmistress."

Fargo saw the anger come into Maxine's face. "You really dislike her," he said.

"That's putting it mildly. We hate her, all of us do. She's the one bringing us out here," Maxine said.

"Whoa, now. Your fathers, your folks, they're the ones sending you," he reminded her. "You don't hate them?"

"Didn't say that," Maxine returned. "They tried to get some others who turned them down. Melinda convinced them she could take us, and for a fancy fee, we're sure. We hate them for what they did. We hate her for what she's doing."

"Sounds as though you'd be happy to get back at all of them," Fargo said.

"Damn right," Maxine snapped.

"Only you really have no way," Fargo said.

"There are lots of ways to do things," she said, becoming enigmatic.

"I'm helping Melinda get you there. You hate me, too?" Fargo asked.

Her face came down to his at once. "God, no. You're only trying to get us there alive," she said and her lips pressed to his in a long, warm kiss. She slid herself downward, running her lips across his body, pausing to caress, to hold, moaning until finally she rolled from him. "I want you to remember this," she murmured as she reached for the nightgown and pulled herself into it.

"I'll remember," Fargo said as Maxine rose to her feet. "Sleep tight."

"I will now." Maxine smiled and hurried away. He watched her until she disappeared in the dark at the base of the hill. Stretching out, he took a few minutes to sleep. The night, for all its unexpected pleasures, had only added more questions to those already wearing paths through his mind. He forced himself to put them all aside and pulled sleep around him. The night stayed still and at the break of day he was awake and in the saddle. He rode onto the plains as the day began to slide over the land and once again, he crossed the plains. He slowed where Carlton's lookouts would see him and then rode on deeper into Kiowa land.

Keeping a steady pace, he was soon deep into Kiowa territory, far beyond the lookouts' sight. He crossed numerous streams, fording a few deep enough to be called rivers. Though the Kiowa roamed the entire plains, this was the heart of their land and his eyes flicked from the ground close at hand to the distant prairie. He'd gone on another half hour when he spied the wide swath where buffalo grass had been flattened. Turning the pinto, he reached the swath and halted as he stared down at unshod pony prints that had trampled the grass down. At least a hundred ponies, Fargo estimated as he studied the mass of hoofprints. They had moved on north, deeper into the heartland of the Kiowa.

Moving on, he slowed as a huge stand of plains cottonwoods rose up directly in front of his path. He drew to a halt, unwilling to enter the forest. Prudence was better than curiosity. It probably screened the main Kiowa camp and he was not about to go nearer in the bright morning sun.

He was about to turn the Ovaro around when he caught the glint of color under a portion of the flattened grass. Dismounting, he explored the grass with his fingers and pulled out a piece of anklet band, stained with earth colors and decorated with quill work designs. He stared at the piece of anklet. It was definitely not Kiowa, he knew as he studied the markings. "Ute," he finally muttered. Pulling himself into the saddle, he retraced his steps along the swatch of pony prints and finally came to the beginning of the grass where he had entered. Once again, the tracks simply stopped and it seemed as though they had been dropped down from the sky. But he thought about the last tracks he had found as he searched the hardy grass beyond the swath. Finally, he managed to spot the faint markings he sought, evidence of tracks that had been carefully covered.

But they had covered tracks that had been in a single file, he saw and these, too, quickly vanished altogether and Fargo was left to swear in frustration. The questions hammered at him more insistently than ever. How were they getting through unseen, taking form only when they were deep into Kiowa territory, on their way to the main Kiowa camp? The answer might mean the difference between staying alive and dying, he realized. The sun had moved into the afternoon sky as he rode back across the plains, this time his eyes scouring the distance until he spotted the plume of dust. Not the pattern of random searching, but the steady path of a troop on patrol. He put the pinto into a canter until he cut across in front of the patrol, which turned out to be Troop A with Lieutenant Buzz Alderson in command. The lieutenant drew the troop to a halt, and advanced alone to greet Fargo. "No more searching, I see," Fargo half smiled.

"No more," the lieutenant said evenly.

"That mean you found what you were looking for?" Fargo asked mildly.

"Yes," Alderson said.

"That make the general happy? That is, if you can answer without divulging military secrets," Fargo said blandly.

Alderson let a smile edge his young lips. "You're a clever man, Fargo," he remarked. "Yes, it made the general very happy."

"Then it makes me very unhappy," Fargo said, his voice tightening. "Talk to me, Lieutenant Alderson. What's he planning?"

"You know I can't answer that," Alderson said patiently.

Fargo's lake blue eyes grew cold as they speared into the young officer. "I know it could mean your life and the life of every man in this regiment," he said.

Alderson's face stiffened. "Sorry," he said, closing up at once.

Fargo swore inwardly but he had dropped another seed. It was all he could do now. He shifted gears. "You touch base with the lookouts?" he asked.

"Always. We have orders," the lieutenant said.

"They tell you they saw a hundred or so Utes?" Fargo tossed out almost airily and he enjoyed watching Alderson's eyes widen.

"No. They said they didn't see anyone," the lieutenant said.

"Well, the Utes are at the Kiowa camp now," Fargo said and was pleased to see alarm join the surprise in the lieutenant's face. "Somehow, they're getting through and your lookouts aren't seeing them," Fargo reiterated.

"Ten lookouts, strategically placed on the territory perimeters? They had to see them." The lieutenant frowned.

"Only they didn't, just the way they didn't see the others that have come. They're massing a force to wipe you out and then clean the plains of every settler, farmer, and wagon train," Fargo said.

"They don't know the general has five hundred reinforcements," Alderson said.

"They here?" Fargo snapped.

"They're due. They could be here by the time I get back."

"Could be. But only five hundred. You don't know how many outside warriors have joined with the Kiowa," Fargo said.

Alderson stared back, his face tight. "I'll tell the general what you've told me," he said.

"He won't believe it. He's got his lookouts. Hell,

you don't know if you believe me," Fargo said with a bitterness coating his words. "There's only one chance to stop this part of the world from going to hell in a handbasket. Stop the general from doing something that'll trigger disaster, if it isn't already too late. Talk to me, soldier."

"I can't, mister. I don't disobey orders," the lieutenant said stiffly.

"Spoken like a true officer and a gentleman of the United States Military Academy," Fargo said, not hiding his sarcasm.

Alderson's eyes narrowed. "I don't think I'll say thank you," he returned. "But you said the right words."

"They'll look good on your grave," Fargo flung back, and spun the Ovaro and went off in a gallop. He slowed only when he was out of sight of the patrol, then he put the horse into a walk and went on across the prairie. The day was drawing to a close when he arrived at the little arbor, and Fargo saw four of the girls preparing a small fire. All wore casual clothes, most in halter-top blouses and all waved as he rode to a halt and dismounted. Melinda appeared and the tightness in her high-cheekboned face answered his question before he asked it. "Jiminy hasn't come back," he said.

"No, he hasn't," Melinda said. "Does this mean we wait another day?"

"It means you stay alive for another day," Fargo returned and Melinda glared back. Maxine and Chrissee came from the supply wagon with tins of beans. Maxine tossed him a polite smile while her eyes spoke to him with their own message.

"You'll eat with us tonight, Fargo. We'll share rations with you. We insist," she said and Chrissee nodded.

"My pleasure," Fargo said and walked to the wide stream to wash as night descended. His thoughts went to Jiminy. He'd expected the little man back by now but he had to realize that Miles may have been in the field when the courier arrived. He finished washing and returned to where everyone had gathered around the small fire. Amy and Josie had made a place for him between them and he sat down across from Lena Baxter's pert, peppery vivaciousness. Melinda sat at the edge of the small circle, but Fargo saw her eyes took in everything with the experienced gaze of a headmistress.

"Tell us about being a trailsman," Josie said as the meal began.

"Not a lot to tell," Fargo said. "Not everyone can do it. You have to have a talent for it or you won't make it. Of course, talent is only a base. You have to build on it with experience."

Lena giggled and her black eyes flashed mischievously. "Sort of like being a good lover. It takes talent and experience," she said.

"That's not a ladylike remark," Melinda cut in with sharp disapproval.

"Doesn't bother me," Fargo said. "It's not a bad comparison, especially from someone who doesn't know much about either."

Lena's black eyes instantly flashed dark fire. "That's not fair," she snapped.

"Is it the truth? That's what counts," Fargo said and met her angry glare with a smile. It didn't pacify her, he knew, but he saw Melinda look pleased at his answer. Lena continued to simmer as the other girls made small talk led by Velma. The meal ended as the little fire burned out, leaving only the two lamps to give light. "Thank you all for the meal and the company," Fargo said as he pushed to his feet. "Waiting is hard, I know, but it's for your own good. Good night."

"We don't mind waiting. We enjoy the stream," Chrissee said as Fargo walked to the Ovaro. Melinda followed.

"You handled Lena's remark very well. She was being provocative," Melinda said. "I'm very pleased with your restraint around the girls."

"You expected something else?" he asked evenly.

"I wondered," she admitted. "They plainly had an eye for you, and you're a man who appreciates women."

"Now, how do you know that?" Fargo chided gently.

"I don't think that's difficult to see," Melinda said coolly.

"How about you? Do you appreciate men?" he asked.

"I've the maturity to separate appreciation from rash behavior," Melinda said loftily.

"Too bad." He laughed and saw tiny bits of color come into her high-cheekboned face.

"I believe in self-discipline," she said.

"Too bad," he echoed. She returned faint disapproval.

"That may be but I'm still pleased to find you can exercise it," she said.

He regarded her with faint amusement. "You're not supposed to do that," he said.

"Do what?"

"Wrap a compliment in condescension," he said as the tiny bits of color spread and flooded her face.

"One for you," she conceded.

"So I get a good mark from the headmistress?" he tossed at her.

"You get an A. For now," she added tartly and left with a toss of her straw-colored hair. He led the Ovaro back to the same spot on the hill, undressed under the half-moon, and lay down on his bedroll in the warmth of the night. His thoughts quickly turned to the day that would come all too soon. He considered another visit to Carlton and discarded the thought. It would only waste valuable time and time was quickly becoming all-important, he decided. He'd use what time he had to try and find out how the braves from outside were arriving as if by magic. That could hold the key to survival.

But right now, only one fact was clear: Both the Kiowa and Carlton were still getting ready. The Kiowa were still bringing in allies, preparing for their attack. And Carlton was still planning to ensure that it happened. That meant there was still a measure of precious time. But how much? A sound cut into his thoughts and he recognized it at once—the rustle of brush at the bottom of the hill. He rose on one elbow to see a figure pushing aside brush, almost marching up the hill toward him. It was not Maxine, but a smaller figure that took form as it drew closer. "Lena?" he muttered aloud as the figure gathered speed, then halted in front of him with hands on her hips, her vivacious face frowning, the halter blouse tight around her breasts.

"That wasn't fair, what you said," she flung at him.

"You sneaked away to come up here and tell me that?" Fargo frowned as he sat up.

"No, but I wanted to say it first," she snapped.

"Simmer down. I said it for Melinda's benefit, to keep her from becoming more suspicious and on guard. It worked. You ought to thank me, all of you," Fargo said.

She stared back for a moment and then her face softened. "I didn't think of that," she murmured. "I'm sorry. Forgive me."

"Done," he said. "Now, why did you come up here?"

Lena folded herself on his bedroll, and slid a little smile at him. "We drew straws again. I won this time," she said.

"Guess I should be flattered again," Fargo said and saw her black eyes roving across his body. "You going to do this every night?" he questioned.

"Every night we can," Lena said. "Unless you object."

"Couldn't do that. Couldn't and wouldn't," he said, and reached out and drew her to him. The halter blouse came off at his touch and two pert, perky breasts faced him, upturned at the cups, her dark pink little nipples reaching out, breasts and nipples so piquant and saucy they seemed to be taunting, daring, teasing. She pushed down on her skirt with both hands and it came off, along with a flash of white bloomers. He took in a small, almost petite, yet strong little figure, everything about her perfectly balanced—a tight little rear, lovely legs, a flat abdomen, and hips with a faint thrust outward that echoed the saucy thrust of her breasts.

Her black eyes flashed a kind of sensuous defiance

at him and her black triangle beckoned, as jet black as the hair that framed her vivacious face. As he stared at her he realized that she seemed to vibrate electricity standing still. She reached out, her arms encircling his neck and he lay backward on the bedroll as she came down atop him, and he felt the heat of her. Black eyes flashing dark fire, she paused for a moment before bringing her mouth to his. "Ummmm, ummmm," Lena murmured, her tongue darting wildly. Her legs rose over him and she slid up along his body until she had brought her pert, upturned breasts to his face, letting the deep pink tips just touch his lips. She stayed there, teasing, tantalizing, and his hands clasped her smooth shoulders and he opened his mouth. "Oh, oh, yes," Lena breathed as she dropped one upturned breast into his mouth. He took it in, closed his lips around it and gently sucked, letting his tongue trace a path around the pink crown. "Oh, oh, ooooh," Lena gasped out, then half rose and pulled away and brought her other pert breast to him. This time she followed it with her body pressing against his, her arms holding his face. "Oh, more, more," she breathed and he felt her torso twist against him.

He turned, swung her over, and was atop her on the bedroll. Her legs opened and clasped around him and he felt her hands fluttering up and down his body. She seemed on fire, every part of her moving, touching, twisting, pressing, her hips making tiny, quivering motions. She let her legs unclasp and straighten, and her hands ran down along his hips, pushing across his groin to clasp around him. She gasped in wonder as she stroked, caressed, pressed, and cradled him, and all the while he could feel her body vibrating with a sensuous intensity. Pushing herself downward, she brought the jet black triangle against him and cried out in delight at the intermingling of touch and senses. Her body continued to vibrate, as though an electric current coursed through her.

His own pulsating warmth pressed harder against her black triangle and Lena half screamed as she pushed herself upward, her sturdy legs lifting to clasp around him. He felt the warm moisture of her seeping against his groin as he slid downward and came to the dark and warm portal, and moved gently forward to feel the tightness of her wrap around him. She gasped and he felt her flinch and he halted but her hands came up to claw at his shoulders. "No, no, don't stop, go on, go on, go, go, go," Lena Baxter screamed and as emphasis, thrust herself forward to encompass more of his pole as she screamed again. He sunk deeper and her arms clenched around his neck and her small body seemed to erupt. Every part of her leaped, bucked, and quivered against him, legs, arms, belly, hips, and he saw her saucy, upturned breasts bouncing and twisting. Consumed with a furious ecstasy, she cried out with each and every movement, reveling in every exquisite sensation.

Truly in a world of her own yet not her own, it was as though some inner force were charging her body and he felt himself sharing in the leaping, bucking, quivering ecstasy of her. When he heard her cries take on new volume, and she somehow found the strength to cling even tighter to him, he was more than ready to meet that spiraling moment when time was no longer time and only sensation ruled. Her final scream ended in a shuddering sound full of rapture and Lena collapsed onto him, her quivering intensity vanishing as a lamp is suddenly extinguished. She lay very still against him and he stayed unmoving until finally, she unclasped her legs and arms and he pushed himself from her and gazed down at her perfectly serene little figure.

Though she lay still, a smile touched her lips and her vivaciousness returned as she sat up, again saucy and pert, her eyes sparkling with dark fire. She pulled his face against her upturned breasts and held him there. "It was more than I ever expected," she murmured.

He smiled, and pulled back to study her for a moment. "Especially when you can't compare," he said not ungently.

"I can compare," she said, pouting instantly. "Well, sort of," she added and found a smile. She gave him a quick kiss and reached for her clothes, turning back when she was finished dressing. "I'm glad I won tonight," she said and was off running down the hillside to disappear in the darkness.

Fargo stretched out on his bedroll. He was flattered at being wanted. They weren't actresses. Their pleasure had been too real to fake. But he found himself wondering if there was something beside pleasure in their eager contests. He set aside the thought and drew sleep around himself. What he planned for tomorrow wouldn't include pleasure.

5

The day had come in on a blistering sun. Fargo had just saddled the Ovaro when he heard a noise at the bottom of the hill. He peered down to see Jiminy hurrying through the brush toward him. He went down, the Ovaro following, and met Jiminy before he had come very far uphill.

"They told me you were here," Jiminy said.

"Who told you?" he asked.

"Melinda said this hill. One of the others whispered where to me," Jiminy said with a pointed look. "They've sure grown up a lot since I left."

"I'll fill you in later." Fargo smiled.

Jiminy drew an envelope from his pocket and handed it to Fargo. "From General Davis," he said. Fargo sat down on a log, pulled the envelope open, and began to read aloud the precise handwriting on official army stationary.

Fargo,

Your letter was bad news. Mine is worse. There's not much help I can offer you, mostly because of the way the army operates. You know well it's made of rules and regulations, many of them the kind that should be thrown out. An officer can be removed from his command for a number of reasons—failure to obey a superior's orders, dereliction of duty, cruel disciplinary acts, gross incompetence in battle, repeated instances of unstable behavior, disregard for the welfare of his men, and a number of other things.

But all of these things require a specific act to bring charges, a concrete example. Some of these accusations require a court-martial to decide. We all know how often incompetence in battle is masked as a tactical error. You've given me no specific acts that would allow me to remove Carlton. Nothing that he's said or done violates regulations. He's been too clever for that. Technically, he's pursuing the Kiowa in his way, a particularly forceful way. Even though you and I know that he's going to drench the plains in blood, army regulations don't address those dynamics. Without a specific act in violation of regulations, I can't remove him.

But it's not completely hopeless. I've sent Carlton an official order to cease and desist his tactics until they can be fully reviewed. If he ignores this, I can have him removed. I've also informed him that Headquarters has turned down his request for 500 troopers. They will have their own courier on the way to him with official notification. This is all standard army procedure. But my courier will reach him first. You can refer to it when you confront him again.

Maybe it'll help you keep the lid on things. Keep me informed.

General Miles Davis, U.S.A.
Fifth Cavalry

Fargo folded the letter and met Jiminy's gaze. "What do you think?" the little man asked. "Will Carlton back off when he learns his reinforcements aren't coming?"

"Any reasonable officer would. But Carlton's a man obsessed. Visions of glory have distorted his judgment. He could still think he can win."

"We know he can't. He'll have disobeyed orders. Miles told you he could remove him for that," Jiminy said. "And that's sure enough for a court-martial."

"A court-martial that will be too late for hundreds and hundreds of innocent victims, a court-martial that will come months after the Kiowa and their allies have ravaged the plains. We may be too late even now."

"You sound like there's no way," Jiminy said.

"That's pretty damn close to it. But I want to know one thing."

"Such as?"

"I want to know how the Kiowa's new allies are getting here without the ten lookouts seeing them. Or without leaving any tracks until they're deep in Kiowa territory. Maybe it'll be important," Fargo said.

"How do you figure to find out?"

"I'm going to visit the Kiowa camp, see what I can hear, see, or smell. Maybe I'll get lucky."

"You'll get dead," Jiminy said.

"I'll try not to do that," Fargo said. He was about to move on with Jiminy when, out of the corner of his eye, he caught the movement upstream. "Shit," he breathed as he pulled Jiminy down into the brush with him, his eyes focused upstream, where six horsemen had halted to let their ponies drink. They were Kiowa, he saw, a hunting party with two deer slung across one of the ponies. Fargo's eyes moved past the braves, along the line of the trees until he spied a horse's head, then another pony. He let a grim smile touch his lips. There were more than two hidden

90

there, he was certain. More likely another six or eight. They were waiting and watching. They plainly weren't letting hunting parties go out without protection any longer.

Fargo remained motionless, watching until the hunting party drew their ponies back from the stream. He cursed silently. If they moved downstream they'd come to the wagons in the arbor. He couldn't let that happen, but he couldn't really stop it. Gunshots would bring the others charging. Perspiration coated Fargo's brow when the hunting party turned and rode out across the plains. He waited until those in the trees moved on also, and drew a deep sigh of relief. But he knew one thing. The arbor was no longer safe. They had found the stream. They were sure to return to it sooner or later and they'd explore it further. He rose and Jiminy walked beside him. "I've got to move them to the high ground, into the hills. The Kiowa won't be looking up there for now," Fargo said.

When he reached the little arbor the girls were sipping coffee from tin mugs and he caught the sparkle in Lena's black eyes. Melinda came out from the Conestoga. "I presume we'll be moving on now that Jiminy's returned," she said.

"In a way," Fargo said.

"What exactly does that mean?" Melinda frowned, hands on her hips, her tall figure stiffening.

"You're going to someplace safer," Fargo said.

"I thought this was safe." Melinda frowned.

"It was. Now it isn't," he said. "Everybody get their things together."

"You'll be with us, won't you?" Chrissee asked.

"Some," he said.

"Some is enough for us," Amy put in, her ample pillowy figure brushing by him.

"I won't be around much, not for a while," he said curtly. His tone didn't seem to have an effect on the girls, as their satisfied smiles stayed in place.

"Get yourselves ready to travel," Melinda said crisply and the others began to gather up their belongings and head toward the Conestoga. Melinda took him aside. "This hardy makes me happy but I'm glad for one thing," she said.

"What's that?"

"You've kept your self-discipline with the girls. That's very commendable," she said.

"Thanks," Fargo said blandly.

"You've developed a very good attitude. I know they've been provocative and you've not let yourself be tempted."

"You do what seems right to do," Fargo said and allowed a modest shrug. Melinda nodded with schoolmarm approval as he turned and climbed onto the pinto. When she took up the reins on the Conestoga, he led the way from the arbor and found a path the two wagons were able to negotiate up the hill. Once atop the hill, where hackberry and shagbark hickory grew densely across a wide, flat expanse, he threaded his way along the ridge. It was after noon when he found a place that was virtually hidden from the world, certainly from any casual observation from below. A small stream trickled by, supplied by a modest high lake fed by underground springs. He directed the wagons into a dense thicket of hackberry, then rode on to check out the lake again. It, too, lay hidden away, with trees growing almost to the water's edge.

When he returned to the thicket, Melinda and the

girls were making camp. Jiminy came up to him. "You figure to go tonight?" he asked.

"After midnight. That'll get me there while it's still dark, and let me be in place when day breaks," Fargo said.

"Want company?" Jiminy asked.

"Sneaking in alone is my only chance. Besides, if something happens, I want you to take them back to Elbow Flats, no matter what Melinda says."

"You think they'll be safe there?"

"If this explodes, nowhere will be safe, but they might have a chance in a town," Fargo answered grimly.

"Good luck, old friend," Jiminy said.

"Thanks. I'll need it," Fargo returned.

Amy, Josie, and Chrissee came by. "You bedding down here with us?" Amy asked.

"No, I'll be by the lake. I'll be riding out while you're all asleep," Fargo said. The three young women exchanged glances and hurried away. Fargo strolled to the Ovaro as Melinda approached. "If I don't get back, you do what Jiminy tells you to do. They'll be my orders," Fargo told her.

"What do you mean if you don't get back?" Melinda frowned.

"Something can always go wrong," he said and was surprised to see her sharp, blue eyes soften with concern.

"I don't like the sound of that," Melinda said. "Not one bit."

He peered at her, saw the concern stay in her eyes. "Well, what do you know, the headmistress has a soft side," he said. "You worried about me or not getting to Montana?"

"How about both?" she returned.

"That's honest. Thanks," he said. "I expect to be back. I'm just taking precautions."

Her hand came up and closed around his in a sudden, impulsive gesture that he felt surprised her as much as it did him. "Be careful," she said and drew her hand away, but her eyes were still soft when she turned and hurried off. Fargo smiled as he led the Ovaro along the top of the hill. They were all made of surprises, he decided. Reaching the lake, he lay down atop his bedroll. It was going to be a long night and maybe a longer day and he decided to take in some extra sleep. The shagbark hickory formed a canopy that kept the direct rays of the sun out of his eyes as he pulled sleep to himself. He stayed in a sound sleep as the day became night, and the moon was beginning to move toward the midnight sky when a sound woke him.

With his wild-creature hearing, Fargo snapped awake, listening. The denseness of the ridge and the thick carpet of leaves made stealth impossible and he drew the Colt from the holster beside his bedroll. He watched the shape move through the trees where they grew almost to the edge of the small lake. Finally stepping out into the open, the figure halted, peered around the lake, and then came toward him. He saw a diaphanous nightgown clinging to a soft, pillowy shape. "Hello, Amy," he said as she halted at the edge of the bedroll.

"Surprised?" Amy asked.

"You girls are full of surprises," he said, taking in her long, dark brown hair that framed her slightly plump face. Full, round cheeks and a wide, sensuous mouth of full, partly open lips and the freshness of youth gave her an attractiveness without actually being pretty. He saw her dark brown eyes enjoy scanning his muscled body. "You draw straws again tonight?" Fargo asked as she lowered herself onto the bedroll.

"Yes," Amy said with a wide smile.

"You going to do this contest every night?" Fargo asked.

"As long as we can. Why, aren't you enjoying it?" Amy questioned.

"Oh, I'm enjoying it plenty. It could be habit-forming," Fargo said. "You won tonight, I take it." Amy nodded vigorously and Fargo glanced at the moon. Another hour would put it in the midnight sky. He hadn't figured to ride until then, he reminded himself. He had time to play his part and he saw Amy's eyes on his body. Suddenly she reached up with both arms, pulled the nightgown off, tossing it aside with a kind of bold defiance. But her hands kept clenching and unclenching, he noted, a certain sign of nervousness.

He reached out, pulled her down on the bedroll, and took in her full, ample breasts that seemed to somehow overflow themselves, a dark red tip looking smaller than it was on each expansive mound. Amy was a full-figured girl, with a shape that was a shade too much, her belly a very round mound, legs that somehow held shapeliness despite a definite extra layer of flesh. A dark triangle seemed small and her hips were full. Yet Amy radiated a sensuousness of her own, not unlike those tropical orchids that overwhelmed you with their lushness. He brought his muscled chest against Amy's softness and her mouth fastened on his as her arms flew around him. Her full lips enveloped his, her tongue moving to press deeply. "Oh, oh, God . . . oh, God," Amy breathed and she pulled his face to her breasts and he found himself buried in pillowy softness.

Long, low, throaty sounds came from Amy as she pressed tight to him and when his lips found one dark red nipple she arched her back and a deep groan escaped her. "Yes, oh, God, yes, yes," Amy said and he found himself being enveloped by her fleshy figure as she moved against him, her thighs opening, clasping against him, falling open again. "Don't wait, don't wait," Amy gasped and her dark triangle brushed back and forth against his throbbing warmth. "Oh, yes, oh, please, please, please," she cried out and her large breasts rubbed against his chest. He felt an almost desperate haste sweeping through her that carried its own brand of excitement with it, as though he were being borne along on rushing tides. He wanted to hold back, let her enjoy the pleasures of patience, but Amy would have none of it.

Amy's fleshy little belly pushed into his groin and her full-fleshed thighs slapped against him as her hands pulled at him and little desperate entreaties fell from her lips in between gasped cries. He moved to find her wet, waiting warmth, and as he slid forward, her groans became a throaty scream. "Oh, oh, oh, God, yes, yes, yes," Amy cried out and suddenly, as he thrust forward, her scream took on a different character, an edge of momentary pain lacing it. But her arms held tight to him and she pushed herself upward, arcing, demanding more, searching for all of him and again he felt himself being swept along. She stretched her body upward, then down, long surgings rippling through her but everything wrapped in her desperate need.

Her headlong, rushing urgency transmitted its own strange brand of pleasure, passion that seemed edged with fear, compelling in its own desperate way. He moved quicker, more harshly, and Amy screamed in pleasure, and kept surging with him, lifting her hips in quickening response. He saw her head fall back, her brown hair falling across her face as her head twisted from side to side, and soon he felt the spasms inside her, and her cry rose into a deep-throated roar. "Jesus, oh, Jesus." Amy surged. "Oh, God, yes, yes, yes, yes!" He stayed with her, and joined in the eternal explosion as she clung to him, her mammoth breasts shaking violently until finally she grew still and seemed to hold her breath. But he detected the faintest hiss of air escaping her full lips and finally she opened her brown eyes that seemed darker and filled with new comprehensions. He studied her for a moment and she met his gaze with a half smile that was edged with sheepishness.

"What were you afraid of?" Fargo asked.

"Why do you think I was afraid?" she answered.

"All that hurrying," he said.

"Maybe it was just wanting," she answered.

"No dice, sweetie. I know wanting. That came later. At first it was being afraid." She gazed back but didn't answer. "First times can make you afraid," he said gently.

Again, she didn't answer the remark but pushed herself against him. "No matter. It was wonderful," she murmured.

"I'm glad," he said and his eyes went to the sky. The moon had reached the midnight mark. "Time to go," he said as he sat up. Amy found her nightgown and pulled it on and he continued to study her. "You know about the pitcher that went to the well too often?" he asked and she nodded. "How long do you think you can do this before Melinda finds out?" he queried.

"As long as we can," Amy said.

"She finds out and she'll keep you roped together at night," Fargo said.

"Let her. It'll be too late then," Amy said.

"Too late?" Fargo frowned.

Amy hesitated for a second. "We'll have had our fun," she said, the answer believable yet he found himself wondering about it. She hugged him, letting her enveloping warmth spread through the diaphanous nightgown before she hurried away.

Fargo dressed, climbed onto the Ovaro, and rode down the steep side of the hill. Reaching the base, he set out across the plains, holding the horse to a steady trot. Nighthawks swooped low over his head as he rode, but the night stayed still. The moon was bright enough for Carlton's lookouts to spot even a lone rider crossing the plains, he noted as he rode through midplains. When he rode into the heartland of Kiowa territory the moon was sliding its way down the blue-velvet carpet of the sky. This time, when he reached the plains cottonwoods, he plunged into the blackness, slowing to a walk as he made his way through the thickness of the forest. He let his ears and nose become his eyes.

Suddenly, he reined to a halt. His nostrils twitched, drawing in the odor of campfires burned down to embers, and the very distinctive smell of charred wood. He slid from the saddle, pulled the Ovaro into a dense thicket, and dropped the reins over a branch. He marked the spot in his mind by the way two of the trees formed their own canopy overhead. Moving forward on foot, he followed his nose and saw the forest begin to thin out a little. Creeping closer, he came to the edge of the trees. The moon had gone down. It was that hanging hour between dark and dawn as Fargo dropped to one knee, waiting, unwilling to go further in the stygian blackness. The sharp odor of the campfires drifted to him and finally he saw dawn send its first probing fingers out in streaks of gray-pink, the soft light slowly spreading across the sky.

The Kiowa camp unfolded before him and he gasped in surprise at the sheer size of it. A double line of teepees took up the main part of the center of the camp, a half-dozen fire pits dug in stone hollows spaced evenly through the camp. A small river ran along the north end of the camp but Fargo's eyes were drawn mostly to the large open space on the other side of the camp. A long string of ponies were tethered there and countless lines of braves slept on blankets at the edge of the flat, open space. At one end, a wickiup had been erected, and marked with shaman's symbols. His brow furrowed as he noted a neat space set in the center of the lines of sleeping braves. It was plainly being held for more visitors. They were expecting more company, Fargo noted unhappily to himself.

As his eyes scanned the camp again, the teepees began to open and braves and squaws began to emerge. From the tallest of the teepees, a figure stepped out, followed by two squaws. The man wore two eagle feathers in his long black hair that glistened with bear grease in the new sun. A beartooth necklace rested on his chest and he wore elkskin leggings. It was plain he was the Kiowa chief, not only by the way others stepped back for him but by his regal bearing. Not especially tall, he had the high cheekbones and the flat-sided face of the Kiowa, along with a sturdy build. The Kiowa, while not as pure-blooded as some tribes, were purer than the average, with an estimated seventy-five percent of their people purebloods. A dozen squaws appeared with baskets of berries and fruit as Fargo watched the rest of the camp come awake. The braves who'd been asleep on the open land began to drift into the main part of the camp.

As Fargo watched, he saw not only the Kiowas but Pawnee, Utes, Osage, Shoshoni, and Arapaho, and he felt sick in the pit of his stomach. Making a loose count, he guessed that with the newcomers, there had to be some four hundred braves. His lips drew back in a silent curse. Carlton couldn't muster more than three hundred men, he estimated, and then only if he included stableboys, cooks, wagon drivers, wheelwrights, and the other miscellaneous personnel of an army compound. Fargo swore as he surveyed the scene again.

The Pawnee and the other newcomers kept mostly to themselves, he noted. They had come to join forces with the Kiowa but it was still a tenuous alliance. Success would give it strength. Failure would make it fall apart, and send the newcomers back to keep and protect their own territories as was their usual custom. He took note of one more thing as he scanned the camp again. They were not yet prepared for full-scale war. Not only were they still waiting for others, but no warrior would ever go into battle without the

Great Spirits blessing them. That meant the all-night war dance ceremony overseen by the shamans.

It also meant there was still a narrow window of time to try to avert disaster, he told himself, even as he knew he was desperately clutching at straws, giving voice to little more than hope. His grim thoughts were cut off by the sound of hoofbeats from behind and he turned to see riders moving through the trees. Flattening himself on the ground behind a stand of tall beggarweed, Fargo peered through the lavender flowers at some fifty riders as they passed within fifty feet of him on their sturdy Indian ponies. His eyes fastened on arms, anklets, and moccasins as they rode by. Pawnee, he muttered to himself as they rode into the main camp to halt as the Kiowa chief greeted them. The new arrivals slid from their ponies and one spoke to the chief as the others listened. Once greetings were exchanged they began to lead their ponies to where the other mounts were tethered.

As Fargo watched, his eyes went to the ponies and he felt the furrow dig into his brow. The furrow became a frown and he found himself staring at the Pawnee ponies, their legs, the underside of their deep chests, halfway up on their flanks. Their hair was uniformly darkened, each and every one of them. The words formed on his lips, and hung there in silence. They were wet. They had been traveling through water. He continued to stare as the meaning of what he saw gathered force inside him. Answers were exploding inside him, explanations suddenly becoming clear, a curtain torn asunder. A long breath escaped him as it all began to come together.

They had come by water, in single file in the dead of night. They had traveled down, probably by the

Platte, then by the dozens of smaller tributaries that spread out across the plains. They had not ridden across the plains in large bands. That's why Carlton's lookouts hadn't seen them, and why they never found any tracks. They had come stealthily through the rivers while letting Carlton's lookouts scan the plains. Suddenly it was all so clear. They stayed in the rivers until they were well past the perimeter of lookouts and deep into Kiowa territory. Only then did they creep onto dry land, advancing far enough from the rivers before carefully wiping away their tracks. That was why the prints he discovered seemed to appear as it by magic.

Fargo now had the piece of the puzzle he wanted. Could he make it mean anything beyond curiosity satisfied? Hiding here any longer wouldn't give him that answer, he realized, and he began to crawl backward away from the camp. He stayed flattened on the ground until he was back where the trees grew thick again. Pushing to his feet, he moved on to find where he'd left the Ovaro. He moved with his eyes turned upward, searching the treetops, and finally he spotted the two entwined cottonwoods that created a unique canopy. He hurried forward and he'd just reached the Ovaro when he froze. The hairs on the back of his neck rose and his eyes stayed on the reins. They were still over the tree branch but not as he had dropped them.

He had his own way of dropping reins over a branch, a special way he tucked them on the underside. These reins had been picked up and then put back, but not in his way. He stood very still, his ears straining for any sound. He didn't take the reins and climb onto the Ovaro. Halfway into the saddle he'd be at a most vulnerable spot, unable to spin, drop, duck, or exert the leverage to leap. He started to edge back as though he were about to go to the other side of the horse and he caught the sound split seconds later, the soft swoosh of air, so faint no other man would have picked it up. But Fargo was dropping as if cut in half, aware the sound was that of a tomahawk cleaving the air.

He heard the tomahawk thud into the tree inches from his head and, springing up, he whirled to see the Indian charging at him, a hunting knife in his hand. Fargo's hand twitched, wanting to go to his Colt, but he forced himself to pull it back. He wasn't far from the camp. A shot would bring a deluge of braves. The Kiowa continued his headlong charge and Fargo measured distances as he braced himself, gathering his muscles. The Indian's charge ended in a leaping lunge, the knife thrust forward as if it were a short spear. Fargo twisted as he ducked away and felt the knife graze his shoulder. He flung out one leg as he hit the ground, catching the Indian's leg as he charged past. Whirling on his back, Fargo saw the Kiowa slam full tilt into the tree, then stagger back, shaking his head. Fargo leaped to his feet and darted forward at his attacker. The Kiowa was still trying to clear his head as Fargo's looping left fist smashed into his jaw.

The brave went backward and down, the hunting knife dropping from his hand. He tried to reach for it with slowed reflexes but Fargo kicked it away and the Kiowa avoided a following kick by rolling across the ground. His head clearing, the Indian rose up against a tree and Fargo started for him, halting as he saw the man reach up and pull the tomahawk out of the tree trunk. His lips pulled back, the Kiowa instantly came at Fargo, the tomahawk raised to strike. Fargo rose on the balls of his feet as the Kiowa closed in, and was ready to dance to his left as the tomahawk swept down in a vicious chop. Recovering, the Kiowa quickly launched the tomahawk to his right, and Fargo managed to twist away as he felt the ax whistle past his face.

The man pressed forward with short, chopping blows and Fargo had to give ground, ducking and twisting away from the chopping blows that came increasingly closer. Suddenly he saw an open moment, and he dropped low and lashed out with a tremendous blow into the Indian's ribs. He heard the man grunt in pain, and drop onto one knee and Fargo stepped in with a long, roundhouse left that caught the man's jaw. The Kiowa went down and onto his back but he kept his grip on the tomahawk. As Fargo came after him, the Kiowa found the strength to bring the tomahawk up in a short uppercut. Fargo had time only to get his arms up to protect the blow that was aimed at splitting his jaw in two.

Fargo gasped in pain as the tomahawk smashed into his arms. He staggered back, his arms suddenly numb and dropping to his sides. The determined Kiowa leaped up, then charged forward with the short-handled ax raised. Fargo drew back, the numbness making his arms useless. He turned and started to run as though he were fleeing and heard the Kiowa's footsteps coming behind him, quickly gaining ground. Fargo's eyes searched the ground as he ran, feeling a slight tingling return to his arms. Suddenly he seemed to stumble, falling forward to the ground and rolling onto his back. The Kiowa was almost over him, and as he started to bring the tomahawk down, Fargo found enough strength in his tingling arms to fling one arm up in a quick, sharp motion. The Kiowa's eyes widened as he saw the hunting knife hurtling at him from where Fargo had scooped it up. He tried to twist away but he was too late.

Fargo's knife sank deep into the brave's abdomen, stopping only when flesh found the small hilt. The Kiowa clutched at the knife, yanked it out of his abdomen, and stared down at the gush of scarlet that flowed from his body. He stared for another half minute before he doubled up, pitched forward, and lay still as a red stain spread across the ground. Fargo took a deep breath as he pushed to his feet and took a moment to reflect on what had happened. The Kiowa, a lone scout returning to the camp, had spied the Ovaro. He'd taken the reins up to lead the horse away, then decided to cleverly wait for its rider to return. Fargo swore as he climbed onto the pinto, keeping the horse at a walk until he finally came to the open plain.

He rode on, gathering thoughts as he did, painfully aware that he had few options left. The shadows of death were growing longer and there seemed no way to turn aside the inevitable. But he had to pay one more visit to Carlton. With what he knew now, maybe he could convince the man to listen. He put the pinto into a trot and forced himself to feel encouraged.

6

Fargo was nearing the fort when the patrol crossed his path, the smooth, young, blond face of Lieutenent Alderson at the head of the column. "Not again," Alderson said as he swung beside Fargo. "You going to try to see the general again? You don't give up, do you?"

"Not with this many lives hanging," Fargo said. Alderson didn't comment as they reached the fort. Lieutenant Nickles greeted them.

"Fargo wants another go at the general," Alderson said. Nickles allowed a wry shrug and walked with them to the commander's quarters. Carlton rose as they entered and eyed Fargo with impatient distaste.

"Now what, Mr. Fargo?" Carlton sneered as Alderson and Nickles looked on.

"Some four hundred Kiowa and their allies," Fargo said.

"Four hundred. How did you come up with that figure?" Carlton asked, his sneer staying on his lip.

"Visited the Kiowa main camp, close enough to see," Fargo answered.

"And you still have your scalp? You're very lucky," Carlton said.

"I'm very good," Fargo returned.

"My lookouts didn't see any of these new arrivals," Carlton said.

"Because they came by river in the dead of night," Fargo said. "Sneaked in when and where your lookouts wouldn't be watching for them."

"If I believed you, which I frankly don't, it's unimportant. My reinforcements are probably arriving today," Carlton said smugly.

"Guess again," Fargo said and enjoyed seeing Carlton's brows lift. "Headquarters turned down your request."

Carlton's surprise turned to angry disbelief. "And how do you know that, Fargo?" he thrust.

"They notified General Davis. He sent word to me," Fargo answered.

"Ridiculous. They'd no cause to turn me down. I don't believe a damn word of this. I wouldn't put it past you and the jealousy of Miles Davis to make this up," Carlton flung out.

"A courier's on his way with official notification," Fargo said and flicked a glance at Alderson and Nickles. They were both listening with rapt attention. His eyes returned to Carlton and he saw the general peering at him as a careful craftiness came into his face.

"On his way, is he?" Carlton echoed and Fargo nodded. "Well, I'll just wait to see him when he gets here before I swallow any of this wild story."

"Fine. Meanwhile, hold off doing anything more until the courier arrives," Fargo said.

"You'd both like that, wouldn't you?" Carlton retorted. "Anything to stop me from doing what no one else has been able to do—break the back of the Indians. How transparent of Miles Davis. Well, I'm not waiting. I'm going ahead with my plans. I told you,

I'm going to shatter their spirits as well as their bodies."

Fargo heard the thought racing to the forefront of his mind. The man was spouting, filled with ambitious pride, wanting to shout his cleverness from the rooftops. It wouldn't take much to push him a step further. "Big talk, that's all it is," Fargo prodded. "Big talk that you know is bullshit."

"How dare you!" Carlton exploded, hot fury in his eyes. "You'll see, you small-minded cowards, all of you."

"You've no way," Fargo pushed and Carlton leaned forward, his face growing livid. "All talk, that's what you are, General. All talk," he pressed. "You've got no plan."

"Plan? You want a plan? How about destroying their burial ground? How about burning that sacred land of theirs to the ground? I'm going to show them that they'll be destroyed in this life, and in the next. I'm going to show them that there's no place to hide unless they surrender to me."

Fargo pinned his eyes on the man and he felt sick to his stomach at the general's pride. It took a moment for him to find his voice. "You can't do that," he said.

"It's as good as done. The Kiowa will get the message. Then the others will get it, all across the plains," Carlton said.

"Message? You'll get back a message of fury and murder like nothing ever seen before. It'll be a bloodbath. Even the peaceful tribes will rise up," Fargo said.

"Nonsense. You'll see I'm right," Carlton said and

snapped his fingers at his junior officers. "Show Fargo out. If he returns, put him in irons."

"Don't do it. For God's sake, don't do it," Fargo flung at Carlton and realized how futile he sounded. Carlton's harsh laugh drove the fact home to him.

"Get him out of my sight," Carlton said and Fargo left, flanked by Alderson and Nickles. They walked in silence beside him until he reached the Ovaro. Fargo turned to them.

"You know General Davis. You served under him. Do you think he's the kind of man that would make this up?" he shot at them. Neither answered but both looked uncomfortable. "Your reinforcements aren't coming. There is a courier on his way with an order from General Davis. Carlton's a man obsessed, an ambitious maniac."

"He's our commanding officer," Alderson said stiffly.

"I feel sorry for you, for every man on this post," Fargo said as he climbed onto the Ovaro. "Where's that burial ground he's going to destroy?"

"We can't tell you that," Nickles said.

"I'd find it myself only I don't have the time," Fargo said.

Alderson and Nickles exchanged tight glances. "Why? What good's that going to do you?" Nickles asked.

"I don't know," Fargo answered honestly. "I'd just like knowing. You can tell me. Carlton already opened that door." Fargo waited, seeing Alderson give an almost imperceptible nod. Nickles spoke up.

"Due west. Go between two rows of black oak, over a hill and across a stream. You'll see it a ways on from the stream," the lieutenant said.

Fargo nodded. It was a victory of sorts, he recognized, a crack in their armor of rules, regulations, and obedience, and he was grateful for it. "Thanks," he said genuinely and put the pinto into a trot as he rode from the fort.

The sun still bathed the plains as he rode, cloaked in a feeling of helplessness. He couldn't stop Carlton and he couldn't halt the towering Indian fury that would surely follow. But maybe he could save something, rescue a shred of victory from the carpet of defeat. He racked his mind as he rode and finally a thought took shape. Not a plan, he realized, more a moment of desperation, a last cry in the wilderness. Perhaps it would be futile, he realized. So much had to conspire to make it work. But he had to try. He had nothing left.

Fargo finally reached the high ridge, skirted the lake, and reined up at the wagons. Dismounting, he immediately sought out Jiminy. "Last chance time. Will you help me?" he asked.

"Can't turn down a last chance," Jiminy said.

"Saddle one of your horses, and take along two or three of your biggest burlap sacks," Fargo said and Jiminy hurried off. Fargo immediately found himself surrounded by six lovely bodies.

"We've been waiting for you to come back. You going to stay tonight?" Chrissee asked eagerly.

"No. I'll be riding out in a few minutes," Fargo said and saw Melinda nearby, watching closely as Amy leaned against him.

"We were hoping you'd stay. When will you be back?" Velma asked.

"Can't say," he told them.

"Hurry," Maxine said and they drifted away as Melinda approached.

"Why are they so interested in whether you're staying the night?" Melinda asked. "This isn't the first time they've been interested in that."

He shrugged. "They like to flirt. You said so yourself," he answered. Her lips pursed as she took in his answer. Her eyes told him she wasn't sure if she accepted it.

"You're back safe. Must you go off again?" she asked.

"I have no choice," Fargo said as Jiminy came up with the two horses.

"Jiminy, too?" Melinda frowned.

"One of us will come back for you," Fargo said, sounding more confident than he felt. Melinda's frown stayed but he saw concern come into her eyes. He squeezed her shoulder reassuringly as he swung onto the pinto and rode away with Jiminy. They headed across the plains, and kept riding as the day ended. Soon they traveled beneath the three-quarter moon. The midnight sky was overhead when, following the directions Nickles had given him, they crossed the stream and came upon the sacred burial ground.

Fargo halted, Jiminy beside him, his eyes sweeping the large plot of ground. The very air seemed different, he could feel it. Not an ordinary stillness but a strangely peaceful quiet. No night insect buzzed, no nighthawks called, nothing broke the strange and eerie silence.

It did, indeed, seem a strange and sacred place, a hallowed ground that seemed to radiate mysterious forces from beyond the ordinary world. Perhaps it was only his imagination working, Fargo reflected.

Imagination was a powerful force yet perhaps it was too often invoked because there were only unsettling explanations elsewhere.

But as he surveyed the sacred ground, Fargo found himself more than willing to accept the red man's beliefs in a place graced by the spiritual world, chosen by man and overtaken by other forces. He let his eyes slowly travel across the somehow throbbing space as he took in the half-dozen scaffolds that dotted the grounds. Jiminy's hushed voice broke into his thoughts. "Never could understand why they put their people up on those high scaffolds instead of in the ground," Jiminy said. "It's their way, anywhere I've been."

"It's traditional. The Indian believes that burial in the ground will interfere with the passage of the spirit to the other world," Fargo said.

"So that's it," Jiminy muttered, letting a wry little sigh follow. "Different folks, different strokes. Everybody's got their own ideas about what finally happens and how."

"You believe what you come to believe," Fargo said. "I'm not much for quarreling with anybody about that."

"You still haven't told me why we're here," Jiminy said.

"I'm going to try something and I haven't any idea if it's going to work, or even if it can. But if it does, it might make the difference between living and dying for a lot of good people. Let's call it a last-chance try," Fargo said.

"Sort of like walking blindfolded," Jiminy said.

"Close enough," Fargo said and let his eyes rove across the sacred ground once more. Three of the scaffolds bore bodies carefully wrapped in blankets with netting strung over them.

"What are all those things on the ground and tied to the scaffold poles?" Jiminy asked, following his gaze.

"The individual's personal, prized, and sacred possessions, things that were favorite and important to him or her in life. I see beads, amulets, sacred bundles wrapped in cornstalks, a favorite bow, or a shawl. Sometimes the head of a favorite horse is hung on a scaffold pole. Don't see any of those, thank God," Fargo said. He swung down from the pinto, his glance taking in the line of ironwoods growing just beyond the burial grounds. "Get the sacks. I want to put every one of their personal possessions in them," he said. Jiminy fetched the sacks he had brought and gave one to Fargo, who began to bag the bundles around the first scaffold, then collected those objects tied to the scaffold poles.

When he and Jiminy finished, they placed the sacks to one side. "Now for the bodies. I'll climb up and hand them down to you," Fargo said.

"It's your show." Jiminy shrugged and watched as Fargo began to climb the first corner pole of the scaffold. It shook and bent, but held, and he pulled himself up onto the high floor of the scaffold. He crossed to the body that lay securely and completely wrapped in blankets, and when he lifted it he was surprised at its lightness. But he knew the meaning of it. It had been on the scaffold a long time and was now largely reduced to bones. Working carefully, he lowered the blanket-shrouded body down to Jiminy and climbed from the scaffold.

He went to the next, then the third, until all of the

blanketed forms lay on the ground. Motioning to Jiminy, they started to carry the first body to the small stand of ironwood just past the burial site and finally had all three and the two sacks stashed in the trees. They had just finished when Fargo heard the sound of hoofbeats and the clatter of rein chains. He stepped to the edge of the trees with Jiminy, and secluded himself behind a tree trunk just as the cavalry troop rode into view. Carlton led the troop with Nickles at his side as they halted at the edge of the burial ground. Carlton's face was flushed with excitement.

"Get at it," he shouted and Fargo watched the troopers ride forward into the burial ground. First they used their sabers to cut down the scaffolding, slicing the corner poles in pieces, and letting the rest topple. Then, as Fargo grimaced, they lighted torches. They set the broken scaffolds on fire first, then began to torch the bushes, the surrounding brush, and finally drew long lines of flame across the grass. It didn't take long before the sacred burial ground was burning from one end to the other. Carlton drew back, looking on with satisfaction shining in his flushed face. Fargo's glance went to Nickles, seeing the lieutenant looking on with his face as if made of stone. "More! Again!" Carlton shouted. "I want every last piece of this place turned to ashes!"

The troopers used their torches to move back and forth across the ground again, finally finishing and drawing to one side. Carlton had had his wish. Where there had been a sacred burial ground there was now only a smoking, blackened expanse. "Mission accomplished," Carlton roared in glee. "We'll see how they like that." He turned and led the troop away, and

Fargo rose when the sound of their hoofbeats died out.

"Help me move everything. This is too far away," Fargo said.

"From what?" Jiminy asked.

"From the fort. That's where they're going to strike first," Fargo said. "Bring the extra horse." When Jiminy returned with the mount, Fargo began to load the three corpses onto it, securing them with a length of lariat. Finished, he handed one of the sacks to Jiminy and kept hold of the other. "Let's ride," he said.

Jiminy swung in beside him as Fargo rode between the double line of black oak and out onto the plain. He turned north toward the fort but swung east before he neared the stockade walls. He went upstream before he crossed to the other side and rode into the stand of black willow and shagbark hickory that grew close to the water's edge. When he was almost opposite the fort, he halted, and with Jiminy's help, lifted the three bodies from the horse. From inside the trees, he peered out again at the dark bulk of the fort that rose some fifty yards from the stream. He carefully hid the three bodies and the two sacks in the trees and, motioning to Jiminy to follow, rode back upstream before crossing back to the other side.

"What are you figuring to do?" Jiminy asked.

"I'm going to see if last chances can work," Fargo said, drawing to a halt and swinging from the saddle. "Get down. I'm going to need your back," he said to Jiminy as he rummaged in his saddlebag and came up with the piece of notepaper and the horn-stopped ink bottle. Using Jiminy's back as a table, he began to write a short note to Miles Davis that said all that needed to be said:

Miles—
    No more time, no more words. The madman has set the fire. Come with whatever you can, even if you can't stay. Ride hard and fast.

Fargo

He folded the note and gave it to Jiminy. "This is for the couriers at Elbow Flats. Then get back to the girls and Melinda. Don't wait around for an answer," he said.

"Where'll you be?" Jiminy asked.

"Waiting for all hell to break loose," Fargo said.

Jiminy climbed onto his horse and rode away without an answer. Fargo smiled. Jiminy was a man who knew when words were superfluous. Fargo turned west, riding until he found a small cluster of shadbush, then he dismounted and entered the dense foliage, setting out his bedroll. There was still time to get in some needed rest. The Kiowa would visit the burial land sometime during the day. They usually had someone pay a visit to the sacred ground. They'd have to take time for a war dance and the blessings of the shamans. Even their rage would not let them do otherwise. He had time to sleep. Hell was not quite ready to break loose.

7

The sun was full when Fargo awoke. He used his canteen to wash, and carefully stepped from the shadbush. He had slept enough for a tired body, but not enough for a despondent soul. A small stand of wild cherries provided breakfast and he slowly rode across the plains as the sun started to near the noonday sky. A thin plume spiraled into the air and Fargo turned toward it, following it over two low hills before he saw the cavalry patrol. Surprise swept through him as he saw hardly a quarter of the usual number of troopers. The company pennant read Troop A, and he rode forward, seeing Lieutenant Alderson bring his few men to a halt.

"This isn't even a skeleton patrol," Fargo commented as his eyes swept the horses and riders.

"We're not on patrol. This is as far as we go," the lieutenant said.

"What are you doing?" Fargo asked.

"Reconnoitering, watching for any sign of the Kiowa in force. If we see them, we've orders to hightail it back to the fort," Alderson said. He fastened a careful glance on Fargo. "You do whatever you wanted to do?" he asked blandly.

"Yes. You do what you had to do?" Fargo returned with equal carefulness.

"Yes," Alderson said. Fargo kept his face expressionless but he was glad to see that Alderson hadn't denied anything. They had exchanged honesty and he'd leave it at that. He saw the lieutenant glance past him, and Fargo turned to see another thin plume spiraling toward them. Moments later he saw Lieutenant Nickles rise over the crest of the hill, leading an equally thin band of troopers. Nickles nodded to Fargo as he halted his men and came over alone. "Told Fargo we were on reconnoiter," Alderson said.

Fargo's eyes took in both young officers. "You're about out of time. Your only chance is to take everyone on the post and get away from here," Fargo said.

Nickles allowed a grim smile. "I don't think General Carlton's going to go along with that," he said.

"Then you take command," Fargo said.

Nickles and Alderson raised their eyebrows in unison. "You lost your mind, Fargo?" Alderson shot back. "We'd be court-martialed and jailed."

"No you won't. You can prove you were doing the right thing. The courier's letter will back you up. It tells Carlton to cease and desist along with the rejection of his reinforcements," Fargo said. "You want to sacrifice yourselves and every man on the post because of an obsessed commanding officer?"

He saw Nickles and Alderson exchange uncomfortable glances. "We could try talking to him again," Nickles said, "but that's all. You're asking too much."

"I'm asking you to stay alive," Fargo said. "The courier's note will show you did what General Davis ordered."

Nickles shook his head. "No, we can't do it. It'd be mutiny. We could get a firing squad. It'd be different if we had the letter, if we'd seen it. But all we have is your word."

Fargo let an oath escape his lips. "Dammit, it'd be just like Carlton to ignore the letter when the courier arrives," he admitted.

"No, he wouldn't do that," Alderson said. "That could get him a court-martial. Ignoring a superior's orders isn't something you can get away with, not even for generals."

"Or lieutenants," Nickles put in. "We'll have to take our chances, do our best."

"You have no chances, dammit!" Fargo flung back. "Listen to me, for your own sakes."

"We're a troop of United States Cavalry. We'll put up a good fight," Nickles said.

"I'm sure you will but you'll all be dead heroes. Don't you see, you won't be just facing an ordinary Kiowa attack. You'll be facing a force of men enraged beyond anything you've ever seen. You'll be facing a force of wild braves fighting out of a fury beyond their ordinary fury. And you'll be outnumbered, too," Fargo said.

"We'll talk to Carlton again, tell him we think we ought to pull out," Nickles said and turned to Alderson. "Let's get back. We haven't seen anything," he said.

Fargo's eyes caught the sudden movement beyond the crest of the second hill. "I see something," he said and both young officers turned and followed his gaze to where a half-dozen buzzards slowly rose into the air, circling in a slow pattern. "I'm going to have a look," Fargo said and sent the pinto forward in a walk. He glanced back and saw Alderson and Nickles following. They'd given their men orders to stay in place, he noted. They were beside him when he reached the crest of the second hill and stared down to where four more buzzards picked at a blue-uniformed figure stretched motionless on the ground.

"Shit," Nickles swore and Fargo sent the Ovaro down the hill. The buzzards swooped away with their usual noisy din of protest as Fargo reached the bottom of the hill and jumped down from the horse. Nickles and Alderson were beside him as he knelt on one knee beside the uniformed figure, seeing that the buzzards had already picked at the man's face that was now little more than a mass of torn flesh. "Jesus," Nickles swore and swallowed hard.

"Never seen buzzards at work?" Fargo asked and received a strangled reply from the lieutenant.

"The courier," Alderson said, pointing to the collar insignia of the man's uniform. Fargo's eyes moved from the round bullet hole in the courier's forehead over to the three arrows that were sticking up from his chest and abdomen. "Kiowa?" Alderson asked and Fargo nodded.

"Rifle and arrows," Nickles muttered.

"They have both. They used both," Fargo said. He pressed his hand onto the man's body. "Sometime last night," he said.

"He was on his way to the fort. This is the way he'd come," Nickles said. "They saw him and jumped him."

"Their luck they happened to be at the right spot at the right time," Fargo commented.

Nickles frowned back. "Luck is luck. It happens," he said.

"Except that Indians aren't much on night riding," Fargo said.

Nickles's frowned deepened. "You're meaning more. Say it," the lieutenant said.

Fargo motioned to where the courier's pouch lay nearby. It was torn open, its insides bare. "They emptied his pouch," Fargo said.

"That's right," Nickles said.

"Only they wouldn't do that. The Kiowa wouldn't give a shit about a courier's pouch. They'd take his gun, his boots, his belt, his knife, maybe his hat and jacket. But they didn't take any of those things. All they did was empty his pouch," Fargo pointed out and felt Alderson and Nickles staring hard at him as he walked further from the slain courier, his eyes searching the ground.

"What are you looking for?" Nickles questioned.

"If they were here, they had to leave prints, even if it was only one or two of them," Fargo said as he continued to scan the ground. Finally he halted. "Over here," he called and Nickles and Alderson hurried over to where he stood, pointing to a spot on the ground. "Prints," he said. "One horse."

"But you found them," Alderson said. "That says something."

"It says the Kiowa weren't here," Fargo said.

"What in hell does that mean?" Nickles said in exasperation.

"These aren't Indian pony prints. They'd be unshod. These are the prints of one horse wearing horseshoes," Fargo said.

"Exactly what are you saying, Fargo?" Alderson asked.

"I'm saying the Kiowa didn't kill that courier," Fargo snapped.

121

"But there are Kiowa arrows in him," Alderson said.

"Kiowa arrows are easy to come by. So's a Kiowa bow. I'll bet plenty have been brought to the fort," Fargo said and Alderson nodded resignedly. "The Kiowa didn't do this. It was made to look that way, by an amateur. A rifle brought him down, then three arrows were fired into his body," Fargo said, watching the uncomfortable looks slide across both Alderson's face and Nickles's now darker countenance. "You said this was the way the courier would take to the fort. The Kiowas wouldn't know that but Carlton would," Fargo said. "Wake up! Look at what I've shown you. It all adds up." He saw the shock in both of their young faces, shock laced with the dark, troubled realization that still they fought against.

"You know what you're asking us to believe?" Nickles said.

"I'm not asking you to believe anything except what you see, to look at what's in front of you and to stop wearing blinders. A Kiowa attack that takes only the contents of a pouch with no Kiowa pony prints anywhere. This was done by the man who wanted what was in that courier's pouch, and that was no Kiowa," Fargo said.

"But that'd mean he'd be disobeying official orders. I told you that'd mean a sure court-martial," Alderson said.

"Not if the courier never reached him. If he never got the orders, he never officially knew his reinforcements had been turned down. A man can't be court-martialed for not obeying orders he never received. He's being real clever and you'll all pay for it. He'll sacrifice all of you because he's obsessed with the idea he can win and be in the clear. God, how long are you going to obey a lunatic?" Fargo said. The two young officers exchanged glances again but this time Fargo saw bitter acceptance in their faces. "I know how hard it is for you but you've got to face it and act on it," Fargo pressed.

"How?" Nickles asked.

"It's still the same. You have to take command of the post. Tell Carlton what you know and that you're taking over. I'll back you up," Fargo said.

"He's not going to sit still for that," Nickles said.

"Then you put him in custody. He's guilty of murder, to say nothing of trying to avoid a direct order and ignoring the welfare of his men. He ought to be in custody," Fargo said. He waited, and soon Alderson nodded, Nickles adding his own assent, both young faces dark with grim realization.

"We'll go back now. Waiting won't make it any easier," Nickles said.

"I'll tag along," Fargo said as both young officers turned back to where their men waited. They set out for the fort at a walk, riding side by side. Fargo drew up at the rear of the abbreviated platoon, his thoughts already turned to the terrible finality that was still to come. There'd be no avoiding that, Fargo knew. Arresting Carlton was perhaps a case of too little, too late, a gesture that would do nothing to stop the bloodbath that was even now gathering itself. Even as they rode, the Indians were in their war dance with their shamans, charging their rage to terrible heights. He didn't give any more thought to Carlton and his mind raced with ways that might prevent the men of Fort Burns from being completely wiped out. But he rode wrapped in a cloak of despair and darkness, and silently cursed every plan that fell apart in his mind.

But finally, a plan formed that offered some slight hope, such as it was. But it was the only one that offered any chance and it took in the men of the post and the greater threat that would turn the plains to red. Yet as the day drew to a close and they reached the fort, Fargo wondered if his plan was little more than a blueprint for failure, an exercise in futility. It was a thought he couldn't shake away as they rode into the fort. Nickles dismissed the squad, and waited as the men hurried off to stable their mounts before he and Alderson started for Carlton's quarters.

"Want to do it on your own?" Fargo asked.

"No. You're part of it. You can see it through with us," Nickles said.

"You've a post guardhouse?" Fargo asked.

"Two buildings down from here. You think we'll need to put Carlton under guard?" Nickles asked.

"You can count on it," Fargo said and saw the distaste reflected in both of the lieutenants' faces. "I know you don't like the idea but this won't be a matter of proper manners," he said.

"We'll try it our way, first," Nickles said. Fargo shrugged as he followed both young men into Carlton's office. Carlton looked up from his desk, his usual expression of faint disdain changing to displeasure as he saw Fargo.

"What's he doing here with you?" Carlton barked.

"Observing protocol, sir," Alderson said, and drew a deep breath. His words then rushed from his lips. "We're sorry to inform you, sir, that we're relieving you of your command."

Carlton frowned, his gaze going from one lieutenant to the other. "You gone crazy, both of you?" he said. "What in hell are you saying?"

"We're taking command of the post, sir," Nickles said. "We found the courier."

"Did you? Then bring him in here at once," Carlton snapped. He was good at playing his role, Fargo admitted silently.

"We know what happened. We know the truth of it," Nickles said and spelled everything out to Carlton, keeping his voice flat. "It would have fooled us, and most everyone, but Fargo drew the real picture for us. He showed us all the things that we wouldn't have picked up," Nickles said.

Carlton's face reddened. "And you're going to listen to this spy for Miles Davis?" he flung at them.

"We're listening to the Trailsman, sir," Alderson said.

"You fools! You goddamn, stupid fools! That's what you are," Carlton shouted.

"Not anymore," Nickles said. "We'll take your side arm, sir."

"You'll do nothing of the sort, you idiots," Carlton snapped.

"Please, sir. We'd like to do this as officers and gentlemen," Alderson said.

"You mean as mutineers and traitors!" Carlton roared and Fargo saw Alderson and Nickles both wince. They were having trouble staying firm. The years of training, loyalty, and obedience reared up inside them. Carlton was gauging them, he saw, quick to see their weak spots.

"Please, sir," Alderson said again.

"You want my sidearm, you come take it," Carlton threw back and Fargo cursed silently. Carlton wanted a chance to draw, and to shoot. That would bring the post running. He wanted to have sergeants and corporals there and order them to arrest Nickles and Alderson. It'd be a stand-off he expected to win. He was the commanding officer. They'd more likely obey his orders than those of a lieutenant, even two lieutenants.

"Your side arm, please, sir," Alderson tried again and neither he nor Nickles reached for their side arms. Quietly, Fargo reached down for the slender throwing knife in the calf holster around his leg, sliding the blade out and bringing it into the palm of his hand as he straightened up. He'd not give Carlton a chance to shoot, he decided as Carlton started to make his move, pulling the Remington-Beals army revolver from the leather holster at his side.

"Come on, take it, you miserable traitors!" Carlton shouted. "Or should I save a firing squad the trouble of killing you?" He had the Remington-Beals out and pointed, but Fargo flung the double-edged, thin blade in a quick, underhand motion. The knife hurtled the short distance before Carlton could bring his revolver up and the gun dropped from his fingers as the blade went completely through his hand. "Ow, Jesus!" Carlton screamed as he clutched at his hand but Fargo was at him in two long strides as he scooped up the gun and pressed it against Carlton's throat.

"Don't move. I didn't learn anything about obedience and loyalty at West Point. I won't think twice about finishing you," Fargo said as he pushed the general's face into the desk. Nickles and Alderson ran over and Fargo released his grip on Carlton. "Put a kerchief around his hand and then put him in wrist irons," Fargo said, and stepped back as Nickles rummaged through a cabinet and came up with a pair of wrist irons that he snapped on Carlton.

"You'll pay for this, all of you," Carlton snarled.

"Take him away. I'll go along," Fargo said and both junior officers walked the general the short distance to a narrow wood structure with two small, barred windows. Inside it was a single room with a cot, water basin, and toilet.

"You'll never get away with this!" Carlton shouted.

"Shut up, sir." Nickles said as Fargo followed him and Alderson outside, where they locked the door and started back to the commander's office.

"Call reveille. Get the men together," Fargo said.

"At this hour?" Nickles frowned.

"The sooner the better. Tell them what's happened. Tell them you've taken joint command of the post. Tell them Carlton's put all their lives in danger and they'll get the details later. Then tell them come morning, they're going to have to fight for their lives like they've never fought before," Fargo said.

Fargo watched Nickles hurry off to find the company bugler and then stepped back into the shadows as Nickles returned to stand beside Alderson. The bugler sounded the call and the men turned out of their barracks to line up in the stockade yard, some sleepy, all surprised. Nickles informed them that he and Alderson were in command, telling them everything Fargo had suggested. When it was over, the men returned to their barracks to wait for detailed orders that Nickles told them would soon be coming. In the command office, Fargo faced both the young lieutenants and thought he detected new lines in their young faces. They were growing up fast.

"The Kiowa and their new allies will hit this place

come dawn," Fargo began. "There's only one chance not to be wiped out. We've got to hit them hard enough to make them hurt, make them take a step back. That means surprise. Staying in the fort would be suicide, and it's too late to run. They'd come after you, and catch you on the plains in the open, their territory. You'd be outnumbered and outmaneuvered."

"Doesn't sound like there's much of a way out," Alderson said.

"There isn't but I've got a plan. It's maybe the only way out," Fargo said. "When you explain it to the men you can tell them they won't be fighting just for themselves but for every town, settlement, and wagon train across the whole damn plains."

"You spell it out. We'll make it work," Alderson said. Fargo nodded with a silent prayer their words would prove right.

8

The silent time had come, that time between dark and day when the night insects ceased their snapping, clacking, and buzzing, and the day insects had yet to begin their own soft din. The day's songbirds still hadn't taken wing, and the night creatures were just reaching their lairs and burrows. The timber wolves no longer bayed at the moon, and even the night's damp winds were giving way to the day's warm breezes. Fargo lay flattened on the ground at the edge of a line of shagbark hickory and black willow. In front of him he could see the stream and, fifty yards beyond it, the dark bulk of the fort.

Fargo glanced to his left along the treeline, then to his right. He saw Nickles and Alderson flanking him but nothing else and he allowed a grim grunt of satisfaction. He had listened to them instruct the men and they had done a good job. He turned to peer deep into the trees behind him. Everything he and Jiminy had brought from the sacred burial site was still hidden there. He had told Nickles and Alderson and watched their eyes grow wide with astonishment. "It's all finally come down to this," he had told the two officers. "Carlton's legacy, you could say. Maybe it'll work in ways he never expected."

Fargo's thoughts shut off as the silence suddenly became less silent. He listened, putting one ear to the ground. The faint sound took on strength, the soft tread of unshod shoes. He reached out and touched Alderson's shoes. "We've got company," he said. Alderson stiffened, and Fargo gave Nickles the same message. The pink-gray of dawn began to spread across the sky, moving with surprising speed. Just when dawn asserted itself, the horde of riders appeared. Fargo's eyes went to the fort, moving slowly across the double row of blue-uniformed figures, each with their army hats pulled low, a carbine jutting out from in front of each figure. They were in place on the stockade walls on all sides, and he brought his eyes to the thundering warriors now charging in at a full gallop.

Their war whoops filled the air as they raced at the fort, a wild, furious attack that saw them charging around the gates at a furious pace while they poured both rifle fire and arrows at the defenders on the walls of the fort. As he watched, Fargo felt his brows raised in surprise as a second charge of warriors raced up, firing cluster after cluster of flaming arrows into the fort. Most were aimed at the wooden gate and the stockade walls but many were lobbed into the interior of the fort. It only took seconds for the stockade to blaze in dozens of places. The gate, Fargo saw, was quickly burning from the concentration of fire arrows that set the dry wood aflame. The attackers were circling the fort, still at a full gallop as they wildly poured rifle fire and arrows into the defenders while the second wave of attackers continued to loose their fire arrows.

The stockade was burning furiously now, Fargo

saw, the single corner blockhouse also ablaze. The gate was consumed by fire from top to bottom and Fargo saw it wavering. His eyes went to the top of the stockade. Only a few of the defenders were still standing in place, all but ignored by the racing braves as they attacked. The loud, hissing crash brought Fargo's eyes back to the gate and he saw it collapse in a shower of smoke, flame, and leaping sparks. He glimpsed the Kiowa chief immediately lead his warriors leaping over the fallen gate and into the interior of the fort. They entered screaming wildly in triumph. Through the noise, Fargo heard Alderson's voice calling out in a harsh whisper. "God, we forgot. Carlton's in there," he said. "I didn't think they'd burn down the fort."

"Too bad," Fargo said and saw Alderson stare in shock at him. "He brought it on. It's only right he pays for it. Besides, they'll say he died a hero," Fargo said and turned away. He reached down and brought up the rifle that lay at his side, raising the big Henry to his shoulder. It only took a minute more before the Indians streamed from the fort, the Kiowa chief in the lead. Fargo saw that many of his warriors waved blue-uniformed jackets in their hands as they halted beside the chief. Two of the braves used their knives to slice the uniform jackets to pieces in fury as other braves broke off firing at the fort and pulled their ponies to a halt. They quickly became a pushing, milling group, and Fargo could no longer see the chief.

But he could hear the Kiowa chief's voice raised, shouting with a new anger. The moment had come. They had stormed into the fort to kill any of the defenders still alive. But they had found no defenders, dead or alive. All they found were blue uniforms stuffed with paper and sheets that had been carefully propped up on the walls of the stockade. In their wild, insensate rage, they'd never noticed that nobody was firing back at them. They'd been too consumed with their own fury. Only now did they realize that their wild attack hadn't killed one of their hated enemies, the desecrators of their sacred soil. He heard the chief's voice raised in a howl of anguish and frustration. Fargo drew a bead on one of the braves surrounding the chief, a Pawnee warrior, and fired as the Indian pitched from his pony.

Almost instantly, the trees behind Fargo erupted as the line of troopers burst into the open, flattening themselves and laying down a furious barrage of gunfire. They poured a hail of bullets into the Indians who were still milling around in shock and surprise. Fargo saw braves falling on all sides and he brought down at least eight in his first volley. He reloaded, seeing three braves start to race to the side, and brought down two of them, who collided as they fell. But the attackers, taken completely by surprise, began to recover. With the Kiowa chief barking orders, they raced away, spreading out as they did to make smaller targets of themselves. Finally they halted beyond the blazing fort, and stayed spread out as they turned to stare across the stream at the line of trees. "Cease firing!" Nickles shouted, Alderson echoing the command as the troopers' carbines fell silent.

"You said we had to hurt them," Nickles said. "By God, I'd say we brought down more than a hundred."

Fargo nodded in agreement as he surveyed the bodies that littered the scene. "You did well, real well," Fargo said. "Well enough to turn away an ordinary attack. But this is no ordinary attack thanks to Carlton. We evened out the odds but that's all. They'll come at us again."

"We'll cut them down. We have a good defensive position. Let them charge us."

"They will, but you can be sure it won't be the way you expect," Fargo said and his eyes cut over to where the Indians had gathered. Staying spread out, they milled around the Kiowa chief. Then half of them dismounted, spread out, and flattened themselves on the ground. They began to crawl forward while the others stayed behind on their ponies. Spread out, they made small, difficult targets as they slowly crawled forward.

"Shit," Nickles bit out as he watched the braves steadily making their way toward the stream in front of him. When they drew opposite the fort, they disappeared in the smoke from the still-burning wood. When they fully came back in sight they were nearing the stream and within firing range. But they were still spread out and small targets. "Fire at will!" Nickles called out and the carbines began to bark again. But Fargo saw that only a few of the shots hit their targets flattened on the ground. The troopers were ordinary shooters firing at targets that needed sharpshooters. Suddenly, as if one, the braves rose on their elbows and fired a barrage across the stream. Fargo ducked and saw at least ten troopers go down.

"Retreat!" Alderson shouted. "You're too good a target out here in front of the trees! Get back into the tree line!" The men quickly ran backward, disappearing inside the trees. Fargo and the two officers scooted back together. Settling down, Fargo peered off into the distance where the other half of the Indian force had stayed on their ponies. As he watched, they split into two groups, one riding east, paralleling the stream, the other west. "What the hell are they doing?" Alderson asked.

"It's called tactics," Fargo said. "They didn't go to West Point, but they're still masters at it."

"You know them best. Can you read their moves?" Nickles questioned. The Indians supplied part of Fargo's answer as they opened up a hail of rifle fire. Not carefully aimed shots at targets well hidden in the trees, but a steady barrage.

"They're keeping us pinned down here. They expect we'll concentrate on answering their fire. Meanwhile, the others have gone to cross upstream and down. When they're on this side they'll come through the trees at us from both ends," Fargo said.

"Sons of bitches," the lieutenant growled.

"Face half your men east, the other half west. Have them hunker down and wait and you'll do the surprising. Keep twenty men returning fire across the stream. That'll keep them thinking you're doing what they want."

Alderson and Nickles moved quickly, positioning their men while Fargo watched the attackers just across the stream keep up their steady fire. He backed deeper into the trees, and found a spot behind a hickory tree, and it was not a long wait before he heard the horses coming through the trees. They rode in as fast as the trees would allow but the troopers were positioned and ready on both sides. The attackers had lost their advantage of surprise. They had been tactically outmaneuvered and found themselves on the receiving end of a barrage of bullets. Surprised and hit hard, they nonetheless reacted, leaping from horses to maneuver through the trees and charging forward for hand-to-hand combat. The tactic worked, as the troopers were taken off guard by the quick-moving, lithe, leaping figures that attacked in swift, darting movements.

Fargo saw two braves charging at him, both Kiowa, and he got the Henry up quickly enough to bring down both, only to whirl as he caught a sound to his right. A third brave rushed at him, his tomahawk raised to strike. Fargo had time only to drop below the arc of the ax as it whistled past his head. He brought the rifle barrel up far enough to dig it deep into the Indian's stomach. The man doubled over in pain and Fargo brought the rifle stock upward with all his strength. The stock smashed into the man's jaw and he went down with his chin hanging loosely in two pieces. Fargo brought the rifle around again in time to cut down a brave charging at him on his pony. He dropped to one knee and picked off two more darting figures when he saw the attackers turn and run, racing through the trees, darting away, leaping onto their ponies, and fleeing.

He turned to Nickles. "We hurt them again but they cost us plenty this time, especially those coming in from the east," the lieutenant said. "It would've been worse if we hadn't been ready, thanks to you." Fargo glanced out at the Indians across the stream, seeing that they had broken off their steady barrage. They began to crawl backward, staying flattened on the ground until they were out of the troopers' range. They soon rose and moved further back as the two groups of Kiowa returned, many nursing their wounds. Fargo watched as everyone gathered around the Kiowa chief, his face tight as he stared at the scene.

"You're looking awfully grim," Nickles commented. "I'd guess they're talking about pulling out."

"You'd guess wrong. They won't break it off. This is a sacred mission. They'll come at us again and again. Maybe they'll be committing suicide but they'll take us along with them," Fargo said. "They have to win, for their dead, for their ancestors, for what you did to their sacred ground." Nickles and Alderson stared back, their faces grave, aware they had lost too many men, also. "Maybe this is the time," Fargo murmured.

"Time for what?"

"To invoke their dead, those sacred ancestors, to make an offering of our own," Fargo said.

"You call it," Nickles said and Fargo took Nickles and Alderson aside.

"I'm riding out alone. I'm hoping the Kiowa chief will be curious enough to meet me. Meanwhile, you get everything I showed you hidden back in the trees. Put the bodies over your horses. When I wave at you, bring everything out," Fargo said.

"Let's hope it works," Nickles said and started away with Alderson. Fargo went into the nearby trees and swung up onto the Ovaro. He peered out across the stream, seeing the Kiowa chief still talking with his warriors. He moved the Ovaro forward, pushing out of the tree line and into the open. Sitting very straight, he walked the horse directly forward. He was seen at once, the Indians turning to watch him move toward them. He reached the edge of the stream and halted, feeling the perspiration coating his forehead. But he didn't move.

Finally, the Kiowa chief rode his pony forward, the others parting for him. With equal slowness, the Indian moved toward the stream and Fargo sent the pinto forward through the shallow waters, halting at the other side of the stream. The Kiowa chief continued to move directly at Fargo until he halted, hardly six feet separating him from his foe. Fargo met the Indian's glittering, onyx eyes, not with defiance, but not with fear. To show fear would be a fatal mistake, he realized. The Kiowa chief, the beartooth necklace still against his chest, stared at him in silence. Words would come, Fargo knew. Not many, but enough. The chief spoke Kiowan, of course, but Fargo was certain he also understood some Siouan, the tongue spoken by the Crow, Dakota, Iowa, Osage, Assiniboin, and at least six other tribes, and used as a general language of the plains. Fargo knew Siouan well enough. Combined with the universality of sign language, he could talk with the Kiowa chief, he was certain.

But their real communication would not be through the spoken word or sign language, Fargo knew. It would take place with messages more understood than given voice, the silent language of feelings communicated by deed and gesture, spoken through the eyes, the body, and the senses. Fargo held his place, letting another minute go by under the Kiowa chief's intense scrutiny, giving Alderson and Nickles a little more time to get ready. Very slowly, Fargo raised one arm into the air, held it there, then slowly brought it down, aware that at least fifty arrows were aimed at him. The Kiowa didn't move, didn't twitch a muscle or blink an eye. Fargo half tuned in the saddle and saw Alderson and Nickles crossing the stream. They led three army mounts, each carrying a blanket-wrapped body.

Fargo's eyes returned to the Kiowa chief and saw the man's strong-boned face lose its impassive mask. The chief's eyes widened and surprise crept across his face. His gaze stayed on Alderson and Nickles as they moved from the stream and began to carefully place each body on the ground at his feet. Next they emptied the two sacks of their sacred bundles, amulets, beads, fetishes, and every other possession of spiritual importance to the deceased. Finally, the Indian brought his eyes back to Fargo. He used sign language to ask the single question: *Why?*

"It is a gift, an offering," Fargo said. "For the chief of the Kiowa, for the Great Spirits."

The Indian repeated the sign. *Why?* he asked again.

Fargo searched for words and felt the Indian's piercing gaze boring into him. "It was a bad thing. It was a wrong thing," he said, using a combination of Siouan and sign language. He gestured to the bodies on the ground with their possessions. "They were saved. Their spirits are with them. We have done this," Fargo said. "They ask only one thing."

"What do they ask?" the Kiowa chief said in Siouan.

"To return to make the sacred ground sacred again," Fargo said. The chief waited a moment, then slid from his pony and slowly put his hands on each of the three bodies and every one of the items on the ground. When he finished, he turned back to Fargo. "Take them. Return them to the ground they will make sacred again. It is what they ask. Only this, not more killing," Fargo said. "Our gift. We give it because it is right to give. There will be no more killing now."

He waited as the Kiowa chief's eyes moved across the stream to where the troops formed a double line. Finally, he returned his piercing gaze to Fargo. "This time. You . . . these others. Only this. Only now," he said.

Fargo nodded and motioned to Nickles and Alderson to follow as he recrossed the stream, where he halted, looking back to see the chief directing others as they took away their dead. "What'd he mean?" Nickles asked.

"It's over here but only here. The offering worked. For us only, here and now. There'll be no peace. Everything will go on as always, attacks on settlements, wagon trains, patrols, anything and everything. But that balance that existed is back, that understanding has been restored. Those unwritten rules are back in place."

Nickles grimaced. "Killing as usual. Fighting as usual. Nothing good there," he said.

"No, but it's better than what was about to happen. We stopped a bloodbath. Putting out fires is better than fighting a holy war. Be grateful for small victories, even negative ones," Fargo said.

"We are, and every man here owes you, Fargo," Nickles said.

"The fort's gone. Set up a field camp for now. I'm sure General Davis is on his way. He'll decide the rest," Fargo said.

Alderson frowned into space. "We took too damn long to see," he said. "Carlton was there in front of us and we kept looking away."

"Don't blame yourselves. You've been trained to

respect, not suspect," Fargo said. "I'll be seeing you again, officers. Good luck, meanwhile."

"And to you," Nickles said as Fargo put the Ovaro into a canter and rode away. He galloped across the plains, glimpsing the Kiowa in the distance. Only a small group headed toward the burial ground and he saw others break off into separate groups and go on their way. Pawnee, Osage, Arapaho, and the others, returning to their own territories. Their experiment in alliances had been a lot less than successful. They'd be returning in anger and he felt sorry for any wagon train that crossed their paths. As Fargo made his way across the plains, he gave a wide berth to any bands he saw. Day still clung to the land when he reached the hills, passing the lake to find the wagons. He found only one, the converted hay wagon with Jiminy standing beside it.

Stepping forward, Jiminy answered the question he knew was coming before it was asked. "Gone. Vamoosed. On her way to Montana," he said.

"Damn. The land's full of Indians looking for victims. Why'd she take off?"

"She had a big fight with the girls. She was real mad. Didn't have anything good to say about you, either," Jiminy said.

"Why aren't you with her?"

"She wouldn't let me go. She fired me, said I was too friendly with you. She loaded the Conestoga with supplies and took off. She won't be making time, not with her wagon that loaded down," Jiminy said.

"I'm going after her. You stay, ride the plains, and keep an eye out for General Davis. You see him, tell him I'm riding northwest," Fargo said and Jiminy nodded as Fargo turned the Ovaro and moved from the hills. Once on the plains, he quickly found the wide, unmistakable wheel marks of a single Conestoga wagon leaving deep tracks. He followed until night fell, then found a spot in a field of burdock and bedded down. He rode again with the new day and wondered what had infuriated Melinda. Had she just grown angry at having to wait again or had something else set her off? She was moving slowly, but she'd had an entire day's head start and the sun was moving across the afternoon sky when he saw the tracks turn to the edge of a forest of red cedar.

The forest turned in a slow curve and the tracks followed. He had just started around the long, slow curve when he heard shots and the high-pitched war whoops. Cursing, he put the pinto into a gallop, slowing as he veered into the cedars. The shots were evenly spaced and the war whoops had an almost taunting quality to them. As he came to the end of the curve, Fargo saw the Conestoga pulled tight against the forest line. A dozen or so Indians raced back and forth on the open plains as they fired at the wagon. Individual braves dashed forward for a closer shot, then raced away. He caught a glimpse of the moccasins. Pawnee, he thought as his eyes went to the Conestoga. Only an occasional shot came from the wagon and, staying in the cedars, Fargo halted and dropped from the pinto just as he saw four braves on foot inside the trees. They were making their way toward the wagon and Fargo drew his Colt and moved forward on silent steps.

The four Pawnee were concentrating on the wagon as they closed in on it, three with their knives drawn. Fargo halted, took aim, and fired. Two fast shots felled two of the Pawnee, hitting the ground less than a foot from the wagon. The other two dived to the ground and Fargo's next shot missed. He glimpsed them pull up behind tree trunks, then dart forward, moving from tree to tree with both speed and timing. Fargo peered out through the trees and saw that the other Pawnees had heard his shots. They halted, disappearing into the trees, but the movement close by and to his left drew Fargo's attention in time to see one Pawnee spring from behind a cedar.

He raised the Colt and his finger pressed the trigger just as he saw the knife hurtling toward him. He dropped low and his shot slammed into a tree trunk as he spun, hearing the second brave charge at him from the other side. The Pawnee was quick, darting from side to side as he raced forward. Fargo's shot only grazed his shoulder. Close now, the Indian leaped into the air as he hurled himself at Fargo. Fargo brought the Colt up and fired, and this time his shot hit the attacker's shoulder. But the man's leap carried him forward and Fargo found the Pawnee's body slamming into him and he felt himself go down. The Colt hit the ground hard and skipped out of his hand.

He tried to dive to reach the pistol but the Indian's fury drove him to slam into Fargo again. This time Fargo fell sideways, and caught a glimpse of the Pawnee. The Indian's shoulder was drenched in red that coursed down his arm, and driven by his insensate fury, he drove forward again, both hands outstretched to close around his foe's throat. Fargo managed to bring one knee up and catch the Pawnee in the groin as he came down. With a guttural sound, the Indian fell to the side, gasping in pain. He tried to rise but Fargo was on his feet first, bringing a roundhouse blow that smashed into the man's jaw. The

Pawnee fell backward, his head hitting hard against a rock, and finally he lay still.

Fargo heard the other Pawnee running at him from his right. He didn't try to turn to meet the charge that would bowl him over. Instead, he dived forward, a lunging effort, but his hand closed around the Colt where it lay in the grass. The Indian had hurtled past him and Fargo saw him turn, the knife in his hand. The Colt barked and the Pawnee staggered backward, the knife falling from his hand before he collapsed in a heap. Fargo pulled himself to his feet and peered through the trees.

The Pawnee in the open plains had halted, hearing the shots, and Fargo saw them listening, watching. They would wait a few moments more, cautious and unsure of what was happening inside the cedars. Fargo seized the moment and ran to the tail end of the Conestoga and peered in. He saw the girls on the floor of the wagon, wedged into every spot they could find between boxes, sacks, and crates. His gaze went to the front of the wagon, seeing the shock of straw-colored hair. She crouched, looking out from the edge of the canvas of the wagon, the rifle in her hands.

Maxine, nearest to Fargo, saw him and started to push to her feet. "Stay down!" Fargo shouted and she dropped back to the floor. Melinda turned at his voice and he saw surprise mixed in with the glare of her sharp, blue eyes. "Trouble?" he asked.

"Smart remarks all you've got to offer?" she threw at him.

"Always happens when I run out of miracles," he said with a derisive snort. "I'm going to try and get them to come after me. If they do, you take this wagon and turn it around and run like hell back the way you came."

"Why that way?"

"They're on their way north. They just happened on to you. I'm betting they won't bother going back to look for you. You disappear, they'll just go their way," Fargo said.

"Do what he says, for God's sake!" Chrissee called out. Fargo turned and left the wagon and ran over to the Ovaro. A glance through the cedars showed him that half the Pawnee had left their ponies and were stealing on foot toward the Conestoga. Fargo took the big Henry, sent the pinto into a gallop, and burst through the trees into the open. He sprayed shots from the repeating rifle in a wide arc and saw three of the Pawnee fall from their ponies. He was racing on as the Pawnee started after him, those on foot running to vault onto their mounts. They were all giving chase as he sent the Ovaro racing across the plains, spraying another volley back at them.

They had done exactly as he thought they would, and Fargo had confidence the Ovaro could outrun any of their short-legged steeds. He kept a steady gallop, not pushing the Ovaro, but the Pawnee's fury made them persistent. They stayed right behind him and it wasn't long before he felt the Ovaro beginning to tire. There was good reason—the horse had been ridden hard and long the last two days. Fargo flung a glance back at the Pawnee. They held to their steady pursuit and he swore but refused to push the Ovaro to go faster. He rode southeast over the prairie and when he glanced back again, the Pawnee had edged a little closer and he cursed silently again.

He'd ridden for another ten minutes when his eyes

grew wide and he saw the large plume of dust moving toward him from his left. He swerved toward the dust cloud and knew the Pawnee had seen it, also. He glanced over at his pursuers and saw them slowing as they realized the dust cloud would cut in front of them if they kept on. Wheeling in a small circle, they raced west across the flat plains and Fargo slowed his horse as the large plume became a wide mass of blue-uniformed horsemen, almost a full regiment. As they came closer, Fargo saw the straight figure of Miles Davis at the head of the double column. Fargo reined up and Miles drew up to a halt in front of him. "You're what they call a sight for sore eyes," Fargo breathed. "Jiminy send you this way?"

"That's right," the general said. "I was on my way to Fort Burns when he found me."

"To what used to be Fort Burns," Fargo said and Miles's brows lifted. "It's a field camp, now. Two young lieutenants in command."

"Alderson and Nickles?" the general asked and Fargo nodded.

"They had a course in growing up quickly," Fargo said and recounted everything that had happened. Miles Davis drew a long breath when he finished.

"Seems as if you outdid yourself, Fargo," he said.

"I put things back the way they were. That's not much of an accomplishment," Fargo said.

"It is if you think about what could have been," Miles said. "I'll see to whatever needs to be done while I'm here. There are a lot of folks who'll never know how much they owe you."

"That's always the way of it," Fargo said. "We never know how much we owe to who, and what."

"Maybe we can find time to sit down with a bottle

of bourbon before I have to head back, old friend," the general said.

"Maybe," Fargo said and Miles saluted him as he put the pinto into a trot. He headed south, then east, and it was nearly dark when he found the Conestoga wheel marks and then the big wagon as it still hugged the edge of the cedars, Melinda holding the reins. She pulled up as he stopped and swung to the ground. He waited as she climbed from the wagon, a smudge of dirt across her forehead, tiredness in her eyes, but still she moved with an easy, fluid grace. "You want to tell me why you went damn fool crazy?" he asked.

"Things I found out," she said haughtily.

"Such as?"

"How you lied to me about your self-discipline. And to think I complimented you on it," Melinda said icily. "You lied to me about all of it. You said things so cleverly. Only they were lies."

"Wrong. I didn't lie. I know what I said. You heard what you wanted to hear," he returned. Her glare stayed. "How'd you find out?" he asked.

"They got too chatty. I overheard them, the little bitches. Yes, they hit at me but they used you, too," Melinda said.

"What are you talking about?" Fargo queried.

"Let them tell you themselves," Melinda said and he heard the malicious pleasure in her tone. She raised her voice. "Out here! Now!" she called and in moments the girls stepped from the wagon, Maxine first, then Amy, Lena, and the others following. "Tell Fargo how clever you've been," Melinda said with icy sarcasm in her voice, then spun on her heel and strode off to disappear behind the wagon.

Fargo took in the six young women, who stared almost sheepishly at him. "I don't hear anything," he said.

"Well, we sort of already told you," Maxine said. "You just didn't know it."

He let his thoughts unreel until they came to a screeching halt inside his mind. "When you said you'd get back at all of them, your folks for sending you, Melinda for taking you?" he said.

"Bulls-eye," Maxine said. "And we have."

"How?" Fargo queried.

"They sent us away to come back obedient, grateful, perfect in every way," Lena said. "The kind of girls they could marry off as they wanted, to the families they wanted. We didn't matter."

"Of course, being untouched, a virgin, was part of being perfect, a very important part in certain circles," Maxine said. "Well, we put an end to all that. They won't be marrying us off, now. They won't be making choices for us."

"We paid them back where it'll hurt and Melinda won't get the full payment they promised her for delivering us in perfect condition," Amy put in.

"And you used me to do it. Melinda was right. Guess I was all wrong to feel flattered," Fargo said a touch ruefully.

Maxine's arms were around him first, then Lena, then the others crowded around. "No, no, no. We didn't use you, not the way that sounds. We wanted you, wanted to do it with you. We wouldn't have done it with just anyone," Maxine said. "We talked often about that."

"Then you came on the scene and God, we all wanted you and suddenly it was all there for us, everything in place. We had to make love to you," Lena said.

"With you it was a chance we'd never have again, the best of two worlds, everything rolled into one," Amy said.

"Sort of like screwing two birds with one stone," Fargo said.

"Yes, exactly," they chortled almost in unison.

"Well, you'll win. You've already won. You're not going to Montana. I'm sending you back East," he said and they showered him with hugs and kisses.

"We love you!" they shouted, stepping back as Melinda came out from behind the Conestoga, her lovely face tight as she walked to Fargo.

"They tell you everything?" she asked him.

"Yes," he said.

"Leave us," she said to the girls and they filed back to the wagon. Melinda turned to him, her sharp blue eyes probing.

"Yes? Is that all you can say?" she asked with disapproval.

"I can live with it. You'll have to. So will their fathers," he said.

"It doesn't bother you to be used?" she speared.

"Not in the way they explained it," he said. "They've won. Get used to it. I'm sending you back East. The plains are still too dangerous, and will be for a good while. There's a stage out of Elbow Flats. I'll take you there. Besides, there's no reason to go on. They've won. It's done."

Melinda let a bitter sound escape her lovely lips. "I guess so," she muttered.

"You didn't come out empty-handed. They paid you a good advance," he said.

Melinda's chin lifted and her eyes held a strange little light as she peered hard at him. "Maybe not," she murmured.

"What's that mean?" he frowned.

"It means maybe it's not over," she snapped.

"It is, believe me. Accept it," he said just as night lowered itself. She didn't answer and strode away to the wagon. The girls came to him minutes later. "This is as good a place as any for you to camp for the night," he said.

"We'll start a fire. You staying with us for the night?" Josie asked.

"I'll bed down a few hundred yards up along the cedars. I hear things better when I sleep alone," he said.

"You expect trouble?" Amy asked.

"No, but just in case," he said. They each kissed him before he took the Ovaro and walked away. He went on perhaps a quarter-mile and found a break in the trees, then unsaddled the horse and set out his bedroll. He ate a stick of beef jerky in the little hollow, and as a full moon rose, he undressed. He was on his bedroll in the warm night, almost asleep when his ears caught a faint sound. He sat up, listening to soft footsteps coming through the trees.

He smiled and wondered. They were still choosing straws. Maybe that was the best proof that they weren't really using him. The figure came into sight, stepping out where the moonlight caught her and he saw hair that was pale straw in the silver light. He was frowning as she came to the bedroll, a thin night-dress around her. She stood before him with a kind of defiance, and suddenly shook her shoulders and the thin garment fell from her, landing around her ankles.

His eyes took in her tall, lovely figure, lean yet not thin.

Square, broad shoulders rose up to a lovely, long neck. Slightly long breasts dipped with a beautiful curve to full, rounded cups, each lovely mound tipped by a small, rose-tinted tip surrounded by a pale rose circle. Her's was a skin of smooth white, almost an alabaster quality to it where it hadn't been tanned by the sun. A flat abdomen contrasted the pronounced ribs and his eyes followed the soft swell of her belly with its little elliptical indentation, offering its own sensuousness. He saw hips that were wide without being heavy, beautifully curved and moving down to long, gorgeous thighs and equally long calves. She might have had a willowy body if it weren't for the strength in it that offered more than just beauty. His eyes went to her dark triangle, a hint of straw-colored strands in it.

She dropped to her knees beside him. "No questions. No talk," Melinda murmured and her lips were on his, pressed gently, then harder. Her arms slid around his neck and he felt her ample breasts press against his chest. "Oh, God, oh, oh nice, nice," she murmured and rubbed herself against him. He felt the tiny rose-tinted tips move over his skin, a tingling delicacy to her touch. His hand cupped one breast, and caressed its softness, circling the pale rose circle as Melinda cried out. "Yes, oh, yes, yes . . . good, so good," she breathed. He brought his mouth down to one little tip and drew it in, pulling gently on it and feeling it swell under his lips, taking on new firmness.

He drew it into his mouth again, sucking it, letting his tongue circle the tip. Melinda's torso moved, lifted, and fell back. Her hands slid across his body, pressing, moving up and down along his torso. He drew his mouth from her breast and she gave a small sound of protest that faded at once as his tongue began to trace a line down her abdomen, nibbling, tickling, sucking. He paused at the little indentation in her belly, caressing it as Melinda cried out. She had her mouth open, drawing in tiny breaths, letting each become a gasp of pleasure. His lips moved down further, reaching the swell of her belly, down to the sensation of her soft fibrous hairs, feeling their filamentous tendrils curl and slide into his mouth and he pulled gently on them.

"Oh, God, oh, Jeez, oh, oh," Melinda gasped and he pressed his face down on the soft swelling that was her pubic mound. Again she cried out and he felt her long legs lift up, offering herself to him. Her hands reached down, grasped his head, held it hard against her Venus mound as little cries of delight escaped from her lips. He let his hand slide downward, resting on the warm, wet moistness and Melinda screamed. "Oh, yes, oh, yes, please, please, oh, my God please!" He crept slowly down further, and caressed the soft outer walls of her sweet and dark portal, and all of her seemed to quiver as she gasped out little screams.

Suddenly her hands were digging into his back, his buttocks, pulling at him. "Jesus, now, please, take me, take me!" she breathed in a throaty whisper and he felt her pubic mound lifting, twisting, her body imploring, the language of the senses demanding to be heard. He released his own pulsating manhood and reached for her, finding the honeyed way and sliding forward as Melinda's scream split the night. "So big!" Her long legs clasped around him in a sweet vise, and she moved with him in a delicious rhythm, and waves of sensation coursed around him and he felt the ripples of her contractions against his rigid pole.

"Ummmm, ummmm, mmmmmmm," Melinda moaned and he saw her eyes were half closed, her luscious breasts rubbing against his chest, her torso moving with the rhythm of her hips. Her mouth found his with a sweet, devouring pressure, her tongue a darting, wild organ of its own. She took his head and pressed it to one full-cupped breast and crushed it there. All the while, the slow, undulating rhythm of her moist tunnel slid forward and back, up and down, her moans made of pure ecstasy. Then, with the suddenness that was always unexpected yet always expected, she uttered a sharp cry and her long thighs rose, fell open, and slapped hard against him. "Oh, God, now, oh, now, now!" she cried out and the slow, wonderful undulations changed, became a furious twisting and urging, and he heard her half crying and half screaming, pleasure rising to heights that only wanted to reach greater elevations.

"Yes, yes, now, now, now!" she screamed and her hands slapped at his shoulders, dug into him, and yet he sensed she was not ready for that single moment of blissful lightning. She continued to cry out and slide against him and thrust herself upward and then, with the suddenness that is always new, she seemed to freeze for a long moment as a scream tore from her throat, circling in the air and trailing away. Another followed, then another, and just as suddenly, she cried out in protest and her hands dug into him. "More, more, damn, damn, damn," she said, clinging to him and the warm wetness of her surrounded him, its own magnificent sensation.

But there was no sudden collapse with Melinda.

She wound down slowly, her body continuing to make its own little urgings, the senses pulling every last moment of pleasure from flesh and nerves. But slowly, she began to grow quiet, but he felt her tongue sliding down his neck, tiny, nibbling motions that carried their own message. She held him to her, inside her, keeping her body tight against his until finally she relaxed and lay almost limply against his strong frame. But she kept one breast against his face, one rose-colored tip resting softly upon his lips. When she stirred, later, she rose up on her elbows, no sharpness in her blue eyes now, only a soft quietness.

He let his own gaze study her. "Why?" he asked.

"You do what seems right to do," she said. "Someone said that to me once." He saw the tiny smile as it edged her lips.

"Good advice," he said.

"I intend to be using it often, like in a few minutes," she said.

"Sounds good to me," he agreed. Her words were not empty promises and soon she was crying out with him again, her long body sliding up and down on his, her hands reaching for him, helping him find that sweet place she offered with eager, total wanting. Finally, when she lay against him again, a dreamy little smile on her lips, she murmured softly.

"Stay with me, for a while, at least, Fargo," she said.

"For a while," he agreed.

"Let Jiminy take the girls back on the stage from Elbow Flats," she said.

"Why not?" he said. She shifted contentedly, making a little niche for herself in his arms and was asleep in moments. He slept with her until the first rays of dawn came. He awoke her gently. "Time to get back to the wagon," he said.

She rubbed sleep from her eyes and sat up, her ample, alabaster breasts swaying beautifully. "I'll go first," she said.

He smiled. "The proper thing. Once a headmistress, always a headmistress."

"No," she said, slipping on the nightdress. "It's not being proper. It's being possessive," she said honestly. "I'm not sharing any of this with them."

"I'll be along." he said as she hurried away. When he dressed and strolled back to the wagon, Melinda was in the driver's seat, the reins in her hand. She gave him a polite nod and he kept the smile inside himself as he waved to Maxine and the others, who peered from the Conestoga at him. The trip back to where Jiminy waited with the big hay wagon was uneventful and Jiminy happily agreed to take the girls back East on the stage out of Elbow Flats.

"Till we meet again, Fargo," he said with a hug and a hand clasp. "You've something lined up, I'm sure."

"Definitely," he said and saw the smug little smile on Melinda's face. He didn't mind. He felt his own stirring inside him. Smugness had its place. As did a lot of other things.

LOOKING FORWARD!
The following is the opening
section from the next novel in the exciting
Trailsman **series from Signet:**

THE TRAILSMAN #226
NEBRASKA SLAYING GROUND

1860—where the great untamed plains
of the New Land brought out both the best
and the worst in men, and proved that
savagery can wear many faces. . . .

"You can touch me if you like."

Skye Fargo stopped in front of the lovely dove who had invited him to sample her wares, his lake blue eyes dancing with mirth. He openly admired her hourglass figure, sheathed in a tight red dress that accented her abundant charms. "Just like that?" he asked. A big, broad-shouldered man in buckskins, he dwarfed the woman's petite frame.

"It's customary," the dove said, nodding to the right and the left. "See for yourself."

The long entrance hall to Bob Potee's gambling den on the second floor of number 3 Missouri Avenue was lined by buxom beauties. As patrons walked by, they touched the lovely lady of their choice where no man had any business touching a lady except in private. But the women didn't seem to mind. In fact, they were enjoying themselves immensely. Joking and laughing, they thrust their bosoms out in flagrant invitation.

"It's done for luck at the gaming tables," the dove ex-

Excerpt from NEBRASKA SLAYING GROUND

plained. "Mr. Potee started the custom when he opened the place." Her voice lowered and she winked slyly. "Of course, you'll have even better luck if you slip me a twenty-dollar gold piece."

Fargo laughed. "Sorry, gorgeous. I'd love to oblige, but I barely have twenty dollars to my name." He'd lost most of his poke the night before in a stud poker game at another one of Kansas City's landmarks, Doc Frame's Gambling Emporium. The city boasted upward of twenty such establishments and was well on its way to becoming the gambling capital of the entire West.

The dove took the news in stride. "Tell you what," she said, studying him from head to toe. "It's on the house. Treat yourself."

"Rather generous, aren't you?" Fargo quipped.

"You're a lot handsomer than most, and I've always had a special fondness for good-looking galoots." The dove arched her shoulders so that her twin mounds swelled toward him like watermelons ripe enough to burst. "My name is Molly, by the way, and I get off at one. In case you'd like some company later on."

Fargo smiled. "I'll keep it in mind." Boldly reaching up, he covered her right breast and gently squeezed.

Molly blushed ever so slightly, her full cherry lips forming a delectable O. "Your hands are nice and warm," she complimented him. "Unlike some of the lunkheaded drovers who waltz through here. I'd swear they were made of ice."

Fargo could feel her nipple through the sheer fabric, the rounded tip as hard as a nail. On an impulse he flicked it with a finger and Molly wriggled in delight.

"Play your cards right and you can do that to your heart's content," she declared.

"Speaking of cards," Fargo said, reluctantly lowering

his arm, "I've got to find a game to sit in on." He had come to Bob Potee's to try and recoup his losses.

Molly leaned forward. Her mouth brushed his ear, her breath fanning his neck as she whispered, "Whatever you do, stay away from the table at the back. One of the regulars there, a big gent called Guzman, is the slickest cheat this side of the Rockies. He'll fleece you dry."

"Thanks for the warning," Fargo said, patting her firm backside.

Giggling, Molly straightened. "I'll be waiting right here at one o'clock and you better not disappoint me."

Fargo touched the tip of her chin, then blended into the stream of new arrivals flowing into the luxurious interior. The owner, Potee, had spared no expense. Plush wine red carpet covered the floor. Mahogany paneling adorned the walls. Overhead, large chandeliers sparkled, while the room was crammed with polished tables and chairs. Up on a small but elegant stage, a balding piano player provided lively music.

At the bar customers were lined up three deep. Fargo waited his turn, ordered a whiskey, and took his drink toward the rear. Sweet little Molly didn't realize it, but her friendly advice had given him an idea.

Four men were seated at the last table. Guzman was easy to pick out. Overweight, with oily hair and flabby jowls, he wore a black frock coat, white shirt, and a string tie. For all his bulk, he handled the cards with casual ease, his thick fingers flowing with superb speed, the trademark of a true professional.

Fargo sipped his drink and observed for a spell, taking his measure of the players. One was a mousy sort who held his cards close to his vest. Another was an older man who always left his on the table after glancing at them. The third had no business playing poker. He wore his cards on his face, as it were, his expression always betraying whether he had been dealt good ones or bad.

They were playing for average stakes, each pot no higher than twenty dollars. Fargo realized he must play carefully until he had enough to make his move.

It was Guzman's turn to deal, and he did so fluidly, his fingers flying with practiced precision. If he was going to cheat, now was when he would do it.

Fargo watched closely but noticed nothing out of the ordinary—at first.

The game was draw poker. The mousy player asked for three cards, the older gent for two, while the third jasper stood pat. That left Guzman, who announced in his gravely voice, "The dealer takes one," and dealt a card to himself, shading the deal, doing it so slickly that no one other than Fargo caught on.

It was an old trick. Guzman started to slide off the uppermost card using his thumb. But the card wasn't halfway off when he used his second and third fingers to propel the bottom card forward in its stead. It was all done in the blink of an eye, so smoothly that it looked as if he had dealt properly. Truly flawless sleight of hand.

Fargo wasn't the least bit surprised when Guzman raised the ante from the usual dollar to two. Nor when it turned out the others had good enough cards to stay in the game, but not good enough to win the final pot, which totaled over forty dollars—twice as much as usual.

Finishing off the rest of his coffin varnish in a single gulp, Fargo pulled out an empty chair. "Mind if I sit in?" he said, sliding down before anyone could answer.

"Not at all, mister," Guzman said curtly. "So long as you don't mind parting company with your money."

The mousy player was more courteous. "Be our guest, friend. Good luck to you. I'm Harold Pinder."

Guzman snorted. "Do you think he cares who you are, you yack? All he's interested in is your cash." Guzman gave the deck to the older player. "Your turn to deal, Simmons."

The fourth man, the one whose expression always gave him away, sorted through his small amount of coins and bills. "Another couple of hands and I'll be busted again. I swear, I have the worst luck of anyone I know. If I had a lick of common sense, I'd give up this stinking game."

"Your luck isn't that rotten, Barkley," Guzman surprised Fargo by saying. "Remember that time you won pretty near sixty dollars? And last month when you almost cleaned me out until I turned the tables?"

Fargo wasn't fooled by the cardsharp's seemingly kind comments. Guzman wanted Barkley to keep coming back because poor players like him were easy to fleece. Fargo guessed that Guzman had let Barkley win so Barkley wouldn't lose interest. There was no doubt about it; the gambler was one slick hombre.

Harold Pinder adjusted his spectacles. "Tell me, friend," he addressed Fargo, "if I'm not being too nosy, what do you do for a living?"

"I've done some scouting, guided a few wagon trains," Fargo said without going into detail. His personal life was no one's business but his own.

"You don't say," Harold remarked. "I thought as much, how you're dressed and all." He gave a tiny cough. "Tell me. Are you perhaps, in need of gainful employment? My cousin is looking for a reliable guide to take him across the prairie. Would you be interested?"

Guzman drummed his fingers on the table. "Is this a card game or a damned church social? You chatter worse than a chipmunk, Harold. You know that?"

Fargo didn't like how the card shark butted in. And

since he had no employment prospects lined up for the immediate future, he said to Pinder, "Where do I find this cousin of yours? I'll look him up tomorrow."

"His name is Jace Carver," Harold responded. "Second cousin on my mother's side. He has his own business, Carver Supply, over on Jefferson Avenue. Can't hardly miss it, what with the huge yellow sign he has out front."

Guzman chuckled. "It's hard to believe you and Jace are kin. The two of you are as different as night from day."

"Oh, I don't know. Everyone says we have the same chin and nose," Harold said defensively. "We're not all that different."

"Neither is a mountain lion and a lamb," the gambler countered and roared at his own wit.

Simmons began to deal. "Here we go, boys. Same as before. A pair or better to open."

Fargo played conservatively, only raising when the cards were in his favor. He learned early on that it was simple to tell when Harold and Barkley were bluffing. Harold gnawed on his lower lip, and Barkley looked as if he were sitting on broken glass. Simmons was inscrutable but he never took risks, never betting more than a dollar or two no matter how good his cards were. As for Guzman, he was a master at manipulating the others, reading them as some people read a book.

By the end of an hour Fargo was seven dollars ahead. Not much, but he now had a total of twenty-five plus some odd cents. He started betting a bit more, and by the end of the second hour he was up to thirty-five.

"I told you," Barkley remarked, tapping what little was left of his pile. "I should have quit long ago."

"Stick it out," Guzman said. "Lady Luck might smile on you yet."

But she didn't. A quarter of an hour later Barkley had barely ten dollars to his name. Simmons had about twelve, Harold Pinder a bit more.

"Tell you what," Fargo said, glancing at Guzman. "Why don't we hike the stakes? Five dollars to open, and each raise must be five or more. What do you say?"

"Going for broke, eh?" Guzman said. "I'm willing if everyone else is."

Barkley shook his head and raked in what was left of his money. "Count me out, gentlemen. If I go home plumb broke again, my missus will take a rolling pin to my noggin."

Harold Pinder rubbed his hands together excitedly. "I'm staying. This is getting interesting."

Simmons shrugged. "It doesn't make no nevermind to me how high the stakes are. I'm in for the duration."

Play resumed. It was Harold's turn to deal and he did so with exquisite care, taking forever to shuffle and an eternity to deal. He counted each card aloud, slowly sliding each and every one across the table as if he were afraid they would break.

"You're about to put me to sleep," Guzman complained. "Any slower and I'd swear you were made of molasses."

"I'm being thorough," Harold defended himself.

"You're being stupid," Guzman snapped.

Fargo ended up with two kings, a queen, a ten, and a two. He debated whether to just keep the pair and finally decided to hold on to the lady, too. It was well he did. He was given another queen—and one more king. Now he had a full house. Only four-of-a-kind, a straight flush, and a royal flush could beat it. But when it was his turn to raise, he only did so by five dollars. He didn't want to clean the table just yet, not when Guzman was due to deal next.

Fargo won the pot, a grand total of thirty dollars. Now he had more than enough to lure Guzman in. Simmons helped by folding. Harold Pinder mulled it over a bit and decided to stick in the game.

"Give me the cards," Guzman said, sweeping them in. He shuffled twice, then cut one-handed, a feat few were capable of. Shuffling twice more, he tilted the deck. Not much, but enough for him to be able to see part of the bottom card. No one noticed except Fargo. Guzman was too crafty.

"Here's where we separate the greenhorns from the longhorns," the gambler declared, bestowing a thinly disguised sneer on Fargo.

"I hope I have enough to hold out," Harold said, frowning. He was down to eleven dollars or so.

Fargo gestured. "Do yourself a favor and bow out while you can."

"What for? It's only money."

"This from someone who makes his living as an accountant," Guzman said, shaking his head. "If your clients only knew."

"I resent your insinuation, sir," Harold said stiffly. "I'd never betray their trust. I'm no swindler."

"Don't have a calf," Guzman responded. "I never said you were." As they talked, the gambler dealt, displaying his usual precise skill.

Fargo picked his cards up and fanned them. He hadn't fared as well this time around. Fate had granted him a four of clubs, a seven of hearts, a ten of spades, a jack of hearts, and a queen of diamonds. Ordinarily he would discard the lower three and hold on to the face cards, but at the last instant he changed his mind and kept the ten of spades, hoping to draw an outside straight. Once again his hunch played out. A nine of clubs and a king of diamonds were slid across, giving him a high straight.

Harold Pinder was gnawing on his lower lip. When it came his turn, he asked for three cards and then smacked them down in irritation. "So much for recouping my losses! I should go beat my head against a wall. I fold."

That left Fargo and Guzman.

"I'll take two," the gambler said.

Pretending to be interested in his hand, Fargo peered at the cardsharp from under hooded eyelids, waiting for the crucial moment when Guzman attempted to deal from the bottom of the deck. He had to time it just right. Too soon or too late and he would be made to look the fool himself.

Then it happened. Guzman started to slide the top card outward. In the flash of an instant he did the same with the bottom card, contriving, as he had before, to slide the bottom one past the top one while simultaneously replacing the top card back.

Fargo's right hand streaked across the intervening space. His fingers clamped on to Guzman's, trapping the gambler in the act of double-dealing.

"What the hell!" Guzman bellowed, trying to jerk away.

"What's going on!" Harold asked in bewilderment.

Equally puzzled, Barkley blurted, "Here now! No grabbing allowed!"

Only Simmons caught on. Leaning forward, he pointed at the two cards wedged between Guzman's fingers. "Son of a bitch! Look there, boys! That slick bastard is trying to cheat!" Simmons shook a fist. "How many times have you pulled that stunt on us before, you lowdown snake in the grass?"

As red as a beet, the veins on his temples bulging, Guzman heaved upward. "Let go!" he snarled, tugging to free himself.

Games at nearby tables halted. Patrons shifted in their seats to stare, those who recognized the dirty dealer, scowling at him in contempt.

Guzman stepped back and yanked harder. His hand slipped loose. In the process, he dropped cards all over his chair and the floor. Glaring balefully, he rubbed his fingers where Fargo had gripped them. "So help me, I'll blow out your wick for this!"

Simmons, Pinder, and Barkley also rose, the older man bobbing his chin at the gambler. "You're the one who should be turned into wolf bait! You rotten cheat! I have half a mind to go to Bob Potee."

"That won't be necessary," interjected a dapper man who materialized from out of the gaping onlookers, his hands on his hips, his countenance a study in indignation. "I warned you, Guzman. But you wouldn't listen."

"Now hold on, Bob—" the gambler said.

"Silence!" the smaller man snapped, his voice like the crack of a bullwhip. As if on cue, two burly characters in dark suits appeared at either elbow, their jackets parted to reveal the pistols they carried underneath.

Guzman was furious but he held his tongue.

"I told you there had been a few complaints," Bob Potee said crisply. "I warned you that if anyone ever proved you were a cheat, I'd have you thrown out and permanently banned." Potee crooked a finger and the two burly characters moved in closer to the fuming gambler. "My men will escort you out. Don't ever step foot on these premises again."

It was too much for Guzman. "Don't you want to hear my side?"

"No. I've been keeping my eye on you, and I happened to see the whole thing. You finally ran up against someone with quicker hands than yours."

Raw hatred blazed in the look the gambler cast at

Fargo. "You've made the biggest mistake of your life, mister. You hear me? This isn't over."

Bob Potee motioned and the pair of burly bouncers each took hold of one of Guzman's arms.

"Wait a minute! What about my money?"

"*Your* money?" Potee said sarcastically. "You fleeced these others out of most of it. Besides, you know how cheating is handled. The cheat's money always goes to whoever he was playing against when he's caught. And since only you and this fellow in buckskins were still in the game, it's all his."

The glowering gambler was ushered out as Bob Potee came around the table. "A word to the wise, mister," he said to Fargo. "A coyote like Guzman isn't about to forgive and forget. He'll lie in wait and put a slug in your back the first chance he gets."

"Let him try," Fargo replied.

Potee gazed around the crowded room, and sighed. "I'm truly sorry. I try my best to run clean games, but I can't be everywhere at once. Occasionally a bad apple like Guzman crops up."

"You can't blame yourself," Fargo said, helping himself to the pot and Guzman's large pile.

"I'm the owner. Like it or not, the responsibility rests on my shoulders." Potee regarded him and the other three. "To help make it up to you, your drinks are on the house for the rest of the night. Just ask the barkeep at this end of the bar. I'll tell him to set you up."

Harold Pinder, Barkley, and Simmons exchanged grins. "That's awful nice of you, Mr. Potee," Harold said.

"Consider it a bribe," Potee said, not entirely in jest. "I don't want any of you going around saying I run a crooked gambling house."

"We'd never do that," Simmons assured him.

"Hell, no," Barkley said. "Everyone in Kansas City knows you're as honest as the year is long."

The dapper owner bid them good evening and melted into the throng.

Fargo had accumulated a small hill of coins and bills. He commenced counting it, laying the bills out in a row according to their denominations and stacking the coins by type. The grand total came to one hundred and fifty-three dollars, not quite as much as he had thought it would be, but enough to keep him in whiskey and women for another week or more. Looking up, he saw the others staring at his newfound wealth as if it were juicy steak and they hadn't eaten for a week.

"He cheated us, too," Harold Pinder remarked rather timidly.

"That he did," Fargo allowed. "But you dropped out."

"It's not fair," Barkley whined. "Guzman took a lot more of our money than he did of yours."

Simmons waved a hand in dismissal of the notion. "It doesn't matter, George. How's this guy supposed to know whose is whose? It's not like those bills have our names on them. He has a right to it all. That's just how these things go."

They went to leave.

"Hold on," Fargo said, and counted out three piles of fifteen dollars apiece. It was approximately how much each had lost since he sat down. "Help yourselves. And next time, be more careful about who you play cards with."

"Thanks, stranger!" Harold beamed. "You're all right. I'll be sure to tell my cousin about you." Stuffing the bills into a pocket, he bustled away.

Simmons took his without a word, nodded gratefully, and headed for the bar.

That left Barkley who didn't know when he was well

off. Hefting his share, he commented, "I should receive more than they did since I lost twice as much."

Fargo doubted it. "Fifteen is all you're getting. Unless you'd rather not have that." The Trailsman held out his hand, palm up.

"No, no, don't get me wrong," Barkley said hastily. "This will do just fine." But his face put the lie to his words. Clenching his fists, his spine as rigid as a board, he departed in a huff.

Since there were too many coins to tote around, Fargo took them to the cashier and exchanged them for bills. Then, never one to pass up a free drink or three, he visited the bar. A clock on the wall revealed it was a few minutes shy of midnight. Another hour, yet, before Molly was done for the night.

A familiar figure stepped to his side. "Simmons just mentioned what you did, mister. Damned decent of you."

"Barkley didn't think so."

Bob Potee snickered. "Some people are so soured on life, they can't get the acid out of their systems. And he's one of them." Potee offered his hand. "I don't believe I caught your name."

Shaking hands, Fargo told him.

The proprietor's thin eyebrows arched. "Do tell. Your reputation precedes you, Trailsman. Had I known who you were, I wouldn't have butted in earlier. I'd have let Guzman go for his gun so the undertaker could plant him six feet under tomorrow." Potee scanned the boisterous throng. "On second thought, the last thing I'd want in here is a gunfight. Too many bystanders. I'd better have one of my boys stand guard out front in case Guzman tries to sneak back in to get his revenge."

"Tell you what." Fargo had an inspiration. "I'll do you a favor and leave, if you'll do me a favor in return."

"Name it."

Fargo did.

Bob Potee grinned from ear to ear. "Consider it done. But keep in mind that when Guzman cuts loose, anyone near you could take a slug. And I wouldn't want her hurt. She's a mighty sweet filly."

"Me either." Fargo thanked him and ambled to the long hall. Molly was still there, still smiling and flirting and parading her bosom as if it had won first place at the county fair. She didn't see him come up behind her, and she jumped when his arm looped around her waist.

"Time to go, gorgeous," Fargo said and pecked her on the neck.

"Are you drunk?" Molly responded, giggling. "I don't get off until one, remember? You'll have to wait a while yet, handsome."

"Potee gave his permission for you to leave early." The warmth of her body and the musky fragrance of her perfume combined to cause a twitching in Fargo, low down. He swung her around so they faced one another, her ample breast cushioned against his broad chest. "Your place? Or my hotel room?"

Molly traced the outline of his jaw, a playful twinkle animating her eyes. "My, my. What *do* you have in mind?"

"Let's put it this way. Potee also gave you tomorrow off, with pay." Fargo steered her through the gilded double doors and started down a flight of carpeted stairs. He wasn't unduly worried about Guzman. If trouble came, he expected it to be outside, and he would be ready for it.

But no sooner did they reach the bottom than a bellowed curse rent the air, punctuated by blasts of gunfire.

MICHELLE REID

Marriage on the Rebound

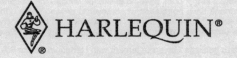

HARLEQUIN®

TORONTO • NEW YORK • LONDON
AMSTERDAM • PARIS • SYDNEY • HAMBURG
STOCKHOLM • ATHENS • TOKYO • MILAN • MADRID
PRAGUE • WARSAW • BUDAPEST • AUCKLAND

ISBN 0-373-11973-9

MARRIAGE ON THE REBOUND

First North American Publication 1998.

This edition published by arrangement with Harlequin Books S.A.

® and TM are trademarks of the publisher. Trademarks indicated with
® are registered in the United States Patent and Trademark Office, the
Canadian Trade Marks Office and in other countries.

Printed in U.S.A.

CHAPTER ONE

THE room had fallen into a terrible silence. No one moved, no one spoke, the horror that was every young woman's worst nightmare jamming the very air that surrounded them.

Shaan had dropped into the nearest chair, her face turned chalk-white with shock. Pressed between her knees and half-buried in the soft folds of pure white silk and delicate lace were her hands. Ice-cold and numb, they were crushing the single sheet of notepaper Rafe had just grimly handed to her.

'Dear Shaan,' it said. *Dear Shaan...*

'How could he do it?' Her uncle's harsh cry broke into the terrible silence, sounding hoarse and stricken and grievously bewildered.

Nobody answered him. Shaan couldn't, and Rafe obviously wasn't prepared to.

He stood by the window, effectively disconnected from it all now his part in the dirty deed was done, while out there, only a few short miles away, was a church packed full of guests, all dressed in their best wedding finery, waiting for a bride and groom who would not be turning up.

By now they would have begun to suspect that something terrible had gone wrong, the fact that Piers and Rafe were not in their places by the altar enough to arouse suspicion alone. Her aunt would be jumping all over the place with worry and Jemma, her only bridesmaid, looking foolish in her pretty pink dress, would be waiting just outside the church for a bride who was no longer wanted.

'My God! He couldn't have cut it any finer, could he?' her uncle raked out angrily.

'No,' Rafe decided to answer that one, though his voice sounded deeply constricted, as though he'd only just got the single syllable past his tensely locked throat.

Shaan didn't so much as move, her eyes—dark, dark brown under normal circumstances—looking so black in her pale face that they seemed utterly bottomless. They were not seeing much. They looked inwards, staring into the cold, dark recesses of her mind where horror, hurt and humiliation were waiting to grab hold of her once the all-encompassing numbness of shock had worn off.

Was Rafe in shock too? she found herself wondering. She supposed he must be. He certainly looked pale beneath that warm, golden tan his skin always wore. And he was dressed for a wedding in a formal grey morning suit. He could not have suspected Piers was going to do anything quite so crass as this.

Piers...

Her gaze dropped to her hands, where her fingers curled tightly around the single sheet of notepaper.

'I'm so sorry to have to do this...'

Her lips quivered, but not the rest of her—that was held in a kind of frozen stillness that barely allowed her enough room to breathe. Her mouth felt dry, so dry that everything had cleaved to everything else. And her heart was pumping oddly—not in her breast but in her stomach, huge, great, throbbing pulses which were making her feel dizzy and sick and—

'God—' Her uncle broke into sudden movement. 'I have to go and warn all those poor people waiting at the—'

'There's no need,' Rafe put in grimly. 'I've already seen to it. I thought it—best,' he finished inadequately, hating the situation Piers had thrust upon him so much that the words came out terse and clipped.

Sure enough, and as if on cue, the sound of a car

pulling up outside the smart London town house alerted them to the first horrified arrivals back from the church.

Too soon, Shaan thought numbly. I'm not ready for them. I can't face—

'Shaan!'

It was Rafe's voice, sounding raw with concern, and a moment later she felt herself being caught just before she toppled sickeningly forward.

'I don't want to see anyone,' she whispered threadily—not actually unconscious, but dizzyingly close to it.

'Of course not.' Rafe was squatting in front of her, holding her slumped upper torso against him, the fine tulle veil covering her thick mane of jet-black hair rustling against his face. He was trembling, she noted vaguely, his heart thundering beneath her resting brow.

'It's Sheila...' Her uncle Thomas had moved to peer out of the window. 'It's your aunt, Shaan,' he murmured soothingly. 'She—'

At that moment the front door burst open, and Shaan began to shake—shake violently. Rafe uttered a soft curse and shifted his big frame so he could gather her deeper into the protective cocoon of his arms as the sitting room door flew open.

'Shaan!' a high-pitched, near hysterical voice cried out. 'Oh, you poor baby!'

'No,' she whimpered against Rafe's shoulder. 'No...' She didn't want this, couldn't cope with it. Not her aunt's grief, not her uncle's—not even her own!

Rafe must have sensed it, because he stood up suddenly, pulling her upright with him, and in the next second she was being lifted into his arms, her ice-cold face pressed into his warm, tense throat.

'She's fainted,' he lied. God alone knew why, but Shaan was grateful to him. 'Her room, Mrs Lester— show me where her room is.'

'Oh, Shaan!' Aunt Sheila—her quiet, soft, super, gen-

tle aunt Sheila who rarely let anything ripple the calm
waters surrounding her life—went completely to pieces,
dropping down into one of the chairs to sob uncontrol-
lably. Uncle Thomas went to her while Rafe muttered
something beneath his breath and strode out of the room
without waiting for direction.

The hall was packed with people. Shaan could sense
their horrified presence even while Rafe kept her face
hidden in his throat. Ignoring them all, he took the stairs
like a mountain climber, the angry adrenaline pumping
in his blood powerful enough to send him up there without him so much as taking a breath.

She heard several horrified gasps, and Jemma's voice,
questioning and sharp with concern. Rafe answered
tightly, but she didn't know what he said. She was hovering somewhere between this world and another, riding
on a fluffy grey cloud just above pained reality.

'Which room?' His voice was terse, rasping enough
to score through the cloud.

But although she tried to concentrate on the question
she couldn't. She was barely aware of where she was.
On another muttered curse Rafe began opening doors,
throwing them wide and glancing inside before moving
on to the next one, until he came to the one which could
only be the bride's room, because of the mad scatter of
wedding paraphernalia all over the place. Once inside,
he sat her down on the end of the bed and then turned
to slam the bedroom door shut.

Then silence hit, the same hard, drumming silence
which had closed them all in downstairs, after Rafe had
delivered his letter.

Rafe just stood there, glaring at her downbent head
for a few moments, then suddenly strode over to grasp
the short tulle veil she still wore. Careless of the amount
of pins holding it in place, he ripped it from her head
and threw it aside.

'Sorry,' he muttered tensely. 'But I couldn't…' Swallowing, he spun away, thrusting clenched fists into his pockets.

Her scalp began to tingle from his rough handling, but Shaan didn't mind. If anything she was glad of the feeling because it told her that she was at least partly still alive. And she even understood why he'd done it. She must look pathetic, really pathetic, sitting here in all her bridal finery while her groom made off in the opposite direction.

Then it really hit—self-revulsion surging up from nowhere to bring her staggering to her feet, the letter, still crumpled in one hand, falling forgotten to the floor as she began a mad clawing at the tiny pearl buttons holding the front of her lacy bodice together.

'Help me!' she pleaded in choking desperation, fingers trembling, body shaking, her expression until now uncannily still breaking into a war of tortured loathing.

The silk ripped as she tugged, but she didn't care—suddenly it was the most essential thing in her life to get out of this dress, remove everything even remotely connected with Piers or her ruined wedding day from her body! 'Help me, for God's sake!'

'Shaan, I can't!' Rafe sounded actually shocked, which brought her eyes jerking up to his face.

'Why not?' she demanded in tight, thick condemnation. 'You've done everything else you could possibly do to ruin today for me. Why can't you help me ruin this dress, too!'

Her sudden attack sent him back a step, set a nerve ticking at the side of his rigidly held jaw. His usually implacable grey eyes going dark with emotion as he opened his mouth to say something—and Shaan's chin came up, dark eyes daring him to deny what she'd said. He couldn't, and his mouth closed again into a hard, tight line of self-contempt.

On a fresh wave of inner violence, Shaan gave a vicious yank at the bodice so that the two pieces of fine fabric sheared apart to send tiny buttons flying everywhere, dropping on the bed, on the floor, one flying across the room to land on the soft mauve carpet at Rafe's feet.

Rafe stared down at it, his dark head lowered so she couldn't see the expression on his grim face. She turned away on a rustle of silk to finish the complete destruction of the dress as, without a single care for its cost, she took malicious pleasure in ripping it from her body until she stood, trembling and cold, in the lovely white lace basque and silk stockings, which was all she wore beneath.

'This feels worse than rape,' she whispered, her arms wrapping tightly around herself.

'God, Shaan. Don't...' he muttered, taking a half-step towards her with his hand outstretched in a kind of distressed appeal.

Then it fell heavily to his side because he knew there was nothing he could say—nothing that could ease the pain and degradation she was suffering right now.

Instead, he turned for the door, his broad shoulders stiff beneath the smooth grey cloth of his formal morning jacket. 'I'll—go and get someone to—'

'No!' The protest rasped from somewhere deep down inside her. And she turned to look at him as he stopped dead one step from the door. 'No,' she repeated huskily. 'You can go if you want,' she allowed. 'But I don't want anyone else coming anywhere near this room.'

It was one thing having Rafe witness her complete downfall, since it was he who had effectively brought it about, but it was quite another having all those others witness it too. She wanted nobody here. Nobody. Not her best friend, Jemma, nor even her aunt.

She didn't care about Rafe, or the fact that she was wearing next to nothing in his presence. Rafe had openly held her in contempt from the very first moment Piers had introduced her as his—

'No.' Thoughts of Piers brought the sickness back, churning around in her stomach, so that she had to heave in some deep, controlling breaths to stop it overwhelming her altogether. Her nails bit into the soft flesh of her upper arms with enough cruelty to draw blood.

Then she felt something cold press against her skin, and remembered. Her long lashes flickered upwards as she unclipped her left hand from her arm and spread the cold and trembling fingers out in front of her.

A huge diamond winked tauntingly back at her, and with an angry tug she wrenched it from her finger and spun to face Rafe again, her black eyes spearing bitterness into his tensely guarded grey ones.

'Here,' she said, and threw the ring at his feet. 'You can give that back to him when you see him next. I don't want it; I don't ever want to see it again.'

Turning away from the image of Rafe slowly bending to pick up the ring, she walked quickly into her small bathroom, where she wilted shakily against the closed door. Her insides felt thick and heavy, as though every functioning organ had collapsed in a throbbing heap deep in the pit of her stomach.

Nausea enveloped her, followed by a black dizziness, followed by a raking sense of self-disgust which had her body folding right in on itself. Then, with the sudden jerky movements of one whose mind was not functioning with any intelligence at all, she was stiffening upright and lurching drunkenly away from the door.

She needed a shower! Her cold and trembling skin was crawling with revulsion and she desperately needed to wash it away.

It was only as she wrenched the fragile white silk basque from her body that she saw the pale blue satin- and lace-trimmed garter still clinging lovingly to her thigh, just above one white silk stocking, and a smile twisted her bloodless mouth when she realised just how

ridiculous she must have looked to Rafe, making her
grand exit with this piece of frivolity on show.

Tears blinded her eyes, the first of many, she supposed, and she wretchedly wiped them away with the
back of an icy hand and stepped into the shower cubicle.
Trembling fingers found the tap and turned it until the
burning-hot hiss of water gushed down on her. Then she
stood, not moving, just letting the stinging heat wash all
over her, eyes closed, face lifted up to it, not caring if
she scalded herself so long as she scoured every last hint
of the bride from her body.

How long she stood there like that, she had no idea,
because she refused to allow herself to think, or even to
feel much. But through the tunnel-dark recesses of her
consciousness she was vaguely aware of intermittent
knocks sounding on her bedroom door, of voices—one
her aunt's, sounding high-pitched and shrill, another one,
crisp and clear was Jemma, sounding demanding.

Rafe's darkly resonant murmurs intermingled with
them, saying God knew what. She didn't know nor care,
so long as he kept them all away from her. Then, eventually, the silence fell again, a solid kind of silence
which soothed her flurried heart and helped keep her
face turned up to the hot, hissing spray.

There would be time enough to endure all those pity-
ing glances and murmured platitudes which were bound
to come her way. These few minutes were for herself,
herself alone, to try to come to terms with what she now
was.

A jilted bride.

A nerve jerked at the corner of her mouth. Humiliation
sat in the empty hollow where her heart used to be. A
fool, more like, she corrected herself ruthlessly, a fool
for ever believing that Rafe Danvers would let her marry
his brother.

She had known from the first time she stood there in
front of him, with her hand caught possessively in Piers'

hand, that Rafe was going to do anything in his power
to break them up.

Piers...

Oh, God, she thought wretchedly as his handsome,
smiling face loomed up to torment her. How could he?
How could he do this?

'Shaan...' The loud knock sounding on the bathroom
door made her jump, her feet almost slipping on the wet
tiles at the deep, husky sound of that voice.

So, Rafe hadn't given in to all those other concerned
voices and made good his escape like his brother had,
she noted grimly. He was still here, standing just on the
other side of her bathroom door, as always ready to see
his responsibilities through to the bitter end. She had told
him she didn't want anyone else near her and he had
taken her at her word—which therefore meant he could
not desert her himself until he was satisfied he had seen
this responsibility through to its conclusion.

Which was—what? she asked herself.

Rafe. The older brother. The more successful one. The
head of the great Danvers empire. A man with shoulders
more than broad enough to take whatever was thrust
upon them.

And Piers had certainly thrust her upon Rafe today,
she thought with a bitter little smile.

'Shaan...'

The voice came from much closer and she opened her
eyes, turning her head to stare blankly through the thick
bank of steam permeating all around her—to find Rafe's
grim figure standing with a towel at the ready just outside the open shower cubicle door.

'Who said you could come in here?' she said, too
numb to care about her own nakedness—both inside and
out. The water was still gushing over her.

He didn't move his gaze from her face—not even to
make a sweeping inspection of her naked body.

'Come on,' he said quietly, the towel held outstretched between his hands. 'You've been in there long enough.'

She laughed—why, she didn't know—but it was a sound that fell a long way short of humour and probably sounded more bleak and helpless than anything else. Long enough for what? she wondered. After all, I'm not going anywhere, am I?

Closing her eyes, she lifted her face back to the spray, effectively dismissing him.

'Hiding in here isn't going to make it all go away, you know,' he said quietly.

'Leave me alone, Rafe,' she threw back flatly. 'You've achieved what you set out to do; just leave me alone now.'

'I'm afraid I can't do that.' One hand dropped a corner of the towel so he could reach into the cubicle and turn off the water.

The new silence was engulfed in steam, emanating up from the wet tiles at her feet, and she glanced down to watch it swirl around her body, coiling up her long, slender legs and over the rounded contours of her hips, caressing as it wound around the firm swell of her breasts.

'He didn't want me,' she murmured dully. 'After all he said. He didn't really want me.'

The towel came softly about her shoulders, Rafe's hands holding it there as he gently urged her out of the cubicle and turned her into his arms. 'He wanted you, Shaan,' he told her huskily. 'But he loved Madeleine. In all fairness, he had no right to promise any other woman anything while he still loved her.'

Yes, Madeleine, she thought emptily. Piers' first and only love… 'And you had to bring her back into his life,' she whispered accusingly.

'Yes,' he sighed, his hand moving gently on her back. 'You won't believe this, Shaan, but I'm sorry. I really am sorry…'

For some reason his apology cut so deeply into her

that she reared back from him and, with all the bright, burning, bitter condemnation bubbling hotly inside, she threw her hand hard against the side of his face.

He took it, took it all, without even flinching. He didn't even release the hold he had on her, but just stood looking back at her with those cool grey eyes opalescent in his graven face, his mouth a thin, grim line.

She wanted to cry, but she couldn't. She wanted to kick and scream and hit out at him again and again and *again,* in an effort to release all the hurt and anger culminating inside her, but she couldn't. That one brief flash of violence seemed to have taken what bit of energy she had left from her. All she could do now was stand there in the circle of Rafe's arms and stare up at him through huge black haunted eyes, wondering if that grim look he was wearing hid satisfaction or any guilt at all for what he had done.

Rafe had warned her—as long as six weeks ago, he had warned her he wouldn't just stand aside and let her marry his brother. From the first moment their eyes had met across the elegant width of Rafe's luxurious home, his contempt for her had been there, vibrating on defences she hadn't even known she possessed, until she clashed with that look.

Until that moment she had just been Shaan Saketa, loving daughter of the late and much missed Tariq and Mary Saketa, proud of her mixed blood because she had never been made to feel otherwise—until those silver ice eyes had gone sliding over her.

Then, for the first time in her life, she'd experienced what real prejudice felt like, and the rare combination of thick, straight jet-black hair, dark brown eyes and skin as smooth and pale as milk, which had been turning people's heads in admiration all her life, suddenly became something to be sensitive about. She'd had to steel herself to actually take the hand Rafe had held out to her in formal greeting, knowing by sheer instinct that he had no wish to touch her or even be in the same room as her.

Yet, oddly, not only had he taken the hand but he had held onto it—and clung to the new, very defensive look in her liquid brown eyes—the dark, dire expression in his had managed to chill the blood in her veins in appalled acknowledgement of what his grim expression was telling her.

It had been the moment when Rafe Danvers had made sure she was rawly aware of her complete unsuitability to become one of the great Danvers family.

Well, today he had won his battle. And now he could afford to be a little charitable, she supposed. Lend comfort to the defeated.

She moved out of his arms, clutching the huge bath sheet around her trembling figure as she went back into her bedroom.

Miraculously, there wasn't a single sign of bridal attire about the place. The whole room had been completely swept clean of everything while she'd been hiding in the bathroom. The dress, the mad scatter of bits and pieces were all gone, leaving only her rose-pink bathrobe folded on the end of the bed, and her suitcases—so carefully packed the night before—still stacked neatly beside the bedroom door.

She dropped the towel and picked up the robe, uncaring that Rafe had followed her back into the room and that she was once again exposing her nakedness to him. It didn't seem to matter, not when the sight of her body held no interest for the man in question.

She turned to glance at him, though, as she cinched the robe belt around her narrow waist. He was standing in the bathroom doorway, not leaning, but tense, his hard eyes hooded.

'Your suit is wet,' she told him, sending a flickering glance along his big, hard frame where the pale grey showed dark patches where she had leant against him.

He shrugged with indifference and moved at last, walking across the now neat bedroom to her dressing table. 'Here,' he said, turning back to her and holding out a glass half-full of what could only be brandy.

She smiled wryly at it. 'Medicinal?' she mocked, taking it from him and lowering herself carefully onto the end of the bed. From being rubber-limbed with shock, she was now stiff with it—so stiff, in fact, that even the simple act of sitting down was a painful effort.

'Whatever you want to call it,' he replied. 'As it is…' He turned again, lifting another glass in rueful acknowledgement to her. 'I'm in need of the same.' And he came to sit down beside her. 'Drink it,' he advised. 'I can assure you, it will help.'

She swirled the dark amber liquid around the glass for a moment before lifting it to her bloodless lips. He did the same, sitting close to her, his arm brushing against hers as he moved it up and down.

It was strange, really, but, having spent the last six weeks avoiding touching her at all costs—except for that one brief contamination when they had been formally introduced—Rafe now seemed quite happy to be as close to her as he could get.

She glanced at him from beneath her thick black lashes, seeing the rigid tension in his square jaw, in the harsh line of his strong profile. He was nothing like Piers to look at. The two brothers were as different in every way as two men could possibly be. Where Rafe was dark, Piers was fair—so fair, it hadn't come as a complete surprise to her to find out later that they were only half-brothers. Which also answered the question as to the ten-year gap in their ages. Piers was the handsome one of the brothers, the one with the uncomplicated smile which went with his uncomplicated character.

Or so she had believed, she amended grimly as she took another sip at the brandy. It burned as it went down, and the taste was gross, but it did at least put some warmth back inside her.

'What happened to everything in here?'

Rafe glanced around the pristine, tidy room. 'Your aunt and your friend cleared it all out while you were busy in the bathroom,' he explained. 'They—needed to feel useful.'

'I'm surprised Jemma didn't throw you out,' she murmured.

'Not your aunt?' he queried curiously.

'No.' Shaan shook the thick, wet pelt of black hair. 'My aunt has never been rude to anyone in her home in her life.'

'Unlike me.'

'Unlike you,' she agreed, not even trying to work out why they were sitting here having this stupid conversation in her bedroom of all places—he being who he was and she...

'Jemma tried throwing me out,' he admitted, taking a quick sip at his drink. 'But I—convinced her that you would handle all this better with me here rather than anyone else.'

'Because you don't care.' She nodded understandingly. She knew exactly why she had clung to Rafe rather than anyone else.

'That isn't entirely true, Shaan.' He sounded gruff all of a sudden. 'I know you won't believe this, but I knew from the beginning that Piers was not the man for you. All right,' he conceded at her deriding glance, 'I'm relieved he came to his senses before it was too late. But I am not proud of the time he took to do it. Nor will I forgive him easily for the way he's hurt you today. No one,' he finished roughly, 'has the right to wound another human being like he has done... If it gives you any satisfaction at all to know it, I can tell you that he and Madeleine are not proud of themselves for—'

'It doesn't,' she cut in, rising abruptly to her feet. 'And I really don't want to hear it.'

Lifting the glass to her mouth, she tossed the full contents to the back of her throat, then stood, back arched, eyes closed, breath held, while she absorbed the lick of liquid heat and waited for it to begin numbing her again.

She didn't want to feel anything yet. She wasn't ready. She didn't even want to think—not about herself, not about Rafe, and especially not about Piers and Madeleine.

'All right, Rafe.' Putting down the glass, she turned suddenly on him. Her eyes were still too big in her pale face, but her mouth was steadier, the colour beginning to ease back into her shock-whitened lips. 'I know this has all been an ordeal for you, and I thank you for the bother you've taken with me, but I'm going to be all right, and I would like you to leave now.' Now, before it all came hurtling on top of her, before the real hurting began, before…

But he gave a grim shake of his dark head, not even attempting to get up, and Shaan jumped in alarm when his hand snaked out to close around her wrist, the sudden tingle of her defences warning her that she wasn't completely numb as he pulled her back down to sit beside him.

'I'm not going yet,' he informed her bluntly. 'I have a proposition to put to you first. And I want you to hear me out before you say anything. I know you're in shock, and I know you can't possibly be capable of making decisions of any kind. But I'm going to force this one on you for the simple reason that I think, if you agree, we can at least save your pride if nothing else from this mess.'

He paused, then turned to look directly at her, those grey eyes of his very guarded but unwavering as they caught and held onto her own gaze.

'Will you marry me instead of my brother, Shaan?' he requested gravely.

CHAPTER TWO

FOR a single, short, breath-locking moment Shaan experienced a complete mind black-out. Then, '—Have you gone mad—?' she choked. 'Why, you despise the very sight of me!'

'That isn't true, Shaan,' Rafe denied.

Not listening, she tried to get up, but found her legs wouldn't let her. Her whole body had turned to crumbling stone, the shock waves of the past couple of devastating hours beginning to crack her wide open inside.

His hands came out to capture her own, closing all four of them tightly together on her lap and compelling her to turn around and face him. He looked tense, as white as she felt, but determined. She was trembling so badly now that even her head shook, quivering on the slender curve of her neck, her breathing gone haywire because of the tight contraction of her lungs.

'I know I'm not Piers,' he grimly conceded. 'Nor ever will be for that matter. He's my half-brother, and as different from me as—as Madeleine is from you. But—'

Madeleine! The name was beginning to haunt her, like the face—that sweet, gentle face, with its big blue vulnerable eyes surrounded by a cloud of soft golden hair. Madeleine was the archetypal pocket Venus, the fine porcelain doll. While Shaan—she was the—

'She's right for Piers, Shaan!' Rafe said fiercely, as though her thoughts were so open to him that he could easily make them his own. 'She always was! They were childhood sweethearts, young lovers before a stupid misunderstanding had Madeleine flying off to live with her mother in America last year...'

'I told you I didn't want to hear any of this!' she cried, trying desperately to struggle against the black cloud threatening to completely overtake her.

'All right!' he rasped, sucking in a tense breath, then letting it out again. 'Listen to this instead,' he insisted. 'In three days' time, your aunt and uncle should be leaving on a three-month long world cruise. Do you think they'll even consider going now, after what's happened to you today?'

She stared at him, having forgotten all about her aunt and uncle's delighted plans to take their dream cruise now the niece they had taken care of so lovingly for the past nine years was leaving the fold, so to speak.

'They don't have to worry about me,' she said shakily. 'I'll tell them—'

'Tell them what?' he challenged when she fell silent, her mouth moving soundlessly. 'That you'll be fine sitting here all on your own for the next three months grieving?'

'I don't intend to grieve,' she denied, stiffening in affront.

'Good.' He nodded his dark head in approval. 'I'm glad to hear you've got more spirit than to do that. But would you leave *them* on their own if something as devastating as this had happened to them? Of course you wouldn't.' He answered for her. 'And if you did manage to convince them to go, do you think they'd enjoy themselves, knowing how they'd left you behind?'

'I'll go and stay with Jemma...'

'Jemma is getting married herself in a few months,' he reminded her.

'How did you know that?' she gasped in shaken amazement.

He shook his head, dismissing that question as insignificant. 'Let's just leave it that I do know. To inflict yourself on Jemma now would spoil the excitement for her, because your own ruined wedding day will sit over you all like a thick black cloud.'

'Which doesn't mean I need to *inflict* myself on you instead!' she cried, hurt by the cruelly blunt way he had made her face that fact.

'Why not?' he demanded, grimly determined grey eyes boring straight into her wounded brown ones. 'If anyone deserves it, then I do. You said yourself that this was all my fault, and I damned well know it!' he admitted roughly. 'It was me who called Madeleine to warn her about you and Piers. It was me who advised her to get back here if she still felt anything for my brother. And it was me who encouraged them to see each other at every possible moment I could arrange, to make Piers see what a dreadful mistake he was making by marrying you!'

'God, I hate you so!' she choked, turning to fling herself face-down on the bed, her poor body hurting in so many different places that she actually shook with it.

'Listen to me!' To her surprise he lay back too, stretching out beside her as though he had every given right to be this close to her, when only yesterday he had shied away from even looking at her! 'Shaan...' His hand came out to stroke down the silky wet pelt of her hair, his fingers trembling slightly. 'I admit it. I feel lousy about it all. Guilty, if you want to call it that. I owe you. Let me help you get through this with at least some dignity.'

'By offering yourself in your brother's place?' She laughed, the sound shrill with near hysteria. 'How old are you?' she demanded, turning onto her back to glare bitterly up at him.

He grimaced. 'Thirty-four.'

'I am twenty-two years old,' she informed him. 'Piers is twenty-four.'

'All right,' he bit out, jerking up and away from her. 'So I'm no bargain when compared to my brother! I'm not asking you to love me instead, just—give me a chance to help you through these next few months while you get over this.'

She didn't think she would ever get over this.

'And what will you get out of it?' She hadn't spent the last three years of her life working for the Danvers company without learning very early on that their revered chairman didn't do anything without a damned good reason for doing it!

'Like you,' he said, 'I save the family face.'

'You're that concerned with family honour?' Her sceptical look made his mouth grow tighter.

'My brother should be whipped out of town for the way he used you, Shaan. It makes the Danvers name dirty.'

Used... She sank back against the pillows, her eyes clouding over darkly. Yes, Piers had used her; all along the line he had used her, with his declarations of undying love and passionate promises.

He hadn't just used her, he had grossly defiled her. And the only saving grace she could glean for herself out of it all was the knowledge that he hadn't given in to her pathetic little pleas to make love to her before they married!

'God, I feel sick!'

Rolling dizzily off the bed, she ran, stumbling, into the bathroom, where she was horribly and humiliatingly sick while Rafe stood there beside her, holding her hair away from her face, grimly taking her weight while she leaned weakly over the bowl.

Here she stood, she flayed herself bitterly, a virgin on her wedding day—with no groom to care one way or another that she had saved herself for him!

The bitterness welled up and sliced through her eyes as she ran the cold tap so she could splash her clammy face with water.

Rafe was wrong about one thing if he thought himself

no bargain compared to his brother. He was worth ten of Piers—and that had nothing to do with looks or charm, or even the love still throbbing in her breast for his brother, despite all the hurt he had inflicted on it.

It had to do with this—this deeply inbred sense of responsibility he possessed. The kind which had made him warn his brother's ex-lover about what Piers intended to do. It had to do with this—this need to put right what one of his own had messed up.

Her life—the family name. Their mutual honour!

'I won't marry you, Rafe,' she said, leaning heavily against the wash basin. 'Not to save your face or my own face. I won't degrade myself any further by pandering to just another Danvers method of exploitation.'

'I'm not trying to exploit you,' he denied gruffly.

'Yes you are.' She lifted her head to stare bleakly at his grim, hard face in the bathroom mirror, then just stood there, staring instead at the empty void which was her own unrecognisable face.

The tears began to burn at the backs of her eyes, and she covered them with her hands, her body beginning to shudder in another bout of weak self-pity.

Rafe's hands were firm on her shoulders as he turned her into his arms. And she felt his heavy sigh as she struggled against the onset of tears once again.

'I have nothing left...' she whispered bleakly. 'Nothing...'

'But you will again soon,' he murmured reassuringly, and suddenly his arms were tightly crushing bands around her. 'Come away with me now, Shaan,' he urged her huskily. 'At the moment, only you, me and Piers know what he actually said in his letter. Only we three know the real reason why there was no wedding today. Even your uncle didn't really understand—only that Piers had decided not to marry you.

'We can tell them he found out about us, that you and I had fallen in love. Piers won't try to deny it. He'll just be relieved that we've found some way of making him come through it smelling cleaner. They're already speculating down there as to why you wanted me with you rather than anyone else. Let's go and tell them that you and I are going away together to marry quietly somewhere. Let's give them something to cling onto, Shaan—a bit of hope!'

'Everything has been packed,' she whispered into his shoulder. 'I h-haven't got anything to wear.'

'We can soon remedy that,' he said, the tension seeping out of him when he recognised her words as a statement of defeat.

His arms tightened on her in a short moment of encouragement, then he was taking her back into the bedroom and over to the stack of suitcases waiting by the door. 'Which one shall I open?' he prompted huskily.

Shaan stared down at them. Her trousseau, she thought emptily. The clothes she'd spent weeks gathering together for the express purpose of pleasing Piers.

Pointing to one of the cases, she turned abruptly away, shuddering, because the very idea of wearing anything she had packed in those cases filled her with horror now.

Rafe glanced sharply at her, but didn't say anything, his face tightening with a new aggression as he picked up the small weekend case and laid it on the bed so he could flick open the catches.

Shaan came to stand beside him, looking into the case with him. Inside lay a variety of female fripperies, from the expected toiletries to a neat pile of brand-new silky underwear, and the tension lying between them began to pulse with a new knowledge.

This was the case she would have used for her wedding night. It contained only the kinds of things a new bride would want to have around her on such an important occasion. Soft, delicate, sexy things, to tantalise her new husband with.

Without a word, her lips sucked back hard against her

tightly clenched teeth, she reached down and selected a
pair of white silky briefs and matching bra. Then she
took out the uncrushable silk Jacquard suit in a bold
apple-green colour that she had packed to wear after
their stop-over in Paris. After that they had been supposed to go on to the Seychelles for a month-long
honeymoon. Then she turned, walking away towards the
bathroom, her dark head held high.

The door closed behind her and Rafe stood, staring at
the closed door for a long time, before turning slowly
back to the case. Then, on an act of violence which
would have startled Shaan if she'd been there to witness
it, he sent the small case flying to the floor with a single,
vicious swipe of his hand, glaring down at the tumbled
array of feminine items scattered at his feet.

When she came back, though, dressed, her hair contained in a simple knot at her nape, she found the room
neat and tidy.

Rafe was standing by the window, looking big and
dark and forbidding, with that black scowl on his face.
But the moment he saw her he smiled, albeit grimly, and
came over to her side.

'OK?' he asked.

She nodded, knowing she shouldn't be allowing this
to happen, but somehow unable to find the strength to
put up any more opposition.

Rafe was right about one thing—he was the only person she felt she could share the torment with because he
had been the one to instigate it in the first place.

'Leave the talking to me,' he advised as he turned her
towards the bedroom door.

She didn't answer—couldn't have if she'd tried—but
she nodded. She had to trust in him to be the sane one.
It was the only way she could cope right now.

They went to the sitting room.

Her aunt, her face red and swollen with crying, looked
nothing like the bright, happy, if over-excited woman

Shaan had watched leave for the church earlier today. Gone was the hyacinth-blue dress she had been wearing, and the huge, frivolous hat Shaan and her uncle had teased her about the day she had brought it home and showed them.

She came to her feet as they entered, still so shaken that she needed her husband's help to do so. And suddenly they looked old and frail, so utterly unable to cope with the horror and emotion of it all.

For nine years of her life these two people had loved and cared for her, taken up the responsibility of Tariq and Mary Saketa's child after she'd been left orphaned by a dreadful accident. Even though they had been well into their fifties then, and unused to having children around them, they had been good and loving towards her, had given her everything it was in their power to give her, put their own lives on hold for her sake, and been happy to do it.

Seeing Shaan safely married to Piers had meant the end of their commitment to her. And while she had been busy planning her wedding day, these two wonderful people had been just as excitedly planning their dream world cruise like two teenagers set free from parental control at last.

And Rafe was right, she couldn't spoil that for them as well.

'Shaan...' Her aunt's hoarse and trembling voice brought fresh tears to Shaan's eyes as she hurried forward to gather her into her arms.

'I'm all right,' she assured her, closing her eyes because she couldn't bear all this. Couldn't bear their pain along with her own pain. 'Really I am.' Over the top over her aunt's soft grey head, Shaan looked at her uncle. 'I'm so sorry,' she whispered, unable to stop herself from saying it.

Rafe moved up beside her, his hand slipping around her waist in an act of grim support. 'Mr Lester...'

'I hope your brother has it in him to feel shame for what he's done today,' Shaan's uncle said tightly.

'With all respect, sir,' Rafe came back politely, 'my brother was at liberty to change his mind right until the last moment—just as Shaan was at liberty to change hers also,' he added succinctly.

'Oh, my poor child!' her aunt sobbed, and, using what was left of her depleted banks of energy, Shaan helped her back to the sofa, aware that she was unable to support herself for very much longer.

Rafe let her go, his hand dropping to his side as he stood watching the gentle way Shaan seated both herself and her aunt before gathering the older woman close while she cried softly.

'Nevertheless, he should be made to face up to his obligations,' Shaan's uncle continued, aiming the blunt criticism directly at Rafe. 'If only in his duty to let my niece down less cruelly than waiting until she was ready to leave for the church before pulling this treachery!'

'In this case, I'm afraid that kind of duty doesn't count,' Rafe replied, his grim gaze not reacting to the outright attack. 'You see,' he went on coolly, 'my brother refused to marry Shaan because he had discovered that she is in love with me.'

Shaan leaned her head back against the soft leather headrest and closed her weary eyes. She had never felt so drained and empty in her whole life.

Rafe drove the car in silence, grim faced and withdrawn now the worst of it was over. Oh, he had been very clever, very alert all the way through the ordeal. He had not allowed her to be spoken to alone, he had not even allowed her uncle to question her on any of Rafe's tersely delivered statements.

And, oddly, her uncle had seemed to respect the way Rafe had been determined to protect what he was now claiming as his own.

Rafe had just told them in crisp, simple English that he and Shaan had fallen in love on their first meeting, that the two of them had been trying to fight their feelings ever since, and that—as her uncle would expect of her—Shaan had refused to turn back from a marriage she felt already committed to. In the end, out of desperation, Rafe had said, he himself had approached his own brother to plead with him on their behalf only that morning.

That Piers had, of course, backed out of marrying a woman who was in love with his own brother was perhaps only natural under the circumstances, they'd been told. He was sorry for all the heartache and embarrassment they had caused everyone, he'd gone on. But he was not sorry for stopping the wedding from taking place.

Rafe had then calmly told them that he was now going to take Shaan away and marry her himself, quietly, and that, like themselves, they intended leaving the country on a long honeymoon until the fuss died down.

And now they were driving to—she had no idea, nor did she care. She took with her the small consolation of knowing that somehow Rafe had managed to convince her uncle and aunt that everything had been done for the best. That, far from being broken in two by Piers' desertion, Shaan was actually relieved that she had not gone ahead and married him.

She had left their house knowing that they would be taking their world cruise as planned, in the knowledge that their niece, whom she suspected they were disappointed in, was in safe and loving hands.

But, although Rafe might have saved her from being labelled a jilted bride, he was mistaken if he believed his solution had done anything to assuage her pride, because it hadn't. For now she knew she looked like the jilter rather than the jilted, and really that was just as bad, just as unacceptable to those people who mattered.

On top of that she still felt used, defiled and rejected. And no lies, no matter how convincingly presented, could ease the terrible sense of loss and inadequacy she was suffering right now.

The car drew to a halt, and she opened her eyes to find herself staring at the Danvers family's elegant home, set in its own grounds in this prestigious part of London. Without a word to her, he climbed out of the car, looking faintly ridiculous in his formal clothes as he came around to open her door and help her out, leading her in equal silence into a house she had never felt even the slightest bit welcome in.

As they stepped into the hall, a short, dumpy woman with frizzled hair and a harassed face came bustling towards them. 'Oh, Mr Danvers,' she gasped out in agitated breathlessness. 'I'm so glad you're home. The telephone refuses to stop ringing—' Sure enough, as if on cue, the phone began pealing out even as the woman spoke. 'Everyone wants to speak to you, and I just didn't know what to say to them. They say Mr Piers has jilted his…'

She noticed Shaan then, half-hidden behind Rafe's frame, and went as red as a beetroot, then as white as a sheet. 'Oh, dear, I'm so sorry. I…'

Rafe made a gesture of impatience. 'Pull the bloody plug on that phone, Mrs Clough!' he commanded gruffly, and turned to stretch an arm around Shaan's shoulders. He began guiding her up the stairs and along the upper landing into a room which could only be his own private suite judging by the sheer masculine power of the place.

'Sit down,' he told her, moving away from her and indicating a brown leather armchair placed beside a huge old oak fireplace. 'I won't be long. I just want to change out of these clothes.'

He went, disappearing through another door, leaving her staring numbly at the chair. Her mind had gone blank, reaction setting in to take her off somewhere deep inside herself where no one else could go.

She tried to move and found she couldn't—couldn't remember how to make her limbs work. Her face felt stiff and drawn downwards, her shoulders aching from the rod of tension braced across them. Her head was throbbing, her stomach was queasy, and her eyes were burning in their sockets—not tearful, but hot and dry.

She heard the faint sound of gushing water, recognised it as a shower, but that was about all. Time ticked by, the quietness of the room having no effect on her whatsoever. Her hands hung limply at her sides, the fingers feeling oddly heavy. Her mouth drooped downwards too, as though a weight was tugging on each corner.

She continued to stare blankly at the chair.

Rafe came back, coming to an abrupt halt when he saw her. The smell of clean, male soap permeated the air around them while he studied her through narrowed, faintly worried eyes.

'Shaan.' he said her name carefully.

She didn't turn—couldn't. She heard him, but couldn't seem to respond. The heaviness had transported itself to her limbs now, dragging down on them, holding her like a huge block of wood pinned securely to the ground. And her head felt heavy, the very top of it feeling as though someone was pressing forever harder down on it, trying to push her into the carpet beneath her feet.

Rafe came over to her, the clean smell of soap strengthening as it came with him. It was a very strange feeling, this paralysing weightiness which was disabling everything but her senses. They still seemed to be working fine: her sense of smell, of hearing, even her sense of touch seemed intact, as he reached out to grasp her chin, lifting her face so he could study it.

She saw him frown, saw the grey eyes darken in concern. She saw that he had showered, his dark hair was lying slick against his head now. She saw he had changed into a pale blue shirt and casual linen trousers that fitted cleanly on his trim waist.

'Are you going to faint, by any chance?' he murmured enquiringly.

Yes, she thought, I think perhaps I am. And she closed her eyes at the exact same moment that she swayed towards him. He caught her, muttering and cursing as he lifted her into his arms, and once again she found herself being carried by this man who had ruined her life, through to the next room and over to a huge emperor-sized bed, where he laid her before disappearing into what could only be the bathroom, judging by the sound of water running again.

He came back with a glass of water and a facecloth. He put the glass down on the bedside table, then sat down on the bed beside her to apply the cloth to her clammy brow.

His touch was gentle, the cloth deliciously cool and refreshing; his thigh where it rested lightly against her own was strangely comforting.

'You remind me of a doll,' he informed her drily. 'A rather fragile, very temperamental clockwork doll who's had her key removed.'

Dragging open her eyes, she managed a weak smile for him.

He smiled too. It was a rare sight, something she had never seen him do before, and it changed the whole structure of his face, softening its aggressively male lines and adding an extra dimension to his persona that she found rather perturbing.

Why, she didn't know, and she frowned as she closed her eyes again.

'Here, I want you to take these...'

Her lashes flickered upwards to find that Rafe was

now holding the glass of water in one hand and two small white pills in the palm of the other.

Shaan stared at them for a moment, then shook her head. 'No,' she refused. 'I don't want sleeping tablets.'

'These are not sleeping tablets as such,' he assured her. 'They're simply some very mild relaxants you can buy over the chemist's counter without a prescription. I use them to get me through long plane journeys,' he explained at her dubious expression. 'You won't sleep unless you want to, but they will help you to relax. You're as strung up as piano wire, Shaan,' he added gently, and touched the back of her hand.

It was shock. Not so much his touch, but the sudden realisation that both her hands were clenched into white-knuckled fists at her sides. Her arms were tense, her shoulders, her neck, her legs—all locked in a tension so strong that she was literally trembling under the pressure.

'And anyway,' he added softly, 'you aren't being given a choice...'

And before she could do anything about it he had pressed her chin downwards and popped the two pills into her mouth.

She almost choked on the water which quickly followed the pills. 'Sorry,' he apologised at her accusing look. 'But you need to be bullied a bit right now. It will save you from having to think for yourself.'

Yes...she had to agree with that. Thinking meant hurting, and at the moment she was hurting enough—more than enough.

On a sigh that seemed to come from some deep, dark place in her, she let her eyes close again, shutting him out—wanting to shut it all out and just let the pills do whatever they were supposed to do.

It was shock—the delayed kind of shock you hear of people experiencing where they get hit by a car then get up and walk away, only to discover they should not have been walking anywhere because they were so badly injured.

That was what she had been doing since Rafe had arrived this morning to smash her whole world apart. She was one of the walking wounded, not quite ready yet to face what had really happened to her.

Which meant when she did find the courage to face it she was going to fall apart. And when that happened she could well find herself involved in a second accident. One which trapped her so completely that she would not be able to walk away even if she wanted to.

'We shouldn't be doing this, Rafe,' she murmured worriedly. 'It isn't right. It isn't—'

'I thought we'd just decided that I was going to do all the thinking,' his quiet voice interrupted. The hand still covering one of her clenched ones, squeezed gently. 'Trust me, Shaan,' he murmured. 'And I promise you I won't let you down.'

On a sigh that signalled the end of her small burst of spirit, she retreated into malleable silence again.

Rafe remained where he was for a few moments longer, watching her. She could feel his eyes on her and wondered dully what it was he thought he was seeing. A pitiable creature called his brother's jilted bride? Or that other Shaan, the one who had been so completely overwhelmed at their first meeting by his clear dislike of her that the person she really was had literally shrivelled up in his presence?

'Do you dislike me so much because of Madeleine? Or because of my mixed blood?' she heard herself ask, without really knowing she was going to say it.

Still, his response brought her eyes flicking open. 'What—?' he rasped. 'Did I hear you correctly? Were you just accusing me of racial prejudice then?'

She hadn't meant to offend him, yet seemingly that was exactly what she had done. 'You hated to touch me,' she reminded him. 'Or even to look at me if you could avoid it. What else was I supposed to think?'

'Well, not what you did think, that's for damned well sure!' He got up, and she felt oddly lost without him close to her. 'You actually believed me crass enough to dislike your relationship with my brother because of your mixed race?'

He was obviously having difficulty taking that in.

She closed her eyes again, too trapped in this feeling of muscle-locked apathy to do much more than smile ruefully at his resentment.

Because the real point was, if it wasn't her mixed race, then what *was* it he didn't like about her? Because there was definitely something.

'Get some rest,' he said gruffly. 'We'll talk about it later.'

Yes, later, she agreed silently as her muscles began to slacken out of the tension-lock that shock had held them in. They could discuss all of that later...

CHAPTER THREE

'IT'S all arranged.'

Rafe came into the drawing room with his now very familiar aggressive stride, making Shaan jump because it felt as if he had only just walked out before he was back again.

But then, he had not left her alone for more than a few minutes at a time during the last forty-eight hours. And every time she had found herself with a few moments' respite from his aggressively dictatorial presence, it had always been with a terse assurance from him that he would be back in seconds, making sure she knew that she would not have time to sink into the brooding misery they both knew lurked beneath the fragile surface of her hazy existence.

'We get married in the morning just before your aunt and uncle leave for their cruise.'

'Oh.' She went pale, the sudden sinking of her heart telling her that she should not be allowing this to happen.

Rafe glanced at her, grey eyes hardening when he saw the way her small white teeth began to press into the soft cushion of her full bottom lip. 'Jemma has agreed to stand witness for you,' he went on firmly. 'She wants you to ring her; I said you would.' A wryish twist touched his mouth. 'She's worrying in case I'm holding you here against your will, so you'll have to assure her that I'm not—won't you?'

A challenge; she was receptive enough to note the challenge in his voice on that last question. 'I...'

'Have you got anything suitably white to wear inside those suitcases we brought with us?' he asked as she

opened her mouth to answer the first real question he
had asked her in forty-eight hours—only to find herself
utterly thrown by the second one.

'I...yes...n-no... I d-don't know...' She blinked, her
still shocked mind having difficulty keeping up with him
for half of the time—and as for the other half, he just
didn't allow her to keep up. 'W-why...?' she managed
to ask.

'To marry me in,' he sighed, shoving his hands into
his trouser pockets as he glared into her blank black
eyes. 'You ripped your wedding dress to shreds, if you
remember?'

Yes, she remembered, and shuddered. She'd ripped
her lovely dress to shreds in front of Rafe, had stood
totally naked in front of Rafe. She had been physically
sick in front of Rafe, had let him talk her into letting
him take the place of his brother...

She'd let him construct a pack of lies for her family,
let him bring her here to his house, which had been
turned into a positive fortress within minutes of them
arriving. The big iron gates had been locked to any visitors, and the small cluster of reporters who had collected
outside them had been completely ignored.

He was, she was coming to learn, the most amazingly
determined man when he set his mind on something.
From the moment she'd conceded to his crazy suggestion in her bedroom two days ago, he had not given her
a single opportunity to withdraw her agreement.

If she opened her eyes, he was there. It didn't matter
what time of the day or night it was, Rafe was always
there. Sitting, standing, pacing about the room like a
caged animal until she opened her eyes. Then the orders
would begin. Get up, sit down. Drink this, eat that. Take
a shower, get into bed, go to sleep.

Quite simply he had taken her over, and in doing so
demanded her full compliance to his every wish and
command. And if he caught her brooding at any time he

snapped her out of it with the guttural bark of his voice, almost cruel in his methods of keeping her mind off his brother.

Piers. A kind of anguished desolation washed over her, taking what little colour she had in her face along with it.

'Shaan!'

The bark hit her eardrums, making her wince, grating along her nerve-ends as she forced her eyes back into focus to find him glaring at her, eyes like silver lasers boring into her, burning out everything else but the power of his presence.

'White,' he prompted. 'I want you to marry me in white. Think. Have you got anything white in your suit-cases?'

White. Her mind went white, a complete white-out, as she tried hard to remember what her lovely trousseau consisted of. Then she laughed, a high-pitched, slightly hysterical sound that hardened his face as he stood there glaring down at her.

'A white silk nightdress and matching negligée,' she said, and nodded, seeing herself as she had the day she'd tried it on in the exclusive West End lingerie shop. Soft and slinky, it had clung to the slender contours of her body, from the narrow bootlace straps which had seemed too fragile to hold up the two triangles of fine silk that had covered her breasts to her ankles.

She remembered the delicious tremor of anticipation she had experienced as she'd stood there looking at her-self in the full-length mirror in the shop, seeing herself as Piers would see her—the white for purity, the silk for sensuality, its sheerness offering an enticing glimpse of her woman's naked body waiting for him beneath. Breasts full and rounded, nipples duskily inviting. The flatness of her stomach and the narrowness of her waist. The seductive cling of the fabric around the swell of her hips and the hollow of her navel. And the velvety dark shadow at the juncture with her thighs which marked the embodiment of her womanhood.

'I don't suppose you'll want me to wear that,' she concluded, letting out another of those strained little laughs.

His frown blackened. 'No, I don't suppose I would,' he agreed, and abruptly turned his back on her. 'Ring Jemma,' he commanded. 'Get her to pick something suitable out for you to marry me in and bring it with her in the morning. God knows,' he sighed, 'neither you nor I dare step outside my blasted gates until this damned thing is over.'

Running a weary hand through his hair, he walked out of the room, leaving her to chew pensively on her bottom lip, because she had suddenly realised that this must be just as big an ordeal for him as it was for her.

Well, almost. He hadn't lost someone he loved—he was just marrying someone he didn't.

She rang Jemma as instructed, but reluctantly, because she still wasn't ready to speak to anyone—Jemma perhaps least of all. Her friend was no fool. She'd been well aware of how blissfully and blindly in love Shaan had been with Piers.

'What's going on, Shaan?' Jemma demanded the moment she knew who it was. 'For God's sake, love, what are you trying to do? You can't replace one brother with the other! It's a recipe for disaster!'

My life is a disaster, she thought tragically, and closed her eyes against the never far away threat of tears. 'It's what I want,' she stated quietly. 'It's what we both want.'

'But you don't even like Rafe!' Jemma cried, sounding angry and bewildered. 'You even admitted to being a little afraid of him!'

'I was afraid of the way he made me feel,' she argued, thinking but it was close to the truth; she had always felt Rafe was a threat to her happiness.

'Because you were falling in love with him?'

Love—what's love? she wondered blankly. She was sure she didn't know any more. 'Yes,' she replied.

'And now you're going to marry him instead of Piers,' Jemma concluded.

'Yes,' she said again. 'You should be relieved, not angry,' she said, then added drily, 'You always did hold Piers in contempt.'

'He was devious.' Jemma defended her opinion. 'Someone who smiled as much as he did just had to be hiding something. But I never thought for one moment it would be another woman.'

That hurt, and Shaan flinched. 'Which just goes to show what a lucky escape we all had, then, doesn't it?' she mocked rather bitterly, recalling—as no doubt Jemma was recalling—the headline on Mrs Clough's daily newspaper which had said, DANVERS BROTHERS SWAP BRIDES IN SENSATIONAL LOVE TUSSLE!

What a joke, Shaan thought bitterly. And what a pack of lies for the sake of a catchy headline. Rafe didn't love her, and Madeleine had never been his bride!

She was now Piers' bride, though, Shann recalled dully. The article had said so: 'Piers Danvers married Madeleine Steiner only an hour after he should have been marrying Shaan Saketa'.

Which meant that Piers must have been planning to let her down long before he bothered to tell her he no longer wanted her.

There had been more in the article, but Rafe had happened to walk into the kitchen then, and snatched the newspaper away from her. His black fury at Mrs Clough for bringing it into his house had been enough to turn the other woman white, while Shaan had just sat there shuddering in sick disgust at the depths of Piers' deceit.

'Do you think you'll have time to pick something suitable out for me to wear tomorrow?' she asked Jemma now, dragging her mind away from the only moment since this had all begun when she had been in real danger of breaking free from this numbing shock she was hiding behind.

Rafe had stopped her; he had bodily lifted her off the kitchen chair and marched her into his study, then dumped her down in front of a PC, switched it on and shoved a handwritten twenty-page document in front of her. 'You can type, can't you?' He'd mocked her look of bewilderment. 'So—type. I need it by lunchtime.'

'Yes, of course I will.' Jemma's voice seemed to reach her from some totally alien place outside her muddled thought patterns. 'But I wish you'd take a little time out to think about this before doing it,' she added worriedly. 'You could be jumping straight out of the frying pan into the fire—have you thought of that?'

Of course she had. When Rafe gave her the chance to think for herself, that was. And that had definitely not been yesterday, when he'd heaped piles of work on her, she recalled ruefully.

But thinking didn't help. Nothing helped. She simply did not care what happened to her. So, 'I love him,' she claimed, the reality of the words meaning nothing to her any more. 'He's what I want. Don't spoil it for me, Jemma.'

'All right.' Jemma's sigh was long-suffering but her manner softened a little when she added, 'I'll see you tomorrow.'

Jemma's choice was a Mondi suit in the severely tailored style that particular design house had made its own in recent years. The skirt was daringly short and needle-slim, and the matching jacket moulded Shaan's slender figure to low on her hips and was fastened with gold military buttons to match the military braiding around the sleeve-cuffs and the collar. There was no blouse. The fitted style of the jacket left no room for a blouse, and the shortness of the skirt seemed to add an alarming length to her slender legs, which were encased in the sheerest white silk.

'Too short?' she asked Jemma pensively, giving a self-conscious tug at the skirt-hem.

'Are you joking?' Jemma scoffed, standing beside Shaan to view the finished product in the full-length mirror. 'Rafe'll need holding back when he sees you in this. You look fabulous, Shaan,' she added softly. 'Utterly stunning.'

But Shaan didn't feel stunning. She felt as if she was looking at a total stranger. As if that girl, with the big brown empty eyes and jet-black hair swept sleekly away from her face into a silken knot on the crown of her head, was someone else entirely.

In fact the only thing she did recognise, which said it really was herself standing there, was the fine gold chain around her throat, with its heart-shaped locket suspended from it, which held photographs of her parents' beloved faces.

Cold fingers tremored up to gently touch the familiar locket, and suddenly tears were flooding to blur out the reflection.

'Why the tears?'

With a small start she blinked the moisture away, long lashes flickering down and upwards as she brought her gaze into focus on Jemma's grave face in the mirror.

'I thought brides were allowed to be weepy,' she parried.

'Sure,' Jemma agreed. 'They're even allowed to look all pale and tantalisingly ethereal.' Her voice was loaded with mockery. 'All you have to do now is smile and I might even begin to believe that you really want this.'

'Don't,' Shaan pleaded hoarsely, hooding her too revealing eyes. 'Don't probe, Jemma. I don't think I'm up to it right now.'

'Why?' her best friend demanded. 'Because you know deep down inside that this—marriage, for want of a bet-

ter word for it,' she tossed off tartly, 'won't stand up to
scrutiny?'

Shaan's heart fluttered in her breast—the first sign
she'd had for days that life actually still existed inside
her—as a moment's desperation welled up.

Her lashes flickered again, and a brief glimpse of that
desperation revealed itself to Jemma. On a gasp, she
spun Shaan around to give her a small shake. 'For goodness' sake!' she said fiercely. 'What the hell is really
going on here?'

The bedroom door opened, and as if Rafe could actually sense that Shaan's courage was beginning to fail
her he walked arrogantly into the room, his silver-hard
gaze flashing from one tense female face to the other.

Shaan went hot, then cold, staring at him through a
hazy mist which wasn't entirely due to her lingering
tears. Rafe was wearing a simple dark business suit over
a plain white shirt and dark silk tie. Nothing special. Yet
there was something about him—the red rose he wore
in his lapel maybe—which seemed to make a statement
of possession in itself, that trapped the air in her lungs
and sent a prickling sense of awareness tripping though
her.

'Shaan, you look beautiful,' he murmured brusquely.
'Shall we go?'

Like a woman in a trance, she nodded mutely and
walked obediently towards him, feeling Jemma's silent,
pleading, helpless protest following behind her in urgent
waves but unable to stop herself.

In a few mad days, Rafe had made himself so indispensable to her that she could deny him nothing. He was
the rock she clung to in the storm-wrecked destruction
that had taken place inside her.

As if he knew it, he took her hand as soon as she was
in reach, drawing it firmly into the crook of his arm and
holding it there with his own hand.

There, you're safe now, the gesture seemed to say,

and she lifted her bruised eyes to his and smiled—albeit weakly, but it was a smile.

She didn't hear the soft gasp her friend uttered when she saw that smile, nor did she see the hard look of triumph Rafe sent Jemma, because she had already lowered her head and was lost in that hazy world of nothing, relying totally on this man beside her for her very survival.

It was a brief civil ceremony—a relief to Shaan, who didn't think she could have coped with anything more. Her aunt and uncle were there. They hugged and kissed her and told her to be happy, but she saw the look in their eyes and knew they were still suffering a similar shock to herself over what had happened.

Jemma was more direct. She took hold of her friend's shoulders and made her look directly at her, taking her chance while Rafe stood across the room talking grimly to a man he had briefly introduced as, 'Saul, my second in command.'

'Anything,' Jemma said urgently. 'If for any reason you need me for anything—you just call and I'll come. Understand?'

Shaan nodded, her eyes huge and dark and empty in her pale face. 'Thank you.' She leaned forward to brush a kiss across Jemma's warm cheek. 'Please don't worry about me, Jem,' she pleaded as she drew away again. 'Rafe will look after me.'

'Will he?' Jemma's sceptical gaze lifted to take in the man in question. 'He better had, or the Danvers family will have me to contend with.'

Shaan managed to smile at that, recognising the threat for what it was—a weak one, since Jemma was in no position to do the Danvers family any harm. But the meaning was clear—Jemma was not fooled. She was puzzled, but not fooled, and she considered the Danvers family had done enough to her friend without hurting her any more.

There was no wedding breakfast. Rafe rushed her straight into a waiting limousine the moment they left the register office. He said it was because they had a plane to catch, but Shaan had to wonder if he was rushing her away because he knew their deception would not hold up to any real scrutiny.

And the irritating press didn't help. Their flashbulbs had been exploding in their faces from the moment they had stepped out of Rafe's house, and hadn't stopped since. By the time the chauffeur-driven limousine sped away from the kerb, Shaan was wilting with fatigue, the act of playing the blissful bride having drained her to the very dregs.

'All right?' Rafe enquired, his hand covering her cold ones where they lay together on her lap.

She nodded, sighing as she leaned back into the soft, squashy leather seat. 'Will our picture be splashed all over the papers again tomorrow?' Her tone alone said she didn't relish the idea.

'That depends,' he replied, 'on whether there's a disaster between now and then. We are classed as expendable news.' He answered the puzzled look she sent him. 'The juicy fill-in to help sell their rags if nothing better comes along—vulgar, isn't it?'

'How do you live under such constant notoriety?' she asked with a small shudder.

'I don't—usually,' he replied, and she shuddered again, in bleak recognition this time that it was her fault that he was having to endure it now.

'I'm—sorry,' she whispered.

'Why should you be sorry?' he clipped. 'It wasn't you who caused this particular sensation, Shaan. It was me.'

'And Piers,' she added hollowly.

'The Danvers brothers, then.' He nodded, and leaned forward to press a button on the console in front of him which sent the sheet of glass that partitioned them off from their driver sliding downwards. 'Make sure you lose them before we head for the airport,' he commanded. 'They've had their floorshow; now they can take a running jump.'

The man nodded and glanced in his rearview mirror, and swerved neatly into the outer lane, taking a right turn at the next set of traffic lights, then a quick left, appearing to anyone who knew London well that he was taking them directly back to Rafe's London address, his sharp gaze constantly checking his rearview mirror. But after a while he changed direction, sweeping them out of London and toward Heathrow.

'You've just got time to change out of that suit before we board,' Rafe told her when they'd booked into the first class departure lounge. And he handed her a flight bag before directing her to the ladies room.

She nodded and went, coming back ten minutes later dressed in a soft cream cotton shirt and a pair of buff-coloured trousers that Mrs Clough must have packed for her, because she certainly hadn't done it for herself.

She found Rafe lounging by the wall not three feet away. He hadn't changed, but, then, his outfit was not so obviously bridal. The red rose had gone from his lapel, though, and his face was wearing that harsh, implacable look she hadn't seen at all that morning.

His eyes glittered oddly as they glanced over her, sprinkling her with a strange sense of intimacy that she found unnerving simply because she did not understand it.

Then he was reaching out to take the flight bag from her, and the odd look was gone. 'We're running late,' he said, curving a hand around her arm to begin guiding her through the milling throng of fellow travellers. He was rushing, and she had to run to keep up with him as he strode towards the long row of departure gates linked by a moving pathway.

They entered the plane via a connecting corridor. Their seats were the best in the first class section of the

747. Feeling slightly bewildered, and not a little harassed after all the rushing about, it felt to Shaan as if they'd only just got settled when the plane was in the air.

And it was only then that she realised she had no idea where they were flying to. 'W-where are we going?' she questioned.

'I wondered how long it would take you to ask that.' Rafe's smile was tight. 'A long way,' he answered. 'To Hong Kong, to be exact.'

Hong Kong? She blinked. 'How long will that take us?'

'Fifteen hours if we're lucky, seventeen if we're not.' He hailed a passing hostess and ordered some soft drinks, then sat back, fishing in his jacket pocket for something. 'Here, take these.'

Automatically she held out her hand to receive the two small pills. 'But...'

'No buts,' he said. 'It's a hell of a flight; better to sleep as much of it away as you possibly can.'

The hostess returned with their drinks; she had a gentle smile and oriental eyes. Rafe took the drinks and held one of the glasses to Shaan's lips. 'Pop the pills, Shaan,' he ordered flatly.

Without bothering to argue, she did as he told her, then drank to wash them down.

'And maybe it's a good time to warn you that those two pills are the last you're going to get,' he informed her as she settled back into her seat with a sigh. She turned her head to look at him questioningly. 'It's time to begin standing on your own two feet, Shaan,' he explained quietly. 'Pill-popping only dulls problems; it doesn't cure them.'

'I never wanted the pills in the first place,' she reminded him. 'It's you who's been forcing them onto me.'

'Well, not any more,' he promised. 'Now, tell me

about your parents,' he requested. 'Your father was a Lebanese doctor, wasn't he?'

How did he know that? she wondered as she nodded in confirmation. 'But he trained here in London,' she informed him. 'Which is where he met my mother. Sh-she was a nurse working at the same teaching hospital... They were killed,' she murmured, a fine-boned hand drifting up to her throat to close over the little gold locket she always wore there. 'By a car bomb in Beirut whilst they were out there working for an international aid agency.'

'How old were you?'

'Thirteen.' She smiled sadly. 'I was staying with my aunt and uncle at the time, so I simply—went on staying with them. They've been very good to me,' she added on a soft sigh.

'But you still miss your parents,' he quietly concluded.

'Yes.'

'Shh,' he murmured, when her dark eyes glazed over with a wall of warm moisture.

He did a strange thing then. He reached up to gently take the gold locket from her fingers, lifted it up, brushed it against her lips like a kiss, and carefully lowered it back to her throat again.

'Go to sleep,' he commanded gently.

It was the last thing she remembered.

The lift she was travelling in suddenly dropped ten floors in as many seconds. Her eyes flew open, that awful sinking sensation leaving her stomach alive with butterflies. Then she just stared, completely bewildered as to where she was. It took several more troubled seconds to remember, then that now familiar feeling of desolation washed over her. If needed several more minutes of grim, taut stillness before she managed to contain it enough to take an interest in her surroundings.

The cabin was in darkness, the distant hum of the plane's powerful engines barely impinging on the quietness surrounding her. Someone had reclined her seat and covered her with a lightweight blanket, and a pillow had been positioned beneath her cheek. The shutters were down on the porthole windows, but it only took a glance in that direction to realise it was as dark outside as it was inside the plane.

Turning her head slowly, she found herself looking directly into Rafe's sleeping face. His unexpected closeness caught at her breath. For some reason she hadn't expected him to be asleep. Over the last few days she had never seen him anything but aggressively alert, and she found it rather disconcerting to see him like this.

Like her own, his seat was reclined, his dark head relaxed on his shoulders and facing her way. He had removed his jacket at some point during the flight and his tie had gone too. The top few buttons of his shirt had been tugged loose and the sleeve-cuffs rolled up to reveal the crisp, dark covering of hair on his tanned forearms. His hands lay in a loose link across the flatness of his stomach, the gold ring he had insisted she place on his left hand gleaming softly in the dimness.

She glanced at her own hands, clasped in a similar way to his, and studied the matching ring she was wearing.

Married, to a stranger.

A wry smile touched her lips and she turned to look back at him. What did he think? she wondered. What did he really think about the crazy liaison they had embarked upon?

His face told her nothing, as usual. Even in repose it still kept its thoughts to itself. Yet, with his winter-grey eyes hidden beneath lowered lashes that formed two shadowed arches against his high cheekbones, there was a gentler look to him, while those tough lines of aggressive determination were eased away by sleep. And

his mouth looked softer, kinder, the lips forming a
smooth bow shape that suddenly struck her as surpris-
ingly sensual.

Surprising because she had never thought of Rafe in
that way before. But now she felt something begin to
stir inside her, something like the fine brushing of fingertips on the lining of her stomach, and her heart gave
a low, droning thud in response.

No; she denied it and closed her eyes again, blocking
it out—blocking him out. Rafe might have made himself
virtually indispensable to her very existence at the moment, but she didn't want to start feeling like *that* about
him. It smacked too much of desperation.

And her emotions were traumatised enough.

Piers. A sigh whispered from her, saddened and
pained.

'Are you awake?'

She opened her eyes again to find herself staring directly into Rafe's, smoky grey and less probing in the
darkness.

Did he actually know the very moment she began
thinking of his brother? she wondered. It was certainly
uncanny the way he always managed to interrupt her
thoughts before she had even got as far as conjuring up
Piers' smooth, handsome face.

'Yes.' She softly stated the obvious. 'How long?' she
asked him.

He lifted an arm, eyes narrowing as they squinted at
the luminous hands on his watch. 'Eight hours, give or
take,' he informed her. 'Not bad.'

His hand came up, fingertips brushing a stray strand
of black hair away from her cheek. The action startled
her—not because he had touched her, but because that
same fluttering sensation skittering around her stomach
had made her flinch defensively away from it.

She could not have offended him more if she'd suddenly started verbally attacking him, she realised on a

rush of aching remorse. All hint of softness disappeared from his face, and in the next moment he was sitting up, his seat drawn into its upright position, and he had flicked on the overhead light.

Shaan stayed where she was for a few moments longer, guilt squeezing at her chest. Then she sat up slowly. 'I'm sorry,' she murmured. 'I—'

'I suppose you're ready for a drink.' Cutting right through her apology, he pressed the call button for the hostess, and Shaan grimaced, acknowledging that perhaps she deserved it. Rafe had been nothing but steadfastly supportive towards her; it was only natural that he should like to believe he could touch her without her reacting so violently.

The rest of the journey was an ordeal. Mainly because she found she couldn't sleep any more of the long hours away, and had to sit quietly beside Rafe while he immersed himself in paperwork. He had produced a briefcase that Shaan had not noticed him bringing with him until he'd pulled it out from beneath his seat. And, other than to join her for the odd light refreshment to break up the tedium, he proceeded to ignore her for the rest of the journey.

She only just managed to contain the next nervous start, when he suddenly reached across her, his warm body brushing against hers as he flicked the cover away from the window. 'If you want to see one of the most spectacular sights you're ever likely to see, then look out there,' he suggested, moving smoothly back into his own seat.

Her eyelashes fluttered, a moment's blank incomprehension holding her completely still while she fielded the light tingles the innocent brush of his body had activated in her. No, she told herself confusedly. It was surprise which had caused the sensation, not—

'Shaan?' he prompted.

She sucked in a shaky breath and pulled herself together, glancing to her right—then she gasped.

The sun was shining, and below them the waters of the famous Victoria Harbour glistened gold in the bright light. And stretching as far as she could see stood the buildings. Tall, individual things, of all shapes and sizes, packed in tightly, one on top of the other, yet exuding a strange kind of beauty that excited the senses.

'Meet Hong Kong,' Rafe said quietly. 'The undeclared jewel of the south China seas. Anything that is worth anything is traded here. For a tiny outcrop of rock, it wields more corporate power than most of the world's governments would dare to admit.'

She could believe it, Shaan thought as she stared in awe at the kind of skyline that could give Manhattan a run for its money.

'Over six million people live and work in that tiny plot of land,' he continued. 'And on some days you can believe it,' he added drily. 'Yet, having said that, I have been coming here almost all my adult life, and I've yet to see a scrap of paper on the floor or a hint of vandalism anywhere. Hong Kong is proud of itself and its achievements, and the people reflect that pride in the way they care for their city.

'They have a transport system that puts London to shame, whether it be the old-fashioned trams that run packed to the gunnels for hardly any charge at all, or the Star Ferry which connects Hong Kong itself with the Kowloon peninsula, or the underground system, efficient, spotlessly clean and beautifully air-conditioned. In other words, you can go anywhere with the minimum of effort—so long as you don't go by road,' he added ruefully.

'But that really wasn't what I meant when I suggested you look,' he said as the plane banked suddenly, then flattened out again. 'I was actually meaning—this...'

His timing was perfect. Her hand went out. It was

purely instinctive to want to grab hold of something, and it happened to be Rafe's arm as she let out a sharp gasp in utter dismay. 'My God, Rafe,' she breathed. 'We can't be more than ten feet from the tops of those buildings!'

'Hair-raising, isn't it?' He grinned, watching her expressive face instead of the view of Kowloon that seemed to come up to meet them as they flew in. 'They consider it the most dangerous airport approach in the world, yet its safety record is impeccable. We'll make it, never fear,' he assured her softly.

It was then that she realised just how fiercely her nails were curling into his arm, and on a sudden flush of colour she unclipped them. 'I'm so sorry,' she mumbled. 'I just didn't—'

In answer, Rafe took hold of her hand, placed it back on his arm and held it there. 'I thought you knew, Shaan,' he murmured. 'You can cling to me as fiercely as you like. It's what I'm here for. It's what I want.'

Her lungs drew in air on a soft gasp at the expression in his eyes. But, no; she denied it, shaking her head. Rafe didn't want her—couldn't want her. They might be married, but it was no ordinary marriage. It was simply an exercise in saving face. She couldn't bear it to be otherwise. Not now, not yet. Maybe never...

CHAPTER FOUR

OUTSIDE, the humidity hit Shaan like a hot, wet blanket being slapped into her face.

'Come on.' Rafe took her arm as she paused, having to fight to drag the thick, humid air into her lungs. 'There's a limo waiting; let's get inside it before we melt.'

Once they were inside, the car moved off with a silent smoothness and Shaan let her head fall back against the soft leather cushions. She felt like a limp rag, whilst Rafe looked as alert and as fresh as he had when he'd escorted her out of his house this morning—or had it been yesterday morning? She couldn't remember, hadn't taken the trouble to find out what the time difference was.

'What time is it?' she asked, totally disorientated.

'Almost noon,' he said. 'Local time,' he clarified when he caught her expression. 'About four in the morning to us.'

No wonder she felt dead on her feet! Her eyes were having difficulty even focusing, they felt so tired.

The car battled its way through the snarling traffic and into a tunnel which she assumed was taking them beneath the water to Hong Kong itself. Then they were moving along the rows of tall buildings where the modern splendour of plate glass and forged steel stood alongside old and crumbling colonial stone.

There seemed to be no rhyme nor reason as to why one building plot had been transformed into a plate glass towerblock while the one beside it bore the resemblance of a slum. Yet between them both, they only added to the charm of the city which was already beginning to spark her interest.

They pulled up outside the elegant-looking place with a porticoed entrance and white uniformed porters waiting to jump to open the car doors for them.

'Welcome, Mr Danvers, Mrs Danvers.' The young Chinese man who bowed to them surprised Shaan with his personal knowledge of who they were, but it did not seem to surprise Rafe at all.

'My wife is exhausted, Lee,' he said with the brisk informality of one who came here a lot. 'Are we in my usual suite?'

'Yes, sir.' With a snap of his fingers, Lee had two more porters running to get their luggage from the boot of the limo. 'If you will follow me, we will deal with the formalities.' With a jaunty lilt to his stride, he moved off in front of them, leaving Shaan feeling slightly overawed by all the special treatment as she followed mutely behind, with Rafe's hand possessively on her arm. She had always known he was important—after all, he was head of the great Danvers Corporation. But she thought this kind of treatment was reserved for government dignitaries and film stars only!

Signing in took mere seconds, then Lee was leading them off towards the lifts and politely inviting them to precede him inside before he stepped in with them and set the lift moving.

Shaan felt so tired she was in danger of wilting. And, indeed, when Rafe's arm came about her shoulders to urge her against him, she didn't bother to struggle; it was that necessary to let him take at least some of her weight for her.

'Hang on a little longer,' he murmured understandingly. 'Then you can have a nice long shower to freshen you up before we go in search of lunch.'

Lunch? 'All I want to do is fall into bed,' she told him on a stifled yawn.

'No can do, I'm afraid,' he refused. 'The best way to combat jet lag is by fighting it. Get through the rest of today without sleep and you'll feel a whole lot better for it tomorrow. Trust me,' he added at her protesting look.

'Trust me'. His favourite two words, she thought as she subsided wearily against him. A small smile touched his mouth as he watched her, but there was no hint of softening. That solid chin of his still jutted out in stubborn determination, and she let out a stifled sigh. 'One day soon I'm going to put a stop to your bullying, Rafe,' she promised him on another yawn.

'Really?' he said. 'Good. I'll look forward to it.'

Shaan glanced up at him, looking for the expression that should have gone with that disturbingly sanguine tone, but, as usual, his face told her nothing.

The man was an enigma, she decided. A total enigma.

Their room was a luxurious suite, with a rich rose carpet and creamy damask furnishings. She barely had time to take in the spacious sitting room, with its soft, curving settees and elegant dining table complete with candelabra, before Rafe had hold of her arm again. Lee was dismissed, and Rafe took her through another door.

It was a bedroom, furnished in the same soft colours but with a huge double bed covered with a creamy satin quilt.

'The bathroom is through there,' Rafe indicated with a nod of his dark head. 'Go and take a shower, wake yourself up, while I check on the bags.'

Twenty minutes later, wrapped in a snowy white bathrobe she had found hanging behind the bathroom door, she came back into the bedroom to find that everything had already been unpacked and put away for her.

And hanging on the wardrobe was a fresh set of

clothes—yet another display of Rafe's peremptory manner.

He'd selected a plain linen shirt-waister dress in a natural wheat colour, with brown leather buttons up the front and a matching brown leather belt. She had never seen it in her life before—or the matching brown blazer that hung beside it.

Or the brown leather shoes sitting neatly to attention on the floor, and the cream silk underwear draped on the bed.

With a puzzled frown, she stepped up to the wardrobe and slid open the door.

It was a shock. She recognised nothing of her own in there.

What the hell...? she wondered in a moment's blank incomprehension, then felt the first rumblings of mutiny begin to bubble inside her.

From the moment she'd left her aunt and uncle's house she hadn't seen a single piece of her own luggage. Some of the clothes she had so lovingly bought for her honeymoon with Piers had appeared in the wardrobe back at Rafe's house, but a lot of them hadn't, and the suitcases she had never seen again.

Even her flight bag had been a different one. Instead of the black leather bag that matched her old luggage, Rafe had come up with a velvety soft tan one, made of the finest kid leather, in which he'd told her to place her personal items.

'Feeling better now?'

Rafe appeared in the doorway to the bedroom.

Shaan pushed her hands into the deep robe pockets and turned slowly to face him. 'Where did these come from?' she demanded.

There was a moment's pause. 'Why?' he countered casually. 'Don't you like them?'

'It isn't a case of like,' she said. 'I just don't recognise them.'

'Ah,' he said. 'They're new,' he explained. 'I had your sizes faxed out here, so everything should fit...'

Faxed? Faxed out where, and to whom? 'But where are my own things?'

'Back in England.' He shrugged and glanced pointedly at his watch. 'I have one or two phone calls to make before we—'

'Rafe!' She stopped him before he could turn away. 'Have—have you discarded *all* my other stuff?' she asked him incredulously.

'Did you want to see it again?' he asked, disturbing her insides with the narrowed coolness of his regard.

'I...no,' she admitted, feeling the colour recede from her face. 'But—'

'There is no but,' he cut in. 'You hated the sight of those things and I hated them too. So I got rid of them, OK? And even if it isn't OK it's too damned late. You're my wife now, Shaan,' he added grimly. 'Not Piers'. And things you bought to please him will certainly not please me.'

'But all that money, Rafe!' she cried. Whether he was right or wrong, she was horrified by the unnecessary extravagance.

'What money—Piers' money?' His mouth turned down into an ugly sneer when Shaan lowered her eyes in guilt.

Yes, Piers had paid for her trousseau. She had been nothing but a very junior secretary who needed every penny of her income just to live. As Piers had pointed out to her when they'd discussed their honeymoon, she would be his responsibility by then, so why shouldn't he pay for the kind of clothes he would expect to see his wife wearing?

'Well, then, don't trouble yourself about it,' Rafe said

tightly. 'Because any money Piers spent on you initially came from me, so the—"extravagance" is my problem, not yours. Get dressed,' he commanded, anger flashing across his eyes as he watched her sink heavily onto the edge of the bed. 'We have a business dinner to attend this evening, and we have to get across the city to my offices to pick up some papers I need to study before we meet these people.'

'We?' Her head came up sharply, alarm making her catch her breath. 'But you don't need me to—'

His harsh sigh cut her short. He strode over to her then bent to lift her back to her feet, his fingers hurting where they pressed into the delicate structure of her shoulders.

'Listen,' he said. 'In the eyes of everyone who matters, we are man and wife. And in the role of wife it is your duty to be at my side when I entertain. Is that asking too much?'

'I... No, of course not,' she answered stiffly.

'Good.' He nodded. 'So, do you come with me to my offices, or would you prefer to sit here moping over your lost trousseau?'

It was meant to cut, and it did. What she didn't understand was why he was suddenly attacking her like this. It didn't make any sense.

'I'll come with you,' she conceded dully. 'Just for the record,' she added on a sudden flash of rare defiance, 'I couldn't care less what you did with my other things. But I do object to you implying that I was some kind of gold-digger! I was in love with Piers! And I was marrying him for the man I thought he was—not for what I thought I could get out of him!'

'Yet you use the past tense already,' he threw back coolly. 'Does real love wither into the past tense that quickly, Shaan?'

She lowered her head, the cruel taunt killing that small

flare of defiance as neatly as if he had taken it between his finger and thumb and snuffed it out.

'Look,' he continued, turning impatiently away from her, 'if you could hurry up in here, I would appreciate it. Only I need a shower and a change of clothes myself before we—'

'W-what do you mean?' Shaan gasped, beginning to feel dizzy with all the shocks he seemed hell-bent on laying on her.

Rafe was slowly turning back to look at her, his eyes narrowed and very guarded as he prompted carefully, 'About what, exactly?'

One of her hands made a fluttering movement out in front of her. 'Rafe,' she breathed, a deep sense of unease sending the tip of her tongue on a moistening foray around her suddenly dry lips. 'I... We aren't—sh-sharing this bedroom, are we?'

'Of course,' he confirmed, eyes narrowing even further when what bit of colour she had left in her face drained away. 'This is a one bedroomed suite. Of course we have to share it.'

Shaan stared at him in horror. A one-bedroomed suite, she repeated feverishly to herself. With only one bed! 'No,' she whispered as alarm shot like a thousand sharp needles through her. 'That's not fair. I—I've done everything else you've expected me to do, Rafe. But I will not sleep in the same bed as you.'

'And why not?' he demanded, sounding so arrogantly surprised that she wanted to hit him! 'There is no sin that I know of in a man and wife sharing the same bed.'

'In this case there is,' she disputed, trying hard to keep her voice as even as his, so he wouldn't know how close to hysterics she was actually becoming. Sleep with Rafe—close to Rafe? She shook her long mane of hair. She just couldn't do it, and she was hurt that he was expecting her to! 'We have a deal, you and I. A deal which involves saving face and nothing else!'

'Exactly,' he agreed, sounding annoyingly calm and logical in the face of her quivering alarm. 'This is the best one-bedroomed suite this hotel has to offer. It's the one I always use when I come here. People know me in this hotel, Shaan,' he said grimly. 'How do you think it would look to them if I suddenly asked them for one of their two-bedroomed suites when they know I've just taken myself a lovely bride?'

She swallowed, understanding him exactly. In this particular situation, Rafe was saving his own face. And she knew—knew even as every sense she possessed was clamouring in opposition to it—that she did not have a single protest she could offer against him doing that.

Rafe knew it, too. The way he stood there, drawing out the new throbbing silence between them to deliberately punctuate her numbing defeat, said it all.

Then the telephone in the other room began to ring. 'Be a good girl and get dressed,' he said as he turned to go and answer it, adding casually over his shoulder, 'I may as well order us some lunch here now the hour is getting so late. Ten minutes, Shaan,' he concluded peremptorily.

No wonder he was such a brilliant businessman, she thought as she was left staring blankly at the empty space Rafe had left behind him. The man could cut any argument to shreds without even having to try hard!

And she should have remembered that, she told herself grimly, flopping back onto the bed to stare at the ceiling with a feeling of stunned helplessness.

Working for the Danvers Corporation herself, she would have to had to be blind and deaf not to know all about the man who paid her wages. Not that she had ever had any contact with him—nor so much as set eyes on him in that vast multi-storey office block where the top-floor chief rarely set foot in the unhallowed halls of his working minions.

Except once, she recalled, thinking back to that one brief moment in time, before she'd even met Piers, when her eyes had clashed with those of Rafe Danvers.

A day when she had found herself accidentally tangled up in a sudden wall of bodies that had come surging out of one of the managerial offices on her floor.

She'd been walking down the corridor, her arms full of files she had just picked up from the filing department. Restricted as she was, she'd had no hope of darting to one side as they'd come like a herd of cattle upon her. They'd tried to avoid her, she allowed. But one rather bullish-looking man wearing an aggressive scowl on his face had looked right through her as if she hadn't been there, knocking so violently against her arm that she'd staggered, the files going one way, she going the other. He hadn't even apologised, striding off without so much as turning his head to see the destruction he had left behind him.

It had been Rafe who had paused, Rafe who'd turned to see what all the clatter was about. Rafe who'd come back and apologised for the accident, and enquired if she was all right.

The knock had left her breathless, and the fact that she'd recognised him instantly as the big white chief few ever saw off his own executive floor had only made her more flustered. She could remember blushing, remember sliding her eyes quickly away from the hard impatience glinting out of his and mumbling some incoherent assurance that she was fine as she'd bent down to gather together the scattered files.

She had expected him to leave her then—had wanted him to, so she could rub her arm where the other man had barged into her. But he hadn't. Instead he too had come down on his haunches, dark trousers stretching across his powerful thighs as he'd helped scoop papers back into spilling files.

And that had basically been it, she recalled. Except for her mumbling a breathless thank you when he'd silently handed her back her files, and he nodding in acknowledgement before rising back to his full, daunting height again.

It was then their eyes had clashed—just one tiny speck of time when she'd glanced up and he'd looked down and the world had seemed to grind to a dizzy, swirling halt as those sharp silver points seemed to pierce right into her. Then he'd nodded his head again and strode off, leaving her standing there staring blankly after him as he went to join his impatiently waiting herd.

That should have been the end of it as far as she was concerned. So she'd been surprised when later on that day the man who had knocked into her turned up at the side of her desk and coughed uncomfortably.

'I believe I owe you an apology,' he'd said, his bullish face tight, as if apologies did not come easily to him and he resented giving this one.

Shaan had just blinked up at him, wondering who had sent him and, more to the point, how they'd found out who she was. She was, after all, nothing but a very junior secretary amongst a whole army of secretaries who filled up all the desks in the huge typing pool.

It was a few weeks later, when she'd been sent to do some urgent processing for Piers, and they'd suddenly discovered an attraction for each other, that he had referred to the incident himself, then grinningly filled her in with what had happened afterwards.

'Rafe hit the roof,' he'd told her. 'The moment he got us all back upstairs, he turned on poor Jack Mellor and tore him to shreds!' His expression alone had said he found it all rather amusing. 'Said if Jack wasn't capable of applying even the basics in good manners then what the hell was he doing working for him? Jack just stared at him, wondering what the hell he'd done to bring on such a raking attack. So Rafe told him—in that neatly slicing way he has of diminishing someone to the ranks of idiot without having to try very hard—and poor Jack was ordered off to find out just who you were, apologise personally and then report back to him.'

In her mind's eye, Shaan could still see the way Piers had shaken his fair head ruefully. 'I don't think Jack will ever forgive Rafe for showing him up like that in front of the rest of us. Since we were all a bit taken aback by his reaction over such a silly little incident, we half expected to hear that you'd been rushed to hospital or something, with at least some broken bones for your trouble. But you didn't even receive a scratch, did you?' he'd quizzed curiously.

But it was only now, as she lay there across the bed she was going to have to share with Rafe tonight, that it occurred to her that the way Piers had been talking had put him amongst that trampling herd that had come bearing down upon her. She hadn't realised that before—certainly hadn't noticed him. And only Rafe had cared enough to stop. Only Rafe had considered it more than just the 'silly little incident' Piers had obviously considered it.

Piers. A weight pressing heavily down on her chest sent the air seeping painfully from her lungs. Piers, the younger one, the more handsome and sunny one of the Danvers men. Piers, the less intimidating and far less complicated one.

And, she now knew, the shallower, more selfish and—

'Shaan!' The sound of that harshly rasping voice calling from the other room brought her eyes jerking open in startled surprise.

'Coming!' she answered shakily, jerking off the bed to stand, swaying with a mixture of utter fatigue and miserable confusion as to where her life was going to take her from here on.

She looked down at the bed, imagining two dark heads on the snowy white pillows—and shuddered in utter rejection of what next went skittering through her mind.

'No,' she whispered to herself. 'No. Never. Rafe doesn't want me like that. I know he doesn't.'

And with that comforting thought she made herself get dressed, determined to be as cool and collected about all this as he was being.

Even if it killed her to do it.

Their lunch was just being wheeled in as she let herself into the other room. Rafe's voice sounded impatient as he instructed the waiter to leave the heated trolley by the dining table before dismissing him.

Drawn by the delicious aroma of freshly ground coffee, Shaan walked over to the table and sat down, her eyes carefully averted from the lancing, probing look Rafe sent her.

The telephone rang again while she was pouring herself a cup of coffee, and it was only as Rafe strode across the room that she realised there was a huge cedarwood desk she hadn't noticed before, the top of it already lost in a mound of paperwork.

No wonder he looks so impatient, she thought ruefully. While I've been hogging the bedroom, he's been working like a dog!

'Coffee?' she offered, striving to sound at ease when really she was strung up like piano wire. 'Or would you prefer to shower first?'

He glanced at his watch, grimaced, then sighed. 'Coffee,' he decided. 'Black, no sugar.' And he made a visible effort to relax some of the tension out of his shoulders as he came to join her.

He had only taken one step when the telephone began ringing yet again. On another sigh he turned back to the insistent machine and snatched up the receiver. 'No more calls for the next half hour,' he instructed whoever was on the other end, then dropped the phone back on its rest, his expression long-suffering as he came to sit down opposite her.

Mutely, Shaan handed him a cup, her gaze watchful as she sipped slowly at her own. He glanced up, caught her studying him and gave a tight, wry smile.

For some reason that smile melted something inside her—gave her courage to smile back and ask quietly, 'Do you always have to work at such a pace?'

'One of the trials of being a high-flying businessman,' he drily mocked himself.

'All work and no play,' she joined in the joke.

His eyes came to life suddenly. 'Not all work,' he corrected, and watched the embarrassed colour sweep her cheeks as his meaning hit home.

Piers had told her all about his women. And if Piers was to be believed—which she wasn't sure of any more—Rafe's women were very beautiful, very sophisticated, and very independently successful—women who did not cling and understood that they took second place in his life to his job.

'A whole collection of them,' Piers had described very mockingly. 'Spread out in a string across the world, all happy to make themselves available to him when he happens to be in town.'

One in every port, Shaan mused ruefully. Did that mean he had a woman in this port?

'Here,' he said, placing a covered plate in front of her and removing the domed lid to reveal the lightest, fluffiest omelette she had ever seen. She stared down at it and decided she did not want it. In fact her stomach had just closed up at the very thought of food entering it.

She swallowed tensely, aware of his eyes on her, aware that her sudden lack of appetite was due to the sudden suspicion that he had indeed got a woman tucked away somewhere in this crowded city.

And why should that bother her? she asked herself grimly. His private life was none of her business!

'Eat,' Rafe commanded, after watching her stare at her food for too long.

She ate, forcing each morsel into her mouth and having to work at swallowing it.

It was a relief when the phone started ringing again, so that she could desert what was left on her plate when Rafe got up to answer it.

'Right.' He turned towards the bedroom the moment he came off the phone. 'I'll be about ten minutes. If the phone rings take any messages and tell them I'll get back to them as soon as I can.'

'But I don't speak Chinese!' Shaan protested in alarm as he reached the bedroom door.

Amazingly he was grinning when he turned back to face her. 'You idiot,' he chided. 'This is Hong Kong—the most cosmopolitan city in the world! There isn't a person on this crowded little rock worth their salt who can't speak better English than we do ourselves!'

'Oh,' she said, feeling foolish.

'Ten minutes,' he repeated, and was still laughing at her when he disappeared into the bedroom.

When he came back, she was standing by the window gazing across the bay towards the less famous skyline of Kowloon.

'No calls?' he asked.

She turned to find him standing there in a beautiful slate-grey suit and pale blue shirt, with a slim navy tie knotted at his throat. His hair was still slightly damp, his tanned jaw swept clean of the shadow that had darkened it before. He wasn't looking at her but was concentrating on tugging his shirt-cuffs into a neat line around the cuffs of his jacket, and so missed the silent gasp she couldn't hold back as her senses reacted to how unnervingly attractive he was.

'No,' she answered, feeling slightly breathless.

He glanced up. Perhaps some of her agitation was showing in her voice. His eyes narrowed on her face, coolly assessing as they explored her pale, rather confused, expression. 'What's the matter?' he demanded.

'I...nothing,' she denied, looking quickly away from him. 'W-will I need my jacket?'

'Maybe not outside,' he answered, after a short, sharp pause that said he did not believe her. 'But the buildings are all air-conditioned and it can be quite cool inside them. And, anyway,' he added as he strode past her to hook her jacket off the back of the chair she had draped it on, 'despite the heat, people dress conservatively here. Without the jacket you look like a tourist. With it,' he added, settling the silk-lined linen across her shoulders, 'you look like the elegant wife of a businessman.'

He came round to stand in front of her, the clean smell of him further disturbing her already disturbed and confused senses. He stood a full head taller than she did, putting her eyes on a level with his square, cleanly shaven chin.

'Shaan...' he murmured slowly, '...if you're worrying about you and I sharing a bed tonight, then don't.'

'I'm not!' she denied.

'No?' he mocked. 'Well, something is certainly troubling you.' He lifted a hand to her chin, his fingers gently urging her to look at him.

'It—it just doesn't feel right,' she explained shakily. 'All this—enforced intimacy with a man I hardly—'

'Like?' he inserted.

'I never said that!' she denied, lifting protesting eyes to his. His expression was disbelieving and she sighed, wishing he would just give her a little space so she could untangle the mess her emotions were in. 'You're difficult to—'

To ignore, she had been going to say, but stopped herself because she knew he wouldn't understand. But that was exactly the right way to describe the problems she was struggling with just now. She needed—wanted—to be able to ignore him as a living, breathing sexually attractive male, but she couldn't, because with each passing minute she spent in his company she was becoming more and more aware of him.

A man she could quite easily tumble headlong into love with.

No! The way her brain flashed that frightened protest at her made her stiffen up like a board. 'Can we just go now?' Her eyes pleaded so anxiously that he grimaced, then sighed in exasperation.

'Sure,' he agreed. 'Why not?' And he let go of her, leaving her very aware that she had just managed to offend him—again.

CHAPTER FIVE

IT WAS a trying afternoon, if only because Rafe was so determined to fill every second of it.

He discarded the idea of using one of the hotel's chauffeur-driven cars in favour of travelling on the underground.

This was an experience in itself to Shaan, after being used to London's aged underground system, but she would have appreciated it more if she hadn't been so tired—and if that last little scene in their hotel suite hadn't placed some stiffness between them.

They left the underground at a place called Central, which brought them smack bang into the middle of corporate Hong Kong. And the moment they stepped outside it was like having that wet blanket slapped in her face again.

'Two minutes and we'll be out of it,' Rafe assured her, and, with a hand on her arm, rushed them across a busy road and in through a pair of huge plate glass doors which led—thankfully—back into blissful coolness.

His Hong Kong branch office was situated in a building that resembled a futuristic space rocket straight out of a Jules Verne novel. Shaan left her stomach behind when the lift rocketed them up thirty floors in half as many seconds. Then the doors opened, and she found herself staring at the most beautiful oriental woman she had ever seen.

Smiling in welcome, her lovely sloe-shaped eyes were fixed directly on Rafe. She sent him a bow and said something in Chinese to him, which he replied to in the same language. Then she looked curiously at Shaan.

'Shaan, meet Su Ling, our Far Eastern sales director. Su Ling,' he smoothly concluded, 'my new wife, Shaan.'

The woman wasn't surprised, and as she bowed politely to Shaan, Shaan ruefully presumed the news of their very public marriage had preceded them even this far. 'I am happy to meet you, Mrs Danvers,' she murmured in a beautifully accented, sensuously soft voice. 'May I offer you both my sincere congratulations?'

'Thank you,' Shaan answered awkwardly, feeling like a fraud.

Thankfully, Rafe started demanding attention, asking quick-fire, well informed questions as he guided Shaan across a gracious foyer of pale whites and greys and in through a door to an elegant room walled almost completely in glass.

It was an office, sumptuous in its ultra-modern design, furnished almost entirely in grey. Grey carpet, grey walls, grey cabinets, grey leather sofas and chairs. A large grey desk took up almost the whole of one plate glass wall, and the standard office paraphernalia that was set neatly on top of it was simply a darker shade of the same nondescript grey.

'Coffee would be nice,' Rafe murmured, and, with a smile and a bow, Su Ling went off to organise it, leaving Rafe and Shaan alone. 'This shouldn't take long,' he promised, guiding her over to one of the soft leather sofas and seating her on it.

The moment she was seated, his attention left her, shifting over to the big desk where a neat pile of files drew his interest. Shaan sat quietly watching him as once again he immersed himself in work, sitting behind the desk on a high-backed grey leather office chair, his lean face sharpened by concentration.

He wasn't a handsome man, she decided as she studied him. Not in the true, classical sense of the word anyway. Piers was that—a truly handsome man with a classically perfect profile whereas Rafe's attraction was due more to the irregularities of his features than their perfect symmetry.

His nose, for instance, was long and thin, with a bump in the middle of it that suggested he must have broken it at some time in his life. As if to confirm that theory there was a scar to the side of the bump—just a tiny, thin white line. There was nothing sinister about it, but it prompted curiosity as to how it had got there, suggested that Rafe had not always been a man who relied exclusively on his mental strength, as he did these days. That maybe, in his past, he had been quite willing to use a bit of physical strength, too.

But by no stretch of the imagination could Piers be called a physical man. Like the perfect contours of his face, his body was whip-cord lean, with no obvious muscle to spoil the line of his clothes, whereas Rafe's clothes—expensive and beautifully tailored as they were—could not quite hide the expanse of hard muscle that made up his bigger frame.

Both brothers were about the same height, but when they were standing side by side Rafe physically overpowered Piers in every way, with his broader shoulders, wider chest and a definite angle to his torso where it narrowed down to lean, tight hips.

The line of Piers' body was smoother, sleeker, but it lacked that air of masculine power that Rafe exuded. Even their hair was different. The silky, straight fairness of Piers' hair suited the kind of man he was, just as Rafe's thick, dark, slightly wavy hair suited him.

Piers smiled a lot, but she could count on the fingers of one hand how many times she had seen Rafe smile, and she had yet to see him smile with any real humour. Piers could find humour in just about anything—whether the moment deserved it or not.

In fact, she realised suddenly, when she really thought

about it Piers had a nasty habit of laughing at others' misfortunes—like the time he'd laughed at Jack Mellor's discomfort at being ordered to search her out and apologise.

Younger, she reminded herself. Piers was ten years younger than Rafe and therefore looked at life from a different perspective. And, because he was younger, perhaps she was not being fair in trying to compare him with his older, far more sophisticated and wordly brother. Yet—

She frowned, finding herself coming up against a solid wall which blocked out the answer to that 'yet'. Yet what? she wanted to know, and found it frustrating to have no answer.

'How good is your shorthand?'

Shaan blinked, bringing her big eyes back into focus to find Rafe studying her narrowly.

'I...' She didn't really know how to answer him. Her shorthand was good, very good, but by Rafe's high standards that might not be good enough. 'Adequate, I suppose,' she compromised warily, wondering why he wanted to know.

'Adequate enough to take down some notes for me while I'm running through these?' He flapped a sheaf of papers at her, with an odd smile playing around his mouth that almost hinted at wry appeal.

'I—suppose so,' she answered uncertainly, getting nervously to her feet.

'Good. Thanks.' Dropping the papers, he reached down and opened a drawer in his desk, pulled out a notebook and a couple of sharp pencils and slid them across to her. 'Pull up that chair, then, and let's give it a go,' he invited, waving her towards a straight backed chair standing at right angles to his own.

She did as he bade, moving nervously to get the chair then sitting down on it, before picking up the notepad and pencil. Rafe barely glanced at her, his attention seemingly fixed on the papers in front of him. There was a moment or two's silence while he gathered his thoughts, and she had to stop herself chewing nervously on the tip of her pencil. Then he began, voicing remarks in clear, precise tones that she had no difficulty transcribing for him.

In a matter of minutes her nervousness had gone, swept away by the quick-fire way he dealt with the information in front of him. It soon became clear that he was reading some kind of sales projection report, and she was deeply impressed by the way he coolly and shrewdly picked it to bits, asking questions and making pointed remarks that were going to make the poor person who had compiled it squirm in their seat. Because even in her small experience there was one thing she was sure about—and that was that by the time this report landed on Rafe's desk it should have been absolutely question-and comment-free.

Su Ling appeared at one point, loaded down with a tray of coffee things. She paused, surprise showing in her lovely eyes when she realised what was going on, then Rafe waved her impatiently across the room, dismissing her with thanks that bordered on the brusque. She had barely closed the door behind her before he was back at work, his use of acid wit as he ripped the report apart drawing more reluctant appreciation from Shaan as she noted it down. It went on and on, pages of questions and comments that held her so engrossed she actually jumped when Rafe spoke to her directly.

'Do you think you got all of that?'

Her head came up, her dark brown eyes warmed by a light that hadn't been in them for days now.

'Yes!' she said, then smiled a little wryly at the note of surprised pleasure in her voice. 'I may be trained to take dictation...' she shyly explained the surprise '...but since I joined your company I've had very little opportunity to use it. I work mainly for your army of salesmen, and they tend to dictate onto their mini-recorders then pass the cassettes on to be transcribed.' She gave a little shrug. 'I expected to be a lot rustier than I was.'

In fact, she remembered silently, the only time she'd had cause to use her shorthand skills recently had been for Piers, and he had such an easy, laid-back attitude to dictation that it really had not been any kind of test of her abilities. Not like just now—not like Rafe, who—

'Shaan?'

She blinked, bringing her mind back to the man sitting at right angles to her. He was watching her narrowly and she realised that, once again, he had known the very moment when Piers' name had popped into her head and was responding accordingly—snapping her out of her reverie before it took too tight a hold.

'Do you think,' he went on once he had her full attention, 'you could transcribe that lot for me if I find you a word processor to use?'

'Of course,' she said, feeling more comfortable with this boss-secretary relationship than their other, much too intimate one.

'Good.' He nodded, then bent down to open the large bottom drawer in his desk. To her surprise he came up with a lap-top computer which he put down on his desk in front of her. 'Ever used one of these?' he asked, and at her mute nod dumped a set of cables on her lap. 'Then I can leave you to set it up while I pour us some coffee?'

He got up, stretching out his lean frame in a long, lazy way which drew her reluctant gaze to the muscles flexing along the rigid walls of his stomach. Her mouth went dry and she looked quickly away, fingers suddenly all thumbs, because a strange kind of heaviness was attacking her own muscles.

Jet lag, she decided firmly. The sensation had nothing

to do with Rafe. After all, his constant closeness was something she had become more than familiar with over the last few days.

Yet, when he moved away, she let go of the breath she had not realised she had been holding until that moment and frowned, not liking the suspicion that she was becoming more and more aware of him as a real flesh and blood man.

By the time he brought two cups of coffee back to the desk, Shaan had the lap-top jumping into life. The machine was loaded with the same kind of software she was used to using, and she opened up a new file and set her mind to the task in hand while Rafe immersed himself in yet more paperwork.

They worked in companionable silence for a while, he flicking through papers, picking up his pen to score the odd remark across a paragraph, or just lazing back in his chair to read.

It was a strange kind of situation, Shaan mused at one point when she paused to sip at her cup of coffee. Here they were, strangers—enemies to a certain degree—but newly married and, as far as any outsider was concerned, supposedly here on their honeymoon. Yet at the first opportunity he got, Rafe kept on putting her to work!

'What's the smile for?' His deep voice intruded.

Did the man ever miss anything? she wondered ruefully as she glanced up to find that far from concentrating on his own work, as she'd thought him to be doing, he was sitting back in his chair, concentrating on her instead.

'I was wondering what your staff must be thinking of you, putting me to work like this,' she told him truthfully.

'I would rather know what you think of me,' he countered softly.

Shaan lowered her eyes, cheeks suffusing with self-conscious colour. 'I think you're a slave-driver,' she said lightly, deciding to put his potentially loaded remark in the context she had placed her own remark in.

But the colour remained high in her cheeks for a long time afterwards, and every time she glanced up she found him still sitting there just watching her.

It was disturbing. It was troubling. It made something deep down inside her coil up tightly, as though it was making ready to spring wide apart at the slightest provocation.

Jet lag; she blamed it all on that once again—desperately. I'm going mad with the need for sleep, she told herself firmly. That's all it is.

An hour after that they were back in the lift. Then swiftly back to the futuristic foyer.

'Where to now?' she asked, hoping he was going to say back to the hotel for a rest.

But he didn't. 'To get you fixed up with some clothes.'

'Oh, Rafe!' she groaned. 'Please, no!' She was so tired she was almost dropping. 'You've just dumped a whole load of new clothes on me without my knowing it. I don't want any more!'

'There's a shopping mall across the road from here,' he said, as if she hadn't spoken. 'You can buy anything from Chanel to Joe Bloggs there.'

Two hours after that, he had her sitting in an Italian-style café in the same mall, sipping strong black espresso to help keep her awake.

'I think I hate you,' she murmured when she caught him watching her with an annoyingly wry smile on his face. 'Why are you doing all of this?' By 'this' she meant the criminal array of exclusive designer bags stacked all around them both. 'It's not as if I'll ever get around to wearing them all!'

'I had to keep you awake somehow,' he replied, seemingly indifferent to the amount of money it must have cost him to 'keep her awake'. 'No pills tonight, remember?'

'Keep your silly pills,' she told him. 'Just find me a cushion, and I'll fall asleep right now, with my head on this table. How long have we been awake now, anyway?'

He glanced at his watch. 'Only twelve hours since you woke up on the plane,' he said blandly.

'It feels like a lifetime.'

'Drink your coffee.' He grinned.

'And you can stop that, too,' she snapped. 'Ordering me around like a puppet.'

His eyes narrowed, the silver behind them glinting as he studied her thoughtfully for a moment. 'Do you still work for me?' he asked curiously.

'Do you mean "work" as in am I still employed by your company?' she asked.

He nodded.

So she did. 'I'm due back in the office three weeks on Monday.'

'Then stop arguing with your boss,' he commanded.

'I'm on holiday,' she reminded him.

The way he reached across the table to grab hold of her hand was so unexpected that she jumped in surprise. 'You're on *honeymoon*,' he corrected, with softly taunting emphasis. He watched her go pale at the reminder and knew she was thinking of Piers, not of him. He dropped her hand again. 'And don't flinch every time I touch you,' he added, in yet another harsh reprimand.

'I'm—sorry,' she murmured, every hint of new-found spirit draining right out of her.

Rafe let out a heavy sigh of irritation. It was odd, really, but she had a feeling it was aimed at himself rather than her.

'Come on, let's go,' he said grimly.

It should have been a relief to get back to their suite, but it wasn't. She was in desperate need of some space on her own, without the threat of Rafe Danvers invading it, but he wasn't having that.

He made her hang up all her new things. He made her sit down with him in the sitting room and share a pot of coffee. He made her watch CNN news with him on the TV. And every time her eyes started to close he made them open with some remark that required concentration and an answer.

Did the man never need to relax himself? she wondered crossly when, at last, she was allowed to escape to the relative privacy of the bathroom while she showered and got changed for dinner.

Dinner! Out to dinner! With other people—strange people!

As if she hadn't been through enough today to make her want to sit down and weep at the stress of it all, they were going out to dinner with a large group of his business colleagues!

'Oh—damn you to hell, Rafe Danvers,' she muttered as she fought with hair that did not want to go up in the neat bun she was trying to pin it into. It took a good half-dozen pins to eventually secure it—a half-dozen too many pins, judging by the way her scalp was protesting.

Half-dead on her feet with jet lag, face flushed with impatience at her hair, and literally dancing inside with the state Rafe had put her nerves in, she stood and stared at herself in the full-length mirror.

The dress she was wearing was a strapless short black silk and tulle cocktail dress, which tightly moulded her slender figure from gently thrusting breasts to the very apex of her thighs, where it flared out in a mid-thigh-length skirt of rustling black tulle and left too much of her long black-stockinged legs on show for her liking.

But Rafe himself had chosen it—of course—only this

afternoon. He'd forced her to try it on for him, then further discomfited her by allowing his eyes to linger on her much longer than they should have done before he'd said, 'Wear that for me tonight,' in a roughened tone that had set the muscles in her stomach tingling—because the tone had matched the expression in his eyes, and she hadn't liked that either.

The knock sounding at the outer-suite door made her jump in alarm—another indication of how strung out she was, she realised tensely as she listened to Rafe's long stride as he went to answer it.

Then she stood, staring blankly at her own face without seeing the vulnerable tilt to her soft ruby-painted mouth, or the way her beautiful black eyes revealed how utterly defenceless she felt. She only saw how exhaustion was hollowing out her cheeks, and how she'd had to do a careful bit of covering up to hide the dark circles around her eyes.

Did the straight line of this bodice sit too low on the creamy slopes of her breasts? she wondered anxiously. And the skirt was definitely too short, she decided, biting pensively down on her full bottom lip as she gave an experimental swing of her hips and watched in the mirror the way the fluffy skirt billowed out to show even more leg.

'Very nice,' a deep voice murmured huskily from behind her, and she almost cried out in alarm because she hadn't heard him come into the room. Now her wary gaze flickered upwards to clash with his in the mirror.

'I—' That was all she managed; she was suddenly struck breathless and dumb by the height of him, the width of him, the powerful attraction in that dark, tough, aggressively handsome face looking back at her over the top of her own dark head.

Having to fight with herself to do it, she dragged her

eyes back to her own reflection and glared at the dress. 'It's too short,' she complained. 'And too tight.'

'Rubbish,' he dismissed. 'It's perfect.' Then in a dusky voice that set her nerve-ends tingling, '*You're perfect.* Or you will be when we've added this...'

He stepped to one side, moving out of the mirror's range and directly into her full, unprotected view as he came to stand in front of her.

And her heart gave a quivering flutter.

He was wearing black, like herself—a conventional black dinner suit and a slender black bow-tie tied neatly around the collar of a snowy white dress shirt that did nothing to hide the expanse of solid flesh bulging beneath it. He smelled different too—of something warm and spicy, sensual, very alluring—and she found herself suddenly overwhelmed by the sense of his dark presence—by the sheer maleness of the man.

By the power of his sexuality.

Oh, God.

'Here,' he said, bringing her eyes into focus on the small high-domed box he was holding in his hand. And she went perfectly still, her blood running cold as she recognised the box for exactly what it was.

No, she begged silently. Please, no.

But even as she made the aching plea Rafe sent the lid flicking upwards, and her heart quivered, then fell like a stone to her stomach as she stared at the contents.

An engagement ring—it just could not be anything else—sitting in the centre of a black velvet cushion. Even her novice eyes recognised the quality of the big oval ruby nestling in its circle of bright, sparkling diamonds.

'Your hand, please, Shaan,' Rafe requested quietly, with no idea of the horror she was feeling inside as he lifted the ring from its velvet bed.

As things stood between them now, they merely had

a bargain, drawn up on practical grounds with a simple gold band to seal the civil contract they had both signed. But this—this beautiful ring of dancing fire suggested so much more!

Too much more.

It suggested love, romance, a hot, sparkling passion. It made a glowing, unmistakable statement of ownership—possession in the most intimate sense of the word.

But it was a lie—such a dreadful lie! Like the beautiful diamond ring Piers had given her!

'Shaan?' Rafe prompted when she made no effort to lift her hand.

She shuddered, feeling sick, compelled to look at him simply because she had become conditioned over the days to responding to that tone in his voice. But her eyes were dark pools of anguish when she lifted them to his, her soft mouth trembling in wretched appeal.

'Please, Rafe,' she whispered, 'don't make me wear it.'

'Why not?' he demanded in frowning surprise. 'You're my wife. It is expected that you wear my ring.'

'Yes,' she conceded. 'But...' She sucked in a tight breath of air, trembling so badly now that even her breasts quivered. 'But it means nothing, does it?' she burst out painfully, her eyes willing him—begging him—to understand what she was trying to say here. 'I just can't wear something as s-special as that when it means nothing!'

He said nothing for a moment, his eyes holding that pained appeal in her eyes until she thought she might pass out as the cruel clutch of emotion she was experiencing made her ribcage ache at the tight band of tension wrapping around it.

Then, quite ruthlessly, he said, 'You wore my brother's ring and that meant nothing.'

Shaan closed her eyes, almost swaying as that particularly cruel thrust hit home. 'But I didn't know it was worthless when I accepted it,' she whispered thickly.

'Which is not the case with this one,' he brutally pointed out. 'So give me your hand.'

A heavy sigh shivered from her. He was so immovable, so damned intractable! About as sensitive to her feelings as a wall of solid rock!

'Shaan.'

Damn.

Her hand lifted. His fingers were warm and smooth against her own, steady where hers trembled, as he slid the lovely ring home. Mutely, she stared down at it. The dark stone flashed in what felt like mockery where it settled against her plain gold wedding band. The air around them began to throb with something that brought tears springing into her eyes, though she was bewildered as to what that something was.

'Let's go,' he said, and stepped around her, leaving her standing there, frowning, wondering if she had misheard that new, roughened note in his voice.

It was a nightmare. The whole wretched evening was just another waking nightmare. A long, exhausting round of warm congratulations and smiling thanks and, worse, the curious looks which made it clear that everyone present here tonight knew that Rafe had married his brother's bride.

And, on top of all of that, from the moment they all met up in the elegant foyer of one of Hong Kong's top restaurants, Shaan knew she was way, way out of her depth with these people.

There were four couples, including themselves. Not Chinese, but British. British expats who had made their homes in Hong Kong. And all of them were of Rafe's ilk, which placed a whole generation between herself and the quick-witted, sophisticated conversation that flashed from one to the other, leaving her feeling like a bemused spectator standing on the very perimeter of it all.

The men were slick, smooth operators, with an air of power and success about them that was clearly stamped into their female counterparts too. They were beautiful women, expensive women, with unimpeachable class and style, sleek smiles, and a sharp eye for what was going on around them.

It was no wonder Rafe had wanted her to look good. Next to these women she must appear very young and very gauche—not that they went out of their way to make her feel like that, she had to acknowledge. If anything, they tried their best to make her feel one of them, their smiles warm and genuine—like the questions they put to her in an effort to draw her into their sophisticated circle.

But she felt too awkward, too self-conscious and shy to respond with any ease. And it didn't help that she found no consolation in Rafe's solid presence, because he was as much a stranger to her as the rest of them were.

Yet the way he kept her clamped to his side, with an arm at a supportive angle across her back and his fingers resting in the trim curve of her waist, as they stood in a group sipping pre-dinner drinks, made a statement to the contrary.

As did the warm smiles he kept sending her—and what he did when their first drink arrived and everyone lifted their glasses to them in a congratulatory toast. He brought her to stand right in front of him, held her shy gaze with a dark intimacy that set her senses flurrying, touched his glass to hers, watched while she sipped self-consciously at her simple dry vermouth—then bent his head and kissed her.

The feel of his mouth, warm and smooth against her

vermouth-moistened lips, made her quiver in surprise. It was just an act; she knew that as she struggled not to show how unfamiliar those lips were to her. Rafe was simply acting out his role as loving bridegroom while she—she was left feeling troubled and confused by the brief burst of pleasure she experienced.

Jet lag; she blamed the unexpected response on it as she stood, eyes lowered, so no one could read what was going on inside her. It was simply jet lag that was making her legs feel unsteady and her insides curl up with some unfamiliar tension.

But, no, she had experienced this odd feeling before, she recalled. On the day when she'd been presented to him as his brother's future wife. It had felt then as though she'd received a high-voltage electric shock, a feeling overlaid with a sudden burst of dread that had held her white-faced and still and sent her shifting closer to the protection of Piers' comforting presence.

Yet Piers had not been the protector she'd believed him to be, she reminded herself dully. And the flash of angry contempt she had seen in Rafe's eyes then had not been aimed at her personally, but at the disastrous situation he must have seen looming up on the horizon because of what his brother was doing.

And Piers. Piers had been so triumphant, so—smug in the way he had introduced her to Rafe. And it was only now, as she allowed herself to replay that scene knowing what she now knew, that she realised he had not been like that because he was proud to present her, but because of some secret little battle he'd been having with his brother which had revolved around Madeleine and what Rafe knew about Piers and the other woman.

'Shaan.'

She glanced up, pain and contempt for Piers showing in her dark, dark eyes. Rafe saw it, and his fingers flexed against her waist, his eyes flashing silver murder at her just before the fingers dug in painfully to pull her angrily against him and his mouth swooped in another brief but punishing kiss that totally silenced their small group of onlookers.

'Forget him,' he muttered as he slid his mouth to the sensitive hollow of her ear. 'Piers is no longer yours to dream about!'

Blushing fiercely, and totally disconcerted by his sudden attack, she gasped. 'But I wasn't—'

'I think we should feed these two quickly and let them go,' one of their guests murmured teasingly.

Rafe managed a laugh, his moment's anger smoothly hidden by a cloak of rueful humour Shaan wished she possessed too. 'It is, after all, technically still our wedding day,' he drawled. 'Though goodness knows,' he added on a sigh, 'it has to be the longest one on record!'

Still? Shaan repeated to herself as everyone's amused laughter wafted around her. It couldn't really be this morning that they'd married in that little civil ceremony which was such a hazy memory to her that she could barely recall it?

It was a relief that the waiter came to show them to their table then; she was beginning to feel so stressed out that she needed to sit down or she had a feeling her legs would give up on her.

But the meal was interminable, course after course of exquisitely presented Chinese dishes appearing in front of her for her to pick at, while the conversation seemed to eddy to and fro with her barely registering most of it.

She felt lost and marooned, so totally out of her depth that it took all she had in her to smile, to concentrate on the questions put directly to her and answer them with at least some hint of intelligence.

No one was cruel or uncaring, yet she felt battered and bruised by the easy camaraderie she just could not join in with. If Rafe noticed—and she was sure he must have—he said nothing. But each time she happened to glance at him his eyes were on her, utterly inscrutable but on her, and she felt even more uncomfortable because she knew he must be seeing how totally inadequate she was for this.

'Come and dance.'

The light clasp of his hand on her arm as he propelled her to her feet was a sheer relief. Dance, he'd said, and she was ready to do anything just to get away from the ordeal she was wallowing in.

The music was slow and easy, the dance floor a small circle of polished wood set in the centre of the cluster of dining tables.

Rafe drew her into his arms, pulling her close so her chin brushed against the lapel of his jacket, and urged her into a slow, swaying movement, one hand resting lightly on her waist, the other lightly clasping one of hers close to his heart. She could feel his breath disturbing the fine hairs at her temple, warm and faintly scented with the dark red wine they had been drinking. Her other hand rested on his shoulder, low down where the muscle curved towards a bulging breastplate.

'Now you can relax,' he suggested, making her heavily aware that the tension she was suffering must have been very noticeable.

'I'm sorry,' she felt constrained to say. 'I know I'm not making a very good impression for you with your friends.'

'You're not here to impress my friends,' he responded. 'You're here because it's where I want you to be. And, anyway,' he added softly, 'they are utterly enchanted with you, so stop fishing for compliments.'

'I was not!' she denied, flashing a protesting glance up at him, only to sigh ruefully when she saw his teasing expression. But she still felt compelled to add, 'I still think that they think you've gone a little mad, marrying someone so obviously out of their league as I am.'

'And you think I care what they think?' he countered.

No, she accepted, on another small sigh. This man did not care a jot what anyone thought of him—or he wouldn't have married his brother's jilted fiancée in the first place, would he?

'You all seem to know each other very well,' she remarked.

'That's because I used to live here,' he murmured, smiling briefly at her look of surprise. 'I returned to London to run the company after my father died. But I've been commuting here on a fairly regular basis ever since. And we all tend to meet up at least once for dinner like this while I'm here.'

She frowned. 'But I thought you said this was a business dinner.' Not that she'd heard much business mentioned during dinner, she realised.

'It is in a way,' he confirmed. 'They are all business colleagues as well as friends. That's how it works, I'm afraid,' he added rather ruefully. 'Business and friendship tend to melt into one at our level. Which is why I couldn't afford to offend them when they offered us this—a wedding celebration dinner tonight.'

Was that what it was? Shaan suddenly felt even more guilty for not managing to rise to the occasion.

'I'm sorry if it's all been a bit too much for you.'

'It hasn't,' she quickly denied, knowing it was a lie even as she said it. 'They all seem very nice people. It's just that I'm so—tired,' she finished lamely.

'Well, a few more minutes of this,' he murmured as he drew her even closer to the solid warmth of his body, 'and I think we can leave without offending anyone.'

It was an assurance that took some of the tension out of her as they continued to sway together like that.

Though it felt strange, very strange, to be held this close by a man she hardly even knew.

She was used to dancing with Piers, but Rafe was so much bigger than Piers—harder than Piers, she added, with a new feeling of breathlessness as her senses registered the tight firmness of the well-structured bone and muscle she was being pressed gently up against.

With Piers, who was so much more slender and lithe, she'd used to feel quite equal to him when they had danced like this. But with Rafe she felt small and rather delicate—'female' was the surprising word which flashed into her mind. No match at all, in fact, for the latent power he exuded.

And where Piers had always been laughing, chatting, teasing, full of a light-hearted exuberance she'd always found easy to respond to, Rafe was quiet and more controlled about everything he did.

Yet, she realised, though she might have found Piers easier to be around, in a situation like this, where she felt stressed out, vulnerable and tired beyond belief, she would rather have Rafe's quiet, solid presence than Piers' noisy exuberance.

'Rafe,' she thought contentedly, and didn't even know she had sighed his name out loud as she relaxed more heavily against him.

But he heard it. His expression was difficult to define, but the way he gently lifted her hands up and placed them round his neck before he gathered her in even closer was a message in itself—if Shaan had been alert enough to pick up on it.

As it was, she simply lifted her face to smile at him— then found herself drowning in a pair of darkened grey eyes which held her utterly transfixed.

It was desire she read there, a desire Rafe was doing absolutely nothing to hide from her. It made her lips part on a soft, breathy gasp as full awareness shivered through her. Then, as if that soft gasp was the answer to some question he'd been asking, Rafe lowered his mouth down onto hers.

She stopped moving, the arrival of that mouth rendering her utterly breathless while she absorbed with a shock how pleasant she found the contact.

But this was Rafe, she told herself hazily.

It made no difference; his lips began to move gently on her own and she found herself instinctively responding.

And in the middle of a dance floor, in the middle of a restaurant packed full of people, something began to slowly erupt inside her.

The eruption of an answering desire.

It went quivering through her like a feathery caress on her most intimate senses. She arched her spine so she instinctively moved closer to its source, her fingers curling into the silk-fine hair at his nape, her heart breaking into a clamouring stammer.

It didn't last long, barely more than a few seconds, but her breathing was fractured by the time he drew away again, and her eyes were glazed by confusion.

'Now you look as a woman should look on her wedding night,' he murmured. And, with that one softly voiced sentence, broke the spell completely.

Was that why he'd done it? Kissed her like that simply to create the right impression for the benefit of his friends?

Relief swept through her—followed so quickly by a disturbing sense of acute disappointment that it actually stunned her for the few moments it took her to pull herself together.

No; she denied it. Don't be stupid. Rafe doesn't want you. And you certainly don't want Rafe! You're just so tired at the moment you're capable of mistaking anything right now—even a light kiss aimed exclusively at adding a little authenticity to this relationship!

'Can we leave now?' she asked a little desperately.

'Of course,' he agreed. 'I would even go as far as to say it is expected of us that we do leave.'

Because he had achieved what he had set out to achieve, she acknowledged suddenly, feeling so heart-sore and weary that the tiredness she had been trying to hold at bay all evening dropped over her like a big black cloud.

CHAPTER SIX

SHAAN had almost totally succumbed to the cloud by the time they got back to the hotel, and Rafe had to prop her up in a corner of the lift and hold her there with his hands while they were transported upwards.

The sound of his softly amused laughter was like the final nail in the coffin of her sense of exhaustion. 'It isn't funny,' she protested, complainingly. 'You've put me through hell today, and I think you did it all quite deliberately.'

'Maybe,' he half conceded.

'I feel like I've been awake for ever,' she sighed.

'Shaan...' he said softly. 'It's only ten o'clock in the evening.'

'What?' Her lashes flickered upwards so she could stare at him in disbelief.

He arched an eyebrow in mockery at her, his eyes still laughing. It surprised her, because she had never seen laughter in his expression before, and it was nice, contagious. She found herself smiling with him, albeit ruefully.

'People tend to eat late here,' he explained. 'They like to make a night of it. But I only agreed to that dinner if we ate early, otherwise you'd only be looking at your second course by now.'

Good grief. She shuddered. 'Aren't you tired?' she asked him then. After all, he had been awake as long as she had.

He didn't answer for a moment. Then, 'I'm used to it,' he answered casually.

Then the lift stopped, and she was having to drag

herself upright—with Rafe's help again, his arm sliding around her waist to offer support during the walk down the corridor to their room.

It was sheer bliss to step inside there and know that this was it. No more diversions. She could crawl into bed and just die.

She didn't even care that they were going to have to share that bed tonight. The way she was feeling right now, Rafe could even have his evil way with her—so long as he didn't wake her up while he was doing it.

She felt that done in.

Someone had turned down the bed while they'd been out, and an oyster silk nightdress had been artistically arranged on one side of the bed, a pair of black silk pyjamas on the other.

Stubbornly ignoring the pyjamas, she picked up the nightdress and took it with her to the bathroom. Five minutes later, hair brushed loose, face scrubbed clean of make-up, she crawled into the bed, pulled the sheet over her shoulder and dropped like a stone into a deep, dark pool of warm slumber...

She drifted awake once during the long night. And she awoke frowning, aware of the alien presence of a weight lying across her body. Her eyes fluttered open then just stared, and a tingling sensation shivered through her when she found herself staring directly into another face, lying no more than a foot away from her own.

Rafe.

Rafe, sleeping beside her, his thick lashes lying in two graceful crescents on his prominent cheekbones, mouth relaxed, lips slightly parted, breathing deep and soft and steady.

Sharing a bed with anyone was a new experience for her. Sharing a bed with a man was totally alien and strangely...intriguing—that she could lie here like this reasonably assured of her own safety while he was obviously so unaware.

In the still, quiet darkness she could just make out a naked shoulder and the shadowy outline of dark body hair on his wide chest, the sheet having been pushed down to somewhere between the beginnings of his ribcage and his lean, tight waist.

She could feel his breath on her face, feel the warmth coming from his body and the weight of his arm where it rested in the curving hollow of her hip. She could see through the dimness the rich gold colour of his skin, see the way his body's natural oils laid a polished sheen over well developed muscles—

No pyjamas, she realised with a sudden widening of her eyes in shocked consternation. He had dared to climb into bed with her wearing nothing!

Or at least nothing on his top half. But—no, she told herself. Surely he wouldn't be so insensitive as to have left off his pyjama bottoms too?

Well, one thing was for sure—she wasn't going to check.

But her eyes drifted lower, to the long, curving shape of him hidden by the covers. And, on a tell-tale moistening of her lips, she found herself wondering what the rest of him was like, her mind conjuring up pictures that had her blushing even if they were only pictures in her own mind.

She had never once caught herself imagining what Piers would look like undressed. For all their sometimes quite passionate interludes, she had never felt this almost uncontrollable urge to touch his naked skin, experience its warmth and its texture, as she was having to struggle against doing now with Rafe.

But then, she added heavily, she had never lain like this with Piers. He had never allowed things between them to get this far before carefully cooling things down, smiling—always smiling, his excuses full of words like 'love' and 'respect', telling her what they had was 'too special to rush'.

But now, with hindsight, she had to wonder if it had merely been indifference. If there had been no light of passion to make him want to touch her more intimately.

Or to have her touch him.

A shadow moved over her heart—the dark knowledge of inadequacy that she had a horrible feeling was going to be the real legacy Piers' rejection had left behind him.

'Shaan?'

As always when thoughts of Piers tormented her mind, Rafe's voice, deep and husky, broke through the heavy clouds, catching her exposed, vulnerable, as she lifted tear-washed eyes up to his face to find him awake and studying her sombrely.

'Forget him,' he said gruffly. 'He isn't worth the heartache.'

'He didn't want me,' she whispered bleakly, laying bare for this man of all men what should be her darkest, deepest secret.

His sigh was heavy, his smoky-grey eyes darkening with shadows of his own. Then that arm moved, tightening across her waist and drawing her closer to that warm, hard body she had been wanting so badly to get closer to. His mouth found hers, moulding it, gently searching, and she didn't pull away, didn't stiffen in rejection, didn't do anything but let herself sink into the comfort he seemed to be offering her.

It went on and on, like a warm blending in the darkness, where pleasure overlaid sadness and instinctively she was drawn even closer towards it. Her hand reached up, touching the warm, tight flesh of his upper arm, then his shoulder, fingers sliding in a slow, tentative exploration which stopped when they reached the cording in his neck, where they curled and clung at the same time as a shaky little sigh broke from her and her lips parted.

Rafe lifted his head—only enough so he could look deeply into her dark, vulnerable eyes. 'I want you, Shaan,' he murmured. 'I want you so badly, I'm prepared to take anything you want to give me.' He moved, gently turning her onto her back so he was half leaning over her. Her hand was still curled around his nape; his reached up to cup her cheek. 'And in return I can promise to wipe Piers right out of your mind,' he vowed. 'The point is, do you want me to?'

Did she? Shaan gazed into those eyes that had gone almost as dark as her own, and was overwhelmed by a desire to simply dive right into them. He was telling the truth when he said he wanted her; she could feel it in the unsteady throb of his heart against her breast, see it burning in the darkness of those eyes and the way his fingers were trembling slightly where they rested against her cheek.

Rafe wanted her, and her own senses responded by turning to warm, sensual liquid that began to pump desire through her body, an answering desire she was just too vulnerable to resist.

'Yes,' she heard herself say in a soft, breathy murmur. She wanted to feel that mouth warm on her own again, feel that same rush of pleasure, lose herself in it. Lose herself in him. 'Yes, I want you to…'

He didn't pause, didn't give her time to have second thoughts about that decision. His mouth closed on hers again, and she did not try to fight him. Instead she let her palms slide over tight, corded muscles, felt the spread of a warm pleasure unfold inside her, and on a soft sigh offered herself in full surrender.

Rafe desired her. And for her there was no stronger aphrodisiac than to know she was desirable to someone.

Though not just anyone; she made that fine but important distinction for the sake of her own self-respect.

This was Rafe. The man she was married to. The *only* man she should give herself to.

Oh, God, make this good for me, she prayed silently as Rafe received all the right messages and deepened the kiss to a sense-searing passion. Make it good for him.

His hand slid down over the taut wall of her stomach, along her silk-covered thigh, until he found the hem of her nightdress. With an economy of effort, he stripped the whole thing from her body. And for one more brief moment, as she lay there naked and exposed to the burning lash of his gaze, she was given the chance to change her mind about this.

Then his hand was caressing her, his head lowering to pull one pulsing nipple into his mouth, and the moment was lost in the turmoil that took place inside her.

He explored her as no man had ever explored her, with mouth and tongue and knowing fingers, feeding the steadily growing ache inside her until it was impossible to lie still without...something—she didn't know what—and a soft whimper of distress broke in her throat, her hands reaching out in search of that elusive something.

Rafe put himself there, his strong arms closing around her as he claimed her mouth with a hunger that took her breath away.

'Rafe,' she whispered in near desperation at the speed with which she was being carried along with him.

'Yes,' he breathed, as if in answer to some question she wasn't aware of asking. 'I know, Shaan. I know...'

No, you don't, she thought hazily as his mouth came back to ravish hers and his caresses grew bolder, more sure in their understanding of what could send her wild with uncontrollable pleasure. Then, with a low, deep groan of helpless frustration, she moved restlessly beneath him.

He shifted his weight, coming to hover above her, the muscles in his arms braced either side of her as at last he lowered himself between her thighs. And she was sliding her hands up the wall of his chest—feeling the pound of his heart as it thundered against his ribs, the heat of his skin, the tremor of need held under rigid control—and she exalted in the whole of it.

This was for her. He was experiencing all of this because of her!

But she had a moment's fear when she felt the physical evidence of his desire for the first time. And, though his entry was gentle, she clutched at his shoulders, fingernails digging into firm muscle, tense, breathless, her body quivering in anxious anticipation of that telling final thrust.

It halted him. He withdrew a little. 'Shaan?'

No! She shook her head, her eyes pinched tightly shut in denial.

'Shaan!'

The voice of command. She responded to it, lifting dark lashes to find his expression so achingly sombre that she let out a wretched little whimper of despair.

He knew the truth. He saw the truth. He now knew that Piers hadn't even wanted her enough to take this from her.

She saw his kiss-softened mouth pull down slightly at one corner in a wry little gesture that brought a wash of tears to her eyes. 'Please, Rafe,' she whispered, too terrified that he was going to withdraw altogether to care that she was begging.

If anything, his eyes went blacker, a flash of terrible sadness crossing them, and, wretchedly, she knew that sadness was for her.

'You fool,' he muttered. 'You beautiful fool.'

Then he bent down to kiss her once, very gently. And, with a firming of his features, pushed deeper again, taking what she was offering him in a single, smooth thrust that broke more than the seal of her virginity. It broke for ever her belief that you had to love someone to feel as wonderful as this.

The short, sharp shock of pain was nothing. The blinding shaft of sensual pleasure which followed it was everything. He filled her, and she gloried in the sensation, her thighs widening, drawing him deeper, legs wrapping round his taut, thrusting frame. And her arms brought him even closer, close enough for her mouth to fix itself onto his.

And, in that hot, tight, all-encompassing joining of body and mouths and minds, she willed the wild rhythm to take them over. The pounding beat of his heart and the gasping rasp of his breath against the bruising crush of her mouth were all-necessary, so necessary to the very substance that was driving her—a need to be wanted like this. A need to know she had the power to drive a man out of his mind like this.

Rafe drove harder, and on a bursting leap of triumphant exultation she felt herself catch hold of the supreme goal. It sang through her blood like the skittering crackle of electric lightning, then burst into a fire-flood of unrestrained rapture.

And, on a sudden blinding, bright flash of insight, she knew that Piers' rejection had been his own misfortune, not hers!

She had survived it. She was whole. She was a warm and sensual, desirable woman.

Rafe followed her, the tight, pulsing muscles dancing wildly inside her driving him to a deep, hot, throbbing release that convulsed his body and locked the air in his throat as they fused together on that wild, wild leap into ecstasy. It kept them like that throughout the whole dizzy, spiralling downward journey back to sanity, where they lay in a tangle of hot, sweat-slicked, muscle-wasted limbs, his body heavy on her, hers turned to a warm, somnolent liquid as their hearts thundered and their heaving lungs struggled to recover.

Then the silence came, and with it reality.

Rafe eased himself from her. Shaan kept her eyes closed, aware of the tears hovering behind her eyelids, aware that she couldn't bring herself to look at him. She knew that although he might have started it it was she who had damned well finished it, driving him on with excuses that seemed utterly inadequate now the need for them was no longer there.

Suddenly she began to shiver, feeling ice cold as reaction set in. Rafe reached out to tug the tangle of sheet from beneath her and covered them with it. But even as she huddled greedily into it he was pulling her to him, his hand firm as he stayed her struggles, flipped her over, curved her into the possessive hook of his body and held her there while she shook like a terrified animal.

'Try not to think,' he murmured with a husky, low note to his voice. 'Just lie still and let me hold you.'

Don't think. She daren't think. She had been thrust back into a deep state of shock.

Only this was a different kind of shock. The shock of discovering the driven depths of her own sensuality.

She fell asleep like that, lost in the tumbling shock of her own discovery.

Next time she awoke it was to sunlight pressing at the closed curtains, casting a rosy-pink glow over the whole room, and the familiar tones of a voice sounding harsh and angry.

'No—just do it!' It was Rafe, sounding slightly muffled by walls and distance, but it was most definitely his voice, tight with impatience.

Still half-asleep, she responded with instinctive auto-mation to the hard, tough command in his tone, sitting up and sliding her feet to the floor before she was even aware that she'd done it. Then she realised she was na-ked—remembered *why* she was naked—and grabbed hold of the sheet, dragged it round her, and then just sat there shuddering while a jumbled mass of fragmented pictures tumbled across her sleep-scrambled mind.

Awful pictures, humiliating pictures, of her virtually offering herself to Rafe—of herself almost begging Rafe!

'Oh, God.' A trembling hand flew up to cover her eyes in burning mortification as his voice came again, deep and angry.

'I don't care if it causes problems!' he snapped 'Yes, I know,' he answered to whatever had been said to him. 'But it will just have to stay on the backburner until I get back... I don't know when,' he sighed. 'When I'm ready— When *she's* ready...'

And Shaan slowly straightened, the hand sliding from her face as she realised he was talking about her here.

'Piers?' His hard voice gave a crack of deriding laugh-ter. 'Since when did he give a damn about anyone else but himself?'

Oh, damn. Feeling that dull thud as her heart dropped at the mere mention of Piers' name, she came to her feet and just stood, swaying dizzily.

'Of course he saw it,' he muttered. 'Hell—didn't they *all* see it?' he growled in rough derision. 'What do you think it was all about? He wanted to ruin things for me in revenge for Madeleine... What? Yes, of course I still love her,' he sighed. 'You can't turn love on and off like a bloody tap just because she happens to love someone else, you know...'

Madeleine? Eyes hot and burning, Shaan stared out at

nothing and saw the cruel, bitter truth leering knowingly back at her.

Rafe was in love with Madeleine.

'My mistake was in not realising that he would sink that low just to get back at me,' Rafe's voice continued bitterly, while, as if she'd been pulled helplessly through the frames of a very bad dream, Shaan found herself walking over to the bedroom door.

With the bedsheet clutched to her in one cold, trembling hand, she reached out to grasp the edge of the door with the other, pulling it towards her so she could step silently into the next room.

He was standing at the desk wearing only his bathrobe. He had his back towards her and a telephone clamped to his ear.

Angry tension pulsed from every muscle in his long, lean frame. 'You think I don't already know that?' he muttered. 'But he gave me no time, no space—nothing to work with! Shaan's feelings certainly didn't matter to him. As far as he was concerned they were expendable...'

Expendable, she thought painfully. Was that all she was to Piers—just an expendable pawn in a fight he had been having with his brother over Madeleine?

'Yes, well...' Rafe sighed. 'At least he got what he wanted out of this bloody mess. Which means I can do what the hell I like with the leftovers...'

Leftovers. Her. Oh, God, she couldn't hold back on the choked gasp of distress that particularly cruel word had dealt her.

He heard it and spun around, eyes flashing silver sparks of anger her way—until he realised just who he was looking at, then the look changed to one of utter, absolute, jaw-locking consternation.

She didn't speak—couldn't. Her voice felt trapped in

her own horror-stricken throat, and neither, it seemed, could he say a word.

What he did do was drop the phone onto its rest without even warning the person on the other end that he was going to break the connection. Then he made a gesture with one hand—a short, angry, half-helpless gesture.

'Don't even begin to think you understood what that was all about,' he clipped out gruffly. 'Because you couldn't possibly have done.'

She'd understood enough. More than enough. 'You're in love with Madeleine,' she told him in a stark, broken whisper.

If anything, he looked even more disconcerted. Colour shot across his high cheekbones; his eyes turned from silver to dark mirrors of shock. She'd clearly hit accurately on the truth.

And while she stood there, staring at him through a haze of deep personal humiliation, the whole thing slotted together like the end of a whodunnit movie.

He hadn't urged Madeleine back to England to bring Piers to his senses, but because he must have believed it safe to bring her back for himself, with Piers effectively committed to another woman!

And he hadn't suggested this marriage between the two of them simply out of a sense of family honour and guilt—but because his own pride had been slighted!

'That makes us both someone else's leftovers,' she said, then laughed as it appeared that once again the quick-thinking Rafe Danvers had been rendered utterly speechless. Because he just continued to stand there staring at her across the full length of the room, his clever mind seemingly gone perfectly blank!

'My God...' she choked, leaning weakly back against the frame of the door as full appreciation of the whole morass of deception took the strength from her legs. 'What a mess,' she whispered. 'What a damned mess.'

'You don't know what you're talking about,' he muttered.

'No?' Her dark eyes flashed a look at him—and saw a completely different person from the Rafe Danvers she was used to seeing. Not that he'd changed, exactly. It was her own perception of him that had taken on a radical alteration.

So, she thought bitterly. This is it. This is him. The real Rafe Danvers. The head of the great Danvers empire. The older brother, the darker brother, the stronger brother. The one with a finger on the pulse of every single thing that went on in his tightly controlled sphere. And the one who showed no hint of weakness anywhere in his make-up.

Not like Piers, or so she'd let herself believe. Nothing like Piers. The younger brother, the extrovert. The one who smiled at lot where the older brother rarely ever did. The one with the poetically handsome features that half the female population swooned over, the one who liked to be liked and even went out of his way to make sure that he was liked.

But she'd always seen Rafe as the kind of man who couldn't care less what people thought of him—as a man who stood apart from the rest, protected by an impenetrable ring of strength he wore around himself.

Now she realised that, far from being protected, he was as vulnerable as the rest of them!

And who to? Madeleine. His younger brother's childhood sweetheart. A small, sweet, gentle creature, with wheat-blonde hair and corn-flower blue eyes. The kind of woman who incited a man's primitive need to love and protect.

The kind of woman men like Rafe *and* Piers, for all their character differences, preferred.

The absolute opposite to herself, in fact.

She shuddered, hating herself—despising Rafe.

Did Madeleine know how he felt about her? Had Piers known? From what she'd overheard of that recent conversation, then, yes, the whole world except Shaan seemed to know! Which must hit right at the very heart of Rafe Danvers' ego.

It was no wonder he had jumped in with this marriage thing. It was a simple case of damage control—not for her sake, particularly, but for his own damned sake!

So why did he make love to me? she wondered on a wretched clutch of pain that had her fingers crushing the sheet where it covered her breasts. Had he been simply using her—was that it? As he'd accused Piers of doing? Had he been getting a bit of his own back?

My God; she closed her eyes, her body swaying slightly as she pushed herself upright from the doorframe. 'I want no more part in this,' she whispered, and stumbled back into the bedroom, only to stand looking around her in blank incomprehension of what she was going to do next.

'No part in what?' It was his turn to prop up the doorframe, looking more in control of himself now in the way he had his hands resting casually in the pockets of his white towelling robe.

But she knew better now. Everything about the Danver brothers was a damned cleverly erected lie. Piers with his warmly smiling, open expression of love, Rafe with his you-can-depend-on-me façade.

Lies. Damned lies.

'I won't play substitute for yet another damned Danvers man,' she declared.

'No one is expecting you to,' he said quietly.

'No?' Her chin came up, dark brown eyes shrouded in bruises of deep personal pain as she bitterly contested that.

The shocked look had gone, she noted, the consternation at being exposed now wiped clean from his face.

But he was wary—very wary—she could see that in the way he was looking at her, as though he wasn't quite sure what was going to come out of this.

'Are you in love with Madeleine?' she demanded outright.

He didn't answer for a moment, the expression in his eyes shaded by some deep thinking of his own he seemed to be doing. 'I don't see what that has to do with this situation,' he replied carefully at last.

'Yes, you do,' she argued. 'Because if you're in love with her then it makes you no better than your brother.'

'Because I wanted to marry you in his place?'

She made a sound of scorn at that. 'Don't make this a bigger farce than it already is, Rafe. You didn't *want* to marry me. You merely wanted to save face.'

'Your face.'

'My face—your face.' She shrugged away the difference. 'Whatever, you were still using me to cover up your own failures.'

'And you weren't using me in exactly the same way?'

Oh yes, she acknowledged heavily. Very much so. 'At least you *knew* my reasons!' she flashed at him angrily. 'But you had no intention of revealing yours to me, did you?'

'I didn't see them as relevant,' he replied.

'Well, I do!' she cried.

'Why?'

Why? Shaan stared at him blankly, the question totally throwing her, because she didn't really know why any of this was relevant. Only that it was—very relevant.

Then the answer hit her, and a sudden cold shiver shook her, sending her arms inside the sheet wrapped round her slender frame in protection.

'Madeleine,' she whispered thinly. It all revolved around Madeleine. Piers loved Madeleine. Rafe loved

Madeleine. Neither loved Shaan, but both were prepared to use her for their own purposes!

'Jealous of her, Shaan?' Rafe taunted silkily.

'Yes!' she cried, tears washing across her eyes at the blunt, cruel way he'd made her face that. 'Don't you think that it's humiliating enough to know she took the man I loved away from me, without knowing she was there haunting every moment we shared together last night?'

'And Piers *wasn't* haunting every moment along with her?' he threw right back in shrewd comparison, and watched stark realisation wipe what was left of the colour from her face, leaving her totally exposed and painfully vulnerable.

For some reason her reaction infuriated him. He strode forward, his hands cruel as they fixed on her shoulders. 'Well, let's get one thing straight,' he gritted. 'No other man haunts *my* bed, Shaan. And if you've a modicum of pride inside you you won't allow another woman to haunt yours!'

'Never again!' she agreed. 'No!'

His eyes narrowed. 'What's that supposed to mean?' he demanded

'Get your hands off me, Rafe.' She tried to push him away.

But he wasn't letting go. 'Explain what you meant,' he insisted grimly.

Her chin came up, brown eyes flashing with a blaze of that pride he had just challenged. 'Since it won't be happening again,' she informed him stiffly, 'neither of us has to worry about any resident ghosts—which also renders this discussion redundant!' Once again she tried to shrug him free, and once again his grip tightened.

'Because you overheard something you didn't like?' he prompted derisively.

Her eyes flashed again. 'Because it shouldn't have happened in the first place!' she snapped, still struggling.

'But it did happen,' he pointed out. 'We made love, Shaan—'

'We had sex!' she scathingly corrected his interpretation.

'Sex, then,' he conceded. 'But incredible sex! Mind blowing, out-of-our-heads sex!'

'Which you would know, wouldn't you?' she threw at him bitterly.

'Yes,' he sighed. 'I would know.' Then his eyes darkened to a look that was almost primitively possessive. 'But you wouldn't know,' he added succinctly, and watched the colour rush into her cheeks as his meaning sank in. 'So I am telling you this so you won't be labouring under any misguided notion that what we shared last night could be had with anyone, because it couldn't!' he stated gruffly. 'It was special—too damned special for you to mock it!'

She wasn't mocking it; she was doubting it.

'But that is not the point at issue here,' he went on grimly. 'The point at issue is whether, when you took me inside you with all that—' He stopped, something crazily like agony raking across his hard, handsome face. 'With all that wretched, begging passion,' he finished rawly 'were you pretending to yourself that I was my damned brother?'

'No!' She hotly denied that, managing at last to pull herself free of him and almost tripping over the trailing sheet as she did so.

The action tautened one corner, tugging it loose from her fingers so it dropped down to expose one creamy shoulder and the globe of her breast, where the nipple still protruded, tight and sore after last night's ravishment.

'Oh!' she choked in wretched dismay, embarrassed

heat pouring into her cheeks as her fingers grappled with what was left of the sheet in an effort to cover herself.

But Rafe's hand was there first—not helping, but claiming possession of that exposed mound with long fingers that stroked arrogantly, then cupped, so his thumb-pad could run a knowing caress over that cruelly sensitive nipple.

And suddenly the angry mood flipped over into something much more dangerous as she stood there staring down at those tanned fingers against her creamy flesh and felt the hot sting of desire drown out any ability to protest.

He stepped closer. Her eyes flicked up to plead with him, then stuck when she saw that same dark, rousing heat burning in his eyes.

'Please don't,' she wrenched out shakily.

But he shook his dark head. 'Your body wants me, Shaan,' he stated huskily. 'Even if your mind wants to reject that fact.'

Her body wanted him. Tears slashed across her eyes. Her body wanted him so that made it all OK, did it?

'Don't you understand?' she choked. 'I feel as if I'm betraying myself!'

'Because you don't love me?'

'Or you me,' she threw right back.

'We both tried love once,' he stated brutally. 'And what did it bring us but a load of pain and heartache?'

'And you think this is a less painful option?' she flashed back.

For an answer, his thumb moved on the pulsing tip of her nipple, she sucked air into her lungs on a sharp gasp of pleasure.

His mouth stretched in a glimmer of a satisfied smile. 'It seems to me,' he murmured huskily, 'to be the perfect option.'

And before she could think to stop him he reached up with his other hand and stripped the sheet from her body.

Naked, exposed, quivering, aroused, she made her eyes plead with him as he took that last vital step which brought him hard up against her. 'Rafe——' she managed to gasp out in a last-ditch plea, before his mouth covered hers.

'No,' he muttered. 'You want this as much as I do.'

'But it *feels* wrong!' she groaned.

'Where is the wrong in you and I helping each other get through a bad time in our lives?' he questioned.

Her eyes glazed over with tears of pain—his pain, her own pain; the two were beginning to blur into one now. 'Was she there instead of me last night?' she heard herself ask him thickly.

'No.' It was utterly unequivocal, his darkened eyes never wavering from her own helplessly vulnerable ones. 'I can honestly say, Shaan,' he went on huskily, 'that Madeleine never so much as entered my head last night. I didn't want her there. I wanted *you* there!'

'But——'

'No,' he said again. 'No more soul-searching.' And he crushed whatever she had been trying to say to him back into her mouth with the urgent pressure of his lips.

The bed waited. He lifted her onto it, then knelt, straddled across her, while he stripped the robe from his own body.

Her heart slammed once, hard, against her breast as she lay there staring up at him. He was so magnificent to look at—big and lean, dark and tanned, with that curling mat of body hair arrowing downwards to the potent proof of his sex.

Her own senses stirred, that slow, deep, salacious curl of excitement spiralling up from the very pits of her stomach, flooding heat into her flesh as touch-sensitive nerve-ends crowded to the surface of her skin in eager anticipation of his remembered caresses.

He was so aroused!

But then, she realised hopelessly, so was she. There was an alien moistness forming between her softly throbbing thighs that seemed to be begging for his touch.

Unable to resist the need, she let her hands come up, sliding into the thick silken mat of hair at his chest, feeling warmth and life and strength as they travelled slowly upwards until they could reach no further, stilling on the solid mass of muscle at his breastplate. Then, lifting bottomless black eyes up to his, she stared at him in mute surrender.

He accepted it with a growling triumph that put the seal on her fate.

He devoured her then; there was no other way to describe it. He stormed her, invaded her, conquered and devoured her.

'This is it, Shaan,' he slurred into the bone-melting aftermath. He was still lying on top of her, holding her trapped by his physical strength and the dynamic strength of his sensuality. 'This is what we have. Which is a darn sight more than most people have. And if you've any sense you'll try to build on that instead of pining for the unattainable.'

He meant Piers and she knew it. Did that also mean that he was not going to let himself pine for the unattainable?

'What time is it?' she said. 'I'm so dreadfully thirsty.'

It was another surrender. He knew it, she knew it. His mouth came down to take hers once again in a single hard, bruising kiss meant to claim that surrender.

'Come on.' He smiled, getting up and pulling her with him. 'Let's go and order some breakfast.'

CHAPTER SEVEN

THREE days later, showered, hair pulled into a simple ponytail, and wearing a plain white sleeveless sundress, Shaan was sitting at the dining table nibbling at the last slice of toast while she waited for Rafe to shower and get dressed himself.

Breakfast, Rafe called it. Sustenance more like, she thought, and grimaced as she swallowed. Making love gave you an appetite— She felt her cheeks grow hot as she sat there hardly able to believe the person she had become.

Or been turned into, she corrected that thought bemusedly. They had hardly moved out of these rooms for the last three days and nights. The man, she had discovered, was virtually insatiable—and if anyone had told her that a shy, almost reticent young-for-her-age twenty-two-year-old could become a slave to her own body pleasures so quickly, she would have scoffed them out of the room!

'Now look at yourself,' she murmured, and had to stand up as that now familiar restlessness began attacking her insides again.

You can still feel him deep inside you, she admitted shamefully, going to gaze sightlessly out across the glittering waters towards the Kowloon skyline.

And it feels wonderful. Warm and heady. Your breasts are still alive with the pleasure of his touch, the nipples pulsing a delicate plea for his mouth to close around them.

In fact, if he came in here right now and said, 'Let's do it again', you'd be ripping your clothes off!

And Piers? she thought suddenly. What has happened to your feelings for Piers within all this new self-awareness?

Gone, she realised with a shock that filled her with a new sense of horror. She could barely manage to conjure up Piers' face now, never mind that deep well of love she'd used to experience every time she thought of him.

So, what did that make her? she then wondered bleakly. Fickle?

Or just a very vulnerable woman on the rebound from a broken heart and desperately grasping at the first bit of feeling somebody tossed her way?

It was not a question. She refused to make it a question because if she did she would have to answer it. And she didn't think she would like the answer any better than the thought.

Because she had an uncomfortable suspicion that 'fickle' would win over 'rebound'.

And that love was something she really knew nothing about. Because if she had to describe the emotion then she would have to now call it—Rafe.

As if on cue, his hands slid around her slender waist and closed across the flat of her stomach. 'What have you seen that's so fascinating out there?' he enquired lazily.

She blinked herself quickly back into focus. 'A sampan—look.' She pointed with a finger towards the boat making its slow way through the water. 'For the first time I feel as if I'm near China.'

'It's a junk,' he corrected humorously. 'And Hong Kong belongs to China now, in case you've missed the world news for the last five years while Britain wrangled with them over their takeover.'

'That's right.' She sighed censoriously, lifting her mood to match his. 'Make me feel like a thick-headed bimbo. I am only a very poorly paid junior secretary, you know,' she said teasingly as she turned in his arms to face him. 'I don't have your— Oh,' she finished on a small surprised gasp.

'What?' He was smiling, puzzled—so different from the man who had walked out of this room a mere fifteen minutes ago that he rendered her breathless.

He had showered, shaved and smelled deliciously of something spicy. His hair was still damp and combed right back from his face. And he had swapped his bathrobe for a pair of lightweight linen trousers and a white collarless shirt that was both casual and classy, and did things to her metabolism that she was beginning to recognise with dread.

'You look—nice,' she murmured shyly.

'So do you,' he returned. 'Nice enough to eat—only, I think we've both eaten enough of that particular dish for a while at least,' he added wryly.

She blushed at his meaning. He bent down and kissed her. It felt different, this kiss. Warm and slow and tender. More like the kiss they had shared the other night on the dance floor. And her hands reached up, just as they had done then, found his head and held it there to prolong the pleasure. His hands were clasped at the base of her spine now, gently urging her closer, and the world faded away on a beautiful moment she knew she would treasure for ever.

He broke it—reluctantly—his mouth returning almost immediately to touch hers again in a strangely poignant gesture. And his eyes when she dared to look into them were darkened by a mood she couldn't quite define.

'You're—special,' he said gruffly. 'Do you know that?'

So are you, she wanted to say, but didn't have the courage. So instead she reached up to return the small touch of lips and was blushing shyly as she drew away again.

The rest of the day went like that—soft, easy, almost romantically perfect—as Rafe took her out to show her Hong Kong, and seemed quite content to play tourist with her, enjoying her fascination with all the new sights, sounds and smells.

They ended up on the Kowloon side via the Star Ferry, which looked so old she worried it might sink halfway across but in actual fact sped them over the water with an exhilarating efficiency.

They ate an early dinner in a small Chinese restaurant in a backstreet Rafe knew about that looked rather dubious to her but served the best Chinese food she had ever tasted. Afterwards he decided to show her the Temple Street night market.

'Keep close to me,' he warned as they turned a corner into a positive sea of market stalls and people. 'And watch your pockets.'

'I haven't got any,' she informed him laughingly.

They hadn't been back to the hotel all day so she was still wearing the simple white sundress, her only accessory a tiny white leather bag strung at an angle from her shoulder on its long, thin strap across her body. All that held was a lipstick and a handkerchief, so any thief stealing that would be disappointed.

But she held tightly to Rafe's hand as they plunged into the Kowloon equivalent of London's Portobello Road.

They wandered down through long rows of stalls hung with top designer wear, ladies' wear, men's wear—most of which were illegal copies of the most exclusive brandnames. Pure silk suits were sold off the peg, with an old treadle sewing machine at the back of the stall to make instant alterations. Camera stalls, electrical stalls—all held state-of-the-art merchandise. Jewellery stalls sold a quality of product that to her novice eyes was exquisite. And her eyes began to glow with excited enchantment at the whole mad kaleidoscope of shapes and sounds and colours.

It seemed to her wonderfully bewildered mind that you could buy anything here, from the most expensive perfume in the world to the most expensive watch in the world—all for next to nothing.

She paused by one stall, spying something that caught her eye. 'Rafe, have you got some cash you can lend me?' she asked him impulsively. 'Only I've not had the chance to cash a traveller's cheque, and I want one of these.'

'What—a watch?' he quizzed, sounding lazily indulgent.

'Mmm,' she nodded. 'I left mine behind in your house in London, you see,' she explained.

He stared down at her for a moment, his expression comically dubious to say the least. 'You are joking, of course?' he murmured eventually. 'You don't seriously want to buy one of these cheap copies?'

'I am not joking!' she declared. 'And I do want one. They're not expensive,' she added quickly when he gave a rather contemptuous shake of his head. 'I just heard someone pay only five Hong Kong dollars for one— that's hardly anything in sterling, is it?'

'If you want a watch, Shaan,' he said drily, 'then we'll go and find a proper jeweller's and I'll buy you one. A real one,' he added, with a glance of derision at the stall stacked with cheap copies.

Her eyes widened at the derision, then snapped with impatience. 'Oh, don't be so stuffy,' she said. 'I'll pay you back tomorrow when I cash a cheque.'

She turned her head then, to catch the vendor's eye, having no idea how her 'stuffy' quip had caught Rafe on the raw. It turned him to stone for the few moments it took him to come to terms with the unhappy fact that she was right and that he *was* being stuffy.

By then she was deep into bargaining with the vendor, knocking his price down as she had watched others doing. And with a mocking little smile which was aimed entirely at himself, Rafe took a metaphorical step to one side to enjoy watching this twenty-two-year-old woman he had married sportily play the vendor at his own game.

She enjoyed it too. It showed in the sparkle of her dark brown eyes when she eventually remembered him. 'Right,' she said briskly. 'We've struck a deal.'

'How much?' Rafe asked languidly.

He had his arms folded across his chest, one ankle resting on the other one, and his eyes were alight with irony.

'Two dollars fifty,' she declared triumphantly.

He pulled a wry face. 'Well done,' he complimented her, and slowly unfolded his arms to dig a hand into his trouser pockets. Then, as if it went against his masculinity to let her close the deal, he turned to the vendor and handed him the two dollars fifty.

The vendor handed Rafe something that had him struggling to keep the horror off his face.

It was a watch, all right, he conceded ruefully. A watch with a wide bright pink plastic strap, a black face—and Minnie Mouse hands.

She hadn't even gone for a classy fake—she'd chosen this...a fake toy!

'I don't believe this,' he muttered

'It's cute,' Shaan told him, holding out her arm so that he could fasten the watch to her wrist with a fatalistic twist to his mouth. 'Is it telling the right time?' she enquired when he'd finished.

Rafe checked the time on his own genuine solid gold Rolex, looked at the time Minnie's arms were indicating, and grimaced. 'To the nearest second, by the look of it,' he conceded rather caustically.

'Oh, good.' Extending her arm out in front of her, she

made quite a drama out of studying her brand-new purchase. 'For the first time since I arrived in Hong Kong, I will actually know what time it is!' she declared in clear satisfaction.

Rafe frowned. 'Is that why you wanted it?'

'Mmm,' she confirmed. 'And because I liked it,' she added, even white teeth pressing into her full bottom lip as she lifted gravely innocent eyes to his, because she knew exactly what he was thinking and was enjoying teasing him about it.

For a moment he took the bait—but it was only for a moment. 'You provoking little madam,' he accused.

'Mmm,' she said again.

And then it happened—just like that. The playful mood flipped over into something else entirely. In the busiest, most crowded place in the universe, their eyes locked and they suddenly stood alone, lost in the heated grip of a stunning mutual awareness.

Someone accidentally jostled her from behind. It pushed her forward a step towards Rafe. His arm came out and around her in instinctive protection. Their bodies touched. The heat sparked like static all over both of them. She quivered. His chest moved in a hard, tight gasp for air.

'Let's go,' he said huskily.

She didn't argue, but let him fold her beneath the possessive crook of his arm, and like that they forged a path back through the crowds, making for the nearest train station.

The train was busy. Shaan stood with her back to a piece of metal wall by some doors while Rafe stood in front of her, a hand braced on the rail while the other hand rested at her waist. He didn't speak and neither did she, but she could feel the tension building between the two of them as the long train snaked its way towards their stop. By the time they got off, she was finding it difficult to breathe. Rafe's face was taut, unsmiling, as they rode the escalators up to street level.

Their hotel was a few short steps away. There they had to share the lift with several other couples. No chance to speak—say something light in an effort to ease what was throbbing between them.

Rafe stood very close beside her, half-turned her way, so she could feel the warmth of his breath on her cheek, feel the tight, pulsing tension in his powerful body. Flicking a nervy glance upwards, she felt her breathing cease altogether as she clashed with a pair of glittering dark eyes that sent a wave of prickly heat chasing through her.

He wanted her, and he wanted her badly. Suddenly she could feel him deep inside her again, hot and throbbing.

It was awful—shocking! She looked quickly away, her mouth going dry, her heart pumping madly in a confusing mix of tingling excitement and real alarm at the sheer ferocity of it.

Maybe the others in the lift felt it too—she wasn't sure, but there was a silence in the compartment that seemed to throb with shared tension. And she spent what was left of the short ride to their floor with her dark head lowered so her hair could hide the self-conscious heat she knew was burning in her cheeks.

Rafe's hand caught hers again the moment they stepped into the corridor, pulling her along the thick carpet to their room, then inside it. He didn't stop until he strode into the bedroom, where he let go of her at last, closed the door, then leaned back against it, eyes closing, chest heaving on a tense sigh of what she supposed was relief, though it didn't seem to relieve anything.

Then his eyes snapped open, and she was taking a startled step back at what she saw burning there.

'Rafe!' she gasped as he started to walk towards her,

not sure whether she found all this compulsive desire incredibly exciting or absolutely terrifying.

Whichever, he was too lost within whatever it was that was driving him to notice any apprehension on her part as he reached for her and began grimly opening the buttons down the front of her dress.

As it was her body's senses were not giving off negative signals; her breathing was ruptured, her pulses racing, breasts already swollen and tight in aching anticipation of what they craved the most.

The two pieces of the dress parted. His eyes burned a searing path down her body, which was covered by the flimsiest scraps of white silk at her breasts and hips. He released the front catch on the bra, bent his head and sucked the throbbing tip of one breast into his mouth. As her spine arched on a sharp, stinging shock of gasping pleasure his arm hooked beneath the dress around her waist and hoisted her backwards onto the bed.

What happened next left her lying stretched out across the bed, unable to move in the thick, clamouring silence it left in its wake.

Rafe was lying beside her, his shirt hanging open, an arm thrown across his face, chest still heaving from the power of his own dynamic climax.

They hadn't even got as far as removing any clothes. She still had her dress on, the two pieces of her bra were lying open either side of her, and her briefs were—somewhere; she didn't know where. And as she lay there, exactly as he had left her, with her thighs parted and the soft, pulsing throb between them a reminder of the hard, hot, savage way he had driven them both to the edge and over, she was aware that she had just been utterly ravished by a man who had been completely out of control.

A man who was now finding it difficult to come to terms with what he had done.

'Rafe—' She touched his shoulder in a tentative attempt to reassure him.

He jack-knifed into a sitting position as if her touch had stung him, his hand grasping at the back of his tense neck while he glared at the floor, and her fingers fluttered tremulously as they slowly lowered again.

'I'm sorry,' he said gruffly, after another strained pause. 'There was no excuse for behaving like a—' He stopped, lost for words apparently, his jaw clenching on a snap of self-contempt. 'I apologise,' he clipped out. Then got up, walked into the bathroom and shut himself inside.

Without so much as glancing at her once, Shaan noted painfully.

Oh, she wasn't hurt by the stunning swiftness with which desire had taken him over—it had done the same to her. And, after all, she'd enjoyed it, quick as it had been; she'd been right with him all the way. So what if they'd never quite managed to get their clothes off?

Or so she would have thought, and passed it off as yet another mind blowingly new variation on the wild joys of sex—if he hadn't reacted like a guilty man.

And a guilty man was usually a man who had set out to punish. Was that what Rafe had been doing while she had been so gloriously out of her head with it all? Had he been punishing her for something? Punishing her for—what?

Madeleine.

The name slunk like the icy draft of a ghostly spectre across her flesh, and she shivered, grabbing the sides of her dress together and curling tightly onto her side.

'Go away!' she whispered wretchedly to that other woman's beastly presence.

The sound of movement from the bathroom had her rolling off the bed to quickly strip the dress from her body and replace it with her satin wrap. Her fingers shook as she belted it around her, teeth gritted behind tightened lips as anger began to bubble up inside her.

I've kicked Piers out of this marriage, she thought bitterly to herself. Rafe can damned well kick Madeleine out!

The bathroom door opened and she stalked towards it, with chin up and eyes flashing in bright, blinding, bitter fury. 'Don't ever—do that—to me again!' she spat into his tense pale face, and stepped past him into the bathroom, slamming the door shut behind her.

Her breasts were heaving, her fingers clenching and unclenching at her sides, that green-eyed monster called jealousy so completely overwhelming her that she wanted to scratch his damned lying eyes out!

He was the one who'd insisted that Piers and Madeleine were to stay out of their bed!

He was the one who had forced this damned sex thing on her in the first place!

She railed on furiously as she stripped off what was left of her clothes, stuffed her hair into a shower cap and stepped beneath the shower.

He was the one who—

'Oh.' A huge sob broke from her; she couldn't seem to stop it. Then another—and another. It was like being on an emotional roller coaster and she didn't think she could take much more of it.

And suddenly she was doing what she hadn't done even when Piers had jilted her. She was sobbing her heart out beneath the warm hiss of water.

And once again he was there. A hand switching off the shower. A hand closing around her arm, drawing her out of the cubicle and against his chest. Next thing the shower cap came off her head and a bathrobe settled over her shoulders with his arms closing round it.

He didn't say a word, not a single word, as she leant

there against him and just let it all come pouring out of her.

She felt limp afterwards, limp and lifeless. And still he didn't say anything in the ensuing dull throb of silence that followed her emotional storm. He just fed her limp arms into the sleeves of her robe, folded it around her body, tied it snugly, then lifted her into his arms and carried her to bed.

She fell asleep wrapped in a bathrobe, wrapped in his arms, gaining a peculiar kind of comfort from the fact that Rafe did not remove his own robe so they lay in a snug bundle of soft white towelling.

In the morning she woke to find him gone, not just from the bed but from the suite, with only a brief note which told her where he'd gone but gave no clue as to how he was feeling about her foolish breakdown the night before.

And foolish she did feel in the cool light of day. Rafe was a man of thirty-four, for goodness' sake! He was used to slick, smooth, sophisticated women in his bed, who knew how to respond to a complex man like him.

He was not used to an over-emotional female falling into a hysterical fit because he'd indulged in a bit of rough sex with her—which she had enjoyed anyway, she reminded herself.

It was Madeleine's ghost she couldn't cope with. And even her arrival in the bedroom last night had been at *her* bidding, not Rafe's.

She sighed, hating her own sense of failure. And hating Rafe for ducking out on her this morning, leaving her to sweat alone on what his mood might be.

Then almost instantly her own mood flipped over to a chin-lifting defiance. If he could escape a showdown then so damn well could she!

'Business meeting', his brief note said. 'Be back around one o'clock and we'll go for lunch'.

Well, she wouldn't be here at one o'clock! she decided. Though where she would go she had no idea.

All she did know was that the need to get away from this damned suite of rooms was growing stronger as each second passed by while she hurriedly hunted through her flight bag for her passport and traveller's cheques.

Ten minutes later, dressed in a simple white soft cotton blouse and a pair of white cotton trousers held up by a contrasting cerise belt, she was travelling down in the lift with her passport and traveller's cheques safely stashed in her shoulder bag, along with a pair of sunglasses and her purse.

Exchanging a cheque for some Hong Kong dollars was made easy by the hotel's own *bureau de change*. It was while she was waiting her turn there that she was drawn into conversation with a sweet old American couple who were standing in the same queue.

They were, Shaan discovered, about to embark on an organised tour of the island with a whole group of fellow Americans. It was pure impulse that made her ask if there might be room for one more on their coach.

After that, the final decision was taken right away from her, because her newly found friends simply took over.

'Though why a lovely young thing like you is alone in Hong Kong is incredible,' the lady remarked as they went to search out the tour guide.

'My husband—' that felt strange to say out loud, she thought as something tightened up inside her '—is involved in business today,' she explained.

'Business? Isn't that just like a man?' was the scathing reply to that one. 'Well. My name is Sadie and this is my husband, Josh.' Sadie made the introductions.

A spare seat was happily found for her on the coach,

and half an hour later Shaan found herself surrounded by twenty friendly Americans who made the day a sheer delight after too much of Rafe's abrasive company.

They began the tour with a hair-raising trip on the Peak Tram to the top of Victoria Peak that made Shaan wish she'd brought a camera with her. The view from the top was spectacular, the journey back down nerve-racking. From there they visited Aberdeen Harbour, where the big floating restaurants were moored and the water was like a floating city of residential junks in itself. After that they travelled along the coast to a place called Stanley, and Shaan marvelled at the abrupt change from heavily built up Hong Kong to a tropical paradise. It was beautiful on this side of the mountains, hardly a building to be seen, and the air was less humid.

Stanley had its own huge market—nothing like as fascinating as the night market Rafe had taken her to, but, still, she found a cerise silk scarf that matched the belt around her waist, and bought it. Then on impulse she bought her aunt and Jemma a similar one each, plus a small jade Buddha she spied that she thought her uncle might like. On further impulse she bought one for Rafe, too.

Guilty conscience, she recognised, even as she did it. Only, she'd happened to glance at the time and realised with a shock that it was already way past one o'clock. He should know by now that she'd escaped, and a tiny shiver trickled down her spine as she wondered how he was taking the discovery.

They lunched in Stanley itself, and by the time they all climbed back onto the coach it was already well past three o'clock. They travelled back via Victoria Peak again, where they stayed to watch the sun go down.

'I've been in some beautiful places in my time,' Sadie murmured softly beside her, 'but I've never seen a sunset as glorious as this one.'

And it was, beautiful—magical, mystical. And while Shaan stood there, feeling the power of it sink into her very bones, she suddenly wished Rafe were here with her to share it. Wished it so much, in fact, that she began to regret coming on this tour at all.

Which rather defeated the object, she ruefully acknowledged as they all climbed back on the bus so they could be ferried back to their hotel.

In the foyer, Shaan thanked her new friends and said goodbye to them, because they were leaving Hong Kong for Singapore first thing in the morning. Then, tired, but feeling more at peace with herself than she had felt since Rafe strode in and took over her life, she rode the lift up to her floor. She only began to feel anxious when she opened the suite door.

The lights were on, the curtains not yet drawn, and Rafe was standing in front of the window, stiff backed, tight-shouldered, with his hands stuffed into his trouser pockets.

He swung around the moment she stepped into the room. 'Where the hell have you been?' he bit out furiously.

Her chin came up, automatic defiance taking over from any idea she might have had of smiling at him. 'You know where I've been,' she replied. 'I left a message for you at Reception.'

'To hell with that,' he said angrily. 'Have you any idea how humiliating it was having no idea where my wife—my *new* wife—had gone when I brought some people back here to meet you? Your message arrived five minutes after we did!' he tagged on stingingly. 'By then I was already tearing my hair out!'

With anger, not worry, Shaan grimly assumed. 'Look.' She tried for a bit of placating. 'I'm sorry. It wasn't my fault if the message arrived late. But if it will make you feel better, I'll apologise to your friends for not being here.'

'You'll damn well do that!' he snapped. 'In exactly—' he stabbed a silver glance at his watch '—one hour from now, since we're meeting them for dinner!'

CHAPTER EIGHT

DINNER! Out to dinner! With total strangers—again! And with him in this mood.

'Oh, damn it,' Shaan muttered as she fought with hair that did not want to go up in the French pleat she was trying to put it in, and, in the end, she dropped her aching arms to her sides and just stood staring at herself in the full-length mirror.

The dress she was wearing was another new one bought by Rafe since they'd arrived here. It was a pure silk, slinkily cut traditional mandarin dress that seemed to mould just about every sensual curve of her figure. It was deep, dark red in colour, and piped in black with gold-threaded embroidery. With her loose black hair she looked even more exotic than she'd ever seen herself look.

It was a shock—a big shock—because the woman standing inside that mirror had 'seductress' written all over her.

There was no way she could go out looking like this! she decided on an upsurge of stomach-clenching dismay which had her fingers reaching for the high-buttoned mandarin collar with the intention of unfastening it.

Then, what's happened to you? she paused to ask her own unrecognisable reflection. Where's the meek and conservative little mouse you used to be—gone? What even made you choose this dress from all the other less provocative dresses hanging on the rail?

I don't know, she answered herself with a wretched kind of helplessness. I don't seem to have any idea who I am or even *what* I am any more!

'Shaan!' She jumped, that harshly impatient voice raking across nerve-ends so on edge they literally vibrated.

He was back to snapping out commands at her, she noted on a tension-packed little sigh.

And she was back to jumping to order, she tagged on grimly as her fingers snapped away from her collar. And instead of taking the dress off she gave her reflection a final, helpless glance before forcing her shaky legs across the bedroom floor and into the other room, hoping to God that *he* wouldn't see what she'd seen when she looked at herself.

He did, or at least something very like it, because his silver-grey eyes raked angrily over her and he muttered a string of muffled curses beneath his breath.

But all he actually enunciated clearly, was, 'Can we leave now?' He said it grimly, tightly—so damned sarcastically she wanted to hit him.

Her tiny black patent evening bag clutched tightly in one hand, she spun stiffly towards the suite door. She heard him let out another strangled curse, and realised with stinging, helpless, wretched despair that her back view was no less provocative than the front view owing to the way the centre back split in her skirt showed more leg than it had a right to do.

But—what the hell? she told herself angrily. It was Rafe who had helped choose the damned dress in the first place! He who'd created this new monster called Mrs Shaan Danvers, who was such a complete antithesis of the old Shaan!

So he could jolly well put up with her, she decided mutinously as her nerve-ends began screaming as he came up behind her.

But all he did do was reach around her and swing the door open so she could precede him out into the corridor.

She swept past, head high, angry defiance sparking in

her ebony eyes. By the time he'd closed the door and joined her, she was already standing at the wall of lifts.

'Where did you go?' he demanded.

'Go to hell,' she said tightly. 'You had your chance for an explanation and missed it. There won't be another one.'

'At least tell me who you went with!' he bit out.

'No.'

The lift doors opened. Shaan stalked inside, turned and kept her eyes glaring directly ahead, completely ignoring Rafe as he stepped in beside her and stabbed at the lift console as if it were one of her eyes.

The doors closed. They were alone and the tension was sizzling. 'All your note said was that you'd gone sightseeing with some new friends you'd met,' he snapped.

Your note said even less, she thought, but kept her lips clamped tightly shut.

'What new friends?'

No answer.

'Where did you meet them?'

No answer. But her senses began to buzz warningly because she could feel the angry frustration in him reaching out towards her.

'Was it a man?'

'Yes!' she flashed at him. 'It was a man! An American: wonderfully mannered, attentive to a fault! And he smiled a lot!' she tagged on with a sting to her tone. 'Which was a darn sight more pleasant than being scowled at!'

His hand, hitting the 'stop' button on the lift console, set her heart hammering and her eyes blinking as he spun round angrily to face her.

'Now listen,' he muttered, clamping hard hands on her shoulders. 'You're angry. I'm angry. We need to talk, but we can't do it now because we're already late for dinner, and it's very important to me that we give a good impression of married bliss—got that?'

'Yes.' She refused to look at him, her eyes flashing all over the place rather than clashing with his.

She was pulsing inside with a desire to break free of something—all of it, she suspected. Giving in to that bout of weeping last night had only been the tip of the iceberg. Now it was all beginning to bubble up inside her. Outrage at the cavalier way Piers had jilted her. Resentment at the way Rafe had so gallantly stepped into his brother's shoes like some white knight to the rescue of the poor heartbroken maiden! Then had come the sex. 'Incredible sex', Rafe had called it. 'Mind-blowing sex'! So she must not forget the sex, must she?

Or Madeleine, come to that—dear, sweet, blue-eyed, blonde-haired Madeleine must not be left out of this carnage her life had become.

'Shaan—'

'Stop doing that!' she snapped, letting her eyes clash with his for a brief second before flicking them away again.

'Doing what?' He was taken aback, which was very gratifying.

'Saying my name like a teacher who is about to reprimand a child,' she said, almost dancing on the spot with her need to let it all blow now.

He frowned. 'Is that what I do?'

'Yes, all the time.'

'And you don't like it?'

'No, I do not.'

'Then I apologise,' he said stiffly.

'Well, there's a first,' Shaan drawled, and knew even as she said it that she was behaving more like the child in need of reprimand than she had ever done.

He must have thought so too, because he let out a heavy sigh, his eyes closing as he seemed to make an effort to get a hold on himself. 'We'd better go,' he muttered grimly. 'Before this thing degenerates into a real fight.'

'What—another one?' she taunted recklessly. 'I thought we had one last night.'

His face tightened, the shaft hitting well and truly home, which almost immediately made her feel ashamed of herself for using it.

Then he reacted.

His hands caught her around the waist and physically hauled her up against the wall of the lift before she'd done more than gasp in surprise. Her eyes widened, real alarm showing in their turbulent dark depths while he stood there in front of her, pulsing with—something— though she wasn't quite sure what.

'Look—I'm sorry about last night, all right?' he bit out tautly. 'I didn't mean to upset you. In case you didn't notice it, I also upset myself.'

'I…' From feeling reckless with provocation, she now found herself feeling wretched with remorse. 'I didn't understand why—why you were so angry,' she explained a little unsteadily.

'I know.' Something flashed across his eyes—more anger, she suspected, but couldn't be sure, and the fingers he lifted to touch her cheek were incredibly gentle. 'But I wasn't angry with you,' he said. 'I was angry with myself, for losing control like that.'

'I thought you must have been wishing I was Madeleine.'

However she'd expected him to react to that honest little confession, it was not how he did react. His eyes closed, his mouth clenched, his big chest moving up and down on a fierce tug of air.

'Oh, hell,' he muttered, and looked at her again. 'Shaan—about Madeleine—'

'No!' Her fingers jerked up to cover his mouth.

'Please don't,' she whispered, sudden tears shining in her eyes. 'I don't think I could bear it if you...' She couldn't finish what she had been going to say because it revolved around his love for Madeleine, and that was exactly what she couldn't bear. 'Can't we just forget it ever happened and go now?' she pleaded anxiously.

He continued to stare grimly at her for a few moments longer, taking in the ready tears, her quivering lips, and lifted a hand to clasp her fingers that still covered his mouth.

He said very huskily, 'You beautiful fool.' And bent his head to kiss her.

He said that to me once before, she recalled hazily as her lips parted in helpless surrender to the needs of his mouth. 'Forget Madeleine,' he murmured gruffly as he drew away again. 'I have.'

As she realised she had forgotten Piers? she wondered, and felt a new warmth suffuse her as hope began to blossom.

Hope for what? She didn't know. She didn't even want to bother searching for the answer, because she could suddenly feel him as though he was deep inside her again, and she wanted him there in reality.

'Do we really have to meet these people?' she murmured huskily. 'I could plead a headache and you could put me to bed and tuck me in, you're very good at doing that...'

He let out a soft laugh, his hands splaying over her slender hips where they were sensually moulding themselves to his. 'And to think,' he murmured ruefully, 'I thought you were such a shy little thing.'

'Disappointed?' she asked.

'No—enchanted,' he replied, and captured her mouth again.

'Does this mean we can go back upstairs?' she questioned hopefully some long, very satisfying minutes later. And, like a woman with a brand-new weapon in her possession, she began seducing him with soft, clinging kisses interspersed with, 'Please?' Her fingertips ran inside his jacket so they could stroke long, sensual caresses along his lean ribcage, and her slender hips slowly gyrated against the steadily building tension in his.

'Please...?' she kept on whispering. 'Please, Rafe—please...?'

Until the kisses grew longer and stronger and deeper, and her new-found powers of seduction grew bolder when it became clear that he wasn't going to bring a halt to what she was inciting here in the hotel lift of all places. Her fingers began to slide loose the black bow-tie at his snowy white collar and he didn't do a single thing to stop her.

And here it was, yet another variation on the act of loving, where she seduced him, not the other way round. Where she made his heart pound with desire and made his skin burn beneath her delicate touch.

Triumph whistled through her when, on a painful groan, he reached out and hit the button which would take them back to their floor again—the triumph of knowing that she had the power to make him want her above everything, even his precious business dinner.

'You are a witch,' he muttered unsteadily, as if catching hold of her thoughts and answering them. 'You've cast a damned spell on me.'

The lift stopped. The doors slid open to reveal a Japanese couple waiting to come inside. They looked rather shocked as Rafe grimly pulled Shaan past them and back down the corridor to their own room.

'I'll never live this down if anyone finds out,' he muttered once he had them safely locked inside their suite again.

'I won't tell,' Shaan promised softly, her fingers already busy with his shirt buttons.

Her fingertips ran light, scraping caresses over hair-roughened flesh, felt muscles inside him dance with pleasure, felt the heat bouncing from him, felt the need throbbing in him, and pulled the shirt free from the waistband of his trousers. With a boldness that managed to shock even herself, she ran her hands over his hips, down his long, powerful thighs, then sensually back up again over the swollen evidence that was the very essence of the man himself.

He shuddered violently, his mouth leaving hers so he could release the air from his tense lungs on a pleasurable hiss. And in all they had shared during these last few dynamic days she had never felt so aware of her own femininity as she was at that moment.

Because he was enjoying this—losing himself in it. His eyes closed, expression taut with a passion that would have alarmed her if her own hungry passions hadn't been as throbbingly intense.

And it was those hungry passions that gave her the courage to go for the kill. With her eyes locked on his face and the delicate pink tip of her tongue probing between the provocative set of her even white teeth, she reached for the clasp on his trousers, flicked it free, then smoothly slid down the zip—and touched him.

It was a shock. No matter how intimate they had become over these last few days, this was the first time she had actually voluntarily touched him like this. And the shock was in the fierce heat of him, the unbelievable tension, the power of him pushing against the final barrier of stretchy black underwear.

'Don't stop now,' he murmured huskily when her fingers went suddenly still.

'Don't stop', he'd said, and she didn't want to stop. She wanted to overwhelm him with the power of her sensuality just as he had done countless times to her. But...

She glanced up, found his eyes open, saw the twin fires of desire burning in their smoky depths and just stared rather helplessly at him—begging, she suspected, for him to take over now her courage was beginning to fail her.

But Rafe shook his dark head in refusal. 'This is your seduction this time, Shaan,' he said gruffly. 'You began it, you finish it.'

He meant that what had happened the night before had been entirely his seduction and, since neither of them had liked what had happened then, he was therefore relinquishing all control this time to her.

But she suddenly discovered that she didn't want it. She liked him to overwhelm, overpower and devour her. She liked to kid herself that he allowed her no choices in this wild, sensual madness that formed the very crux of their relationship.

She liked to see herself as the innocent victim of the ruthless Danvers brothers because if she didn't see herself in that way then she would have to start looking at what she really was.

Fickle. That word came back to taunt her. Fickle in her feelings, fickle in her allegiance. Fickle in the way she could supposedly love one man yet be like this with another.

Fickle.

Then he moved, one of his hands coming up so he could gently comb his fingers through her long, loose hair, and her whole body shivered on a shaky sigh, breasts heaving behind their tight covering of silk, and she turned her mouth into that warm, male palm as her senses went haywire.

Fickle or not, she told herself fatally as she wound her arms inside his gaping shirt and reached upwards for his mouth again, she wanted this—needed it now—so badly that nothing else seemed to matter.

And through all of it came the one telling little truth that had supported her own actions throughout the whole of this thing with this man: the knowledge that he wanted her, desired her, couldn't get enough of her, Shaan, jilted bride of his brother. No matter what Madeleine meant to him, Rafe still wanted her.

And if that made them both fickle then so be it. Because at this moment in time she wanted him more than she could ever remember wanting anything.

Anything.

Wanted this—this wonderful, heady sense of elation she was experiencing as her hands went back to caressing his body, feeling his pulsing responses, his muscles rippling with pleasure when her fingers brushed over them, finding his mouth again time after time, drowning him in hot and moist, wanton kisses.

'What about your friends?' she managed to recall in the middle of their next wave of heated passion.

'I'll ring them,' he muttered. 'Later.' He shuddered at the sensual rake of her nails down the satin smooth skin of his back. 'Much later,' he added, and bent to scoop her up in his arms, then carry her through to the bedroom.

From there on Rafe took over—of course he took over; he would not have been the forcefully virile man she wanted if he had been content to lie back and let her do all the seducing. And what followed was a slow, hot, flesh-stirring loving that was the complete antithesis of what had gone the night before.

It was as if he needed to demonstrate to her that he could be warm, gentle, beautifully controlled, and still be devastatingly passionate. He kissed her all over, left no place untouched, until she lay there a weak, boneless mass of pulsing sensation before he slid slowly inside her.

Then stopped.

It brought her eyes flickering open, blackened by desire, to find his face wearing a sombre cast to it that actually hurt something deep inside her.

'You're beautiful,' he murmured huskily. 'I adore you.'

Was adoring something similar to love? she wondered hazily. Well, if it wasn't, it was close, very close—close enough for her to feel the exact same way about him.

So, 'You too,' she whispered, and watched his eyes turn to silver, felt him swell inside her as if her simple reply had the power to incite him, and she closed her eyes as her body turned to liquid again.

A moment after that he was moving in her with deep, slow, rhythmic thrusts that filled her with a magical sense of both his and her own entity.

It was wonderful. It was special. It was all the more enriched by those few small words of mutual caring which seemed to transcend the mere physical which they had been relying on until now. And the climax, when it came, was more like a gentle flood than a wild torrent, engulfing her in a warm, lazy sea of sensation that seemed to go on and on and on into a softly pulsing world of pure ecstasy...

'Are you going to tell me where you were today?'

He was lying propped up on an elbow beside her, watching her make that slow, sinking journey back to earth again while the back of one finger gently stroked her heated cheek. It was a nice, soothing, almost tender gesture, and so beautifully in keeping with what they had just shared together.

She opened heavy eyes, too sensually languid to do much else, and found his own eyes, darkened by similar satiation, resting on her.

'Not if you're going to start shouting again,' she warned. 'Because I'm just too content to listen.'

His small huff of laughter accompanied the soft slide

of his finger across her kiss-swollen mouth. 'If I promise not to shout, then?' he offered lazily.

'Josh,' she said. 'I was with an American called Josh.' The caressing finger went still. 'He has a wife called Sadie and they are both in their seventies. I asked if I could join them on an organised tour of the island. They agreed, and I had a lovely time into the bargain.'

He didn't say a single word for the space of several taut seconds. 'God, you know how to punish a man,' he muttered then. 'You deliberately let me imagine you swanning all over Hong Kong with some hunk of a guy!'

'You promised not to shout,' she reminded him poutingly.

'So I did,' he ruefully agreed, and the finger began moving again, sliding across her cheek to begin gently stroking her hair behind her ear while something else passed across his eyes—she wasn't sure what, but it warmed a special spot inside her to see it.

Tenderness; that was what it was. Tender amusement. And wry indulgence for her teasing. And—

'So, where did you go with these nice Americans who took you under their wing?' he murmured.

She told him, giving him a detailed account of her whole day—then she remembered something when she reached the part about Stanley market. Suddenly she jumped off the bed to run naked across the room and collect the carrier bag of the purchases she had made today.

'I bought you a present,' she said, explaining her sudden fit of energy.

'Not a new watch, I hope,' he drawled mockingly, his eyes lazily indulgent as they followed her.

'No—not a watch,' she said, turning to teasingly wrinkle her nose at him.

He was still lying as she had left him, reclining on

his side with the sheet negligently draped over his lean hips while the rest of him was wonderfully naked.

He looked so gorgeous it stopped her breath for a few throbbing moments, and then she came back to sit cross-legged on the bed near to him so she could place the bag on her lap while she rummaged inside it.

'Now, let's see...' she murmured, producing first the cerise scarf she had bought for herself, which she draped around her neck, then showing him the ones she had bought for her aunt and Jemma. Next came the tiny jade Buddha for her uncle, and, finally, the slightly larger one she had bought for Rafe.

'They're supposed to be lucky,' she explained. 'If someone else buys one for you. So...' Feeling suddenly awkward and shy, she handed the palm-sized sculpture to him. 'Be lucky, Rafe,' she murmured softly.

For a few moments he didn't move a muscle, and she couldn't see his eyes to know what he was thinking because he had them lowered while he stared at her small pale green offering.

Her stomach muscles began to knot, her chest growing tight in tense anticipation, white teeth pressing into her full bottom lip as the silence stretched without him so much as saying a word.

OK, she began thinking anxiously. So it wasn't the best jade the world could offer, and it certainly hadn't cost the earth to buy, but the thought counted for something, surely? Even with this man, who could afford the very best in anything he wanted?

Then his eyes lifted and she saw it—and her heart flipped over. He was moved—actually moved! His free hand snaked up, caught the two edges of her new scarf and tugged, pulling her face down towards him.

'Thank you,' he said gruffly, and kissed her. And it was special, this kiss, because it held not a hint of sexual passion. Only—

'Shaan…' he murmured as he drew away again, with a sombreness that did not quite fit the occasion. 'I want you to know that I'm not playing games with you here. I want this marriage to work. I want *us* to work.'

'Can it work?' Considering the way it had started, Shaan didn't really think it had a chance.

'You mean because we started with nothing?' he asked. 'Well…' A powerfully muscled shoulder moved in a shrug. 'We can build on nothing. In fact, I would go as far as to say,' he added, 'that it's probably a darn sight easier to build on nothing…' He paused. Then, on a small sigh, he concluded, 'I suppose the point I am trying to make is—do you want to try?'

'You mean I'm being given a choice here?' She tried mocking the seriousness out of the moment.

It didn't work, though he did allow himself a grimace at the justice in her taunt, because they both knew that until now Rafe had not really given her any choices about anything that had happened between them.

But, 'Yes,' he replied, and his eyes remained serious—deadly serious.

Her eyelids lowered while she thought about what he was actually telling her here. He was talking permanence. He was *offering* permanence. 'Is it what you want?' she asked.

'Yes.' It was gruff and it was sincere.

'Piers and Madeleine—'

'No.' His warning tug on the cerise scarf stopped her. 'They no longer belong in the equation,' he stated firmly. 'This is between you and me, and what we've discovered we can have if we just try to work at it.'

'Sex' was the word Shaan would use to describe it. But then it was her turn to grimace, because she'd tried love without sex and had got nothing back from the relationship. So maybe Rafe was right, and they did have a chance of building from nothing—with sex as their foundation instead of that more intense emotion called love.

'Are you a faithful man, Rafe?' she asked him quietly.

'Yes,' he replied.

And she found she believed him. There was something about this conversation which insisted on honesty. But, still, she wanted clarification on that point. 'No other women on the side? No little stop-overs in brief ports of call?'

'Who's been talking?' he sighed, then grimaced. 'Or don't I need to ask?'

'Just answer the question,' she insisted. 'I've been fooled by one man in that way too recently to let another one walk me into the same trap.'

'Rumours about my love life have been greatly exaggerated,' he informed her satirically. 'But, no, no other women.' His eyes caught hers again. 'Just you, me and a chance of something special.'

Something special. Something special sounded tempting. Something special was what she was already beginning to feel for this complicated man with his hard crust of ruthlessness and his mind-blowing sensuality, and this—this warming show of honest sincerity was perhaps worth more than all the rest put together.

But...

Lowering her eyes away from him, she contemplated her fingers while her mind tried to come up with a catch in all of this. Because there had to be a catch, didn't there? It was all just too good to be true—too darn easy—and that prodded at another little sore point she had been struggling with.

This quick, this right and this easy—that did make her fickle.

Or gullible? she suggested to herself soberly. Gullible in a lot of ways. Gullible to Piers' false kind of charm, gullible to Rafe's more aggressive kind, and gullible to—this, this need to be wanted as hotly and as passion-ately as he clearly wanted her.

Could they build on that? Was it at least worth trying, or was she just asking for more heartache at the end of it all?

'Well?' he prompted when she took too long to an-swer.

'OK, we'll work on it,' she heard herself surrender.

His eyes flashed, and in the next moment he was push-ing her onto her back and coming to lie across her, his mouth hot and urgent as it covered hers.

When she lifted her arms so she could bury her fingers in his hair and hold his mouth on hers, he caught one hand with his own, his fingers pleating with her fingers as he pressed them back against the bed.

And it was only when she felt the cold, solid press of something sandwiched between their two warm palms that she remembered the little Buddha she had just given to him.

For luck, she had said. She only hoped there was some truth in it, for she had a feeling they were going to need it if they were to make anything of this odd liaison that never should have begun in the first place—or come as far as it had done since.

And maybe Rafe's thoughts were moving along simi-lar lines, because as he guided them both through yet another storm of heated passion he kept that little Buddha pressed between their heated palms, and even afterwards still kept it there as they slid into a languid sleep.

Oddly, she felt comforted feeling it there. Maybe there was more to its myth than mere fiction. She hoped so; she really hoped so.

So they worked at it—both of them. Worked at it through the rest of their two-week stay in Hong Kong and the weeks following when they returned to London.

And it went very well—aided and abetted by the fact that they kept themselves very much to themselves for most of the time, which meant that no outside influences could put a spanner in the works. And they also utilised to its fullest potential the main ingredient that kept it going.

The sex, to put it crudely. Sex in the morning, sex in the evening, sex when a certain look or a touch would set the whole cauldron of desire bubbling up without warning.

Sex, sex and more sex. It seemed to completely take her over. She thought of little else, she *wanted* little else, and it never occurred to her to question the sense in such a blinkered view of their marriage.

Because she had firmly locked away, in a mental box somewhere inside her head, all the reasons why sex could not and should not be enough to support a relationship. Locked away the fact that what she had actually done was accept physical love in place of emotional love. The relationship really didn't stand a chance, and was just begging for something or someone to come along and smash the blinkers from her eyes.

CHAPTER NINE

'WELL—?' Jemma demanded. 'Are you in love with him or aren't you?'

Dressed in a wheat-coloured trouser suit that was supposed to be casual wear but still managed to look outrageously expensive, Shaan sat at a small table in what had used to be her favourite London wine bar, watching the busy turnover of lunchtime customers mill around in front of her while she decided how best to answer that.

It was odd, she mused idly, but she felt quite out of place here now. In fact, she would go as far as to say that she didn't even know who Shaan Saketa was any more, because Mrs Rafe Danvers was an entirely different being altogether.

She had been back in London a week, after spending two weeks in Hong Kong, and it was during those first two weeks that Shaan Danvers had been created—moulded by clever hands to suit the man she was now married to.

In every sense of the word.

Her clothes, the way she carried herself, the way she looked at life and even the way she perceived herself had all completely altered.

But, perhaps most significantly of all, gone was the strained-faced, empty-eyed, lost-looking creature Jemma had worried so much about the last time she had seen her, and in her place sat this alluringly beautiful woman whose dark eyes now wore the look of disturbingly sensual self-knowledge. A fact any of the men present in the crowded bar would eagerly vouch for.

She seemed to glow with fulfilment. It was sexy. It

was enticing. It talked to a man's sexual antennae and told him that there sat a woman who knew how to make a man feel fantastic about himself.

In short, she was special. And she belonged to someone special, if the way those sexy eyes barely noticed any other man was a judge. And, whoever the guy was, the rest of them envied him and hung around perhaps longer than they should in the hope of getting a glimpse of this member of their sex who was lucky enough to have her.

'Is the answer that difficult?' Jemma mocked drily when the silence between them went on too long.

'Yes, actually,' Shaan murmured, bringing her eyes back into focus with a smile so sensually enigmatic that it almost made Jemma gasp. 'It is that difficult.'

'You said you loved him,' she reminded her. 'Before you married him, you promised me that you did.'

'Ah.' Shaan relaxed back into her chair, taking her glass of chilled white wine with her. 'But we were all playing at make-believe then, weren't we?' she ruefully pointed out. 'Pretending everything had worked out perfectly because it was the only way we could deal with the true horror story.'

'And now?' Jemma might not be a man, but she wasn't blind. She too could see the new sensual awareness glowing in those luxurious eyes—could feel it too, almost pulsing in the very space Shaan occupied.

'The horror story is no longer a horror story,' Shaan answered simply. 'Rafe and I—understand each other.' She decided this said it best. 'We're happy.' In our own little world so long as no one else tries to infiltrate it, she added silently.

'Happy with a lot of things, by the look of you,' Jemma grunted, not comfortable with any of this—not the new Shaan she was being offered here, or the answers that new Shaan was giving her.

But then she hadn't been comfortable with it from the beginning, she recalled. And that discomfort had included Shaan's association with Piers Danvers, never mind his older, tougher, and far more formidable brother.

'What's the matter, Jemma?' Shaan questioned lightly. 'Don't you think I should be happy? Is that it?'

'How do I know when you won't tell me anything?' Her best friend sighed in exasperation.

I've told you more than I've told anyone else, Shaan thought. 'I refuse to tempt providence by dissecting what we have,' was all she actually said, then carefully turned the subject. 'Tell me how the wedding plans are going.'

It was a brush-off in anyone's books, and Jemma noted it as such, but was determined to have her final say anyway. 'Well, I think you're heading for a mighty fall if you don't watch out,' she predicted. But, having merely received one of those annoyingly enigmatic smiles back in return, she allowed the conversation to be turned to the less titillating subject of her own wedding day which was due to take place in a couple of months.

And maybe Shaan should have listened to that final warning. But as it was she was happy, and when you were happy you didn't go and spoil it all by thinking unhappy thoughts, did you?

So she and Rafe continued to enjoy what they seemed to have found in each other, and for the next few weeks everything drifted along beautifully.

Shaan did not return to work for him. It was her own decision, because she felt it wouldn't look good for Rafe if his new wife still worked in his typing pool while he lorded it—as she teasingly called it—up there on the uppermost floor.

And she wasn't a fool; she knew the people she used

to work with would not feel comfortable having her around them now that she was the chairman's wife.

Funny, really, because she hadn't suffered the same qualms about continuing working there as Piers new wife. But then, Piers was not the big boss, only a little boss. He had headed the company sales team, which put him in daily contact with the Danvers' lower echelons, which in turn made him more accessible.

And Piers liked to be liked, was always quick with the light joke and the easy smile which helped put people at their ease with him.

Rafe wasn't the kind of man who cared if he was liked or not. He was the man at the top who everyone else looked up to. The big decision man. The man who could hire and fire the rest, promote their careers or ruin them if he felt so inclined.

And never in a million years could Shaan see Rafe strolling down to his own typing pool to blithely plonk himself on the corner of her desk for a light chat the way Piers had used to do without anyone else so much as batting an eyelid.

In other words, Rafe was a man to be in awe of—not to be comfortable with. So it therefore followed that no one was going to feel comfortable with Shaan working with them any more, knowing that she would be listening in on all their conversations, hearing their gripes and groans and perhaps reporting them to Rafe.

Like a spy in their midst.

And even though Shaan knew she wouldn't dream of telling tales on any of them she in turn would feel like a spy.

Nor did she fancy having to face the kind of curious speculation that must be running rife around the building about the bizarre events leading up to her marriage. So, in the end, the decision not to go back to work there was easy. And the fact that Rafe didn't try to change her mind had to mean that he, too, didn't fancy the idea of having his wife working for him any more.

But neither was she prepared to sit in his house like some pampered doll, with nothing more to do than fill her days making herself desirable for him when he got in from work each night. So she joined up with a secretarial temping agency and, once she got used to moving around from place to place like a transient, found she rather enjoyed it.

She enjoyed the fact that it gave her a bit of anonymity, because she was never at one place long enough for anyone to grow curious enough to start asking her questions about her personal life, and therefore inevitably put two and two together with the Danvers name and the sensational headlines which had appeared in the tabloids several weeks earlier.

And, to top all of that, it also gave her an interest and a sense of independence—and something to talk about in the evening with this passionate man she had married which didn't revolve around bed and sex.

Bed and sex—the only two things they really had in common, if she'd only had the sense to take the foolish blinkers from her eyes. But she didn't, so everything jogged along perfectly for those few more blissful weeks. And if Jemma's caution did pop into her head once or twice, to try to warn her that this extended honeymoon could not go on for ever, she ignored it. Ignored, too, what the warm glow of pleasure she experienced every time Rafe walked into the room was trying to tell her.

Because to face it meant threatening the precarious little boat of contentment she was happily sailing in.

So fate did it for her. Fate, cruel fate, took the decision to reach out and rip the blinkers from her foolish eyes. And the fact that it happened in the middle of a busy London street was a further cruelty, because it left her so open and publicly exposed to what she was being forced to see.

Rafe was supposed to be away—a three-day business trip to the States, he had told her. It was the first time they had been separated since the day they had married, and Shaan missed him beside her in their bed every night—missed him dreadfully.

He rang her, though. Every night before she went to bed he would call to say goodnight, his voice warm and tender, huskily sincere when he said how much he was missing her. In fact, his whole manner towards her had become warm and tender over the last few weeks, the passion tempered to something which verged almost on loving.

Just another illusion fate decided to shatter.

So it was perhaps fortunate that Jemma was there to catch Shaan when she finally saw the full depths of her own delusions.

It was Wednesday, and she and Jemma were on their way to their regular Wednesday lunch together at their usual wine bar. Rafe was due back tonight, and Shaan was lost in her own thoughts as they walked along, thinking of his return and all the plans she had made to surprise him when he got home. It was Mrs Clough's day off, so she was planning to a cook a very special dinner for them herself, and she had bought a new dress that was hardly more than a couple of scraps of choco-late-brown silk, the fabric so fine that it didn't allow anything else to be worn beneath it.

In short, she planned to seduce him from the moment he walked in through the door. Her eyes glowed with a darkly luminous anticipation for the moment as she walked down that busy London street, hardly hearing a word Jemma was saying to her about table arrangements and flowers and all the other wedding details which were filling her best friend's mind.

Then she saw them coming out of a hotel entrance on the other side of the street and everything—*everything* living inside her—slammed to a stark, shuddering stop.

It was Rafe with Madeleine.

They paused on the hotel steps. He turned towards her at the same moment that she turned towards him—a tiny creature who had to tilt her golden head right back so she could gaze into his lean dark face.

Her hands came up, touching his lapels as she murmured something urgent to him that made him bring his own hands up to cover hers while he made some equally urgent reply.

The golden head shook as she murmured something else, and, on a sigh that seemed to rasp from the very depth of his soul, he muttered something tightly—then lowered his dark head to kiss her.

'No,' Shaan whispered, still trying for denial.

Yes, insisted fate. This is it. Truth time. Look at it. Look at it.

And to make sure that she did the veil of self-delusion was ripped cleanly from her eyes so that she was seeing—seeing it all—in a wild, wretched kaleidoscope of cruel images. All of them revolving around Rafe.

Rafe, the man she'd married. Rafe, the man she had given herself to night after night after night. Rafe, the man she had come to trust and believe in.

The man she had fallen madly, blindly—*stupidly*—in love with while he still loved Madeleine. Had never stopped loving Madeleine.

She must have staggered, though she wasn't aware of it, but something alerted Jemma. 'Shaan?' she questioned sharply. 'What the hell—?' Then, 'My God,' she gasped out rashly. 'Isn't that Rafe over there with that woman…?'

Shaan heard no more, because she was suddenly running—running madly, blindly, in an effort to get away before she fell apart inside.

'Shaan!'

She ignored Jemma's sharp call of alarm, ignored the muttered complaints from people she bumped into, ignored everything as she ran, swerving around corners and crossing busy roads without looking, running away from herself as much as she was running away from Rafe.

'Shaan!' It was Jemma's hand closing around her arm and yanking fiercely on it that stopped her from running out beneath the wheels of a car. 'For goodness' sake!' she gasped in shaken fury. 'What are you trying to do—kill yourself?'

'I have to—get away,' Shaan panted, beginning to shake—shake violently.

'You have to calm down,' Jemma countered sternly. And, keeping a firm hold on Shaan's arm, she glanced impatiently around her. 'Come on,' she said. 'We're only a step away from the wine bar. Let's go and get you a stiff drink, then you can tell me what the hell all of this is about...'

Grimly she guided Shaan along the street and in through the wine bar doors. 'Now,' she said once she had secured them a table over in the corner of the room and set a stiff brandy in front of Shaan. 'Who was that woman? Did you know her?'

'That was M-Madeleine,' Shaan whispered shakily.

'You mean the same Madeleine Piers married?' Jemma said frowningly. 'But what's so wrong with that? She is Rafe's sister-in-law, after all.'

'He's in love with her. He always has been.' Always will be, she added silently, and closed her eyes as she began to shake again, so badly that Jemma picked up the brandy glass and put it to her lips.

'Drink,' she commanded. 'You need it. Drink.'

Almost desperately, Shaan drank, felt the burning va-
pours permeate through her system, and at last began to
get a hold on herself. The terrible shaking slowed and
the colour in her face returned, easing into something a
little less corpse-like.

'Now explain what you mean,' Jemma insisted grimly
after watching all of this happen.

Explain. Shaan's long lashes fluttered open to reveal
dark brown irises gone utterly bottomless with a shock
and horror Rafe would have instantly recognised if he
had been there to see it happen.

But as it was Rafe was with Madeleine.

'Rafe is in love with M-Madeleine,' Shaan repeated
threadily. 'I th-think they even got together for a time,'
she added. 'Until M-Madeleine became confused as to
which brother sh-she really loved and ended up running
away f-from both of them to her mother in the States.'

'And how do you know all of this?'

'Rafe told me.' And, if it was possible, her eyes went
even blacker. 'I—overheard s-something he said on the
telephone and—and faced him with it.' She swallowed
thickly. 'So he told m-me...'

Jemma stared at her, shocked—yet not shocked, because she had always suspected that there was some hidden reason why Rafe Danvers had taken his brother's
place.

But because he loved his brother's wife?

'And you've stayed with him?' she muttered as anger
began to burn up inside her. 'After finding this out?'

'I'd just lost Piers,' Shaan answered lamely. 'And
Rafe had lost M-Madeleine.' She couldn't even say the
other woman's name without stumbling sickeningly over
it. 'As he said, why not console each other...?'

'Oh, very cute,' Jemma angrily derided. 'The schem-
ing rotter!' Her eyes began to flash. 'Didn't he bother to

consider what an arrangement like that was likely to do
to you after what you had just gone through with Piers?'

'We both went through it,' Shaan corrected. 'And
h-he's been very good to me,' she added defensively—
though why she was defending him after what she had
seen today, she didn't know or understand. 'I can't believe he would do anything to deliberately h-hurt me.'

'So why are you sitting here right now—*hurting* so
badly you can barely cope?' Jemma mocked all of that
tightly.

'Don't...' Shaan whispered, lowering her dark head.

'Don't?' Jemma repeated. 'I'd like to throttle the devious life out of him, the underhand bastard.'

'He can't help loving her, Jemma,' Shaan choked out
thickly.

'Oh, no?' She mocked that too. 'So if Piers happened
to walk in here right now, you would feel justified in
falling into his arms, would you?'

No; Shaan shook her bowed head. 'Not Piers,' she
whispered. But if Rafe should walk in here....

'Oh, no,' Jemma breathed, beginning to catch on at
last. 'You fool, Shaan,' she muttered. 'You damned
bloody fool...'

And fool just about said it, Shaan accepted bleakly.
She was a fickle, blind, gullible fool.

'Here.' The brandy glass appeared in front of Shaan
again. 'Drink some more of this.'

She was trembling again, she realised as the glass
chattered against her teeth.

'So, what are you going to do now?' Jemma asked
her quietly.

I don't know, she thought, and closed her eyes
again—then wished she hadn't when she saw Rafe's expression just before he'd kissed Madeleine.

It had been pained. It had been racked by an angry,
helpless, useless frustration. And it split Shaan's heart in

two, because it had been the look of a man who was angrily aware that his love was unrequited.

She recognised it because she knew the feeling, and it hurt—hurt like hell.

Yet what right did she have to be sitting here feeling hurt and betrayed when she'd always known where Rafe's true feelings lay? It wasn't Rafe's fault that she had done the stupid thing and fallen in love with him.

He hadn't asked for love from her, had he?

But he had insisted that both Piers and Madeleine were kept out of their marriage, she grimly reminded herself. And him being with Madeleine was a betrayal of the trust she had placed in him to keep his side of that vow.

'Are you going to leave him?'

Leave?

Panic swept through her. A terrible, terrible panic that filled her with a sickening horror that turned her flesh to ice.

Oh, God help me! she prayed, when she realised just how far she had fallen. 'I can't think now,' she whispered, pushing trembling fingers to her burning eyes. 'I need some time—some space to—'

'What you need, Shaan—' Jemma cut in with a blistering impatience '—is to get those damned blinkers off! Wasn't it bad enough when you wore them all the time Piers was around, without you doing the same thing with his thankless brother?'

Shaan's head came up. 'W-what do you mean?' she gasped at the angry outburst.

Jemma glanced away, her eyes flashing with a bitter disdain that literally shook Shaan to her very core. 'Piers made a damned mockery out of you from day one,' she bit out tightly. 'Everyone else could see it—see those charming smiles of his and that easygoing manner was all just an act. But you, you fell for it all like the trusting

little fool you are, and got well and truly hurt for it!
Now you've been doing the same damned thing with his
brother!' she sighed out angrily. 'So do yourself a favour, Shaan,' Jemma finished huskily, 'and get out from
under it all before the damned Danvers brothers really
tear you apart!'

Too late, Shaan thought tragically. They've already
torn me apart.

'What do you think they were doing, coming out of
that hotel in the first place?' Jemma questioned suddenly.

Oh, my God! Shaan stood up, unable—just unable—
to cope with the obvious answer to that one. 'I h-have
to go,' she murmured shakily.

'No, Shaan!' Jemma's hand, grabbing hold of hers,
stopped her from moving, her eyes full of a pained remorse because she knew she had just cruelly hit Shaan
below the belt. 'I'm sorry I said that. Please!' she
pleaded. 'Sit down again while we discuss this! You're
in no fit state to go anywhere just yet!'

No fit state.

She was still in no fit state by the time she let herself
into Rafe's house over an hour later.

She should have gone back to work, but she hadn't
been able to. What was the use when she could barely
think, barely walk, barely do anything with any intelligence, she felt so utterly frozen inside.

But neither did she want to be alone in this house, she
realised from the very moment she entered it. It had
begun to feel like home over the last few blissful weeks;
now it was back to being the most alien place this earth
had to offer her.

And as she stood there in the middle of all its polished
wood luxury her mind flicked towards another home, a
real home—not a place built around an illusion.

The only home she wanted to be in at this precise moment in her life...

When the doorbell started ringing around eight o'clock that night, Shaan was expecting it, but still found it took a concerted effort to make herself get out of the chair she had been sitting on the edge of while supposedly watching television. But she had really been waiting for this.

A showdown with Rafe.

Dry-mouthed, her face composed but very pale, she made herself leave the sitting room and walk down the hall towards the front door. She could see his tall, dark bulk superimposed against the leaded glass in the door, felt his anger reach through the barrier as he gave another impatient stab at the doorbell, and she ran decidedly shaky hands down the sides of her faded jeans.

She hadn't worn these jeans since she'd left here—her aunt and uncle's house—almost two months ago—or the simply knitted waist-cut blue top she had on. Both were part of the hodgepodge of personal items she had left behind here and never quite got around to coming to collect.

Now it was Rafe's house where clothes of hers had been left hanging. In fact, she hadn't brought anything with her, had not been able to bear the thought of walking into the bedroom they'd always shared to go and pack them.

So all she had done was go into his study so she could write him a note which she had sealed in an envelope along with her beautiful engagement ring. Not her wedding ring—she felt her official status as his wife compelled her to continue wearing that—but as for the rest...

She had taken nothing from that house—nothing—leaving her set of house keys and the envelope on the hall table so he would see them the moment he came home.

The note was short and to the point—by necessity—because she needed to finish this with at least some semblance of pride left intact, and the only way she could do that was by not telling him that she had decided to leave him only because she had discovered that he had betrayed her first.

So, 'I can't go on living a lie like this. I'm sorry', was all she had written.

And now here he was, as she had expected, come to make her face him with the whys that she had no real answers to if she wanted to conceal the truth.

The truth. My God, she groaned inwardly as the full, wretched truth of it all went washing through her on a wave of utter misery.

You're a fool, Shaan, she told herself grimly as her shaky fingers fumbled with the door lock and slowly drew the door open. You stupid, gullible fool.

Then her heart quivered, the morass of pained emotions all tying themselves into knots just as they had always done from the moment she had ever set eyes on this man.

He was standing there in the same clothes he had been wearing when she saw him with Madeleine. The same iron-grey suit he had crushed the other woman against when he'd bent down to kiss her. Same bright white shirt, same striped blue tie—only the fine silk had been yanked loose about his tense, tanned throat and the top few buttons on his shirt had been impatiently tugged free.

His face wore the grim, tight mask she recognised from somewhere, but at the moment she was just too strung out to want to recall where. His grey eyes were flat as they searched her set pale face for a sign that this was all just some kind of very bad joke.

But it wasn't, and he seemed to accept that it wasn't. 'May I come in?' he requested quietly.

With her long dark lashes flickering downwards to cover her too-revealing eyes, she took a small step sideways in silent permission for him to enter.

He did so, making her heart stop beating altogether when he came to a halt directly beside her. Her fingers tightened into a white-knuckled clutch on the solid brass door lock. And for a moment they continued to stand there like that, locked into a circle of unbelievable tension, while the full power of his magnetic presence bombarded her with all the weak reasons why she should not be doing this.

Then his hand came up, making her stiffen in silent rejection because she thought he was going to touch her and she couldn't bear him to touch her. Because she knew that the whole roller coaster of emotion would spring free from the tight band of control she had it trapped in. And if that happened she would fall apart—she was sure of it!

But all he did was carefully take the door from her clutching fingers and quietly close it before moving off towards the sitting room. Leaving her standing there trembling and shaken, needing to take a few more moments to pull herself together again before she found the courage to go and join him.

CHAPTER TEN

RAFE was standing in the middle of the room, jacket pushed back, clenched hands resting on his hips in a posture that could only be read as aggressive.

'Now you'd better explain to me what this is all about,' he said. 'And it had better be good, Shaan,' he tagged on warningly. 'Because I am tired and I'm jet lagged and I'm in no mood for any of this.'

She could see that. She wasn't a fool. She could see that he was angry—pulsing with it, actually. Throbbing. 'I told you—in my note,' she said. And looked down and away from him—simply because it hurt too much to look upon that big, lean body and that hard, handsome face, look upon the man who, somewhere along the line, she had allowed herself to imagine really did belong to her.

And that had been her biggest mistake, she realised now—forgetting how they'd begun all of this and believing the illusion.

'About living a lie? Is that what you think we've being doing, living one big lie?'

'Yes.' It was that honest, that simple. She didn't even need to expand on it.

But neither could she continue to just stand here, loving him—hating him. Wishing she had never seen him with Madeleine.

Because all she could see now was him holding Madeleine. And it hurt—hurt so damned much that she had to do something, anything, to override that vision.

It was then that she noticed the television set talking away to its lost audience, and she used that as her excuse, moving stiffly across the room to reach down and switch it off—then almost immediately wished she hadn't when a new kind of silence began throbbing in the laden atmosphere.

'So you leave me, just like that,' Rafe pressed into that thickened silence. 'No discussion. Without even the slightest hint that you may feel like this. You just wake up this morning deciding that we've been living a lie and calmly walk out on me?'

His anger and contempt and derision cut into her like a knife, and she responded instinctively. 'What would you have preferred me to do?' she turned to flash back at him. 'Continue pretending until *you'd* had enough?'

That shocked him, the real bitterness in her tone hitting him on a raw spot that expanded his wide chest in a sharp intake of air.

But it also made him look at her—really look at her—which in turn made her wish she had held her tongue. Because she knew he was now seeing the strain in her face, the pallor, the black orbs of pain that would remind him of another time when he had witnessed her hurting as badly as this.

Sure enough, his eyes narrowed shrewdly. 'There's something else going on here,' he decided. 'I've done something, haven't I?' His perception stunned her. 'I've unwittingly done something that offended you so badly you just walked out on me!'

Shaan's heart contracted. 'Isn't it enough that we've spent the last two months living out a lie together?' she shot back defensively.

'No, it isn't,' he grimly denied, starting towards her. And she had to steel herself not to back off, there was so much latent anger in his manner. 'Because what we share every night in our bed is no lie, Shaan, and you know it!'

'There's more to a marriage than basic sex, you know,' she denounced as he reached her.

'Yes,' he nodded. 'There's a thing called sharing—the good and the bad things. And another called talking.' His hand came up, cupping her pale cheek. 'As in discussing our problems and trying to resolve them.'

'I've already resolved mine,' she snapped. 'By leaving.'

'Why?'

'I've told you why!' Angrily she slapped his hand away from her cheek before she did something stupid like turning her hungry mouth into it.

He simply put it back again. 'Then try again,' he suggested. 'And keep on trying until you come up with something I can accept as the truth. Because if you expect me to believe, Shaan, that you can't stand me touching you, then you're a fool, and, worse, must think me a damned fool!'

And to prove his point his other hand snaked round her waist to pull her against the solid heat of his body. It was awful. She couldn't even control the sharp intake of air into her lungs as the sweet, hot sting of awareness shivered through her.

'It was wrong, Rafe!' she burst out in sheer desperation. 'I did tell you from the beginning that what we were doing felt wrong to me!'

'"Wrong."' His eyes began to burn. 'Four nights ago you lay in my arms with your legs wrapped around me and your eyes drowning in my eyes while we shared the most—perfect experience we have ever shared. And you *dare* to tell me it was wrong now?'

Oh, God. She closed her eyes, swallowing as a dry lump of pain lodged itself in her aching throat because she was suddenly seeing him lying with Madeleine like that, and she couldn't bear it—she couldn't!

'I never said the sex wasn't good!' she responded wretchedly.

'Then what are you saying?' he persisted relentlessly. 'That it isn't enough any more?'

'It was never enough!'

Not for either of them, obviously! Or he would not have needed to have secret meetings with Madeleine, would he?

Once again she tried to tug free of his grip.

Once again he refused to let her go. 'OK,' he murmured. 'Then tell me what it is you do want and I'll do my best to give it to you!'

And his voice was tense—dark and tense—roughened by a bone-melting urgency that almost had her believing that he must care more than she thought he did.

Then she saw him with Madeleine and it all fell apart. 'You can't give me what I want,' she whispered bleakly.

There was silence while he absorbed the full, brutal thrust of that, a long, taut, agonising silence while she stood against him and throbbed with the agony of her own unrequited love for him.

'My God,' he breathed then as a sudden thought hit him. 'It's Piers, isn't it?'

'What?' Shaan frowned in confusion. 'I don't—'

'Shut up!' he cut in, and suddenly let go of her, spinning away, a hand going up to rake through his hair before it clamped itself around his nape and stayed there while he glared down at the floor beneath his feet. His big shoulders, body—every part of him—was locked in a rigid pose of tension that held her breathless and silent.

Then he let out a soft, angry huff of laughter. 'I should have guessed straight away,' he muttered, more to himself than to her. 'The bastard arrives back in London on Monday and you've left me by Wednesday!'

'But I haven't even seen Piers,' she denied, not seeing that he was offering her a way out of this ugly scene until it was too late and the denial had already been made.

It didn't matter, because he didn't believe her. 'Liar,' he sighed, unclipping the hand from his nape so he could clench it into a fist which he pushed to his brow. 'Of course you've damned well seen him.'

Had he come to that conclusion because of his own clandestine meeting with Madeleine? she wondered. And would have laughed at the irony of it—if she had been up to laughing.

But she wasn't because she was closer to weeping.

Then he let out another of those laughs, as if he too saw the bitter irony in the whole wretched mess. 'What did he do?' he flashed sourly at her. 'Shoot hotfoot round to see you at the first opportunity he had, knowing I was out of the country which therefore made the weasel feel safe enough to bare his soul to you and beg forgiveness?'

Well, that's rich, Shaan thought, coming from the man she had seen with her own eyes begging something from Madeleine! And in an act of sheer defiance she lifted her chin, her mouth flattening into a tight little line in an outright refusal to answer him.

So he made up his own answer. 'The bloody worm,' he gritted. 'How long did it take him to slither his way back into your heart, Shaan?' he taunted jeeringly. 'A couple of minutes? An hour, playing the poor, confused lover?'

'You're beginning to sound jealous, Rafe,' she hit back tightly.

It had the most unbelievable effect on him.

His eyes changed, turning almost as black as her own, and heat poured into his face as if she'd just exposed some terrible, dark secret that forced the top off his barely held anger. And it was the sight of that anger which had her stumbling back a step in real alarm in an effort to avoid the hard hand that suddenly shot out towards her.

But she was too late to stop it from curling around the back of her neck and tightening as he yanked her up against him. Then his mouth landed on hers, hot, hard and merciless.

And everything special she had ever felt for him dropped like a wounded bird to the pit of her stomach and lay there quivering as he proceeded to plunder her mouth with a ruthlessness that utterly reviled everything they had ever shared before it.

By the time he let her go she was actually sobbing, her tear-filled eyes almost filling her whitened face.

'Get your things out of my house,' he gritted as he spun away from her. 'I don't want to find a single sign that you've ever been there by the time I get home tomorrow night—got that?'

Got it? Oh, she'd got it, all right, Shaan acknowledged with a blistering fury of her own as she watched him stride angrily for the door through a bank of hot, stinging tears.

What was OK for him was unacceptable for her!

'And just for the record,' he added tightly as he reached the door, 'you can warn Piers from me that if he hurts Madeleine with all of this then I'll personally sort him out.'

Ah, thought Shaan with a strange little smile pulsing across the fullness of her kiss-swollen lips. So we come to the nitty-gritty of all this aggression. Poor Madeleine. We must not upset Madeleine.

'You utter hypocrite,' she derided.

It stopped him mid-stride, turned the full blast of his black fury back on her as he spun to face her. 'What was that supposed to mean?' he demanded.

'I saw you with Madeleine!' she flung at him accusingly.

'What?' It was his turn to frown in confusion. 'When?'

'Today.' Why, she wondered jealously, have there been other occasions when you've met up with her? 'On the steps of the Connaught.' On a flash of shaking contempt she continued, 'So don't you dare stand there taking the moral high ground over Piers and me when you are no better yourself!'

Then instantly she wished she had held her stupid tongue when she saw his expression take on a sudden and radical change as all that dark, angry violence was replaced by a sharp, shrewd intelligence.

Angry with herself, she spun her back to him. 'You were about to leave, I think,' she prompted into the new stunning silence, in the vague hope that her dismissal would throw him off the scent.

No chance.

'That's it, isn't it?' he breathed, putting all that sharp intelligence he was so renowned for into words. 'It's what all of this is really all about—not you and Piers, but me and Madeleine!'

Madeleine! God—she physically shuddered at the damned, blasted name. 'Will you just get out of here?'

'Not until I get the truth out of you!' He was suddenly standing right behind her again, making her nerves sting, making her heart ache, making the wretched tears burn at the back of her throat because she wanted so badly to just turn round and throw herself on him!

Throw herself and lose herself. Find blissful relief in the illusion again.

Rafe did it. It was Rafe who took hold of her, turned her, drew her into the tight confines of his arms and held her there while she tried desperately to struggle free.

'Let go of me!' she choked out wretchedly.

'No,' he grunted, tightening his grip. 'I want the

truth!' he insisted. 'Have you seen anything of Piers since you married me?'

She wanted to lie and shout yes because she knew it would hurt him. No matter what he still felt for Madeleine, she knew now that she still had the power to hurt him with Piers.

But she couldn't lie, not any more; she'd had enough of all the lying! 'I did tell you I hadn't seen him!' she snapped out in raking derision of the quick way he had jumped to all the wrong damned conclusions.

It was a derision entirely wasted because he just ignored it. 'But you saw me with Madeleine today,' he persisted. 'And on that one sighting you decided to leave me without even bothering to demand an explanation! Is that it?'

'I did warn you, Rafe, that I would not live with Madeleine's ghost hanging over me.'

'And you think I could live any easier with Piers' ghost hanging over *me*?'

'You have no reason to see his ghost!' she flashed at him bitterly. 'Since I haven't so much as mentioned him—never mind been secretly meeting him!'

'It was no secret meeting.' He denied that one.

Shaan just shrugged within his grasp. 'It doesn't matter. You met her, I saw you, and now I can't live with you any more. It really is as simple as that.' She tried to get away from him.

'The hell it is,' he muttered. 'It's really as simple as—this...'

'This' being his mouth as it closed over her own again. 'This' being the well of helpless dark need that surged up over all the anger and hurt and self-contempt she was desperately trying to deal with, drowning it, smothering it, tossing her into that helpless vortex of desire she couldn't seem to contain, no matter how badly he hurt her.

'Do you kiss Madeleine that ruthlessly?' she retorted as he drew away.

She had said it to cut, but all it did was bring a strangely mocking smile to his kiss-warmed lips, and made his darkened eyes burn a trail from her own angrily accusing eyes to her mouth, where her lower lip visibly pulsed now with the power of his two heated kisses.

'Madeleine,' he mocked, 'wouldn't know real passion if it jumped out and bit her. Like this,' he added softly, and took that pulsing lower lip into his mouth and sucked so sensually on it that she groaned in hateful pleasure. 'Whereas you, my darling, just can't live without it.'

And he set out to make her face the humiliating truth in that remark by holding his mouth a mere fraction away from hers then simply waiting—waiting until she couldn't stand it any longer and had to be the one who hungrily closed the gap.

He had her then, and he knew it. The way her arms snaked up and round his neck confirmed it; the way her fingers scraped into his silky dark hair so she could keep that mouth clamped fiercely to her own confirmed it. And the way her slender body began to pulsate sensually against the hard length of his most definitely confirmed it.

And the way he had to use brute strength to break the kiss and bodily put her away from him gave the ultimate confirmation.

'I hate and despise you,' she whispered in pained mortification as she literally shook from head to toe in sensual deprivation.

'Strange emotion, hate,' he drawled, mocking her with the hard triumph glinting in his eyes. 'It has a nasty little habit of overwhelming everything, even love, in the end. Now, get your coat,' he added, arrogantly turning his back on her. 'We're going home.'

'No!' Shaan protested on an upsurge of a completely new set of emotions as real horror at what he was suggesting ran like acid through her heated blood. 'I'm not coming back to you, Rafe!'

She would not live under Madeleine's shadow any more!

'You're coming,' he insisted.

'But why?' she cried. 'When you know you don't really want me there?'

'You don't know what I want,' he derided with a contempt that actually managed to reach something wretched inside her—because he was right. She didn't know—except that he still wanted her body, of course. For all his taunting love-play a moment ago, Rafe had not been able to hide his own desire as it sprang up to meet with hers. 'But it's time—damned well past time— you found out what it is I do want,' he added grimly. 'So you've got ten minutes to close this house up. Then we go home—if I have to tie you up and gag you to get you there,' he added threateningly.

And she believed he would do it, too. There was something about the hard resolve written in his tight expression that warned her he would.

'Ten minutes,' he repeated when she continued to stand there, trying to work out what he had in store for her when he did eventually get her home—besides the sex, of course, she acknowledged. That part was so stingingly obvious to both of them that it wasn't even worth denying it.

And maybe that was all he did want, she suggested to herself as she reluctantly left the room to go and do as he had ordered. Maybe it was all he ever wanted with any woman. And that included Madeleine, she decided on a small sting of pure female triumph over the other woman. Because, whatever hold Madeleine had over Rafe's heart, she didn't move him sexually; that much was clear from the way he had mocked her lack of passion just now.

'I'm ready,' she said stiffly, coming to stand at the living room doorway in time to catch him pocketing his mobile phone.

The action made her frown, made her wonder just who he had been talking to. But it was clear from his closed expression that he was not going to enlighten her as he sent a swift glance around the room, which, Shaan realised, had already been made safe for their departure.

Then he was walking towards her, one hand going proprietorially about her waist while the other went to switch off the overhead light.

Her spine arched as he touched it, sending that now familiar prickle of awareness chasing through her.

'Next time we come here,' he murmured meaningfully, 'it will be to welcome your aunt and uncle home.'

Shaan said nothing. What could she say? That hand resting on her tingling spine knew it all anyway.

She belonged to him. His sex slave, she mocked herself grimly. If he changed his mind and decided to take her here and now in this tiny hallway she would let him, and they both knew it.

But, 'I still hate you,' she whispered as he closed the front door on them.

'I know,' he smiled. 'Hell, isn't it? Hating someone you can't get enough of?'

Was that empathy she heard there? she wondered dully. Did Rafe feel exactly the same way about her?

The car journey to his home was completed in a grim kind of silence neither of them attempted to break. She wasn't sure why, but he was very tense, getting more tense the closer they got to his Kensington home. And that in turn made her tense, as if she were having to armour herself against some unseen horror she was about to be forced into facing.

As instincts went, she had to acknowledge that hers were working extremely well today, she noted as they pulled up beside another car parked in the driveway.

She didn't recognise it, but that didn't stop her filling up inside with a dark sense of ill omen.

'Someone else is here,' she pointed out absolutely unnecessarily. 'Who is it, do you think?'

Rafe didn't bother to answer, his lean face tightly closed as he climbed out of the car and came around to help her alight. Maintaining a grip on her arm, he unlocked the front door and guided her inside, then down his beautiful hallway to the sitting room door where he seemed to pause for a moment as if to gather himself.

Then he was pushing the door open and grimly inviting her to precede him inside.

And it was then, and only then, as her eyes locked on the man who stood waiting inside the room, that she realised what that pause had been about.

Piers.

Piers—looking stiff and uncomfortable, the expression in his classically handsome face very guarded to say the least as he flicked his wary blue gaze up to his brother then back to Shaan again.

He didn't speak. No one did. And behind her she could feel Rafe's tension pulsing all over her as he stood there in the sudden clamouring silence, watching both of them.

Then something vital seemed to crack wide open inside her, stopping her breath and holding her pinned like a weighted piece of wood to the spot while her mind came to terms with what Rafe was doing here.

Making the jilter face the jilted.

And, from somewhere within the stunning tension holding all three of them captive, Shaan reacted. 'Well, well,' she drawled. '*Both* Danvers brothers. This is nice.

All we need now is for Madeleine to appear and we can do a bit of bride-swapping.'

Piers flinched. 'Don't, Shaan,' he mumbled uncomfortably.

Don't? she thought furiously. So what would he prefer I do—fall into a fit of broken-hearted hysterics? 'I don't need this,' she muttered, spinning back to the doorway.

But Rafe stood solidly in her way. 'You're staying,' he insisted, using his hands on her shoulders to keep her there. 'You said you couldn't live a lie any longer, so we're going to see if you can live any better with the truth.'

The truth?

'Do you honestly think I'm about to believe a single thing Piers has to say?' she demanded bitterly.

'You will if he values his position in this family,' Rafe stated grimly—and that was said for Piers' benefit, not Shaan's. 'He knows why he's here, and he knows what's at stake here.' His eyes, gone stone-grey with resolve, fixed on her own accusing ones. 'So you stay,' he repeated. 'You listen. Then he goes and we talk.'

With that arrogant proclamation, Rafe unclipped his hands from her shoulders then turned and walked out of the room, firmly closing the door behind him.

And the new silence throbbed with a pulsing reluctance on both sides.

It was Piers who decided to break it. 'I think the *unspoken* implication there was that I leave horizontally if I dare to upset you,' he suggested drily.

It was an attempt on his part to make light of it all. But Shaan was in no mood for his unique brand of wit, as her icy expression told him when she turned round to face him.

He saw it and acknowledged it with a rueful little grimace. 'Don't find me funny any more, Shaan?' he quizzed.

'No,' she replied. 'And neither do I have anything to say to you,' she tagged on coolly.

'I didn't think you would.' Another grimace. 'But big brother insisted—or at least,' he added, 'he maintains that I have a lot to say to you.'

'Well, I have no wish to hear it,' she countered stiffly. 'In fact, I'll even make it easy for you, Piers, and tell you that you did me a favour walking out on me the way that you did.'

'Because you got Rafe instead of me?'

Her chin came up. 'I adore him,' she declared with absolute honesty. 'Within a week of being with him, I'd even forgotten what you looked like.'

He winced at that. 'So, what's new?' he said, on a sigh that took with it every vestige of humour. 'Rafe has been upstaging me all my life, so having you fall out of love with me to fall in love with him is no real surprise, Shaan. In fact,' he added grimly, 'I always expected it.'

'What is that supposed to imply?' She frowned, not following where he seemed to be leading.

'Just what it said.' And with a small shrug of his elegant shoulders he turned to walk over to the window. It was dark outside, so dark he surely couldn't see much further than the paved terrace. Yet Piers managed to fix his gaze on something out there.

'All my life I've been in competition with Rafe over something,' he told her heavily. 'When I was younger, I was competing for my father's approval, to be an equally worthy son—the unattainable,' he mocked, 'since everyone including myself knew I could never be to him what good old Rafe was. His first-born.' He said it drily. 'The big, tough, incredibly clever one. It was the same at school,' he added, thrusting his hands into his trouser pockets, while Shaan quietly moved over to the nearest chair and lowered herself into it. She was

interested in what he was saying—despite not wanting
to be.

'I attended the same schools where good old Rafe had
been before me and left behind him the kind of legacy
that was almost impossible to live up to—though I tried,'
he confessed, with yet more of that grim self-mockery.
'I did at least try to compete with the damned legend—
and failed again.' He huffed out a gruff bark of laughter.
'It was the same at work. Rafe Danvers the super-
heavyweight versus Piers the lightweight...'

Shaan found herself beginning to feel just a little sorry
for him, because he was right and she couldn't even lie
and say that he wasn't. Piers was classed as the weaker,
less effective brother. The easier one to be around because he didn't strike awe into all who met him.

'The only person,' he went on, 'I felt with an absolute
certainty cared more for me than she did for my brother
was Madeleine. She was mine.' His voice was gruff with
possession. 'Had always been mine from the first moment we met each other at some silly teenage party at
the age of fifteen. When Madeleine looked at me,' he
declared huskily, 'she saw no one else. Not any other
man but me. Mine!' he repeated. 'Yet, in the end, even
Madeleine betrayed me with Rafe.'

Shaan's heart squeezed with an aching empathy because, no matter what Piers had put her through, she
could understand what that must have meant to him—
simply because she knew how painful that particular betrayal felt.

'Rafe would have nothing to do with her, of course.'

Her head shot up, eyes widening in disbelief on the
back of Piers' fair head. He must know—surely—that
Rafe was in love with Madeleine?

Seemingly, he didn't. 'He just wouldn't do that to
me—though it's taken me these last few months of
Madeleine's constant nagging to make me acknowledge

that fact,' he confessed, with no conception of what Shaan was thinking. 'I'd become so used to blaming Rafe for every failure in my life, you see, that it just didn't occur to me that really he was the only person who truly loved me. Truly cared about me and my feelings and would never betray me...'

Oh, I wish that were true, Shaan thought heavily. How she wished it were all true. For Piers' sake.

Because she knew that, no matter how she had been treated by both Danvers brothers, Piers had worse coming to him if he was now seeing his brother as the noble knight in this terrible farce they were all taking part in.

Had he never heard of Lancelot and Guinevere?

'But before I let myself see all of this you happened,' he continued. 'With you, I saw my chance to make Rafe hurt as I believed he had made me hurt. And I'm sorry, Shaan.' At last he turned to face her. 'But I went for it without giving a single thought to how my actions were going to hurt you until it was too late to do anything about it.'

'Me?' Shaan frowned, having completely lost the thread of this. 'But why should you think that I could give you the power to hurt Rafe in any way?'

He frowned too, as though her question had thrown him. 'We all saw it, Shaan,' he proclaimed, as if that should make it all clearer. 'Every one of us that was involved in that bit of bulldozing we did at work the day we all bumped into you. We all stood there and watched in stunned disbelief the great man himself fall like a ton of bricks for the little typist from his own typing pool!'

He let out a grim crack of laughter while Shaan came slowly to her feet as the full, ghastly extent of Piers' revenge plan on his brother began to take shape in her head.

'You mean...?' She had to stop to swallow, having difficulty pushing words through the sudden bank of an-

ger beginning to pulse inside her. 'You mean, you sin-
gled me out and made me fall in love with you simply
because you believed you were stealing something that
Rafe wanted for himself?'

He didn't answer—didn't need to—because it was all
so horribly clear now.

Piers had cynically used her, played on her feelings,
coolly stretched the whole farce out to their actual wedding day before deciding to put a stop to it—and all
because he'd believed he was getting one back at Rafe?

'But Rafe was never in love with me, you cruel, crass,
blind fool, Piers!' she spat at him angrily. 'You put me
through all of that for nothing!'

'Of course he is,' he maintained—and had the damned
gall to start grinning at her! 'It was the buzz of the year
around the executive offices! Rafe of all people,' he murmured with cruel, dry satire, 'losing touch with his usual
impregnable cool while he bit Jack Mellor's head off
and scrambled around looking for an excuse to send him
off to apologise to you so he could discover who you
were without being too obvious about it!'

He let out a rueful laugh, his blue eyes alight with
enjoyment at the memory of the whole novel experience.
'If he hadn't been flying off to Hong Kong that same
day, he would have been laying siege at your door,
Shaan, I'm telling you,' he insisted. 'He was hit that hard
and that badly.'

Could it be true?

The very suggestion was enough to take Shaan's legs
from under her. She sank back into the chair as she began to teeter on the very edge of a desperate hope.

'But what about Madeleine?' she whispered.

'Madeleine?' Piers stiffened slightly, and all sign of
that sardonic humour was wiped clean from his features
as he suddenly became gruff-voiced and defensive.
'She's over him now,' he said. 'It was all just a silly

female crush she had on him,' he explained, 'which Rafe tried telling me often enough without me wanting to listen,' he added. 'But it hurt that Madeleine of all people would turn away from me towards Rafe. And I think Rafe had to be quite brutal with her in the end to snap her out of it.

'But,' he sighed, 'by then I wanted nothing to do with her, so she ran away to her mother in Chicago, and we didn't see each other again until Rafe dragged her back here when he realised what I was trying to do with you.'

None of which meant that Rafe was not in love with Madeleine himself, Shaan told herself firmly. Only that he had too much integrity to steal the woman his brother loved.

Unlike Piers; she made the grim comparison. 'Tell me, Piers,' she questioned quietly, 'would you have gone ahead and married me if Madeleine hadn't come back?'

His shoulders hunched inside the elegant cut of his jacket, his fair head dipping so he could stare down at his feet for a moment. 'I didn't pull back from marrying you for Madeleine's sake,' he told her. 'I did it because Rafe came to me and begged me not to do it to you.'

'Oh, come off it, Piers!' Shaan crossly denounced that. 'You'd already arranged to marry Madeleine on the same day you were supposed to be marrying me!'

His head came up, guilty colour heightening his cheekbones. 'I was going to leave Madeleine standing at the altar, not you, Shaan...'

And he acknowledged Shaan's shocked and horrified expression with a grimace of real self-contempt.

'I would have done it too,' he admitted. 'If Rafe hadn't come to me that morning looking desperate and so damned wretched that I...' He stopped to swallow, then on a tense sigh went on. 'You're right, Shaan. I am crass. I know it, you know it, and, my God, but Madeleine and Rafe both know it!'

There was another pause, another self-contemptuous grimace that said he wasn't liking this person he was revealing himself to be. 'Rafe laid his damned soul bare for me that morning,' he said hoarsely. 'And I've never felt so damned despicable in all my wretched life for forcing him, of all people, to have to do that.'

Rafe had actually gone to Piers that morning and begged him not to marry her?

'So you'd better damned well love him, Shaan,' Piers muttered threateningly. 'Because a man who is prepared to lay his pride at the feet of another man for the woman he loves deserves only the best kind of love back in return.'

He's got it, she thought as a warm glow began to suffuse the very centre of her being. Oh, yes, he's most definitely got it!

CHAPTER ELEVEN

IT TOOK Shaan a while to find Rafe because he wasn't in any of the rooms downstairs, though she checked inside them all. Eventually her search took her upstairs to their private suite of rooms—where she found him reclining in one of the big armchairs by the fireplace with his bare feet resting on the low coffee table in front of him.

He had just taken a shower, she assumed by the dampness still clinging to his silky dark hair, and he was wearing nothing more than his white towelling bathrobe. A glass of what looked like his favourite whisky sat on the carpet by the chair—untouched by the look of it, because he seemed to have fallen fast asleep of all things!

Jet lag, she remembered, and felt her heart flip in sympathy because he looked so utterly weary, even in repose.

Being careful not to wake him, she tiptoed further into the room and quietly closed the door behind her, then just stood there, taking a moment to lovingly drink in the sight of him while he couldn't know she was doing it.

This man loved her, she told herself warmly. This man loved her so much that he had gone to his own brother and begged him not to marry her. This man loved her so dynamically that he had then taken her over, married her himself, possessed and devoured her in his quest to hold onto her.

He had wrapped her in luxury, cocooned her in the dark, disturbing heat of his powerful sensuality. He had fought for her, made a fool out of himself for her in the

eyes of his peers, and finally, and perhaps most beautifully of all, he had put his pride on the line a second
time by letting Piers expose the truth to her.

The truth.

Her arms went wrapping around herself so she could
tightly hug that precious truth.

A truth that deserved truth back in return, she decided
as she stood there simply drinking in the lovely sight of
him.

And suddenly she was remembering the last time she
had found him stretched out in that chair like this. Only
he hadn't been asleep then, just relaxing with a whisky.

It made her smile, because she could still hear the
echo of her own teasing laughter as she'd strolled in here
from the bedroom wearing nothing but his cast-off shirt,
left hanging open on her own brazen nakedness, and
with her hair in wild disarray over her shoulders because
she had just been made wonderful love to. Which was
why he'd been sitting in that chair, wearing a look of
pure masculine gratification on his hard, handsome face.

'You look as if you've just been ravished,' she'd
heard herself murmur teasingly.

'There's a wicked witch living in this house,' had
been his sardonic reply. 'She's sex-mad. I need sustenance.' And ruefully he had lifted the whisky to his lips.

'So does the witch,' she'd responded, with so much
sensual provocation that she felt her cheeks grow warm
as in her mind she watched that wicked creature stroll
over to him and straddle his outstretched legs before she
took the whisky glass away from him and bent to replace
it with her own hungry mouth.

How long ago had that been? Two—maybe three
weeks? Yet she could still feel the electric contact of his
hands closing on her naked hipbones so he could draw
her down on top of him. Once again could feel him

throbbing, deep, deep inside her, pulsing as he strove to give her all of himself.

All of himself.

Shaan hugged that thought to herself too, but with more meaning than ever wrapped in its warmly sensual glow now she knew what she did know.

All of himself...

The words had a magical taste to them that filled her with a sudden desire to recreate those special moments, and, creeping quietly across the room so as not to waken him, she disappeared into their bedroom.

He was beginning to stir by the time she came back, with her hair hanging loose about her shoulders the way he liked it and her freshly showered body wrapped in a white fluffy robe to match his.

Her heart was beating a little too fast, because it was taking a lot of courage to go over to him dressed like this, not knowing what mood he was in.

His eyes were still closed, but one long fingered hand was cradling the squat crystal whisky glass now.

'Hi,' she murmured shyly, unsure of her welcome.

His eyes were slow to drift lazily open. That face, that beautiful, lean, dark face was grimly implacable as he looked up at her. 'Had your truth now?' he questioned flatly.

'Yes.' She smiled softly.

'And how was it?' He took a sip of his drink.

'Nice,' she admitted.

Then, before he had a chance to protest, she straddled his thighs with her own silken ones, bent to take the glass from his fingers, discarded it and sat herself down on his lap.

'So may I kiss you for it?' she requested. 'Or are you still too cross with me to want me to?'

He didn't answer, that grimly implacable expression

staying firmly in place as he merely closed his eyes again.

And Shaan had to ruefully accept that he wasn't going to make this easy for her.

'I could always go away again, if you're really that indifferent,' she offered.

No comment—again, the ruthless devil. He didn't even flicker a silky black eyelash.

'The trouble is,' she went on rather tragically, 'you're really much too old for me...' She decided to rile him out of his wretched apathy.

It didn't work.

'I know,' he agreed.

Her chest heaved on a small sigh. 'You have twelve whole years more experience than me of how to play these scenes. It isn't fair.'

The eyes opened, focusing directly on her. 'Are you asking me to wait around for twelve years while you try to catch up?' he enquired very drily.

'What use would that be?' she sighed. 'You'll always be twelve years better at it than me.'

'Well...' The eyes closed again. 'If it makes you feel any better, then I don't feel twelve years older—I feel fifty.'

'Oh, poor old man,' she mourned. Then caught his face in her hands and kissed him.

It took him completely by surprise.

But he didn't really stand a chance anyway.

Though, to be fair, he did try to put up a fight, going all tense beneath her, his hands snapping to her waist and trying to pull her away from him while his mouth remained utterly unresponsive against the coaxing pressure of hers.

But, having caught him off guard she was determined to keep him off guard, so she proceeded to press soft, seductively moist little kisses along the unresponsive line of his lips until the tension began to leave him and his hands stopped tugging, and his mouth finally caved in and began kissing her back instead.

'What was that for?' he grunted when she eventually let them both up for air again.

'Because, old man or not, I love you,' she replied, and watched his mouth take on a cynical twist that completely derided that claim.

'Where's Piers?' he asked then, as if he automatically related the word 'love' with Piers' name where she was concerned.

'Gone,' she said. 'Back to his insipid little wife who can't kiss for toffee.'

Silky dark eyebrows arched at that. 'He said that, did he?'

'No.' She shook her head. 'But you did. Though why I should believe a single word that you say when you lie as well as you do, I don't know,' she added sagely.

'Ah.' He was beginning to catch on at last. 'So he told you it all, did he?'

'He feels guilty,' Shaan explained. 'Because he forced you into having to beg him to let me go.'

'Beg?' he said in protest. 'The liar. I threatened to kill him if he didn't put a stop to his stupid games, but I object to being accused of begging!'

Shaan just shrugged. 'Well, Piers saw it as you begging. And...' her dark eyes took on the lustrous quality of wicked, dangerous teasing '...I rather like the idea of you *begging* him to jilt me so you could jump into his place.'

'I'd watch my step, if I were you, Shaan,' he warned very quietly. 'Because I am still damned angry with you.'

'Mmm,' she acknowledged. 'But I've brought you a present,' she announced. 'A peace-offering, if you like, for my not appreciating the lengths you were prepared to go to get me...'

And even white teeth began pressing down into her full bottom lip, liquid dark eyes pleading with him through the penitent sweep of her long dark lashes while she waited for a response.

It was a look he had seen before, right in the middle of the world's busiest street market, and his eyes darkened at the memory of what that look had done to him then—because it was all pure female guile, that look. Maddening, teasing, playful, inciting—and it reacted on his senses like the sirens' song that had been luring men to their deaths through the ages.

He let out a sigh—the mark of his own imminent death at this beguiling woman's hand. 'Go on,' he conceded. 'I'll fall for it. What kind of present?'

Instantly her hands went to the knotted belt holding her towelling robe together.

But one of his hands closing over hers stopped her. 'What are you doing?' He frowned.

'Unwrapping your present,' she said. 'It's me,' she added softly. 'I'm your present. If you still want me after the blindly stupid way I behaved today, that is...'

His big chest heaved on a short tense suck of air, his eyes closing, then opening to reveal irises gone almost as dark as her own luminous eyes as he muttered something hoarse beneath his breath.

'Oh, come here.' He reached for her then, pulling her against him. 'Are you really so blind, Shaan,' he sighed, 'that you really can't tell when a man is heart and soul in love with you?'

'I suppose I must be,' she conceded sadly. 'But I'm heart and soul in love with you, too, Rafe!' she added urgently. 'I've been in love with you so long, in fact, that I can barely recall my life before you took it over!'

'Good,' he said, and caught her mouth in a short, hot,

masterly kiss. 'Keep it like that,' he grimly commanded. 'Because I'm very possessive of every single moment in your life!'

'And you think I'm not the same with you?' she said, then continued on a sudden flash of blistering possessiveness, 'So if I ever see you so much as *peck* Madeleine's cheek again,' she warned fiercely, 'I shall walk out on you and never come back!'

'The woman is a pain in the neck,' he grimaced. 'She was a pain in the neck while she had her silly crush on me a couple of years ago and she was a pain in the neck today, when she met me at the airport so she could spend the time it took me to deliver her back to the Connaught trying to talk me into forgiving Piers for the way he'd used you!'

'Why the Connaught?' Shaan frowned. After all, Piers had his own apartment right here in London.

'It's where she and Piers are staying because they've sold his apartment.' His hand came up to gently smooth the frown from her brow. 'They're going to live in Chicago,' he explained. 'Piers is going into partnership with his father-in-law. And to be honest,' he added heavily, 'I think it will do him good to get out from beneath my shadow.'

'You still haven't forgiven him, have you?' she realised.

His big shoulders shrugged. 'Beneath all that surface charm he's not a very nice person, you know.'

'I know,' Shaan sighed. 'But I think he's beginning to realise that himself, now, if it's any consolation.'

'The only consolation I need right now,' he said soberly, 'is the assurance that I am what you really want, and not just the guy who caught you on the rebound from Piers.'

'Oh, don't,' she murmured as she saw the ache of real uncertainty glint across his eyes. 'I'm sorry if what Piers and I almost did hurt you, Rafe. But I can't think of a way to make that memory go away. Except to say that from the first moment I saw you after Piers and I got engaged I was more obsessed with you and what you thought of me than I was with anything else—and that included Piers. So maybe I was already falling in love with you without really knowing it,' she suggested anxiously. 'Maybe I was even too frightened to look any closer at why you disturbed me so much in case I had to face what a terrible mistake I'd made!'

To her surprise, he started smiling. 'At the risk of sounding arrogant,' he drawled, 'I am man enough to know my own worth. All I needed was time with you. Time I didn't think I was going to get...'

'You said that on the telephone in Hong Kong,' Shaan recalled.

'I also said I was in love with you, only you chose to believe I was talking about Madeleine.'

'I'm sorry,' she murmured.

'Don't be.' He grimaced. 'To be honest, I was never more relieved than when you misunderstood that conversation, since it meant I could at least hang onto a bit of my pride.'

'While you spent the next two weeks ravishing me,' she added accusingly.

'Now that's a moot point,' he mocked, 'as to who actually ravished who most of the time.'

'Now, now,' Shaan protested. 'Be careful who you malign here, because I have a witness!' And to prove it she held out her wrist where Minnie Mouse still kept perfect time.

'Ah, but so do I!' Rafe responded, and dug into his bathrobe pocket to come up with the palm-sized jade Buddha. 'You said, "Be lucky, Rafe"—remember?' he murmured huskily. 'Well, I am, Shaan. Very lucky...'

He kissed her then, long and soft, and so deeply Shaan felt herself sinking right into him.

'Come on,' she whispered, climbing off his lap and catching hold of one of his hands to tug him up with her.

'Where are we going?' he asked, as if he didn't really know!

'To unwrap your present,' she said, pulling him with her into their bedroom.

Their bedroom. Their home. Their life. Their love.

No illusion. Nothing fickle or gullible or dishonest about it.

Because this was it. The real truth. Shaan loved Rafe. Rafe loved Shaan. It really was as beautifully, gloriously simple as that.

MEN at WORK

All work and no play?
Not these men!

July 1998
MACKENZIE'S LADY by Dallas Schulze
Undercover agent Mackenzie Donahue's
lazy smile and deep blue eyes were his best
weapons. But after rescuing—and kissing!—
damsel in distress Holly Reynolds, how could
he betray her by spying on her brother?

August 1998
MISS LIZ'S PASSION by Sherryl Woods
Todd Lewis could put up a building with ease,
but quailed at the sight of a classroom! Still,
Liz Gentry, his son's teacher, was no battle-ax,
and soon Todd started planning some
extracurricular activities of his own....

September 1998
A CLASSIC ENCOUNTER
by Emilie Richards
Doctor Chris Matthews was intelligent, sexy
and *very* good with his hands—which made
him all the more dangerous to single mom
Lizette St. Hilaire. So how long could she
resist Chris's special brand of TLC?

Available at your favorite retail outlet!

MEN AT WORK™

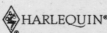

Look us up on-line at: http://www.romance.net

PMAW2

HARLEQUIN ULTIMATE GUIDES™

A series of how-to books for today's woman.

Act now to order some of these extremely
helpful guides just for you!

*Whatever the situation, Harlequin Ultimate Guides™
has all the answers!*

#80507	HOW TO TALK TO A	$4.99 U.S. ☐	
	NAKED MAN	$5.50 CAN.☐	
#80508	I CAN FIX THAT	$5.99 U.S. ☐	
		$6.99 CAN.☐	
#80510	WHAT YOUR TRAVEL AGENT	$5.99 U.S. ☐	
	KNOWS THAT YOU DON'T	$6.99 CAN.☐	
#80511	RISING TO THE OCCASION		
	More Than Manners: Real Life	$5.99 U.S. ☐	
	Etiquette for Today's Woman	$6.99 CAN.☐	
#80513	WHAT GREAT CHEFS	$5.99 U.S. ☐	
	KNOW THAT YOU DON'T	$6.99 CAN.☐	
#80514	WHAT SAVVY INVESTORS	$5.99 U.S. ☐	
	KNOW THAT YOU DON'T	$6.99 CAN.☐	
#80509	GET WHAT YOU WANT OUT OF	$5.99 U.S. ☐	
	LIFE—AND KEEP IT!	$6.99 CAN.☐	

(quantities may be limited on some titles)

TOTAL AMOUNT	$
POSTAGE & HANDLING	$
($1.00 for one book, 50¢ for each additional)	
APPLICABLE TAXES*	$
TOTAL PAYABLE	$ _____
(check or money order—please do not send cash)	

To order, complete this form and send it, along with a check or money
order for the total above, payable to Harlequin Ultimate Guides, to:
In the U.S.: 3010 Walden Avenue, P.O. Box 9047, Buffalo, NY
14269-9047; **In Canada:** P.O. Box 613, Fort Erie, Ontario, L2A 5X3.

Name: _____

Address: _____ City: _____

State/Prov.: _____ Zip/Postal Code: _____

*New York residents remit applicable sales taxes.
Canadian residents remit applicable GST and provincial taxes.

◆ HARLEQUIN®

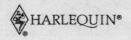

Not The Same Old Story!

Exciting, glamorous romance stories that take readers around the world.

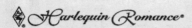
Sparkling, fresh and tender love stories that bring you pure romance.

Bold and adventurous— Temptation is strong women, bad boys, great sex!

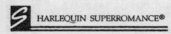
Provocative and realistic stories that celebrate life and love.

Contemporary fairy tales—where anything is possible and where dreams come true.

Heart-stopping, suspenseful adventures that combine the best of romance and mystery.

Humorous and romantic stories that capture the lighter side of love.

Look us up on-line at: http://www.romance.net   HGENERIC

HARLEQUIN ◆ PRESENTS®

Everyone has special occasions in their life—an
engagement, a wedding, an anniversary...or maybe
the birth of a baby.

**These are times of celebration and excitement,
and we're delighted to bring you a special new
series called...**

One special occasion—that changes your life forever!

Celebrate *The Big Event!* with great books by some of
your favorite authors:

September 1998—BRIDE FOR A YEAR
by Kathryn Ross (#1981)
October 1998—MARRIAGE MAKE UP
by Penny Jordan (#1983)
November 1998—RUNAWAY FIANCÉE
by Sally Wentworth (#1992)
December 1998—BABY INCLUDED!
by Mary Lyons (#1997)

Look in the back pages of any *Big Event* book to find
out how to receive a set of sparkling wineglasses.

Available wherever Harlequin books are sold.

HARLEQUIN®
Makes any time special ™